Blond
Cargo

Blond
Cargo

WITHDRAWN

JOHN LANSING

GALLERY BOOKS/ KAREN HUNTER PUBLISHING
New York   London   Toronto   Sydney   New Delhi

G

Gallery Books
An Imprint of Simon & Schuster, Inc
Simon & Schuster, Inc.
1230 Avenue of the Americas
New York, NY 10020

Karen Hunter Publishing
A Division of Suitt-Hunter
Suitt-Hunter Enterprises, LLC
P.O. Box 832
South Orange, NJ 07079

First Karen Hunter Publishing/Gallery Books trade paperback edition January 2015

GALLERY BOOKS and colophon are registered trademarks of Simon & Schuster, Inc.

For information about special discounts for bulk purchases, please contact Simon & Schuster Special Sales at 1-866-506-1949 or business@simonandschuster.com.

The Simon & Schuster Speakers Bureau can bring authors to your live event. For more information or to book an event, contact the Simon & Schuster Speakers Bureau at 1-866-248-3049 or visit our website at www.simonspeakers.com.

Manufactured in the United States of America

10   9   8   7   6   5   4 3 2 1

Library of Congress Cataloging-in-Publication Data is available.

ISBN 978-1-5011-1028-3
ISBN 978-1-4767-9551-5(ebook)

For Loretta and John

Blond
Cargo

1

Jack Bertolino moved briskly down the polished terrazzo floor of the American Airlines terminal at San Francisco International Airport. He walked past travelers who were deplaning, waiting to board, eating, drinking, and queuing up at ticket counters. Through the windows on either side of the crowded terminal he could see a line of Boeing MD-80s and 737s.

Jack had his game face on. One thought only: take down the manager at NCI Corp who was dirty.

Todd Dearling had been hired as one of five project managers, developing a new generation of semiconductors meant to challenge Intel's control of the market. Yet the new engineer was plotting to steal the proprietary architecture for the company's most advanced technology and sell it to an Argentinean competitor.

Jack had done a thorough background check on Dearling and found no skeletons in the man's closet, no gambling issues, no drugs, no priors; it was greed, pure and simple.

Cruz Feinberg, Jack's new associate, had arrived in Silicon Valley two days prior and wirelessly inserted a program onto

Dearling's iPad while the stressed-out manager was sucking down his daily chai latte at the local Starbucks. Any text or e-mail sent to or from Dearling was cloned and sent to Cruz's laptop. A piece of cake to pull off for the young tech whiz.

Jack was being well paid to catch the thief in the act—let the money and the technology change hands, and then drop the hammer.

Todd Dearling had made reservations at the Four Seasons Hotel in East Palo Alto. A car would be waiting at SFO to ferry his Argentinean counterpart to the suite where the exchange was scheduled to take place.

Jack had booked Cruz into that same suite two nights earlier, where he had set up wireless microcameras and wired the room for sound, to be routed to the suite next door, where Jack's team would document the crime.

Jack lived for these moments. Outsmarting intelligent men who thought they were above the law. Badge or no badge, Jack loved to take scumbags down.

Ten minutes ago, Flight 378 from Buenos Aires had flashed from black to green on the overhead arrivals screen. Dressed in a gray pinstripe business suit and wheeling a carry-on suitcase, Jack walked toward a limo driver stationed near the exit door of the international terminal. The man held a sign chest-high that read EMILIO BRAGGA.

Jack reached out a hand toward the driver, who was forced to lower his placard, shake Jack's hand, and make quick work of grabbing up Jack's bag. Jack headed quickly toward the exit, explaining to the driver that he was traveling light and had no checked luggage.

As soon as the two men exited the building, Jack's second

employee, Mateo Vasquez, dressed in a black suit, moved into the same spot, carrying a sign that read EMILIO BRAGGA.

Jack and Mateo had once been on opposite sides of the thin blue line, Jack as an NYPD narcotics detective, Mateo as an operative for a Colombian drug cartel. When Jack busted the cartel, he made Mateo an offer—spend thirty years in the big house, or come to work for the NYPD as a confidential informant. Mateo had made the right choice and Jack had earned himself a loyal operative when he became a private investigator.

Thirty seconds later, the real Emilio Bragga walked up to Mateo, stifled a yawn, and handed off his carry-on. He was short and stocky with a rubbery face.

"*Buenos días*, Señor Bragga. I hope your flight was acceptable?" Mateo asked deferentially.

"Barely. First class isn't what it used to be." Bragga's accented English was spoken in clipped tones. "Take me to the First National Bank. I have business to attend to."

Two hundred and fifty thousand dollars' worth of business, Mateo might have added, but refrained.

———

Jack arrived at the Four Seasons, generously tipped the limo driver, and hurried up the elevator to the suite where Cruz was waiting. Once Jack stripped off his suit jacket, he joined the young genius by his array of monitors.

"They should make these baby ketchup bottles illegal," Cruz said as he tried to pound the condiment out of the room service minibottle of Heinz. Growing frustrated, Cruz shoved a knife deep into the viscous ketchup and poured a heaping red mound onto his fries. Happy with the results, he chowed down on three drenched fries before wiping his hands on his jeans and returning his gaze to the computer.

"It looks like he's getting ready for a date," Jack said as he took a seat. Cruz kept his eyes trained on the four screens corresponding to the four different camera angles of the room they were covering.

"Guy's squirrelly," Cruz said, biting into his cheeseburger.

They watched as Todd Dearling twirled a bottle of champagne in the ice that had just been delivered from room service, along with a tray of finger sandwiches and crudités. He was a slight, pale, middle-aged man with thinning hair that he kept nervously brushing back off his forehead. He shrugged out of his tweed sports jacket, but when he saw the sweat stains in the armpits of his blue dress shirt, he slid it back on. He hurried over to the thermostat near the door, appearing on a new screen, and turned up the air.

Jack checked his watch and then his phone to make sure he was receiving enough bars to communicate with Mateo.

"I'm getting a little nervous. You?" Cruz asked before sucking down the last of his Coke. He crumpled the aluminum can with one hand and executed an overhand dunk into the bamboo trash bin.

Cruz's mother was Guatemalan, his father a Brooklyn Jew who founded Bundy Lock and Key. That's where Jack first met him. Cruz, who took after his mother's side of the family, looked taller than his five-foot-nine frame. Dark-skinned, intelligent brown eyes, a youthful angular face, and at twenty-three, he could still pull off the spiky short black hair.

"I've got some energy going," Jack said, "but it's all good. You'd have to worry if you didn't feel pumped."

Just then Jack's phone vibrated and the number 999 appeared

on his text screen, code for *It's a go*. Mateo and Emilio Bragga had just pulled up to the front entrance of the Four Seasons Hotel.

"We're on," Jack said with a tight grin.

In another minute, a loud rap on a door made Cruz jump. "Is that here?" he asked, and glanced over at the door to their suite.

"No, it's next door. Great sound, Cruz," Jack said, trying to keep his newest charge calm.

Jack and Cruz watched as Dearling's image moved from one screen to the next, went over to the door, unlocked it, and ushered in Emilio Bragga. The man of the hour wheeled his carry-on across the white marble floor, pushed the retractable handle down into the bag, and gave Dearling an unexpected bear hug, lifting the thin man off his feet. Once the blush faded and he had regained his composure, Dearling was all smiles. He could smell his fortune being made.

"First, tell me you have them," Bragga said brusquely, his smile tightening.

"I have them and more, Emilio. There are even some preliminary renderings for the next series of chips. Consider it goodwill," Dearling said.

He lifted the champagne bottle out of the melting ice with a flourish, dripping water onto his dress shirt.

"A celebratory drink and then business."

"No, business first," Jack said.

"No. Show them to me. Now," Bragga ordered, his voice unyielding.

"Now we're talking," Cruz said to Jack, barely able to control his excitement.

The next knock was more subdued than the first, just a quick double knock.

"That's here," Jack said as he slid out of his chair and opened the door. Mateo was thirty-nine years old, tall, handsome, with striking gray eyes, long brown hair, and a thousand-dollar suit. He beamed at his old friend as he walked in, bumped fists, and moved into position behind Cruz, eyes trained on the computer screen.

Emilio Bragga placed his carry-on luggage on the couch as Dearling pulled a slim buffed metal briefcase from behind the table and snapped it open on the tabletop. Inside was a series of blue, red, silver, and gold flash drives, seated in foam cutouts next to three bound technical binders.

Bragga leafed quickly through one of the binders, visibly relaxed, and placed it back inside the case. He looked at Todd Dearling and nodded his head. Then he smiled.

"This is the money shot," Jack said. "Make it the money shot."

Emilio Bragga walked over to the couch, ceremoniously produced a key, and opened the lock. The sound of the zipper ratcheting around the circumference of the bag got everyone's full attention. And then Bragga flipped open the canvas top.

Two hundred and fifty thousand, in crisp, banded hundred-dollar bills. Jack's team could almost hear Dearling's breath catch in his throat.

"You see those appetizers?" Bragga said, gesturing to the tray of crudités. "That is what this is." He turned his gaze to the thick stacks of money like it was nothing. "Antipasto . . . before the meal."

The two men shook hands. The deal was consummated.

It was all gravy now, Jack thought. He would contact Lawrence Weller, CEO of NCI, who would have Bragga quietly arrested at the airport and Dearling picked up outside his condominium, thereby avoiding any negative publicity regarding the security breach that could affect the value of NCI's stock.

"Start taking sick days as we get closer to the rollout date," Bragga advised. "Then you'll take a forced medical leave. I'll set you up with a doctor in San Francisco who's a friend. He'll recommend you spend a month at a local clinic to *recuperate* while we launch and beat NCI to market. Six months later and with two million in your account, you'll give notice and head up my division. Did I ever tell you how beautiful the women in Mendoza are?"

Bragga's speech was interrupted by another knock on the door.

"Room service," a muted voice said.

"We're good," Dearling shouted as he moved toward the door while Bragga instinctively closed the lid of his bag, covering the money.

Jack gave his team a *What the hell?* look. "Who are these jokers?"

"Complimentary champagne from the management of the Four Seasons," intoned the muffled voice.

"Don't open the door," Bragga hissed.

"Don't open the door," Jack said at the same time.

But Dearling had already turned the handle.

Three men dressed in navy blue blazers with gold epaulettes pushed a service cart draped with a white cloth into the room with a bottle of champagne in a silver ice bucket and a huge bouquet of flowers in a crystal vase.

"Three men on one bottle," Jack said as he pulled his Glock nine-millimeter out of his shoulder rig and headed for the door.

"We weren't the only ones who hacked his computer," Cruz intuited.

"Don't leave the room," Jack told him over his shoulder. He quickly exited the suite, followed by Mateo. Cruz nodded, but his wide eyes never left the computer screen.

———————

The lead man pushed the cart toward Dearling, but instead of slowing down, he muscled the cart up against the timid man's waist, picked up speed, and forced him to backpedal across the room. Dearling's eyes bugged, his face a mask of terror. The flowers and champagne tumbled off the cart, and the crystal vase shattered on impact. The champagne bottle exploded. Flowers and glass and water and bubbly flooded the slick stone floor. Dearling's body slammed into the television set on the far wall; his head whipped back and splintered the flat screen. Glass rained down on the Judas as he slid to the floor behind the cart.

Bragga placed himself in front of his bag of cash and took a gun barrel to the side of his head. The gash spurted blood, drenched his shirt, turned his legs to rubber, and took him down onto one knee. The gunman made a fast reach past him for the bag, but Bragga grabbed the thug around one thigh and tried to bulldog him to the ground.

"I'm gonna shoot you, you dumb prick," the gunman grunted, rapidly losing control of the situation.

"So much for keeping it on the QT," Jack said to Mateo as he kicked the door open and followed his gun into the room.

The third uniformed man spun as the door smashed against the jamb and Jack's fist exploded into his face. The man's head snapped back, and blood streamed out of his broken nose. His arms flailed, and his gun was suspended in midair for a split second before the man and the gun hit the floor.

The man who'd pushed the cart turned his weapon on Jack, who fired first, blasting the man in the shoulder. The force of Jack's bullet propelled the gunman's body backward onto the cart before he flopped to the stone floor, landed on his shoulder in the broken glass, and cried out in pain.

The gun discharging in the close confines of the hotel suite stopped the action. The room smelled of cordite, the only sounds heavy breathing and Todd Dearling's whimpering. Mateo picked up the third man's pistol and covered Jack's back.

Jack turned his Glock on the second man. "Give me your gun or your friend's going to bleed out," he stated with extreme calm.

Before Jack could take control of the weapon, Bragga stripped it from the gunman's hand and smashed him in the temple with surprising violence. Then he swung the confiscated Colt back and forth between Jack and Mateo, stopping them in their tracks.

"Nobody move and nobody follow," Bragga said as he half-zipped the suitcase with one hand and picked up the carry-on bag.

"Drop your weapons," he ordered Jack and Mateo through clenched teeth as blood continued to drip down the side of his face. They complied, knowing he wouldn't make it as far as the lobby. Bragga walked around the couch on unsteady legs, muscling the heavy bag. His eyes bored into Mateo, the "driver" who had betrayed him, and ordered him to clear the doorway with a sharp wave of his gun barrel.

Mateo took a half step to the side, gave the short man just enough room to pass, and pistoned with his full two hundred pounds of muscle, leading with his elbow and hitting Bragga in the back of the head, just above the neck. The Argentinean went down hard.

The overstuffed bag bounced on the floor, the luggage's zipper split open, and a green wave of banded hundreds cascaded out onto the polished white Carrara marble.

"That was a cluster fuck," Jack said with disgust as he picked up his Glock and surveyed the carnage in the suite.

Mateo collected the fallen weapons, grabbed a towel off the wet bar, and used it as a compress to stanch the first gunman's bleeding wound. He was all business.

"Call 911 and have them send an ambulance," Jack said to Cruz, who he knew could hear him over one of the multiple microphones.

"That was insane."

Jack turned around and found Cruz standing, wild eyed, in the hall directly behind him.

"Call 911 and lock the door. Did we get it all?"

"I copied Lawrence Weller and you on your cell, iPad, and laptop."

"Good man," Jack said.

"No, really, you, Mateo . . . man." Cruz shuddered as he pulled out his cell and dialed the emergency phone line.

Jack was not one normally given to second-guessing, but at the moment he found himself seriously questioning his new career choice as a private investigator.

Muttering a curse, Jack holstered his nine-millimeter, crossed the room, and proceeded to snap plastic flex-cuffs on the broken assembly of thieves.

2

Maggie Sheffield was having her last gin and tonic of the night, or so she promised herself. She pulled her thick mane of red hair back, out of her eyes; steadied her hand as she added the Bombay; stopped once; and then kept pouring. Well, it *was* the last of the night. She set the blue bottle down and glanced out the kitchen window of her double-wide, perched high atop the cliffs. The moon was a fat three-quarters and reflected brightly on the calm waters of Paradise Cove below.

Maggie thought she saw something cut through the moon's reflection on the water's surface. At the same time she heard the faint hum of an outboard motor through her screen door. Then a huge, echoing, thumping roar as a powerboat blasted through and shattered the reflected light.

She stepped out onto her porch in time to hear the throaty sound of a cigarette boat powering out to sea, arcing left beyond the wooden pier and traveling south at a high rate of speed. Seawater rooster-tailed behind.

Maggie hadn't seen one of those tricked-out boats since her favorite show, *Miami Vice*, went off the air back in the eighties.

It had left in its wake a low-slung boat that was motoring directly toward the black rock outcroppings.

Pull up, she thought. "Pull up," she said out loud. "Pull the fuck up!" she screamed.

The wooden boat crashed into the rocks, rose up, and splintered in half. It violently ejected what appeared to be the boat's pilot onto the rocky shore. The wreck exploded in a fireball that lit up the dark cove and then extinguished like an antique flashbulb.

Maggie carefully set down her gin and tonic. Then she ran inside the house to dial 911.

3

The pink Venus disposable razor cut a clean swath through the Foamy shaving cream down the perfect curve of Deputy District Attorney Leslie Sager's leg.

A fine leg, Jack Bertolino thought as he watched her meticulous preparations from his bed. Hard to believe such a feminine woman could turn into a raging pit bull in a court of law.

He laughed to himself as he looked at her array of potions and creams and cosmetics scattered around the sink. He had offered closet and bathroom space in his Marina del Rey loft, but Leslie came and went, rolling a small piece of carry-on luggage like a stewardess on an international flight.

Their routine was irregular, usually four days on and three off, but they never took their time together for granted.

"When did you get in?" Leslie asked.

"After midnight. You were out cold. Chris canceled on me, so I grabbed the first flight back."

Chris was Jack's son, presently attending Stanford on a baseball scholarship. The two weren't getting along these days, because the Colombian drug dealer Jack had taken down a month ago had decided to get personal and had run Chris down in a Cadillac Escalade. One of the main casualties of the assault was Chris's pitching arm.

As Jack watched Leslie rinse off under one of the double showerheads in his white, subway-tiled bathroom—her shoulder-length blond hair turban-wrapped in a bath towel—he had to think about baseball stats to keep his morning libido in check.

Oh, what the hell, he thought as he jumped out of bed, dropped his pajama bottoms, and stepped in behind her.

"Don't get my hair wet," she said. It was a deep-throated challenge, not an order.

It just got Jack hot. He soaped her back and nuzzled her neck.

"My back's clean," she murmured.

Ever dutiful, he turned her around to lather her front. He found her lips and ran soapy hands down her athletic body as Leslie found *him* and they both experienced early-morning bliss.

Breakfast of champions, Jack thought, boyishly proud of himself as he toweled off, grabbed the remote, and snapped on the local news.

He caught the tail end of a boating accident at Paradise Cove in Malibu but was already knocking back two Excedrin to dull the ever-present pain shooting down his spine. It was a chronic condition brought on by a fall from a steel girder while doing cleanup at Ground Zero. He spooned beans into the Braun coffeemaker and didn't really catch the story. He knew if the accident was an important story, it would be replayed every fifteen minutes for the rest of the day.

Leslie's three-inch heels clicked crisply as she strode across the concrete floor of the loft and slid her arms around Jack's waist. He poured a cup of coffee and turned to her, offering his lips and the coffee.

"Minty fresh," he all but growled after the kiss.

Leslie took a sip of the fresh coffee and gave Jack the once-over. His black hair was longer on the sides, feathered with silver, and now crowded his collar in the back. It tempered some of his innate intensity. She approved and told him so with her eyes.

His chiseled face had a new cut to add to the arsenal. Twenty stitches on his right cheekbone created a small crescent scar that lay flat when he smiled. The handiwork of Hector Lopez, a serial killer Jack had personal contact with on his last case. The bump on his otherwise straight Roman nose was due to a hard right from a crack dealer named Trey. Just one of many gifts he'd collected working twenty-five years on the mean streets of New York.

"I'm relieved you're in one piece. Ice your hand."

"Yes, nurse."

Worry lines marred her smooth forehead. "Why did you enter the hotel room when you knew there were three armed men? You could've been killed. What were you thinking?"

"Things got fluid."

"It was a white-collar case, Jack. That's what you signed on for. That's what you should be doing."

"I'm fine." Meaning, *That's enough.*

"Take the mayor's offer, Jack. It's not too late. He cornered me at the courthouse when you were up north. Seriously, he wants you on his team."

Jack had recently turned down the mayor of Los Angeles's offer to join his security force as a paid consultant. He was promised autonomy and the power of the badge without having to wear a uniform.

"It'll end up being too political," he said.

"Welcome to my world, Jack. Give it some thought, that's all I ask. You're getting too old for this hand-to-hand combat."

"Ouch. I'll give you some hand-to-hand." Jack leaned in close, his brown eyes seductive with a flash of anger Leslie chose to ignore. She pushed him good-naturedly away.

"You have got to be kidding me, Jack Bertolino. I'm late for work. Think about it," she said, eyebrows raised. "Are you free this evening?"

"Let me check my book. I am," he said without breaking cadence or eye contact.

"Then keep your powder dry and you might get lucky."

Leslie flashed her killer smile, finger-combed her hair behind one ear, handed Jack her coffee cup, picked up her briefcase, and started for the door.

"The defense doesn't stand a chance," Jack said as he followed in her wake, not happy with the direction the conversation had taken. He picked up the light scent of her perfume and then the morning paper as he watched her walk toward the elevator, then locked up behind her.

Jack threw the paper onto the dining table and paused to read the headline.

PARADISE LOST IN MALIBU.

4

Jack carried a Subway turkey sandwich, a tall unsweetened iced coffee, a bottle of water, and a smile as he keyed the security gate that led to the dock in Marina del Rey where his boat was moored. The marina was always quiet during the week. Just the way he liked it.

He stopped to admire his twenty-eight feet of heaven before stepping onto his boat's transom and then . . .

"Yo, Mr. B."

Jack never forgot a voice, which explained his reluctance to turn around.

"Yo, yo, Mr. B."

Miserably persistent, Jack thought. He turned to face Peter Maniacci, who was dressed head-to-toe in black. With his outstretched arms draped over the chain-link fence, Peter looked like an Italian scarecrow. The black circles under his eyes belied his youth. The sharp points of his sideburns, his boots, and the .38 hanging lazily from a shoulder holster added menace to his goofy grin.

So close, Jack thought. His only worry that day had been

whether to eat his sandwich dockside or out on the Pacific with a view of the Santa Monica Pier.

"How you doing, Peter?"

"How you doin'?"

Jack let out a labored sigh. "We could do this all day. What's up?"

"That's funny, Mr. B. How's the boy? How's his pitching arm?"

Jack's face tightened. He wasn't happy that Peter knew any of his son's particulars. When he didn't answer, Peter continued.

"Hey, nice boat. I used to fish for fluke off the North Shore. Long Island. I think I must be in the wrong business."

"Count on it," Jack said. "What can I do for you?"

"My boss was wondering if you could spare a few minutes of your time."

As if on cue, a black Town Car materialized behind Peter and came to a smooth, silent stop. The car rose visibly when Peter's boss, a thick, broad-shouldered man, stepped out of the rear seat.

Vincent Cardona. Expensive suit, the body of a defensive linebacker—fleshy but muscled. Dark, penetrating eyes. Cardona looked in both directions before leveling his feral gaze on Jack. An attempt at a smile fell short of the mark. A thick manila envelope was tucked under one beefy arm.

Jack had been aware there would be some form of payback due for information Cardona had provided on Arturo Delgado, the man responsible for the attempted murder of his son. He just didn't think it would come due this quickly. He opened the locked gate and let the big man follow him down the dock toward his used Cutwater cabin cruiser.

As Peter stood sentry in front of the Lincoln Town Car, Jack allowed the devil entry to his little piece of paradise.

"How's your boy? How's the pitching arm?" Vincent asked bluntly. Just a reminder of why he was there.

"On the mend." Jack gestured to one of two canvas deck chairs in the open cockpit of the boat. Both men sat in silence as Jack waited for Cardona to explain the reason for his visit.

Jack wasn't comfortable with Cardona's talking about Chris, but the big man had taken it upon himself to station Peter outside Saint John's Health Center while his son was drifting between life and death. Cardona's enforcer had scared off Delgado, and that might have saved his son's life. The unsolicited good deed was greatly appreciated by Jack. The debt weighed heavily.

"It rips your heart out when your children have problems and you can't do nothing to help," Cardona said with the raspy wheeze of a man who had abused cigars, drugs, booze, and fatty sausage for most of his life.

"What can I do for you?" Jack asked, not wanting to prolong the impromptu meeting.

Cardona, unfazed by Jack's brusqueness, answered by pulling out a picture and handing it to Jack.

"Angelica Marie Cardona. She's my girl. My only. My angel. Her mother died giving birth. I didn't have the heart to re-up. I raised her by myself."

Mobster with a heart of gold. Right, Jack thought. But Cardona's wife must have been a stunner because Angelica, blond, early twenties, with flawless skin and gray-green eyes, didn't get her good looks from her father. Cardona's gift was her self-assured attitude, which all but leaped off the photograph.

"Beautiful."

Jack Bertolino, master of the understatement, he thought.

"And doesn't she know it. Too much so for her own good. You make mistakes, my line of business. Whatever."

"What can I do for you, Vincent?" Jack said, dialing back the attitude.

Cardona tracked a seagull soaring overhead with his heavy-lidded eyes and rubbed the stubble on his jaw.

Jack would have paid good money to change places with the gull.

"I shoulda never moved out here. L.A. I'm a black-socks-on-the-beach kinda guy. East Coast all the way. Never fit in. But I'm a good earner and the powers that be decided they were happy with the arrangement. Everyone was happy except Angelica and me.

"She turned thirteen, didn't wanna have nothing to do with her old man. Turned iceberg cold. I tried everything—private schools, horses, ballet, therapy, live-in help; nothin' worked. She closed up tighter than a drum. I finally threatened to send her to the nuns."

"How did that work out?"

"I'm fuckin' sitting here, aren't I? On this fuckin' dinghy . . . no offense meant," he said, trying to cover, but the flash of anger told the real story. "I hear you're an independent contractor now."

It was Tommy Aronsohn, his old friend and ex–district attorney, who had set him up with his PI's license and first client, Lawrence Weller and NCI Corp. But *Jack Bertolino and Associates, Private Investigation*, still didn't come trippingly off his tongue.

And thinking of the disaster up north, he said, "We'll see how that goes."

"This is the point. I haven't seen my daughter in close to a month. Haven't heard word one since around the time your son was laid up in Saint John's," he said. Reminder number two. "It's killing me," he continued. "I'm getting a fuckin' ulcer. Then this."

Cardona pulled out the L.A. *Times* with the front-page spread reporting on the woman who had died when her boat crashed on the rocks at Paradise Cove. As it turned out, a second woman down in Orange County had washed up on the beach a few weeks earlier at the Terranea resort, scaring the joy out of newly-weds taking photos at sunset. Talk about twisted memories, Jack thought. As if marriage wasn't tough enough. He'd already read both articles with his morning coffee and hadn't bought into the pattern the reporter inferred.

"And the connection?"

"I got a bad feeling is all. She's never disappeared like this before—not for this long anyway," he said, amending his state-ment. "And then . . ." Cardona said, waving the newspaper like it was on fire. "It says here they were both blonds. Both about Angelica's age. They could be fuckin' cousins. Could be nothing."

"Did you file a missing-persons report?"

Cardona gave him a hard side eye. "Jack, don't fuck with me. We take care of our own."

Jack thought before he spoke. "I'm not one of yours."

"Semantics."

"What about your crew?"

Cardona flopped open his meaty hands. "I get angina, I don't call my cousin Frankie, who has a certain skill set but stinks when it comes to open-heart surgery. Look, I get it. You were on the other team. But this is straight-up business. One man to another. One father to another. I need you to find my girl. You got my number. Use it, Jack. Money's no object. Find my baby."

Strike three.

Jack didn't answer. He stared out at the navy-blue water of the marina, past row upon row of beautiful yachts, symbols of dreams fulfilled, and knew they were empty notions compared to family.

Cardona hadn't actually spoken the words *you owe me*, but they filled the subtext of everything he'd said. He was not subtle. The big man had reached out when Jack was in need, and Jack had accepted the offer. Now Vincent Cardona wanted his pound of flesh.

"This is everything I know. Last address, phone numbers, phone bills, e-mail accounts, bank, credit cards, friends, and whatnot. The whole shot," Cardona said, holding the manila envelope out in Jack's direction.

"I have other commitments," Jack stated.

"You look real fuckin' busy, Jack, if you don't mind my sayin'." His eyes crinkled into a sarcastic grin. Vincent Cardona does charm.

Jack accepted the overstuffed envelope with a sigh.

"If she don't want to come back, fine. No funny business, no strong-arm bullshit from my end. You got my word. I just need to know that my blood is alive. I'm fuckin' worried and I don't do worry too good. Sleep on it, Jack. But do the right thing."

Cardona's eyes locked on to Jack's. Jack remained silent. He'd take a look. No promises, not yet.

Vincent's knees cracked and the canvas chair squeaked like it was in pain as he stood up. He covered a belch behind his fist and rubbed his gut as he moved stiffly past Jack. The boat rocked when Cardona stepped off and walked heavily away, his Italian leather shoes echoing on the wooden dock.

The weight of the world. Jack could relate.

Peter Maniacci opened the gate for his boss and then the door to the Lincoln Town Car, which plunged to curb level as the big man slid in. Peter ran around to the other side of the car and tossed Jack a wave like the queen mum. He jumped into the Lincoln, which lurched forward before Peter could slam the door shut.

Jack walked into the boat's deckhouse, grabbed a bottle of water, and downed two more Excedrin. He stretched his back, which was going into a spasm from yesterday's violence, and chased the pills with a Vicodin to stay one step ahead of the pain that he knew was headed his way.

Jack had already decided to take the case.

5

Thirty minutes later, Jack pushed hard on the throttle as he exited the five-mile-per-hour zone of the protected jetty. As the boat geared up, the vibrations ran through his body, and the salty wind whipped his face and hair. Cirrus clouds knifed the bright blue sky and jagged whitecaps stretched to the horizon. As he powered through a mild wake, he felt the stability of his modest craft and started to breathe normally again.

In the rapidly approaching distance he could see the Santa Monica Pier. Its psychedelic Ferris wheel and neon-lit roller coaster remained still in the morning light. The crowds were thin, but it was early.

Ten feet off the boat's stern, a formation of pelicans flew in a V pattern inches above the water, looking like prehistoric birds of prey. The sight cheered him. Jack wasn't in a stellar mood after the unexpected visit from Vincent Cardona, but his day was definitely looking up.

He left the pier behind in his rearview. After Cardona's visit, there was no question where he was headed.

Paradise Cove.

If the incident in the news was an accident, no harm, no foul. He'd have a beautiful cruise up the Malibu coastline. If a crime had been committed, he'd better take a look before the site was picked clean.

Paradise Cove was a special piece of California real estate befitting its name. The protected cove of emerald water was surrounded by rocky shale cliffs draped in electric-red bougainvillea and mescaline-green succulents. Eucalyptus and palm trees fanned out high overhead and framed the high-end prefab mobile homes with their million-dollar views of the Pacific and the Paradise Cove Beach Café below.

Up closer, yellow police tape cordoned off a hundred-yard perimeter where technicians were collecting large pieces of debris from the boat crash and videotaping the scene. A grease stain spread ominously from the site of the explosion, fouling the pristine water.

Jack spotted bloody smears where the young woman had been thrown onto the rocky outcropping, but the body had long since been removed. Jack made a mental note to find out which coroner was handling the case.

Perched high on the cliff, Jack noticed, a middle-aged woman with a tangle of red hair, standing on the deck of her double-wide, was holding court. Her hands moved a mile a minute as she regaled a small crowd and pointed at the accident scene below. Jack decided to get her story after he got the lay of the land.

He dropped anchor, reached into the waves, and snagged a jagged piece of white-painted wooden debris that clearly had once been attached to the wreck. He stowed it for later examination. Then he pulled down the small inflatable Avalon that was secured onto the roof of the boat's cabin.

Jack paddled for shore along the rickety wooden fishing pier. When he hit the beach, he jumped out and dragged the inflatable up onto the soft white sand.

Rows of Adirondack chairs were set up under faded grass-thatched umbrellas fronting the café's picture windows. A smattering of patrons were eating an early lunch, and small groups of people stood on the beach watching the tech crew hard at work in the late-morning sun. He didn't recognize any of the crew. He was just approaching the yellow security tape when he was stopped in his tracks.

"You have got to be shitting me, Bertolino. What the fuck are you doing here?"

"Where's the warmth, Lieutenant Gallina?" Jack said even before he turned around. He couldn't help but grin as Gallina and his partner, Tompkins, a lean, six-foot-tall African-American detective, kicked up a cloud of sand as they drew closer.

Gallina was an acquired taste, and Jack wasn't a fan. A head shorter than his partner, midthirties, with pasty-white skin that hung loose on his jowls. The lieutenant's receding hairline looked to have taken another step back and he'd put on some weight. He didn't have the bones for it, Jack mused, enjoying the observation a little too much. The lieutenant had arrested Jack for a murder he hadn't committed, an event that understandably put a strain on their relationship.

"Tompkins," Jack said with a little more enthusiasm.

"What, things too quiet for you after you set off an international incident?" Tompkins asked, tongue in cheek. He wiped some sweat off his forehead. "Good police work," he added.

"I got pulled in kicking and screaming," Jack said, deflecting the compliment.

"I know you're on the wrong beach and not here to fuck with our crime scene," Gallina stated.

"It was a crime?" Jack asked.

"Leaning that way; we're waiting on the coroner's report," he offered, instantly regretting his decision to share intel.

"Either that or suicide," Tompkins added. "But it looks like the throttle could've been locked down. Too early to tell."

"Any witnesses?"

Gallina exchanged an extended look with his partner. He came to a decision and answered the question.

"Some boozy broad. Gave off enough fumes I was afraid to stand near her when she lit up. Kept yakking about the crush she had on Don Johnson and a *Miami Vice* boat she saw heading away before the explosion."

"She saw the accident. Nothing specific except the direction the other boat was headed. South," Tompkins added.

Jack nodded. He'd had a lot of experience with cigarette boats in Miami. The cartels used them to pick up bundles of cocaine dropped in international waters and then ran them back into Miami cloaked in darkness. He couldn't remember offhand how far a cigarette boat could travel on a tank of gas, but he'd get that information in case there was a connection between the two dead women.

Tompkins raised his eyebrows in a question that Gallina put words to.

"You are blessing us with your presence because . . ."

"I was approached with a missing-persons case this morning. The client, who shall remain nameless, brought up the possibility of a connection. His daughter has the same look and the age is spot-on for both women who turned up dead in the past few weeks.

"I haven't made a commitment yet," Jack said. "Just thought I'd take a look around since I was in the neighborhood."

"If you come up with anything we should know, call. Let us handle it, Bertolino."

"Will do," Jack said as he turned and walked back toward the café. No one believed a word of it.

Instead of heading back to the inflatable, he turned left through the parking lot and hiked up the road that led to the mobile homes.

By that time the crowd had dispersed, and the woman in question was sitting on her front porch in a wicker chair with her eyes closed, burning what wasn't already dangerously tanned on her face. One hand was wrapped tightly around a red metal goblet that might have contained iced tea. Long Island iced tea, Jack suspected. The pink lipstick mark on the rim was covered in beaded condensation. She had red hair that had been augmented with red dye and wore a red zip-up Nike workout suit revealing cleavage that demanded to be zipped up another six inches.

Jack rapped on the wooden railway and the woman almost leapt out of her sun-damaged skin. Not unattractive. Just tired.

"I didn't mean to startle you. I just wanted to ask you a few questions about the accident," he said.

When the woman's eyes cleared from the sun blindness and she focused on Jack, she purred, "Come up." She held out a once-elegant hand. "Maggie Sheffield. And if it was an accident, the woman had to be stoned, dead, or asleep at the wheel," she noted with a nasality that shattered any notion of elegance.

Jack shook her hand, and she held on for an uncomfortable moment too long.

"Jack Bertolino."

"You're certainly easier on the eyes than the other two detectives I spoke with."

Jack would be sure to share her critique the next time he ran into Gallina and Tompkins.

"You saw the actual crash?"

"I heard it before I saw it. Sounded like a mosquito. Small outboard engine. Old wooden boat. Sat low in the water. When I walked out the door, I could see she was headed for the rocks. Stevie Wonder could have seen the rocks. The tide was out and there was no way she could have mistaken them for sand. I shouted, but it didn't do any good. I'm still shaking."

Maggie held out her hand and indeed it betrayed a slight tremor. More booze-induced than from nerves, Jack suspected.

"I can still see that poor girl's body lying on the rocks. She looked broken."

"What else did you see?"

"She was naked. I mean, who goes out in a boat at night dressed in nothing but her birthday suit? It's too damn cold."

The question was rhetorical, but Jack noted Gallina hadn't shared that little tidbit. Both women were found naked.

"And then there was that sexy boat that drove away before she crashed," Maggie said.

"What did it look like?"

"Well, like Don Johnson should have been driving it. Like a jet."

"A cigarette boat?"

"Yes," she said, a little too excited. "That's what they called it on *Miami Vice*. They don't make TV like that anymore. I used to—"

Jack stopped her with, "Color?"

"Colors," she said, annoyed he had interrupted her flow. "Three long thick stripes. Different colors but I couldn't tell you for the life of me what they were. Just different shades of color."

"Did it look like the two boats were together? Did they arrive together?" Jack asked.

"I couldn't say, but the girl *was* butt-naked. They couldn't have missed her. They must have gotten an eyeful, but they sure as hell didn't turn back to help."

"Did you see the pilot? Man or woman, how many?"

"Now that I think about it, there were two. Men, I think. It was too dark to really tell, though, and they were already beyond the spillover from the café's security lights."

"Anything else you can think of?"

"Not offhand, Detective, but why don't you leave me your card? If anything comes to mind I'll ring you up."

Jack knew he might live to regret it, but he pulled out one of his cards and passed it to Maggie, being careful to keep his fingers away from her snapping manicured nails.

Jack didn't trust coincidence. Not when two women, both young, blond, and naked, turned up dead on the seashore. Either they'd been enjoying a good time that got away from them, or someone had deliberately sent them to an early grave.

6

Back before noon, Jack laid out the contents of the manila envelope on the kitchen's center island. Phone bill, no phone. Address of Angelica's apartment, no key. A short list of her friends, with phone numbers. A quick glance found matches on the phone bill. He'd put those names at the top of his list.

He placed a call to Tommy Aronsohn that went directly to voice mail. He filled him in on the Cardona case before snapping on the television, where all of the local stations were covering the discovery of the second dead woman in the past three weeks. Nothing new was being reported, but it was a story that would get churned because the similarity between the two women was startling. No cause of death was reported for either woman, which Jack thought odd because the second woman appeared to have died when her boat hit the rocks at Paradise Cove. And their identities had yet to be released, which Jack thought equally odd because of the time line at play. Three weeks in was more than enough time to notify the next of kin of the first victim. He picked up the picture of Angelica and understood Cardona's discomfort. Same age, same hair color, same type. Jack pulled out a yellow pad and started to make lists.

For a privileged young woman, Angelica didn't have extravagant tastes or shopping habits. The credit cards weren't maxed out. The last purchase made was at the Macy's makeup department in Century City on the seventeenth of April. The bill totaled $129. A reasonable sum.

The apartment was paid in full on the first of every month from a Wells Fargo account in Beverly Hills. Vincent paid for the rent and incidentals so that Angelica . . . could do what?

The last personal check she wrote, in the sum of three hundred and fifty dollars, in perfect cursive, was made out to the Lee Strasberg Theatre and Film Institute, and notated at the bottom of the cashed check was the name Barry Freid.

So that she could become an actress. Ask and ye shall receive, Jack thought. But why didn't Vincent Cardona know that?

Angelica's father was a mobster and she was trying to change her persona? Maybe. Maybe she just had a gift. Or a private dream. At least she was studying, Jack thought. From everything he had read, show business was a really tough racket. Maybe she'd suffered a string of rejections, gotten fed up, and taken a road trip.

Jack picked up Angelica's photograph and was again taken with the intensity behind her green eyes. The girl didn't seem to have any quit in her.

Three-and-a-half-week trip? Could be, he thought. But no phone calls, no credit card receipts—it just didn't feel right.

He would get started with his interviews after he had laid out the ground rules to Cardona.

No money would change hands. The police would be brought in if necessary. No guarantee of success. This wasn't his only commitment. The only outcome Jack demanded was that his debt be paid in full.

It was a take-it-or-leave-it proposition for Jack, who was painfully aware that Vincent Cardona was a man who played by his own book of rules.

The Mafia handbook.

The phone rang, and he saw it was Tommy Aronsohn.

"You have got to be kidding me," was Tommy's opening remark. "What did Leslie say?"

Tommy had been a baby DA working lower Manhattan when Jack was cutting his teeth as a rookie narcotics detective. They had run some wild, seat-of-their-pants cases back in the day and were still thick as thieves.

"She doesn't know yet."

A deep laugh rumbled from his friend like a storm warning. "You're dating a deputy district attorney, Jack. There are politics involved."

"Don't start, Tommy."

"A missing person. What the hell. You should be able to clear that up in a few days. When you find the kid you'll be a hero in the old neighborhood and they'll treat your mother like a saint."

"I thought I moved out of the neighborhood."

"Good luck with that. So FYI, Lawrence Weller chewed off my ear after your undercover operation lit up the airwaves."

"It's a gift."

"But then Larry turned on CNBC and discovered that his stock had ticked up two dollars in after-hours trading. It seems the Street decided he was a proactive manager protecting their investment. Good work, by the way."

"It got hairy."

"The fee got fatter. Hazard pay, I argued. He folded."

"Great. The guys will be happy."

"There's more to come. What did I tell you?"

"Hang out a shingle, you'll keep me busy."

"I did, I will. Now, when's the arraignment?"

"Midweek. I'll spend a couple of days doing prelim on this case before I hit the road again. Maybe I'll get lucky."

"Keep me in the loop," Tommy said, and he clicked off.

———

A large painting of Lee Strasberg was hung high on a maroon wall and appeared to be looking down on the proceedings like a wizened deity.

Jack had entered the lobby of the Lee Strasberg Theatre and Film Institute, filled with men milling around muttering to themselves. They all looked pretty much the same. Same physical type. A little too much like himself, he thought. It was weird but he shook it off and asked a young, gaunt actor type carrying a pile of papers where he could find Barry Freid. He was handed a few stapled pages of what looked like dialogue of some kind, and told to sign in and get into character. Before he could argue, the door to Studio A swung open and a very worked-up young man, breathing hard, in a full-blown panic, banged out of the studio, pushed through the crowd, and all but ran out of the lobby, slamming the double glass doors behind him.

Another acting career bites the dust, Jack thought.

He took the opportunity to step through the door himself.

A single spotlight shining center stage momentarily blinded him. When Jack's vision cleared, he could see that he was standing in a round pool of light, on a black stage, in a theater painted entirely in black. Of the ninety-nine seats in the house, only two were occupied.

A long-legged, long-haired man with the bearing of a monk and a round, shiny bald pate that reflected the spotlight was rubbing his temples with such intensity, it looked as if he were trying to keep his head from exploding.

An overweight, attractive thirtysomething woman wearing a black turtleneck sweater, jeans, and black knee-high boots sat next to him. Her pen was poised, presumably waiting for him to utter something brilliant.

"Take it from the top," was all the man could muster in a tortured voice, not looking up.

"I'm not here to audition," Jack stated.

The man's head shot up out of his hands like it was springloaded, and he looked at Jack for the first time. He wasn't disappointed.

"Did you hear that?" he said to the woman at his side. "I believed him. He sounded like a cop."

"Are you Barry Freid?" Jack asked.

"Guilty," he said with growing anticipation. "Go on when you're ready."

"I'm not here to read."

"That's what I told my class last night. Walk into an audition like you own the stage. Like they can't succeed without you."

The young woman's pen was a blur of motion as she notated his every word.

"Did you study with Lee before he passed?"

Barry said *Lee* with a reverence that most men reserved for the Pope.

"No," Jack said simply.

"Do you hear the way he answered my question?" Barry went on. "Pure, honest, direct, no acting . . . Sandy?"

"Sandy?" Jack asked, like *What the fuck?*

"Meisner."

"No."

"Perfect, I've seen enough. You've got the part. You look like a cop; you're the first actor who walked through the door who sounded like a cop. I can work with you."

"I was a cop; I'm a private investigator. I'm looking for a girl."

"I'm confused," Barry said, his theatrical joy dissipating.

"Angelica Cardona? She's in one of your classes?"

"I have an Angelica, but the last name is Curtis."

If Jack were a betting man he'd have placed odds that Curtis was her mother's maiden name.

He stepped off the stage and held out his hand to Barry, who reluctantly shook it. "Jack Bertolino."

Jack nodded to the woman sitting next to the director. She returned his gaze, unblinking. The door to the theater banged open and the casting director stuck her head in, confused by Jack's presence. She checked her list.

"Give me five minutes?" Jack asked Barry, who nodded and waved off the young woman at the door; she clearly did not appreciate being waved off. Jack showed Barry the picture of Angelica that Vincent Cardona had provided. Both Barry and his assistant clucked in unison.

"Angelica is AWOL. Hasn't been to class in, I don't know, a few weeks?" he said.

"That's why I'm here. She hasn't been seen in close to a month. Her father's extremely worried. I'm sure you can understand his concern."

"She never showed up for her final scene. A semester of grueling work for naught."

"Any idea where she might be?" Jack asked. "I've read that the relationship between an acting teacher and their students can be a very personal one."

"I'm afraid she was a student of limited ability. Not that she didn't have talent. But whenever it was time to pull emotion from her personal life—we call it emotional recall—and confront her past, she'd block and shut down. Beautiful, but that isn't enough for this kind of work. I knew very little about her social history outside of class."

"Did she have any close friends at the institute?"

Barry's assistant spoke for the first time. "She had a scene partner who was very upset when Angelica did her disappearing act. Carol Williams. She felt betrayed. I don't blame her. People don't come here to study because they want to. They're compelled to."

"Disappearing act. You think she just took off?"

"It happens," Barry said. "Students feel overwhelmed. Fear of failure. Fear of success. You don't?"

"Is Carol Williams here today?" Jack tossed back instead of speculating.

"She had an audition technique class yesterday and she works waiting tables on her off days. It isn't inexpensive getting this kind of training. That's why it was so disheartening when Angelica just disappeared."

"Did anyone at the school try to contact her?"

"The registrar, I called a few times, and Carol camped out in front of her apartment."

"You said Carol works as a waitress?"

"At the Mondrian," the woman said. When it was clear from Jack's expression that the name didn't strike a chord, she added, "the Mondrian Hotel on Sunset."

Jack handed Barry and his assistant each a card.

"If anything comes to mind, if you hear a rumor, if she contacts you, anything, this is where I can be reached twenty-four/seven. I'd appreciate a call," Jack said.

"And if you change your mind about the acting," Barry said, "let's talk. I think you've got something."

"I've got something all right," Jack said, amused. "But what I want is to find Angelica."

7

Angelica Cardona's eyelids fluttered then snapped open. Her green eyes were bright and relaxed and then, as she got her bearings, darkened with the speed of a roiling storm cloud blocking the sun. All emotion and color washed out in a heartbeat.

She closed her eyes again and then willed herself awake, uncovering her legs from underneath the white silk sheets and draping them over the side of the king-sized bed.

Her blond hair was feathered across her beautiful face, but she didn't notice. She pulled down her silk teddy. The material was just enough to cover her. Angelica stood up, moved deliberately to a pair of slippers that had been neatly placed next to the wall, and stepped into them. She headed across the plush gray carpet to a full closet, where she shrugged into a silk bathrobe that did more to accentuate her perfect figure than cover it.

The room was well appointed, like a suite in a high-end hotel. Beautiful bed, fluffy white down pillows and comforter, black-lacquered designer furniture, modern prints on three blue plaster walls, but no windows. There was a large kitchenette with a silver tray laden with sweet rolls and muffins, and a coffeemaker that had been set on a timer was now filling a carafe with fresh brew.

No windows.

Angelica filled a coffee mug and paced the length of the room, lost in thought. Coffee mug in hand, taking small, safe sips. Small, safe steps. Losing count. The steps became strides, more exaggerated and more manic as she paced back and forth. And then with volcanic ferocity she spun and hurled the coffee mug.

The mug seemed to explode into thin air. The mass of brown liquid fanned out and flattened like a Rorschach test. It dripped down the perfectly clear, thick Plexiglas fourth wall like the dark tears she would never reveal to her unknown captor.

Angelica strode into the kitchenette, picked up another mug, filled it with hot coffee, and drank. She picked up a sweet roll and ate. She threw the breakfast roll back onto the dish, sucked in a furious breath, hit the rug, and started humping out push-ups. Angelica wasn't in control of much, but she knew that if she didn't keep up her strength, she would die in her Plexiglas cage.

———

Malic al-Yasiri sat Jesuit-straight behind an ornately carved desk. Thirty-eight years old, he weighed in at one hundred seventy pounds without an ounce of body fat. He had short, dark, brush-cut hair, salted with silver, and severe features that rendered him just short of handsome. His mirthless, coal-black eyes were trained on a sixty-inch flat-screen monitor while he sipped thick Turkish coffee. His eyes creased, but it was more a gesture of avarice than a smile.

Malic dispassionately observed Angelica's outburst and her daily morning routine. Twenty-five push-ups, twenty-five sit-ups, twenty-five squat-thrusts, and then repeat. Malic watched like a scientist, one might say. Like a connoisseur, he would argue. A collector.

His eyes shifted to Matisse's *La Pastorale*, lit with a pin spot on the mahogany-paneled wall to his right. The original. Procured through a very private party after the Musée d'Art Moderne heist in 2010. It relaxed him and thrilled him at the same time.

The glint of pure yellow gold caught his eye. A two-thousand-year-old Mesopotamian statuette he had personally pillaged from the National Museum of Iraq.

While the Republican Guard risked their lives repelling American artillery from the upper floors of the Baghdad museum, Malic was cherry-picking some of his country's most precious treasures in the safety of the basement.

A slight knock at the door brought him out of his reverie. He glanced out the window as he touched three buttons on a panel that slid out from under his desktop. The video display of Angelica wiping the sweat off the back of her neck turned to black and disappeared behind the paneled wall. Another mahogany panel slid in front of the Matisse, and a third hid the gold statuette from prying eyes. He stood, straightened his tailored Armani suit, snugged his floral-pattern silk tie, and unlatched the heavy door to his office.

A dark-haired beauty ran in and jumped into her father's powerful arms. Five years old, precocious, spoiled, Saarah. His little princess, and the only real love of his life. She was the collector's prize possession.

Malic looked over his daughter's shoulder and stroked her head as his wife, Kayla, cleared the edge of the infinity pool. He looked with pride, past his wife, to the main house beyond the aquamarine water and the manicured gardens, to the eight-foot wall that surrounded his gated compound and protected what belonged to him.

"If you don't leave now, you'll be sitting in traffic for two hours," his wife said as she appeared in the doorway. She was oval-eyed, exquisite. She wore a multicolored silk hijab head scarf that hung loosely over her natural blond hair and framed her perfect face. She never stepped foot into the converted guest and pool house. Malic was the only one besides the engineer and workers who knew how intricate the conversion had been.

"You are right, my love," Malic said, his voice deep and resonant. He spoke perfect English with a slight British accent. An affectation he had acquired during his studies at Oxford, along with his future bride.

The drive from Orange County to downtown L.A. was always a challenge. "Have Hassan bring the car around. And you," he said, turning his attention to his young charge. "You be a good girl and know that you are loved."

"Okay, Daddy." She put on her best pouty face until he kissed her forehead and handed her off to his wife before securely locking the door behind him.

Malic desired to take one last look at his blond prisoner. She would be stepping into the bathtub right about now. But he really didn't have the time. That was fine, he thought. She would be his alone for as long as it took to complete the deal.

8

Vincent Cardona wasn't happy that Jack had a previous commitment. He wasn't happy Jack refused to accept any payment. But Vincent was really unhappy that his daughter was still missing and reluctantly agreed to Jack's terms.

Cardona slammed down the phone with a fury.

"Follow that fuck!" he raged at Peter, his face purple-red, the vein on his temple swollen and throbbing. "I wanna know what the fuck Bertolino's fuckin' doing twenty-four/seven. And if he finds out you're following him, shoot yourself with your own gun. It'll hurt a lot less than if I get my hands around your fuckin' neck. Now get the fuck outta here."

Peter, having been trained by the best, moved quickly out of Cardona's sight.

———

Angelica's building was located in a lower-rent district of Beverly Hills. The only thing it shared with its rich cousin to the north was the zip code. The Big Man had called ahead and spoken with

Angelica's landlord, who was outside her apartment having a smoke while Jack took a look around.

Apartment 3B was a one-bedroom on the ground floor of a modest, midsixties, well-maintained eight-unit apartment building. Two stories, off-white stucco, green trim, manicured lawn, and mature evergreen hedges.

The front door opened into the living room, and Jack lingered there to get a feel for the place and maybe get a feel for Angelica before he slipped on a pair of disposable gloves and booties and closed the door behind him.

The floors were white oak and highly polished. Angelica's furniture was shabby chic. Overstuffed tan sofa and a large faded blue paisley chair that looked well worn and comfortable. A modern reading lamp with double white glass globes stood sentry between the two pieces of furniture.

A large wicker basket of unopened mail had been placed directly underneath the mail slot located on the wall next to the door. Jack picked out the phone bill and credit card receipts that had arrived in the past few days.

Angelica's laptop was on a small wooden table that looked out onto the heavy afternoon traffic on Beverly Boulevard, but the room remained remarkably silent. Jack pulled out a flash drive and downloaded the MacBook Pro's hard drive. He'd have Cruz tear it apart.

He was most interested in her social media sites, her e-mail accounts, and her Instagram files. It always amazed Jack how much personal information people were willing to share in this environment of increased identity theft and cyber hacking. A digital trail that could follow the youth of America to their graves— or Todd Dearling to prison, he mused with satisfaction. But Jack knew it might also provide valuable clues as to Angelica's where-abouts.

Her bedroom was feminine but understated and perfectly clean except for a few articles of clothing draped haphazardly on her well-made bed, as if she had changed her mind a few times before she left her apartment. Jack was interested in reconstruct-ing her itinerary the day she disappeared.

Her closet was neat. High-end designer fashions on one side, J.Crew, jeans, and workout clothes on the other. A few empty wooden hangers marked the designer side, and from the quality of the blouses that were strewn on the bed, she had walked out the door dressed for show.

Angelica was orderly and composed. An empty suitcase was in the back of her closet; a carry-on bag stood next to her shoe rack. Again, orderly, not too many empty slots. It didn't look as if she had packed for an extended trip. In fact, it didn't look like she had packed at all.

The bathroom was filled with her toiletries. No prescription drugs to speak of except for a bottle of Zyrtec, which could now be purchased over the counter. No spare toothbrushes or men's toiletries under the sink or in any of her drawers. No birth con-trol. Jack remembered that his ex-wife used to carry hers jammed in her overstuffed bag along with the rest of her crowded life, in case she forgot to take one in the morning.

The analgesics reminded Jack that his back was starting to throb, so he dry-chewed two Excedrin and walked into the kitchen in search of water to wash them down.

Other than the dregs in the bottom of a coffee cup that had been placed in the sink, the kitchen was spotless. Jack took a mouthful of water from the faucet and washed down the bitter pills. He opened the cabinet next to the sink and saw orderly rows of wineglasses and coffee mugs and water goblets. The dishes were stacked neatly, according to size.

Some fruit and vegetables were shriveled and growing purple hair in the fridge but nothing unusual for three and a half weeks out. Bottled water, condiments, and a half-drunk bottle of Chardonnay. Again, it didn't look like she had been planning a trip, and from all appearances, Angelica was a woman who took care of the details. Nothing loose about her bill paying. Nothing loose about the way she lived.

Jack fielded a phone call as he walked back into the living room. Carol Williams agreed to an interview after her waitress shift at the Mondrian Hotel. Ten o'clock gave him pause, but he wanted to get as much accomplished as possible before traveling north again.

He moved up to a Pottery Barn–style bookcase that stood next to Angelica's desk. It was lined with: *A Life in the Theatre*, *Stanislavski*, *Stella Adler on America's Master Playwrights*, *The Method*, and multiple biographies of film and theater stars. And then row upon row of paperback plays that were all stamped *Samuel French Bookshop* and were probably used for her scene study work at the Strasberg institute.

Jack pulled out a dog-eared copy of *Cat on a Hot Tin Roof* and flipped through the pages. He had seen a Broadway production of the play starring Kathleen Turner back in the nineties when his marriage was still a success and they were both still trying.

Handwritten notes filled the margins in precise pencil. This was one serious young woman, Jack thought. Nothing frivolous about her.

No family pictures, except one silver-framed photo that had

turned sepia-brown with age. A very attractive woman, probably her mother. He replaced the picture on the shelf and picked up an unframed eight-by-ten glossy headshot of Angelica. It was definitely her mother. Jack could see a clear resemblance in her eyes.

No cell phone; the new bill just had a carry-over balance. No new calls. The few snapshots in the drawer of the desk also seemed older. Jack gathered them up and would let Cardona put names with the faces. No boyfriends, no letters, nothing personal to give Jack any direction at all. He found a spare key that matched the apartment door key and pocketed it in case he wanted another look around.

Angelica's childhood seemed to have been left behind in the Beverly Hills home. Jack made a mental note to ring up Cardona and take a look at her old room. Get a feel for how she grew up.

The gray-haired landlord cracked the door a sliver, peeked his head into the unit, and almost leaped out of his skin when Jack pulled the door the rest of the way open. They both laughed as the startled man feigned a heart attack. He locked up and then showed Jack Angelica's parking space in the enclosed garage.

Everyone's an actor, Jack thought.

Cardona had provided a key for the late-model red Miata, and Jack spent the next twenty minutes combing through the car—under the seats, in the glove compartment, behind the visor, and in the trunk—for anything of interest. The small sports car was as clean as her apartment. He found a few gas receipts and some Post-its with addresses written in ink that had been filed in the car's owner's manual. There were no names, and Jack decided to add the addresses to his yellow pad and track them down at a later date.

The Excedrin was burning a hole in Jack's gut. Either that,

or it was his growing sense of unease about Angelica's disappearance. She'd been missing for over three weeks; Jack knew her chances of being alive were slim. She might have been grabbed, he thought. But no one had come forward with a ransom note, despite her rich father. Jack hoped her acting partner could reveal more secrets about Angelica than her barren apartment had.

9

Jack was sitting in his favorite booth, at his favorite restaurant, across from his favorite woman, who had just pushed her uneaten duck breast to the center of the table, choked the life out of her cloth napkin, and laid it carefully down beside her plate.

Arsinio approached Jack's booth with a smile on his face, but the chill stopped him in his tracks. He turned on his heel and moved back to the bar area. Smart man. The uneaten plate of food in front of Leslie and the one large bite out of Jack's burger said it all to the sage waiter.

Hal's Bar and Grill was buzzing with the west-side after-work crowd. The New York feel, lively bar, and consistent food made it Jack's go-to place. As long as he didn't have the interview until ten o'clock, he figured he might as well enjoy dinner. The large metal sculptures that separated the bar from the restaurant, the museum-quality photographs and first-class art, provided by local Venice artists, set the place apart from the pack. The volume was up in the large open room, and so was the growing tension at Jack's booth with a view overlooking the entire room and the front door. Old cop's habit that Rebecca, the maître d', respected and accommodated.

"So, are we having our first argument?" Jack asked, and then flexed his jaw. He stared straight into Leslie's angry eyes, trying and failing to lighten the mood.

"I'm a DDA, Jack. I work for the district attorney. My boyfriend works for the mob."

"It's not mob business. Angelica isn't in the mob."

"It's all mob business with them, Jack. Who are you kidding?"

"I thought we discussed not bringing politics into the bedroom."

"Good luck on that score."

"Now you're starting to piss me off."

"Great rejoinder, Jack. Next you're going to tell me it's a matter of honor."

"It is a matter of honor. Cardona may have saved my son's life."

But Leslie was buying none of it.

"So you're telling me that you turned down a hundred and twenty K a year from the mayor because you felt too constricted, and you're going to accept a job with a mobster where you won't accept a salary, because you'd feel too constricted."

"Well, if you couch it like that . . ."

"Jack." Leslie threw up her hands, her voice rising in volume. "Remind me not to call you when I make my next deal. You and Tony Soprano?"

Jack shushed her with his hands. People were starting to glance in their direction and Jack was getting hot under the collar.

"He was there for my boy. It's his daughter. I don't care what his history is."

Leslie was giving him no love, just the flinty eyes of a prosecutor. "Jack, I mean, I usually have all the answers, and I'm dumbstruck."

Jack emptied his wineglass, trying to regroup.

"Are you still going to San Francisco?" she asked.

"Tomorrow, for the arraignment."

"Let's talk when you get back. No worries, Jack. I just have to process what's really going on here."

"Yeah, good, take some time," he said, wanting to end the conversation.

And then Leslie threw a changeup: "We've been moving so fast."

Huh. Wrong answer, Jack thought. "It feels right to me."

"And to me," she added quickly. "We want many of the same things, but clearly not all of the same things."

Jack wasn't fast on his verbal feet when his emotions started roiling. And so he chose to say nothing.

"Just to clarify, you're taking on Cardona's case?" she asked, but it was more a statement of fact.

"I don't think his daughter is vacationing. I think she needs help."

"Give it to the cops."

"It may come to that. I'm open to it if need be."

But that was as much as he was willing to concede. Jack picked up the bottle of wine and replenished their two glasses, fighting to keep his anger in check and his mouth shut. Jack had learned through the years that words had power and couldn't always be taken back. And he didn't want to lose the woman sitting across from him.

Leslie took a sip of cabernet and then put the glass down.

"You're not the kind of man who can be told what to do. I understand that, Jack. It's what attracted me to you. It's what I love about you. Your integrity. But that noble sword can cut both ways."

"The last thing I want to do is hurt you," Jack said, sounding oddly hollow to himself.

"I have to make sure that I'm up for the ride. It took a long time to get to where I am in my career, politically. I know *politics* is a dirty word, but it's part of my life and I'm not finished yet. I don't want to be. I'd resent it, and then I'd resent you."

Jack was going to give her as much rope as she needed.

"I have to assess the risk."

And with that she hung herself.

"You do your risk assessment, and I'll go up north and take care of business," he snapped.

"Jack," she said, trying to defuse the tension.

Jack knew he'd crossed that line, and he found himself shutting down. He'd been there before. The divorce had taken a damaging toll, and he didn't want to relive it. Simple as that. His head was swimming and his heart started to pound.

"I'd better go," Leslie said quietly.

No argument from Jack. He tried to control his breathing as she slid out of the booth and walked across the floor of the restaurant. He started losing the battle as the front door of Hal's closed behind her.

Jack took a big pull on his wineglass as his cell phone rang. He was going to let it go to voice mail but picked up when he saw who was calling.

Narcotics detective Nick Aprea, Jack's close friend and only confidant in the Los Angeles Police Department.

"So, Jack," Nick said by way of hello.

"Nick."

"Good news, bad news."

"Yeah?" Jack hated this game.

"You answered the phone."

"And?"

"There's a contract out on your life."

"Oh shit," Jack said, sounding relieved. "I thought something happened to Carmen, you sounded so . . . weird."

Carmen was Nick's beautiful Filipina wife.

"La Eme," Nick stated with gravitas. "Mexican Mafia. Retribution. They blame you for Mando, Mexican Mafia Mando, getting cut down by the Zetas' commando. Go figure. I'll keep my ear to the ground; you grow eyes in the back of your head."

Nick was referencing the drug case he'd worked with Jack a month ago.

Jack had been instrumental in dismantling the 18th Street Angels, a multigenerational street gang that had controlled the drug trade out of Ontario for the past fifty years. Mando was La Eme, but he also ran the Angels. An important asset, from the Mexican Mafia's standpoint.

Jack wasn't surprised there was blowback. Not happy, but not surprised. It went with the territory. After twenty-five years in narcotics, Jack had made some good friends in his career but more than his share of enemies.

"Thanks, Nick."

"*Vaya con Dios*, my brother."

"Let's hope I'm *bueno con Dios*."

Jack clicked off, glancing at the empty booth opposite him, and then checked the front door of the restaurant. Leslie hadn't miraculously changed her mind and come back. Jack let out a long sigh. It was going to be a long night.

10

Club Martinique was in full swing as Jack fought his way through the throng on the dance floor, balancing two glasses of cabernet. He was clearly out of his element. The crowd was filled with twentysomething Hollywood elite and more than its share of wannabes.

The computerized lights strobed with enough intensity to induce a seizure in an epileptic. The numbing volume guaranteed Jack's ears would be ringing for the rest of the night.

He placed one of the wineglasses down in front of Carol Williams and took the seat next to her. They clinked glasses and drank. There were probably better locations to conduct the initial interview, but Jack wanted to put her at ease. Plus, he would get a feel for the last place she had seen Angelica before her disappearance.

Carol was also blond, but in a cute, pixie kind of way. Short but stacked. Blue eyes and a killer figure that could stop traffic. She had just worked a full shift at the Mondrian Hotel and took two large gulps before she came up for air.

"I'm very oral," she said demurely, wiping her sheer plum lipstick off the rim of her glass.

A hell of an opening line, Jack thought.

"This is where we were rehearsing our scene," she continued, referring to the table. "Sometimes it helps, being out in public. Change the environment, keep it natural."

Jack wasn't sure what she meant but took a sip of wine and let her talk. He was still stuck on the "oral" remark.

"Angelica was working on her sexuality. She was too repressed for Barry. And I'm supposed to work on releasing my anger, which I really think is a total crock," she said with enough intensity that Jack believed her. "Sometimes I'm angry through an entire shift."

"Must be good for tips," he deadpanned.

"Oh, they don't know. Because I repress it, or so Barry thinks."

Jack wanted to steer the conversation away from the artist formerly known as Barry. "Did she ever date?"

Carol shook her head and pursed her lips before saying no.

"Did she ever talk about her family, her father?"

"Angelica was tight-lipped. We all knew who her father was. We didn't really care. It was all about the work. I mean, an actress changing her name . . . who cares?"

"Do you think Angelica is the kind of woman who would just take off? Without letting anybody know?"

"No, that's why I was so angry. You see, again, no issues with anger," she said, raising her eyebrows to hammer her point. "There's a lot of pressure in class to succeed. As far as I could tell—I mean as far as she would let on—class was all she had. Her safe place."

"Did anybody hit on you, disturb your rehearsal that night, follow you out?"

"I get hit on all the time," she said without ego as she gestured to her breasts. "Thirty-four C's. They're like magnets."

Jack kept his focus on her blue eyes. Or tried to. "I can see how that might be an issue."

"A blessing and a curse."

"Now, back to Angelica . . . Did you leave the club together? At the end of the night?"

"No, separate cars. I left first. She used the ladies' room."

"What was her mood like? Did she seem preoccupied?"

"No. Oh." She grabbed her cell phone out of her worn black leather bag and pulled up a photo. "This is us, at this table, that night."

Carol leaned in so close their elbows touched as she showed Jack a few shots of Angelica alone at the table looking cool, calm, and collected, and then a few of herself, mugging for the camera. She flipped the screen a few times and pulled up a picture of Angelica and herself seated together with their backs to the bar.

"Could you forward these to me?" Jack asked.

"No problemo. I'm technically gifted," she said with a Cheshire cat grin.

Jack detected a double entendre in her response and didn't want to give her an opening. He stood up to go.

"Can't you stay? I'm wired from work," she said.

"I've got to run, early flight, but if you send me the photos it would be a great help."

Jack planned on blowing up the pictures of Angelica and then talking to the bartenders alone, before the hordes descended. He handed Carol his card.

"If anything comes up. If you remember anything that might help, call."

Carol drained her wineglass and stood up to say her good-byes.

"You want to follow me home?" she stage-whispered, leaning in close enough that Jack could feel her heat.

"Tempting offer," he said, thinking of Leslie and how their relationship was suddenly up in the air.

"I'm not repressed," she said coyly as her breasts grazed Jack's abdomen.

"I can see that."

But however Jack did the math, Carol Williams was twenty years younger. His son's age. Legal, but oh hell, just wrong, he decided.

"Good night, Carol," Jack Bertolino said, moving off before he acted on his much baser instincts.

———

When Jack got home, he thought about giving Leslie a call, but it was the booze talking. Waking up his computer, he saw that Carol Williams had already forwarded the photographs.

He wisely chose to work.

Jack blew up the pictures and then made color prints. As he studied each of the shots under a light in his office, he was reminded again of just how striking Angelica was. He thought about Vincent Cardona and tried to imagine what he was going through. Jack would have been in hell.

Nothing else jumped off the page. But when he tossed the photos onto his desk, the lamplight illuminated the crowd at the standing-room-only bar in the background. One man was staring straight into the camera lens, holding a martini glass. Carol was in the foreground, and the man's gaze was lasered in on the photographer. Probably Angelica, Jack thought.

Who took the picture of both women?

Jack grabbed his phone and punched in Carol's number. She picked up on the first ring.

"Did you change your mind?" she said, flirty.

"Don't tempt me," he fired back. "Who took the picture of you and Angelica sitting at the table?"

"Just some dude, standing at the bar. He came over and offered, and we accepted. Kinda cute. Well dressed. Seemed nice enough. Why?"

"Did Angelica shoot the picture of you?"

"Uh, yeah."

"Pull up that picture and take a look at the man standing at the bar, over your left shoulder."

"Oh, that's him. Oooh. He's got kind of a creepy vibe there."

"That's what I thought. Thanks, Carol." And Jack hung up.

He went back to the computer and transferred the picture to Photoshop. Cropped the man in question and enlarged the photo. It was grainy but clear enough for an ID. He sent the enhanced picture over to Nick Aprea and asked him to see if the man was in the LAPD system. He thanked him ahead of time for the help.

It could have been nothing, but the man who took the photo might have been the last person to see Angelica Cardona before she disappeared. Jack wanted a sit-down.

11

"So you went over to the dark side," Detective Nick Aprea said, unfurling the flour tortilla and pouring some more *muy caliente* salsa into his burrito, expertly rerolling it, and savoring the next bite of egg, bacon, cheese, and hot sauce.

Nick was wearing a black leather jacket, mirrored sunglasses, black leather boots, and unruly pillow hair. His bout with teenage acne had left him with a hardened visage but rendered him more attractive to the opposite sex.

He made the greasy breakfast burrito look so tantalizing, Jack started enjoying his own. Nick hadn't wanted to have the conversation over the phone, and so they shared a wooden bench outside a taco stand that was the size of a shoe box. It was situated downtown, a few blocks away from LAPD headquarters, in the shadow of glass and steel high-rise office buildings. The street was knotted with Angelenos heading to work.

"Eh," Jack grunted in answer to Nick's dark-side quip as he took a sip of steaming hot coffee, burning his lip on the sadistic plastic lid.

"He's a card-carrying scumbag."

"Don't pull any punches," Jack said dryly. "Let's just hope it hasn't rubbed off on his daughter. If she's still alive."

"You gonna file a missing-persons? You should file."

"Then they'll jump all over Cardona's business."

"Do you give a rat's ass?"

"I'm gonna find his daughter and then I'm out. Debt paid in full."

"I know you're loath to do it, but Gallina's the card you should play. He's on the case, not smart enough to disassemble the L.A. mob, but once you're on record, the cops'll back your action. Some of us are good at our jobs."

"Hard to believe."

"You were holding out on me, pard."

"Waiting for the right time."

"Story: I was pumping iron with a steroid-injecting Neanderthal out of vice. Izzy. From New Jersey. He was spotting me. He's on muscle-enhancing drugs and I'm trusting him to keep two hundred and fifty pounds of weight from crushing my windpipe."

"And?"

"My muscles were maxed. I told Izzy to pull off the barbell. And this jamoke, who held my life in his hands, said something that made total sense to me, in a moment of weakness."

Jack gestured with his burrito for Nick to go on.

"No," Nick said simply, and he took another bite of the burrito.

"That's it? . . . 'No'?"

Nick threw Jack a look that told him he was stepping on his story.

"*No. As in, You're not done, Aprea.*

"Izzy helped me push up the weight and then guided it down.

I resisted with every last fuckin' ounce of strength. I wanted to strangle the prick.

"Work the negative, he said. You'll get stronger."

Nick polished off the burrito and nodded his head, waiting for Jack's response to his brilliance. Undaunted by the silence, he belched and soldiered on.

"You, my friend, are *working the negative.*"

"Explain."

Nick's wolf grin split his face as he wiped his mouth and continued. "The picture you sent me is the very likeness of one Raul Vargas. Busted in 2003 for the manufacture and distribution of cocaine. One of thirty arrested from here to Detroit. Daddy—now get this for irony—became a major political contributor, got letters extolling his son's virtues from the governor, the mayor, the cardinal, assemblymen, and oh, what the hell, they all landed on the desk of the president of the United States. And miracle of L.A. archdiocese miracles, the kid was granted a pardon."

"Christ," Jack said.

"Already weighed in and got the prick released from prison. One man out of thirty indicted. Six years served of a fifteen-year sentence. His father called it a miracle. I call it dirty politics. Business as usual. So my guess is, if your old lady's pissed off your client's a mafioso, wait till you start sniffing up the Vargas family tree."

The coffee turned sour in Jack's gut.

"You'll get stronger, even while they're kicking the shit out of you. The effing president. They'll be playing kick the can with your sorry ass, Bertolino. But you know what, my brother?"

Jack waited for Nick's answer.

"They'll have to go through me first."

The elevator stopped on the thirty-eighth floor of the KPMG Tower at the Wells Fargo Center on Bunker Hill in downtown Los Angeles. Jack experienced vertigo as he looked over the receptionist's tailored suit, past the jagged skyline, all the way to the Pacific Ocean, which shimmered like a slash of silver.

"Do you have an appointment?" the perfectly coiffed, officious young woman asked. She already knew the answer; Jack had asked to see the anointed son.

Before he could come up with something pithy, the elevator pinged behind him and the receptionist raised a warning eyebrow to whoever stepped silently off onto the thick pile carpet.

Jack spun, flashed a winning smile, thrust his hand forward. "Raul, how are you? Jack Bertolino."

A wary Raul Vargas, who didn't want to offend, accepted the handshake. "Do I know you?"

"I'm on a case and won't take more than two minutes of your time."

Raul forced a smile, thought about blowing off Jack, and decided to keep up some semblance of goodwill until he knew what the hell this intrusion was all about. And who the intruder was.

"Are you with the LAPD? We've got a lot of friends."

"Good to hear, me too. Retired," Jack said. He lowered his voice. "Working a missing-persons case. Could we do this in your office?" He glanced toward the receptionist, who was pretending not to listen.

"Halle, when am I due at the planning commission?"

"The meeting starts in five minutes."

Good one, Jack thought. Little Halle was well trained.

"It won't take but a minute," Jack said in as unthreatening a manner as he could muster. He already didn't like the man, who had turned on his heel and walked up the hallway toward his office. Jack winked at the receptionist and followed in his wake.

"What a view," Jack said, once inside the palatial office. "Thank you for taking the time."

"What can I do for you, Jack?"

Raul sat back in his black leather chair. King of his domain. He gestured for Jack to sit in one of two Barcelona chairs, but Jack stayed on his feet. The thirty-year-old had a thick veneer that covered a lot of scar tissue, Jack thought. Six years behind bars could do that to a man. His face was handsome enough, but his eyes had that hollow prison stare. A trimmed brown mustache matched his razor-cut longish hair, which couldn't hide Raul's red-rimmed brown eyes.

Jack cut to the chase. He pulled out the picture of Angelica at Club Martinique. He slid it across Raul's glass-and-chrome desk. "Have you ever seen this woman?"

Raul picked up the printout, looked at it thoughtfully. "I don't think so, I don't know. There are so many beautiful women in this town." He handed it back to Jack. "Should I know her? Who is she?"

"Her name is Angelica Cardona. Her father's Vincent Cardona. Owns the Chop House?" Jack asked, voicing a question.

Raul didn't blink, just shook his head.

"You might know her as Angelica Curtis," Jack continued. "Maybe this will help." And he showed him the picture of Angelica and Carol sitting shoulder to shoulder.

"Not really. Cute, but—"

"The bartender said you took the picture," Jack lied, protecting his source, Carol Williams.

Raul's brow furrowed and then he asked, "Where was this?" And then he answered his own question with a question. "Was this at Club Martinique? Oh yeah. Oh *yeah*." He used his best one-man-to-another low, commiserating tone. "I was loaded. Walked by, they were taking photos with their iPhone. I offered to take a picture of them both."

"And?"

"And they said yes. I snapped the shot, tried to work my charm, and they said no. I walked back to the bar with my tail between my legs, where I spent too much time and too much money."

"And you never spoke with either of these women or saw them again after you took the photograph?"

"Are you kidding me? The club was insane that night. Speaking of which, how did you happen to find me?"

"You make quite an impression," Jack said, evading.

"Good to know," Raul said with a weak grin.

Jack thought about showing him the other pictures, but he saw nothing to be gained.

"I'm afraid I have to go," Raul said, tapping his watch. He stood up from behind his desk and extended his hand. "I wish I could have been more help. How long has the girl been missing?"

Jack shook his hand and exerted more pressure than necessary. "The woman disappeared that night."

"That's terrible, really." Raul met the grip and then broke it. "What a city," he said sincerely.

Jack handed him his card. "Do you mind?" And he took one of Raul's cards out of a gold tray that looked like an antique. "In case I think of anything else or you think of anything, a call would be greatly appreciated by my client."

"I'd love to help. But . . ."

Jack took his cue. "Thanks." He casually walked out the door. Yet he didn't think it was the last time he was going to cross paths with young Raul Vargas. An ex-con rubbing shoulders with a mafioso's daughter the night she disappeared seemed like . . . another coincidence.

———

The door to Malic's office exploded open. He lurched out of his seat with a Beretta Sub-Compact in his hand as Raul charged in. He was stopped in his tracks by the sight of the pistol.

"You forgot to knock," Malic said, python deadly. When he realized his life wasn't in any danger, he replaced his favorite Italian weapon in his hidden drawer.

"Get rid of her," Raul said.

Malic sat down comfortably and stared at Raul like he was an amoeba in a petri dish.

"A PI is sniffing around asking questions about the girl," Raul said, sliding Jack's card across Malic's desk. "And her name isn't Curtis . . . it's Cardona," he hissed. "Are you aware of who Vincent Cardona is?" Raul asked, challenging Malic, the red blossoming from his neck to his ears. "He's a 'made man.' A man with a reputation that makes you look like a fuckin' pansy."

Dead silence in the room.

A blush colored Malic's stonelike cheeks. Finally he said, "Who set her up, Raul? Angelica Curtis, you said. A perfect replacement, you said. I believe this is on you."

Raul continued, undeterred. "Vincent Cardona owns the

Chop House on Canon Drive in Beverly fucking Hills. He's in the Mafia. He's got more connections than we do. You have his daughter. You should have checked. We are fucked. No, we are severely fucked."

Malic let his silence hang in the air for effect.

"Did *you* enjoy getting violated in prison before my men interceded?"

"Don't you dare." But the threat was as impotent as his jailhouse bravado.

"If you ever raise your voice to me again, you and your father will lose everything."

He gestured toward the view from the thirty-eighth-floor window. Ground was about to be broken on a new high-rise construction site. A hard-fought addition to the Los Angeles skyline. Without Malic, permits would be denied, loans would be called, construction would cease, and so would Vargas Development Group. Stark reality froze Raul in place.

Malic wasn't finished talking. "It was my infusion of cash that saved your father's business and my connections with the State Department that saved you. Make sure your father is clear on that. It's been brought to my attention that he is meeting with architects next week on a new project, the Spring Street project, and I wasn't brought into the loop. He can't cast me aside now that I've guaranteed his solvency."

Raul's throat was too dry to respond. Malic was turning the screws. He hadn't even mentioned the video that Raul had shot of himself having sex with the woman who died in the Paradise Cove boat crash. That was enough to put him away for twenty years. Added to his commuted drug sentence it would mean life behind bars.

The woman had clearly been unconscious and the act was undeniably rape. How Malic possessed copies of his personal tapes was beyond him. But they now controlled his life.

"And your father, keep him in line," Malic said. "Our partnership is mutually beneficial."

Raul felt like he was drowning. There were no life preservers. Nothing to hold on to but primal self-preservation, and he worried he was losing his grip.

"And in the future," Malic added, "think before you speak or you won't be fucking women that I provide for your entertainment. But you *will* be bleeding from your anus to your throat."

"Get rid of her," Raul rasped.

Malic wasn't happy with this new complication, but he couldn't have Raul spinning out of control.

"Take an early lunch, Raul. No worries." And then, "Everyone has a father. She will be gone in a week and it will be as if she never existed."

Raul stood frozen in place, gathering himself.

"Now, go," Malic said. "I've got a full schedule. And tell your father . . . Raul, concentrate," he said in even, controlled tones. "Tell your father that I'm ready with the numbers. At his convenience, of course."

Malic picked the card up off of his desk and read *Jack Bertolino & Associates, Private Investigation.*

When his gaze shifted, Raul was gone.

12

Jack and his son, Chris, exited the Café Venetia and headed for Sunken Diamond baseball field on the Stanford campus. Chris stood eye to eye with his father, but with his sandy brown hair and blue eyes, he took after his mother's side of the family. He'd lost some weight since the accident, and his T-shirt and jeans hung loosely on his wiry frame.

"I thought I'd have to call Tommy to bail me out again," Jack said, continuing the story he had started in the restaurant. "Having the incident on film didn't hurt. Lawrence Weller made an appearance with a phalanx of lawyers, and I can tell you, the man was not a happy camper."

Jack knew he was running at the mouth, but his son had remained silent through their entire meal.

"What with three ambulances, five arrests, and leaks from the hotel staff about the stacks of hundred-dollar bills papering the suite."

Chris didn't seem to be listening. He tried to adjust the heavy plaster cast on his arm, looking clearly uncomfortable. "I read about it. You made the paper," he said.

"Today was just the arraignment," Jack continued. "It turns out the gunmen were tipped to the scam by a junior from Stanford. A kid in a coffee shop on a phishing expedition. He got greedy and his life's in the crapper now."

"Yeah, I know."

Chris's bored tone of voice was wearing thin, but Jack pressed on.

"With two separate trials, I'll be making more trips up north. Means more time we can spend together."

Chris's silence was thunderous, only equaled by Jack's guilt.

Arturo Delgado, the man who piloted the Cadillac Escalade like a heat-seeking missile, had tried to kill Chris, knowing it would destroy Jack. A reasonable expectation. It would have worked. Delgado was dead, but the pain lingered on.

"Can I borrow your key? Gotta take a whiz," Chris said as they approached the Garden Court Hotel, where Jack was staying.

Jack handed off the key and Chris disappeared inside. Jack had taken a room for the night and was headed back to Los Angeles in the morning to continue the search for Angelica Cardona. The sooner he found his missing person, the sooner he could get back to his life.

He took in the local scene while he waited. The street was lined with upscale boutiques, restaurants, and coffee shops under a thick canopy of sycamore trees. Their mottled bark—patches of tan, gray, and green—looked like Desert Storm camo. The diverse ethnicity of the students, faculty, and locals walking with purpose gave Stanford a cosmopolitan feel. Not a bad place to spend four years, Jack thought.

Then he spotted the only body at rest, sitting at a small table outside a coffee shop, with a newspaper conspicuously covering his face. But his peg-legged black pants, black socks, and pointed black boots screamed Peter Maniacci.

Jack blended with a group of students crossing the street until he was standing at Peter's side. The anxious man lowered his paper and frantically scanned the front entrance of the Garden Court Hotel. He did a near-comic double take when he sensed Jack at his shoulder.

"Yo, Mr. B." Sheepish.

"How'd you find me?" Pissed.

"You made the news, going into court, and then I just figured . . . you look good on camera," he said, deflecting. "I think maybe you missed your calling."

"What the fuck, Peter?"

"I'm what you call in my business between a rock and a Mr. Vincent Cardona. If I don't report on your whereabouts, he'll shoot me. If he knows that you know, and I knew, and withheld said information, he'd also shoot me."

"Do the right thing, Peter: disappear. Now. I've got no time for this."

"Whatever you say, Mr. B. Uh, can we keep this, uh, between . . . ?"

"Now."

Jack crossed the street just as his son pushed through the door of the hotel. When he looked back, Peter was in the wind. Father and son headed up University Avenue toward the baseball stadium.

"You okay? You didn't eat much," Jack said.

"Not hungry."

"You look tired."

"Not sleeping," he said, slipping on his Oakley sunglasses.

"Want to talk about it?" Jack said, knowing the answer. Had to ask.

"Not really."

Jack wasn't crazy about the attitude, but he was too worried to push it. "I need some caffeine. You want an iced Americano?" he offered, knowing it was Chris's favorite.

"Sounds good."

Was that a thaw in the ice floe? Jack hoped. He'd take anything he could get because his son was obviously in turmoil, and it was killing him.

At a break in the traffic, Jack and Chris did a New York dash across the street. A large truck sped up and then leaned on the air horn and brakes at the same time. Chris blanched. He froze in the middle of the road at the sound of the squealing tires. And then he recovered, flipped off the driver with his good hand, and finished crossing. Head down.

Jack pretended he hadn't seen, but they both knew. He threw a protective arm around his son. He couldn't help it. Chris spun, disengaged, and power-walked up the street away from his father.

———

Jack exited the tunnel that led to the Sunken Diamond playing field. Old-growth eucalyptus trees surrounded the well-appointed stadium. The sky was blue and the sun hidden behind huge, white, billowing cumulus clouds.

The Stanford baseball team had been broken into small groups, going through the rigors of batting, fielding, and pitching practice. Five players were running laps and Jack could see one of Chris's teammates give a thumbs-up to a solitary figure sitting in the nosebleed seats in right field.

Jack sat down next to his son and they watched the action in uncomfortable silence. A leggy freshman at the plate went after a fastball and swung from his heels. The crack of the bat and the hustle of the outfielder were usually enough to put a smile on Jack's face. Today, they fell short.

"If it's any help, that truck scared the hell out of me too."

"Doesn't help." And then, "Dad, don't take this the wrong way, but I need to go through this alone. You can't do it for me."

Jack understood with his brain, but not with his heart. He got that after being run down by a seven-thousand-pound vehicle, no warning—one minute you're fine, the next you wake up in an ICU—he got that his son would never really be the same. And he understood painfully well that he was to blame.

He and his ex-wife had set Chris up with a psychologist. Their boy shrugged it off. They couldn't force him to go. His head was as thick as Jack's. He was willful, stubborn, and Jack found himself at a total loss.

"Team looks sharp."

It was all Jack could think to say.

"It's hard to watch. Really," Chris said. "I get rid of this thing in three months and two days," he said, referring to his cast, "and then I can start strength training. They want me to build the muscles in my arm again before they'll let me throw. If I can still throw."

Jack felt the fear, honesty, and anger in that statement and it shut him down.

"Makes sense."

Chris stood up and looked down at his father. Jack met his gaze.

"I don't blame you," Chris said.

73

"Good to know."

"Mom does, but I don't."

Chris eased out of the aisle and started walking down the steep cement stairs. He turned and looked back up at Jack. "I'll call you next week. Don't worry about me. And tell Mommy I'm fine. I don't need the pressure."

Jack fought the impulse to follow. He watched his son walk down the stairs, past his team, and out of the stadium. It felt like a knife through the heart.

————

The Boeing jet looped over the San Francisco skyline. The lights illuminated the Golden Gate Bridge as a thick cloud bank swallowed the stream of incoming traffic.

Jack had checked out of his hotel and caught the first flight back to L.A. No reason to stay. He dug under the seat in front of him, retrieved his small carry-on, and pulled out his dopp kit. His back was spasming from the emotion of the day. The Excedrin wasn't cutting the pain by half. He pulled out his prescription for Vicodin.

Jack shook the plastic bottle and let out a distressed breath. He knew before he pried off the cap—his emotions twisting in the wind—that the pills were light. His son was the only one who had been in his room, and at least four Vicodin tabs were missing.

Jack Bertolino had spent his career working narcotics, and his son, the love of his life, his reason for being, had just stolen prescription drugs from him.

Jack never heard the flight attendant offer him a glass of water.

13

Hassan, a lean, swarthy man with military-cut copper-red hair, a close-trimmed full red beard, and chiseled features, stepped off the multicolored cigarette boat and expertly tied it to the wooden dock.

He wore green cargo pants, black leather boots, and an army-green T-shirt that accentuated his ropy muscles. A lit Camel hung lazily from his lips. He took a last deep drag and flicked the cigarette into the ocean. Then he grabbed two canvas rucksacks filled with provisions out of the boat and started the steep climb up the weather-beaten wooden stairs built into the side of the cliff.

Twenty-five feet up, he stepped easily off the first landing onto a small, flat grassy outcropping and set down his parcels. The stairs continued up the rock face to the top of the cliff and the wall that surrounded Malic al-Yasiri's compound. He eyed the metal door that was set at an angle into the rock and painted a muted camo-brown so that it blended with the cliff face and all but disappeared when viewed from the water. He rifled through his pockets, looking for the key. He caught sight of the sun threatening the horizon and decided to get a move on before he lost all light.

Angelica stiffened and then moved quickly from the bed to the small kitchen table as she heard her jailer's turn of the key. The rusted hinges made a grating sound as the heavy door was opened and then slammed shut. She steeled herself seconds before he appeared on the other side of the Plexiglas wall. It was the same routine every day. His was the only face she saw.

"Did you bring me the cranberry juice I asked for? A bottle of wine?" Angelica asked, her voice dripping with attitude.

Hassan would have been happy to kill her. It wouldn't have been the first time. But it wasn't his call.

The Americans had taught him how to follow orders when they were rebuilding Baghdad after bombing sections of his neighborhood back to the Stone Age. Malic had given him a way out of Iraq before the Shia majority took power, and paid him handsomely for his loyalty.

His brother was now driving a cab in Detroit, attending to gang business, and two of his cousins had been smuggled directly to Los Angeles. They were all Sunnis, all members of the same tribe, all fiercely loyal to Malic, to whom they owed their lives and their livelihoods. The Iraqi gang had been conceived in the slums of Baghdad and migrated to the city of Detroit.

Malic had been raised in an upper-crust Iraqi family, but he was a thug. He negotiated with the gang's leader when he first emigrated, and a deal was struck to form a splinter group in Southern California. Malic's group would serve as the conduit for the drugs that fueled the gang's business, smuggled from south of the border by operatives of the Sinaloa cartel.

Ultimately, it wasn't in Malic's DNA to be anyone's second.

He killed the Detroit boss and successfully merged the two cities together into one Iraqi gang, operating for all intents and purposes under the radar.

Until now, Hassan thought, worried. Dumping those women's bodies was risky business. The first had just been bad luck. The woman was one of their Eastern European imports. Smuggled into the states through Mexico City and on up to Tijuana, where she made the last leg of her journey by panga boat into San Diego County along with a shipment of cocaine.

The woman had gotten greedy, or desperate; broken into one of their parcels; and died with her face buried in a mountain of coke before she could be delivered to Malic's client.

She might well have committed suicide. Stupid woman, he thought dispassionately. A natural blonde. She would have been treated like a queen in Iraq. It was too bad about the tides, though. She should have been shark bait. Instead she'd floated back to Orange County, surprised a wedding party, and made the front page of the *Orange County Register*.

The second woman, Malic had assured him, would be a most persuasive message. Help maintain the balance of power in Malic's new job with Vargas Development Group. It was too dramatic for Hassan's taste. He would have been happy putting a bullet in the back of her head.

And now this demon. He bridled at Angelica's sour disposition and wanted to slap the petulant look off her face. She was the last-minute replacement for the floater. All three women were interchangeable, cut from the same cloth. She would be made available to fill the order for an important Iraqi sheik, one of Malic's oldest friends and wealthiest accounts.

Who was Hassan to argue? He would follow orders and live the American dream. At least he wasn't driving a cab.

He answered Angelica in Arabic. It gave him pleasure that she was ignorant and spoke only the infidel's language. He explained as to a child that she must remain sober and healthy. That alcohol was forbidden in the Koran. Besides, he said with a sneer, drinking would bring down her sale price.

Hassan picked up one of the rucksacks filled with her food and set it on the table.

Angelica attacked with the speed of a viper.

She wielded her breakfast fork like a dagger. It arced down with one hundred and twenty pounds of blind fury and impaled Hassan in the back. Red blossomed on his upper shoulder as he roared with pain and dropped the sack of food, spilling salad, fruit, and cold cuts onto the rugged floor.

Angelica bolted.

Hassan spun wildly and grabbed for her, missed, and then caught her by the hair. She was already out of the door and into the hallway by the time she shrieked with the pain of her hair being yanked.

Hassan grappled with her and then pulled her back against his body, wrapped his right arm around her while flailing with his left hand to pull the protruding utensil out of his shoulder.

Angelica bit down on his wrist, breaking the skin, and pulled free again.

Maddened by pain, Hassan dove for her and dragged her back into the room. He raised a fist—he wanted to kill her, wanted to strangle her, but knew he couldn't damage the goods. And so he threw her down onto the dinette chair, oblivious to his own pain. He efficiently bound her hands behind her and her legs to the chair's legs with the plastic ties he always carried when doing this kind of security work for Malic.

Then he walked into the bathroom and carefully pulled out the fork, growling. Stupid, he chided himself. Never turn your back on an enemy. Had he learned nothing in the Iraqi army?

Malic would have him killed if he damaged the prisoner, but Hassan had learned certain techniques, skills, and he would have his revenge.

But first he applied soap to the bite on his wrist and stanched the flow of blood with a towel. He only hoped she was clean. He might need a tetanus shot. His shoulder was tender and sore, but he had suffered worse shrapnel wounds in the war.

"Let me go," Angelica ordered in even tones, fighting to control her breathing and keep the desperation out of her voice. "Untie me. Now. I can get you money, and my father will let you live to spend it. It's your only hope. I'm your only hope."

But Hassan denied her with a firm shake of his head.

A tightly rolled *Live Orange County* magazine that had been left for her reading pleasure would now take some of the fight out of this spoiled girl.

Angelica did not cry out as Hassan pulled back the rolled magazine baton and methodically beat her with it. Her eyes became moist, but she didn't make a sound. Hassan almost respected her stubborn strength as he hit her again and again, working meticulously up her stomach, stopping short of her breasts, then down her arms and again from her outer thighs to her ankles.

Satisfied, he stopped, unrolled the magazine, and placed it on the table next to her bed as a reminder.

Hassan made sure the beating left no marks. Malic would

take his job, maybe his head, and his wife would have to shop for a new husband instead of Bloomingdale's fashions.

He stepped over the spilled food and grabbed all of the silverware out of the kitchenette and stowed it in the empty canvas rucksacks. Then he pulled out his Leatherman multitool and cut the plastic cuffs off her ankles and then her wrists.

Women, he thought with an ambivalent shrug as he walked out the door and locked it behind him. He was pleased with his work, pleased that his prisoner's anger seemed to have waned.

———

With the clanging metallic sound of the exterior door being slammed shut, Angelica's eyes started to brim with tears, but she willed them dry.

Angelica tried to stand but felt dizzy and sat back down.

This was her twenty-eighth day of captivity. She was sure of that because each night she would place her slippers incrementally farther down the wall, away from the bed, counting the knots in the rug.

Angelica knew she had dodged a bullet. If she had stuck the makeshift weapon in his neck as planned, she might now be free. But he'd stood up just as she struck. Her mistake could have cost her her life. She would be sore for days, but she was still alive. He had been thorough with his punishment but careful. Interesting, she thought. They wanted her alive, but for what?

Twenty-eight nights ago, Angelica had thought she might have a sexual encounter with the man she ran into at Club Martinique. He seemed nice enough at the time. He offered to take a photo of Carol and her. And then he made a clumsy offer of company as she was leaving the club. Why not? she had thought at the time. Agreeing to the assignation wasn't about him. She was exploring. Pushing herself. Trying to unlock her emotions. Inhabit her character.

Back at her apartment, though, all went blank. Had he spiked her drink? Had he even entered her apartment? Angelica couldn't remember.

She'd woken up here. In this room. But where was here? Angelica didn't have a clue. She had no memory of falling asleep that night. She didn't remember having sex. Didn't know what was expected of her now. Was she being held hostage for ransom? Was her kidnapping tied to her father's business? Some kind of Mafia retribution?

She did know she wasn't the first person who had been held captive in this room. That's where her night terror came from. Taking a bath, she had noticed a faint carving in the white caulking above the tub.

HELP.

Faint but unmistakable. Probably carved with a fingernail.

Help.

On that thought Angelica lurched unsteadily to her feet, ran into the bathroom, pushed up the toilet seat, and heaved, turning the clear water in the ceramic bowl bloodred.

14

The loft felt empty, Jack thought as he unpacked his carry-on and contemplated his next move.

Thursday was usually one of the nights Leslie stayed over, and he would come home to find her assembling a meal or throwing on some makeup for a night out.

It was too quiet, and Jack didn't know how to proceed. He sure as hell wasn't going to let a relationship dictate his caseload. When he made a decision, he made that the right choice. Good managerial skills, he thought.

But it was too damn quiet.

He thought about calling Leslie and hashing it out but rang up Tommy Aronsohn—who was on East Coast time and had just finished watching *The Tonight Show*—instead. He apologized for the late-night intrusion.

"No problem. Couldn't sleep anyway," Tommy said, walking the phone into the den so as not to wake his wife. "Damn dog snores like a drunken sailor."

"Duke?"

"Oh yeah. He's bad. I'm thinking about getting him a CPAP mask. But I thought that might be cruel and unusual."

"How so?" Jack asked, playing along.

"He wouldn't be able to lick his balls."

Jack laughed and then filled his friend in on the situation with Chris. Both men decided they didn't want to make matters worse, and Tommy promised to talk to a psychiatrist friend and pick his brain. Then he changed subjects.

"Any movement on the Cardona front?"

"One person of interest, a Raul Vargas, but going after him could whip up a political shit storm."

"Never stopped you before."

"I'm getting a bad feeling. I'm gonna have a sit-down with Cardona. See if there's been any internecine warfare, grudges, whatever. Something close to home."

"Have you filed a missing-persons report?"

"If something doesn't break tomorrow, I'll call Gallina."

"Let me know how that goes. I'll get on the Chris thing and get back to you."

Jack then called Cruz, who picked up on the first ring and thanked him profusely for the bump in pay.

"Anything interesting on Angelica Cardona's laptop?" Jack asked.

"I downloaded the flash drive. She's a looker, I'll give her that. A few close friends, no mention of travel, said she was going to stay in character for forty-eight hours straight, whatever that means. And that was sent to a Carol Williams. They had plans to meet at a few clubs over the last weeks before she disappeared. A slew of unopened e-mails, again from Williams, her father, and some of her other friends. Facebook friends matched the names on the e-mails. No sexting or really personal posts or pictures. Nothing on YouTube. I did a printout, so you can let me know. I'm just playing catch-up. Later."

Jack hung up the phone, stripped off his clothes, stretched out on his own bed, and fluffed up his pillow. By land or by sea. The phrase popped into his mind for some reason. Must have been his trip to Paradise Cove. The more he thought about it, the more a new possibility firmed in his mind. Jack had a stop to make first thing in the morning.

———

The thick salty air whipped Jack's hair as he powered his boat up the narrow channel that led to the main central waterway of Marina del Rey. He steered toward the pastel colors of Fisherman's Village.

He planned on taking the piece of wooden boat debris he had plucked out of the water at Paradise Cove to the Coast Guard for identification. Jack decided to run the errand on the water.

Symmetrical rows of pristine white sailing yachts, the brilliant colors of their nautical flags, the scent of the Pacific, the nylon lines snapping on cold rolled steel masts, and the muffled vibration of his own craft helped center Jack. He knew he had to confront his son and hoped Tommy would weigh in later in the day. He didn't want too much time to pass, but he didn't want to make the wrong move and push Chris farther away.

Right now, though, he had to focus on Angelica Cardona.

The uniformed officer seated behind the gray spartan desk was thirty-two, trim, clear-eyed, and knowledgeable. The metal plaque said CAPTAIN DEAK MONTROSE. He gestured toward a black-framed photo and offered up that his father and grandfather had both been career officers in the Coast Guard. They all shared the same square chin, thick eyebrows, and military bearing.

Deak felt an instant rapport with Jack because of his extensive police background, and he was happy to answer some questions. He typed a few commands into his computer and swiveled his screen so that Jack could look over his shoulder.

A black-and-white rendering of a low-slung wooden boat appeared with the dimensions of the craft in the right-hand column.

Deak picked up the foot-square section of the wreck Jack brought in and examined it thoughtfully. He knew exactly what it came from.

"The boat's called a panga. It's a Mexican fishing vessel and the smuggler's vehicle of choice lately. The Sinaloa cartel is using them to ship drugs and illegals north since the border patrol beefed up enforcement along the U.S.-Mexican border.

"Yours isn't the first we've seen in the Paradise Cove area," he said, referring to the piece of wreckage. "Up in Malibu, on a stretch of coastline known as Smuggler's Cove, we just grabbed another boat with fifteen hundred pounds of pot aboard. We arrested three men there. Plus, we got twenty-two illegals up near Montecito a few weeks ago.

"Desperate times," Deak said with compassion. Handing back the piece of wooden plank, he added, "Too bad about the woman. I heard it was a suicide, but I sure can't figure why she'd choose a fishing boat."

"No sense at all," Jack agreed, but he didn't think she'd chosen the boat any more than she'd chosen to die. They talked for a while about the Orange County body that had washed up on shore, and then Jack had another thought. "Is there any way to get a list of the registered cigarette boats in the L.A./Orange County area? The night of the accident, a go-fast boat was reported leaving the scene, moments before the crash. If you have any stats on the distance one could travel on a tank of gas, it would help."

Deak tapped on the keys for a few seconds, hit Print, and handed Jack a few sheets. One listed the boat's specs and the other a list of the cigarette boats registered in the areas requested, along with the owners' names and addresses. "But just know," Deak said, "if the cartels are using the boats for drug pickups or deliveries, they do custom work on the gas tanks that could double or triple the mileage."

Jack thanked him for his time and walked over to Whiskey Red's for lunch.

Jack grabbed a table on the outdoor patio, near the water, and ordered a cheeseburger. While he waited for his food to arrive, he pulled out his cell and called Terry Malloy, the medical examiner who had handled the grisly crime scene and autopsy of Mia, one of Jack's most successful confidential informants. After an all-too-brief affair with Jack, Mia had been found brutally murdered and Jack had been framed for the crime.

After Jack hunted down the killers and cleared his name, Terry Malloy had called to apologize for his behavior during the investigation.

Jack didn't feel too bad about exploiting a little guilt. He needed some information.

15

Malloy was just stubbing out a cigarette on the side of the Los Angeles courthouse before resuming testimony on a triple homicide. He checked his watch and talked while he and Jack started a circuit around the building.

"I compared notes with my southern counterpart because of the time line and physical similarities between the two women," he said. "The Orange County body had enough drugs in her system to take down a rhino. Dead before she entered the water. No sign of a struggle, but get this. There was lividity on her lower back and buttocks."

"So she died at another location. Someone transported her body and dumped her into the Pacific," Jack said.

"Looks that way. Coroner listed cause of death as an accidental overdose. No distinguishing marks except a star tattoo, just below her bikini line."

"Has anybody claimed the body?" Jack asked.

"No inquiries as far as I've heard. And her face was plastered locally and internationally, as was our Jane Doe's. Same lack of response."

"Rape kit?"

"Really, Jack?" he said, as in, *You've got to be kidding.* "Sexually active but no semen. Don't know where she entered the water, but Frank said the currents were driving north to south. So entry point is anyone's guess."

"There were no overboards radioed in to the Coast Guard that night," Jack added.

They continued walking in silence before Malloy volunteered, "This is strictly off the record; I could lose my job."

"To the grave," Jack responded.

Malloy stopped in his tracks and looked over his shoulder before speaking.

"Our Jane Doe died of severe neck trauma. Two of her cervical vertebrae shattered, severing the spinal cord. She was also sexually active, Jack. Again, no semen, but bruising in her vaginal area and tears in her anus. She tested negative for opiates and cocaine. Traces of marijuana, but nothing serious. Something didn't feel right, didn't mesh, so I went back and ran another series of tests and got a hit. She had traces of pancuronium bromide. It's a neuromuscular blocking agent. I won't bore you with the chemical breakdown, but it's a paralyzing agent. Administered before a—"

"Lethal injection," Jack said, finishing his sentence.

"Not easy to come by."

"So she was paralyzed but conscious before the crash," Jack mused.

"A wide-eyed witness to her own death. Kind of macabre," Malloy said. "I inspected the body for a third time before I found the microscopic entry point. An injection between her toes. She was murdered. She didn't have long to live, though. Stage-four breast cancer. Sad, really."

Malloy checked his watch again. "To the grave, Jack," he reminded him. "Gotta run."

Malloy hoofed it back inside the courthouse.

"Have a steak," Vincent Cardona growled.

"No, thanks," Jack answered.

"For crissakes, eat one of my fuckin' steaks. I got the best beef in town. You're not a cop anymore. Not that it stops any of your 'brothers.'" He made air quotation marks.

Cardona was sitting at the bar in his Beverly Hills Chop House. It had red leather booths, beveled glass windows, a top-tier lounge singer who played a baby grand, and a two-week waiting list. Peter was seated at the far end of the bar with his face buried in a plate of smothered pork chops.

"Vincent, I just ate."

"Whatever," the big man said, flipping his meaty hand like he was swatting a fly.

Jack looked a question at Cardona, eyebrows raised.

"No," Cardona said. "I called New York and Chicago. I talked to my crew here. Nothing. Not everyone's happy, but no fuckin' insurrection. And family's generally sacrosanct. Although with this new crowd, who the hell knows?"

"What about rival gangs?" Jack asked.

"Not that I'd know anything about that, but what I hear is, all is well on the reservation. Was that racist? Not that I give a shit."

"Borderline," Jack said. "No, coming out of your mouth, definitely."

Peter barked a laugh and started drinking from his water glass, evading the dangerous look Cardona threw his way.

"Just wondering why you weren't aware Angelica was studying over at Strasberg's," Jack asked.

Cardona turned up a hand and his thick eyebrows at the same time.

"She pulled away. I didn't push. She wasn't on the streets. She looked fine. I thought maybe she was finding herself."

Vincent might not have been too far off the mark, Jack thought.

He chose not to share his growing suspicion that Cardona might be right about the link between his daughter and the two dead women. Instead he got up off his stool, tossed a ten down to cover his iced tea, and said, "I'll call when I have something."

"It better be soon. And it better be good." A painful flash glazed Vincent Cardona's eyes.

Jack left the big man with his sorrow and headed for Club Martinique.

16

Jack found street parking on Wilcox in Hollywood, fed the meter, and pushed through the doors of Club Martinique. It had an afternoon laid-back vibe. The club was tastefully designed with blond wood, retro lighting, and navy blue seat cushions. Tall, lazy banana palms accented the room. All details that had been hidden by the hordes of partiers the night of Jack's first visit.

A few tables were finishing a late lunch as Jack walked up to the bar and slid onto a designer stool. A lone bartender was busy prepping limes into silver dollar–sized garnish wheels for the club's signature margaritas.

"I need some help," Jack said when it became obvious the bartender wasn't going to offer assistance.

"And I need a sugar daddy," the bartender fired back. "These limes are ruining my hands."

The bartender was six-two, one hundred twenty pounds. Blond tips on his brown, gelled hair, and a face so gaunt it forced you to look twice. Jack wouldn't have bet the farm, but the man's doe eyes seemed to pop dramatically due to a subtle application of smoky eye shadow. Jack pulled out the pictures provided by Carol Williams and placed them on the bar.

The bartender pursed his lips before speaking. "Allan has strict rules about talking to the police about our clients. They come here to chill in anonymity, and we try to respect their wishes."

Jack took the referred-to Allan to be the club's owner. He decided not to go into his own status as retired NYPD and soldiered on.

"This woman was at your club"—Jack did the math in his head—"twenty-nine days—call it four weeks—ago, and was never seen or heard from again. Anything you can do to help . . ."

The bartender glanced around the room surreptitiously and then down at the pictures. He grabbed the photo that Raul took of the two women sitting side by side.

"Oh, girl, that's Carol." The bartender's demeanor turned on a dime. "She serves at my favorite hotel. She's not missing, is she?" he asked with genuine concern.

"No, it's this girl, Angelica Cardona or Angelica Curtis," Jack said as he placed the photo of Angelica on top of the stack. "Do you recognize her?"

"I'm Teddy, by the way," the bartender said, thrusting his thin hand forward. Jack shared his own name and shook, being careful not to shatter the bartender's delicate bones.

"Vaguely," Teddy went on. "Once we start rocking, if you're not well-heeled, a big tipper, and a man, my eyes tend to glaze."

"Then what about this man?" Jack asked, sliding Raul Vargas's picture across the bar. "He said he was parked at your bar for the better part of the night."

Teddy picked up the picture and clucked. "The night the girl disappeared?"

"The same."

"I do. He tipped well, but I took notice because he had the look."

Jack waited for an explanation.

"A little twisted. In denial. But I recognize the look."

"Kindred spirits?"

"Don't judge," Teddy said lightly, comfortable in his own skin.

"I need to know if the two of them left the bar together." Jack pointed to the security camera that covered the bar area.

"Can I offer you a drink, on the house?"

"Diet Coke would work."

Teddy rubbed a lemon peel around the rim of the glass as he set the drink down in front of Jack.

"Let me make a quick call. Clear it with Allan. He may do it as a favor to Carol. He worries about TMZ getting their hands on his videos. Can't hurt to try. This Angelica girl's been gone for . . . ?"

"Four weeks. This could be the difference between finding her alive and . . ."

"Sit tight."

Teddy disappeared for a few minutes. When he returned, he handed Jack a disc. "It's all on the computer, in two-month intervals. I downloaded the last cycle, so you'll have to do a little digging. But this definitely covers the night she was here. I hope it helps."

"Thank you, Teddy. It's appreciated." Jack left a twenty on the bar, always happily surprised when a civilian stepped up to the plate.

Jack jumped behind the wheel of his Mustang, turned over

the eight-cylinder engine—pleased with the sound—executed a U-turn, and headed for home.

Using his Bluetooth, Jack left a message for Lieutenant Gallina at headquarters. If he was going to investigate Raul Vargas, who was his only person of interest to date, he'd take Nick Aprea's advice and lean on the LAPD for support. Angelica had been missing for far too long. If she'd been kidnapped, the chances that she was still alive were slim to none. But dead or alive, Jack vowed to find her.

He'd missed a voice mail from Tommy, who said the shrink advised confrontation with solution. Meaning therapy and rehab, Jack decided. In Chris's case, Tommy went on, the drug theft sounded like a cry for help. Jack knew the clock was ticking and his heart was heavy. He dialed Chris's number, even though he knew calls were a one-way street lately. Sure enough, he got voice mail and left a message.

He went back to his work plan. He had to screen the security video and then go down the list of Angelica's other friends compiled by Cruz Feinberg. He wanted to eliminate as many leads as possible before doing a full-court press on his only suspect.

Jack placed a call to Cruz, who agreed to dig up information on Raul Vargas, his drug conviction, and his commuted prison sentence in particular.

He'd get Mateo on the Vargas Development Group. The two of them had a long history. At one time Mateo had been responsible for the importation of multiton quantities of cocaine into the New York City area, and Jack, who was heading up a group of narco-rangers at the time, took it personally. After a six-month undercover operation Jack shut him down.

Jack's group confiscated 1,870 kilos of cocaine, hidden in

boxes of baby formula; dismantled their money-laundering cell operating out of Forest Hills; and locked up twenty-three Colombian nationals.

Mateo, the head honcho, was caught in Jack's net.

Jack made executive management decisions based on what served the greatest good. When he busted Mateo, he decided it was in the state's best interest to utilize the man's connections and talent, and he became Jack's most prolific CI.

Mateo had changed teams, brilliantly worked off his entire sentence, and lived to tell the story. Not an easy feat. The life expectancy of a confidential informant was worse than that of a fifth-round draft pick in the NFL.

Jack had saved Mateo's life—given him a second chance—and the man was forever in his debt. When retired inspector Jack Bertolino had a problem, Mateo dropped everything and jumped on a plane.

After Mateo finished working off his prison time, he went on to make a legitimate fortune in Miami flipping condos in North Beach while everyone else was underwater. He knew the upside and the dark side of the real estate business.

Jack had just made a hard left onto Glencoe Avenue when his cell phone chirped. The call was from his son.

"I know you know," Chris said in a subdued voice before Jack could speak.

"Chris."

"Think I don't know who you are?"

"Let me pull over."

Jack braked to a stop in front of his building so that he wouldn't lose his cell signal in the building's dead zone.

"I couldn't ask," Chris said. "I can't sleep."

"I love you."

Silence.

"You need to talk with someone," Jack said gently.

Still nothing.

Jack checked his phone to make sure he hadn't dropped the call.

"Maybe," Chris said.

Jack waited out another long pause.

"But not someone Coach knows."

Jack understood his son's fear. He'd known a lot of cops through the years who didn't want to be known as head cases. Some—too many—ate the barrel. Took a bullet from their own government-issue.

"We'll find someone off campus," Jack said, trying to still the beating of his heart.

"It's not supposed to hurt. They all said my arm wouldn't hurt. But it hurts like hell, at night, but I didn't want to go back to the sports doctor."

"Maybe there's nerve damage that wasn't picked up on the MRI."

Then Jack got the real story.

"If the coach finds out I'm damaged goods, I might not get a second chance."

"Not important right now."

"Fuck you."

"Chris—"

"Don't tell me what's important!"

Jack could hear tears and rage in his son's voice. He let Chris do the talking.

"It's not your call." And then, "Why did I get hit? Out of all the people crossing the street in L.A. Why me?"

But they both knew the answer.

"Son. Arturo Delgado is dead . . . it can't happen again."

"But I still hurt. And I don't want to hurt. Goddamn it, I want it to stop. And I can't tell anyone but you. Shit. I got Psych One in fifteen. Maybe they can explain why I'm messed up."

Chris clicked off.

Jack let out a labored sigh. Seeing a blur, he wiped his right eye. And then the other. His damn eyes kept filling. Shit.

When his vision finally cleared, he looked up, into the rear-view mirror, and saw a twentysomething Hispanic male, pumping his bike. Hard. As hard as his attitude.

Jack swiped his eyes again. The bike was thirty feet away and closing.

Jack saw a glint of silver as the rider pulled back his gray hoodie, grabbed his midnight special, and held it straight down, tight at his side. Twenty feet. Jack lurched forward to grab his concealed weapon, under the front seat, but the seat belt cinched and snugged him tighter.

The rear window exploded.

Jack reflexively slipped down in his seat and on a two count, threw the driver's-side door open as the next gunshot blew out the windshield.

The cyclist smashed into the opened door.

He was thrown forward over his handlebars, his pistol fired wildly as the young gangbanger flipped up and over, and landed hard on his back in front of Jack's car. His flopping head made solid contact with the concrete. His pistol skittered against the curb.

The door to the Mustang, ripped off its hinges, went spinning into oncoming traffic that was caught unawares. Brakes squealed. Horns blared.

Jack unbuckled his seat belt, leaped from the car. Rushing forward, he grabbed the kid's pistol. When he ascertained that the gunman was out cold, he popped the lid of his trunk, pulled out a set of plastic cuffs, rolled his would-be executioner over onto his stomach, and bound his wrists. *La Eme* was tattooed on the killer's neck. The Mexican Mafia. Jack sat on the curb and fought to catch his breath.

J.D., the owner of Bruffy's Tow and Police Impound, walked calmly across the street and handed Jack a phone. "Nine-one-one. Can't say you don't keep things interesting around here." He looked down at Jack's prisoner, shook his head, and spit on the ground.

Jack spoke to the 911 operator while J.D. picked up the Mustang's door, kicked the bent bike to the curb, and directed traffic safely around the action.

"I'll tow you to Platinum," he said. "You ought to set up a running account."

J.D. was dead serious and Jack couldn't disagree. He wearily handed him back his phone as two black-and-whites came screaming up Glencoe.

17

"Who is this Big Daddy?" Sheik Ibrahim asked with genuine interest. The diminutive man was a Sunni tribal leader from the Anbar province of Iraq. He had attended private school in London with Malic, and the men were distant cousins—part of the same extended tribe. They shared the same bloodline from three generations past.

They had also shared an affection for an undergraduate student named Kayla. Though Iraqi, she was a rare natural blonde. She was a prize. The sheik was the first to date her, but Malic had won her hand.

The sheik's eyes were glued to his television screen as Angelica Cardona tore up a first-act monologue from *Cat on a Hot Tin Roof*. She was fully invested in Maggie the Cat, and her performance was both poignant and true, with a depth of emotion she had only aspired to before her abduction.

"It will be *you*, most esteemed," Malic said with the ease of a politician. "She is an even better choice. Life happens. But this one, she has seen your picture and is eager to please. That should loosen your purse strings."

"I was frustrated by our last negotiation," the sheik said, horse-trading. "We had a verbal agreement and you did not deliver as promised."

His Excellency was a short, round man in his thirties. Round-faced, round pink mouth, round body. Dark brown pomaded hair and a close-clipped Vandyke that only served to focus attention on his weak chin.

He sat on an overstuffed filigree white silk couch in an expansive, white-columned room with an intricate geometric pattern of cobalt blue, white, and gold wall tiles. The opulence had been paid for in part by an illegal Iraqi oil deal that Malic had brokered between Halliburton and his old friend before he immigrated to the United States.

The highly polished black marble floors reflected the image of Angelica from the sheik's massive flat-screen television.

"Accidents happen. It is an inexact science, but this one is guaranteed to make your other girls jealous."

"I would need a full blood workup."

"Already in the works. She's a talented woman from a warrior's bloodline."

"And what if I'm stuck with damaged goods?"

"Your trainer can handle any contingencies. She is beautiful. She has fire, just like your Arabians. Headstrong, willful, dangerous, a winner."

"But the price?" he asked as if the number physically pained him.

Malic thought it tiresome that Sheik Ibrahim would pay two million for an untested stallion without blinking an eye but negotiate for weeks on end for human flesh and blood. He had already kept his new acquisition longer than was comfortable, but Malic had a keen eye for pricing and refused to sell below market value. He turned up the volume as Angelica lit up the high-definition screen.

The sheik's eight-year-old son walked silently into the room holding an iPhone in both hands. He smiled slyly while pointing the phone toward the television.

"What are you doing, my son?" his father asked, sensing his son's presence behind him.

"Playing Angry Birds." The boy adroitly switched to the games app and showed his father the screen.

"Go, run, to bed," he scolded gently in English. "We are conducting business here."

"Yes, Father." And the boy scampered out of the grand room.

"Tell me again, how I will be protected if this woman is damaged?" he asked, still negotiating.

The digital feed switched from Angelica to Malic's museum-lit Matisse masterpiece. "Collateral. Ten times the value of the woman," he said, aware of the sheik's love of fine art.

"Done," the sheik said. "One million eight hundred thousand dollars. I only hope that she *is* damaged. An oil painting does not talk back. Send me the medical certificates and I will send my jet."

"I'll need the money wired ASAP. The interest on my construction loan is due. We have already delayed breaking ground on the new project once. The deal is tenuous."

"From oil to real estate? A mogul now?"

"One adapts. Seize the opportunity. No?"

"Hold," the sheik said as he set down his phone. He buried his head in a handheld device as if he were nearsighted. He hit a few keys, then a few more; looked up at the Matisse on his big screen;

and ceremoniously hit Send. A cruel smile curled his moist lips as he picked up the phone and resumed his conversation.

"It is done and done. One million eight hundred thousand dollars are now in your account. Don't fuck me, Malic."

Malic feigned offense and started to reply, but the sheik was already on to other business. "Call me," he said, clicking off.

He hit a button on the remote and the Matisse instantly disappeared, replaced by a moving crawl of commodity symbols, oil futures, and stock quotes from trading floors around the world. He stood up and stretched his five-foot-five frame as he had been doing since he was a boy praying to Allah that he would grow tall.

The sheik remained, stubbornly, five foot five.

Malic rang up Hassan.

"I'll need a full blood workup on the girl ASAP. Drop everything else and hand-deliver it to Dr. Khalil. Now, Hassan . . . Then first thing in the morning," he said, frustrated. "I'll drive myself to work."

Malic pushed back in his leather chair, stared wistfully at the Matisse, and said a silent prayer that he would have no problems this time. He would rather lose his wife, the mother of his only child, than the painting.

———

Raul Vargas walked through his father's empty weekend home on the Malibu cliffs with a blazing hard-on. He had taken one hundred milligrams of Viagra, which was the only way he could get it up after his stint in prison. Better living through chemistry, he thought.

The repeated rape he'd endured had been shameful, painful,

and nightmarish. The physical and psychic torture would haunt him to the grave.

He'd never go back in, Raul knew. He'd kill himself first. Or anybody else who got in his way. On that he was clear.

Malic had interceded when he needed help most. His gang offered protection in prison, and the rape had stopped. Instant relief. But like heroin, Malic was now controlling his life. Raul thought about killing the man, fantasized about it, but he wasn't stupid. Greedy, okay, that went without saying. It was what turned him to drug dealing when his life had been handed to him on a golden platter. Raul knew that if Malic suddenly came to a violent end, his gang would connect the dots, and his own death would be savage.

Raul walked out onto the rear patio, which afforded him an unobstructed view of the Pacific Ocean and, directly south, Paradise Cove. Yet he didn't see the waves lapping onto the beach below or the clouds that shadowed the dark horizon. All he saw was the fiery image of the crash in his mind's eye.

Malic had called him moments before the fishing boat smashed into the rocks. Raul had stood in this exact spot as the young woman's naked body was ejected from the boat like a mannequin and bled out on the black rock outcropping. He had held his breath as the splintered boat exploded into a roiling fireball. Malic did have a flair for the theatrical, Raul thought.

The violent image replayed again and again in Raul's head like a needle stuck in the grooves of a vinyl record. A constant, nagging reminder of the intended warning. That warning now sent him back into the house. He needed a drink and he wanted to see the victim one last time, he told himself. He wanted to see the digital video that gave Malic the balance of power.

He poured himself a stiff cocktail, took a monster hit off a joint and slid the disc into the Blu-ray player. He dropped his sweatpants onto the slate floor before settling onto the couch in his father's living room to find momentary relief. He took a deep sip of Grey Goose, hit Play on the remote, and watched his recorded demise.

Raul's erect phallus was partially obscured as he thrust himself slowly between the painted lips of a beautiful woman's mouth. She had perfect skin and blond hair, and her eyes were closed. When Raul's hands entered the frame and he tilted the woman's face toward the camera, it became clear that the young woman was unconscious. Better living through chemistry, he thought again, and laughed this time.

The images on the television jumped as he pulled out before climax, knocking into the camera, until it refocused on a full-body shot of the woman. Raul's hands reached into frame and deftly snapped metal clips onto the woman's nipples. Then the camera panned down and pushed in close on the clear red dildo that had been partially inserted into her vagina. Raul's hand started manipulating the latex toy with one hand and himself with the other. Slowly in and then slowly out at first, and then with increased tempo and building ferocity. There was no sound emanating from the television set but heavy breathing, and then choked gasps filled the living room in the multimillion-dollar Malibu estate.

———

Jack had spent the better part of four hours standing in front of his building being interviewed by an LAPD detective who took copious notes. He was getting used to the disapproving stares from other loft owners returning home from work. They were getting used to seeing Jack surrounded by police, reporters, and helicopters.

Thankfully, Nick Aprea showed up to add what he knew about the contract La Eme had put out on Jack's life. Retribution for shutting down the 18th Street Angels, and more specifically, the death of Mexican Mafia Mando. One of their own. And how Nick didn't think the situation was going to just disappear. Not music to Jack's ears, but it helped expedite the paperwork.

The young assassin was an associate of the Mexican Mafia, vying for full membership. Jack's death was to be his first tattooed teardrop. He was taken to Saint John's, treated for a concussion, and then driven downtown for processing.

The attempted murder of Jack Bertolino started a drumbeat that was heard all the way to police headquarters. After retelling his story for the second time to Gallina and Tompkins, he filed a missing-persons report and gave them everything he had assembled on Angelica over the phone.

He immediately questioned that decision when they lied about the victim at Paradise Cove being a suicide. They told Jack that the boat's throttle mechanism had in fact not been tampered with. And if something like a bungee cord had been used to hold the throttle forward, it had been destroyed in the fire. The company line remained: suicide.

Malloy, the coroner, had set him straight on that account, but Jack could only push so hard without violating his promise of silence.

The pair couldn't explain why they were still on the case if it wasn't a homicide but said they were happy to do a thorough search of Angelica's apartment. Jack would take whatever crumbs he could get. They also agreed to send a tech crew to dust for prints before interviewing Vincent Cardona.

That would give Jack time to give the big man a heads-up.

Both detectives were aware of the Raul Vargas parole. The release had felt like a gut punch to local law enforcement. If they could find his prints in Angelica's apartment, they'd pick him up for questioning. But if there were no compelling reasons to pursue him as a lead, enough said. They didn't want the aggravation it was guaranteed to generate.

Jack decided to work his way down the list of Angelica's high school friends before it got too late. He learned that she had legally changed her last name to Curtis, which was her mother's maiden name, and not much more. She'd been out of touch with her friends since starting her studies at the Strasberg institute. There were no boyfriends of record.

Must have been a hell of a ride for her at school with a gatekeeper like Vincent Cardona.

Jack rose from his desk and went for the Vicodin. He reached for the bottle, flashed on his son, and felt the kind of pain the drugs wouldn't touch. But an afternoon spent dodging bullets forced the issue; he took one pill and chased it with two Excedrin and then a glass of red wine.

He made a mental note to refill the prescription. His doctor had been badgering him to have another back operation, but after three failed attempts, and the months of painful recovery time, Jack vowed never to go under the knife again.

He knew he had to call his ex-wife, Jeannine, and bring her up to speed. He decided to wait until morning to be the bearer of bad news. The conversation would not go well no matter how hard he tried to finesse it.

He slipped the disc into his computer and was about to hit Play but was stopped by a firm rap on the metal front door that told Jack exactly who was standing behind it. He wasn't sure how he felt as he crossed to the door and turned the handle.

Leslie was standing there, back straight, hair perfect, ravishing. In one hand she held a bottle of Benziger, in the other, the handle of her rolling overnight bag.

Silence. Finally.

"Are you going to invite me in?" Her voice was as clear as a bell.

A smile creased Jack's face.

"I heard what happened to you this afternoon," she went on, "and judging from my reaction . . . Well, I'm here."

"What about risk assessment?" Jack asked, not letting her off the hook.

"Oh, I can be a real ass sometimes. I'll be relieved when you're done with the case, and I'm glad you're in one piece, and I don't want to lose this, lose you, and if you don't say something soon . . . better yet, Jack, don't talk. Just take me to bed."

Jack lifted Leslie off her feet. She released the handle of her bag, deposited her bottle of red on the kitchen island in passing, and crushed his lips as he carried her across the room. Jack laid her down on his bed.

Their kiss was deep and sweet. Their lovemaking urgent. The orgasm, dynamite. Makeup sex was just the best thing ever, Jack thought. Angry, desperate, hungry, and passionate.

The best thing ever.

18

"Jeremy, just put Jeannine on the phone."

This was not the way Jack wanted to start his day. He took a quick swig of coffee and waited.

"She's doing dishes," Jeremy informed him, mildly irritated. "Her hands are wet, and she wants to know what the call's about."

If Jack could've reached through the receiver and grabbed Jeremy's throat . . . "Family business," he finally said with too much attitude.

Jeremy was his ex-wife's live-in boyfriend. As in: living in the house that Jack had built with his own sweat equity and paid for while he was a newly minted police officer. The same house Jeannine had taken sole possession of in their contentious divorce settlement.

"Oh, come on, Jack, are we still there? I had hoped we'd moved beyond that."

Jack didn't respond well to condescension. "Just have her return my call. This morning, Jeremy." He hung up the phone knowing full well his rudeness would come back to bite him in the ass.

———————

"That was uncalled-for, Jack," were the first scolding words out of Jeannine's mouth ten minutes later.

"Our son's in trouble."

"What did you do this time?"

Jack worried the inside of his cheek, sucked in a breath, and refused to take the bait.

Yet Jeannine wasn't finished. "Every time there's trouble, it springs from you. What is it this time? Was Chris hit by a bullet that was meant for you, God forbid? And Jeremy is part of the family, Jack, if you hadn't noticed," she said, hammering away. "I think he more than rose to the occasion on our last visit, when you were too busy to help your son."

Just in case Jack needed reminding, which he did not.

"Jack, are you still there?"

"Chris stole some of my Vicodin when I was up north visiting."

"Jack."

Jeannine was a lot of things, but stupid wasn't on the list. She immediately understood the implications and slipped into maternal mode.

"He's in pain," Jack said. "His arm and his psyche. I think he understands that he needs help."

"Dr. Zudiker was so good."

"We need to find someone off campus, not in the system. Chris is afraid it'll be held against him."

"He is a cop's son, isn't he, Jack? I'm sorry for what I just said. I..."

"I deserved it."

"I'll book a flight."

"I don't know if it's the right time. He reached out to me. He's got to get there himself."

"Why don't you go back up?"

"I'm on a case."

"Well, there it is."

She just couldn't help herself.

"I'll work it from my end," Jack said. "Tommy talked to a doctor who's got connections in San Francisco and—"

"You talked to Tommy before you called me?" she said accusingly.

Jack's gloves came off. "Chris did not want you to know. Asked me not to tell you. To worry you. He didn't want the pressure. His words."

"Well . . . thank you, then," Jeannine said, deflating. The fight had gone out of her. "What should we do? I'll fly out."

Jack wanted to ask her if she'd been listening but knew his ex-wife was in shock. He was glad she had Jeremy at times like these.

"When the time's right," Jack said gently. "He reached out. If the therapy takes, then maybe we'll have dodged a bullet. I'll find a neurologist up there, have him do a series of tests on Chris's arm."

"Oh, Jack."

"He's a good kid. He'll be okay."

Jack hung up the phone wishing he believed what he'd just said. He gave Chris another call, got his voice mail. Decided he should follow his own advice and back off.

———

The images from the surveillance camera at Club Martinique were surprisingly high-resolution. Jack was set up with his coffee mug and his computer on his kitchen island, while Cruz Feinberg, on the phone at his apartment, watched the images on his iPad a few seconds behind Jack.

"There," Jack said as he hit Pause.

The crowd at the bar was five deep and he'd spotted fleeting images of Raul Vargas standing, sitting, drinking, and cruising. Definitely a man on the prowl. He downed three drinks in the first hour of the video. Jack could see Teddy dropping off the drinks, making change, and lingering with Raul while the crowds built at the bar. In hour two of the video they saw Raul standing with his iPhone close to his face, like he was looking at an app or a text. And then he surreptitiously snapped a few pictures of someone off camera in the dining room area.

"Got it," Cruz said.

"Now what the hell is he doing?" Jack asked.

"I see it. Hold on. He's taking a picture. Trying to look cool, checking it out, and now, now it looks like he's sending it out."

"That's what I saw. Who the hell was he sharing the photo with? Love to get my hands on his phone," Jack said. "Now hit Play again in slo-mo. There. He's putting a napkin over his drink and walking away from the bar toward the tables. Toward where Angelica and Carol were seated."

Raul's image moved out of camera range.

"If Raul Vargas abducted Angelica that night, he might not have been working alone," Jack said.

"Shit."

"Is right. There's one quick shot of Carol leaving the club, alone, and then a blur of Angelica moving in the opposite direction, toward the ladies' room, as reported by Carol. I don't see Angelica again, or Raul, for that matter. I looked at the video frame by frame. Take a break, and then go over it again. You might catch something I missed."

"Will do. I'll call you on your cell. Where're you headed?"

"I've got to deliver some bad news to Cardona. Gallina is going to pay him a visit today."

"Better you than me, boss," Cruz said. "Later." And he clicked off.

Jack grabbed his keys, ready to face Vincent Cardona. He glanced through the sliding glass doors, past the tight rows of white FedEx trucks, down onto Glencoe Avenue. He started walking back toward his front door when he realized he'd seen an anomaly. He turned on his heel and looked out again.

A green 1970s Chevy Caprice with black-tinted windows—gangbanger written all over it—was parked directly across the street from his building, in front of the Fine Wine Storage facility with a balls-on view of his loft.

Firming his lips, Jack strapped on his leather shoulder rig, checked the load on his Glock nine-millimeter, and shrugged into a loose-fitting black linen jacket to conceal the weapon. No use giving his neighbors a heart attack. Jack was already on their shit list for attracting the wrong kind of publicity for their westside loft community. If they couldn't take a joke, fuck 'em, Jack thought.

He took the back elevator, exited through the rear of the building, and jumped the fence onto the FedEx parking lot. He sprinted past the trucks and then across the street, ending up ten feet behind the Chevy Caprice.

He pulled out his Glock and moved rapidly forward in the driver's blind spot.

Jack tapped the gun barrel on the driver's-side window.

The blacked-out window powered down, and two empty hands shot out and rotated front to back to prove their innocence.

"Friend, not foe, Mr. B," Peter said in his nasal Brooklyn twang. "Just keeping an eye on things. You know, I got you covered, so to speak."

Jack holstered his weapon, relieved it wasn't La Eme.

"Where were you yesterday?" he said, giving the busted gangster a hard time.

"Lookin' for a fuckin' parking space. I saw the action in my rearview. I almost lost my lunch. Parkin' sucks around here. By the time I turned the fuckin' car around, you had everything under control, thank God. I didn't think there was any need to get involved once the cops showed. You know. Why push it?"

"It's the thought that counts," Jack said, tongue in cheek.

"Mr. Cardona was reasonably upset. I mean, you can't very well find his daughter if you're taking a dirt nap. Or he generally used words to that effect. I mean, he's offering you protection and whatnot. You know, demanding it. In the form of me."

"He does have a point," Jack deadpanned.

"You think?" Peter asked, surprised.

"Do you want me to just give you my itinerary for the rest of the week?"

"That would be great, Mr. B," the beleaguered man said.

"Get the fuck outta here."

"What?" Peter said, eyebrows raised, checking to see if Jack was putting him on.

"Get the fuck outta here."

He wasn't.

"Oh ... Uh ... Okay, then. Huh. Let's just keep this little conversation between the two of us. . . ."

Peter was speaking to Jack's back as he watched him dodge traffic and disappear into the lobby of his building.

Two minutes later, Jack's rental, a new BMW 335i, pulled out onto Glencoe and roared past.

Peter gave it a five count and burned rubber as he executed a smoking one-eighty and gave chase.

19

Angelica sat stone straight in the dinette chair. Both of her arms and legs had been plastic-cuffed to the arms and legs of the chair. She had a dreamy faraway look in her eyes as Hassan laid a bathroom towel on the small dining table, opened a zippered pouch, and pulled out an empty vial and a sterilized syringe. Angelica watched him working dispassionately.

Hassan pulled the cap off of the syringe and stepped over to Angelica like a lab technician. He inserted the needle into the flesh of her left arm, looking for a flinch that didn't come. Neither did the blood he was sent to extract for testing.

"Stick it in a vein, you stupid idiot."

Frustrated, Hassan wanted to stick the needle in her heart. Instead he was the good soldier. He rubbed her arm with an alcohol pad and tried again.

This time Angelica let out a grunt but no cry. He prodded and pushed and tried to force the needle into her vein, but it rolled under the diaphanous skin on her arm and the syringe came up empty again.

"Give it to me!" Angelica ordered.

Hassan stubbornly tried again, this time in Angelica's right arm, and cursed in Arabic as he was denied a vein.

"If you can't do it, give it to me! I have very fine veins and they're hard to find. Save us both the aggravation. Please."

Hassan gave that some thought. He walked into the kitchen, opened a bottle of water, and took a long, thirsty gulp. Then he pulled his Leatherman off his waist and snipped the plastic tie off Angelica's right wrist. Trying to remain menacing and careful to stay out of her arm's full range, he handed her the syringe.

Angelica balled her fist; ran her forefinger down the vein in the crux of her arm, like she'd seen her doctor's nurse do; and guided the sharp point home.

Hassan stepped in quickly, taking control of the syringe, and pulled the stopper back, filling the reservoir with hot Italian blood.

Angelica relaxed her fist, her eyes dripping with pure Beverly Hills disdain. And then a realization dawned on her. The people who abducted her wanted to know if she was healthy. If she was free of disease. If she was clean. Oh, my God. Her thoughts screamed, and the ringing in her ears reverberated as loud as a church bell. Her face flushed, and she reeled, light-headed, fighting to control her breathing so that she wouldn't pass out.

Angelica knew at that frightening moment that she wasn't being held for ransom. They didn't want a ransom. It wasn't retribution from one of her father's enemies. Her abductors were going to sell her. She was being kept alive in order to be sold, and from the looks of her jailer, probably to someone in the Middle East.

Hassan felt the change in temperature in the room but ignored it and went about his business. He poked the full syringe into the rubber stopper of the sterile bottle and filled it with her blood. Satisfied with his work, he placed the medical supplies in the waterproof satchel.

"Untie me!" she ordered.

Hassan, who wasn't at all pleased with how this exercise had gone, pulled out the Leatherman again and snipped the plastic cuffs off her legs first and then her left wrist.

Being careful not to turn his back on his captor, he unpacked the day's provisions, zipped up the blood sample, and stepped out of the glass room.

"Do you have a daughter?" Angelica almost whispered.

Hassan heard it loud and clear as he locked the door securely behind him.

Angelica stood on unsteady legs, grabbed one of the alcohol pads he had left behind. As the metal door creaked open and then slammed shut, she started to rub her puncture wounds, slowly at first and then manically. Until her arms were hot, red, and threatening to bleed.

20

Vincent Cardona moved with surprising speed for a man his size. He charged at Jack, who grabbed his forearm before his meaty fist found its mark and used Cardona's forward momentum to slam the big man against the wall. Two Italianate paintings in the foyer were jarred from the impact, and their gilded frames crashed onto the black and white tiled floor. Jack grabbed two handfuls of silk shirt, muscling Cardona off balance as the mobster tried to land a punch.

Jack heard the thuds of chairs being toppled in the back of the house. Leather shoes pounded out of the kitchen. A bullet was ratcheted into the chamber of a pistol and Peter's nasal voice, deadly serious, gave an order:

"Let him go, Mr. B."

"If you shoot him you're gonna shoot me, you stupid fuck," Cardona shouted through labored breaths. "Put the guns down, goddamn it, Frankie. You wanna shoot me?"

Jack glanced down the hallway and saw a man who looked a lot like Cardona, only twenty pounds heavier, holding a cannon pointed at his head. The big man reluctantly lowered his weapon toward the floor. Two angry goons standing behind him also dropped their weapons to their sides.

Vincent Cardona had not taken kindly to the notion of bringing the police into his personal business. Skeletons are a bitch, Jack thought.

He eased off on the pressure and Vincent pushed away from the wall. He pulled down his shirt, which had exposed a thick mat of hair underneath his striped silk Armani.

Jack took one step back, spun, and punched Peter squarely in the face. Peter looked confused as he lost control of his .38, which clattered to the floor, and his equilibrium, which dropped him to one knee.

"Never pull a gun on me unless you plan on using it," Jack said evenly. The implied threat wasn't lost on anyone in the room.

Frankie and the two goons headed back to the kitchen.

Jack turned and laid into Cardona: "If your daughter is still alive, and that's a big if, we need all the help we can get. Time is not our friend, Vincent. Now, you hired me to do a job. Back the fuck off."

Vincent Cardona was not generally at a loss for words. He did the talking and people did his bidding. His face turned a dangerous shade of purple, and he stood mute, breathing hard, contemplating the unimaginable for a father. Finally, he said, "Let's get some espresso before the bulls arrive." He stepped over the broken artwork and started toward the kitchen. He turned back when he realized Jack hadn't moved.

"There's no time. Give the detectives full access. They're not interested in your business, only your daughter. Tompkins is the more reasonable of the pair. They're sending a crew over to Angelica's apartment to dust for prints today. Make sure they can get in. Now, I need to see Angelica's bedroom," Jack said as he moved past Peter, who was dusting off his pant leg and picking up his weapon. "And I need names and addresses to match these faces," Jack said, handing Cardona the photographs he had found in Angelica's apartment.

"Upstairs, on the right."

———

Jack held an oval silver-framed picture in his hand. Angelica Cardona at twelve or thirteen, he guessed. Open, fresh, clear eyed, beautiful, and full of life. Jack felt her father's pain. He thought about his own son and the crisis he was going through.

The bedroom was pink. Larger than Angelica's entire apartment. Filled with every electronic toy and device money could buy. Boy band posters, riding trophies, oversized stuffed animals. A young girl's dream.

The difference between the bedroom she grew up in and her new apartment was startling. Angelica was a young woman looking to redefine her life. Independence. A clean break from her past.

Jack could understand that. It was what motivated him to move out west. Leave his old life behind. It hadn't worked out that way so far, and he hoped Angelica would have better luck. If she was still alive.

Her drawers were empty, and her closets were as neat as in her apartment. She had taken a few keepsakes with her when she moved but left the excess behind. Jack felt an overwhelming sense of loneliness in the room. Strange.

He looked out the second-floor window to the manicured grounds below. An Olympic-sized swimming pool, spa, and English gardens. A life most people would kill for. A lifestyle paid for with other people's blood. Nothing more to be learned here.

As Jack walked down the steps, he was met by Cardona, who handed him an envelope with the photographs.

"All good kids," he said. "They were on the list I gave you on your boat. I marked the pictures with their information on the back."

"I'll find her, Vincent. And then we're done." Jack moved past Peter, who was incongruously working a broom and dustpan, cleaning up the debris from the fallen art. Jack could see a wicked knot developing under his right eye. "And keep him out of my hair," Jack said as he walked out the front door.

Vincent Cardona threw a look to Peter, who propped the broom against the wall; loped down the hallway like a coyote in the wild, checking the load on his .38; and vanished out the back door.

———

The door to apartment 3B stood open. Jack was careful not to brush against any of the black residue that remained on the door handle where it had been dusted for prints.

Gallina and Tompkins glanced over as Jack walked into the living room, wearing disposable booties and gloves. Gallina scowled and turned away.

"The woman lived clean, I'll give her that," Tompkins said by way of hello.

"Lived?" Jack asked pointedly.

Tompkins ignored the question. "My Amy could take a lesson."

Jack didn't know if Amy was the detective's wife or his daughter. It was the first time he had mentioned family.

"No prints on the front door. So, unless she was wearing gloves, someone wiped them clean," Gallina said without turning around.

Black powder marred the windows, the sills, and the locking mechanism. Jack knew the apartment had been photographed and vacuumed for trace, everything. In the kitchen black powder had been brushed onto the handles and surfaces of the kitchen appliances and wineglasses. The tech crew had been thorough.

The lead technician walked in from the bedroom with his heavy black bag in tow. "I bagged that one wineglass with the trace of lipstick on it, and we'll test the contents of the wine at the lab. You want me to lock up?"

Gallina answered brusquely. "I'll handle it."

"Where was the wineglass?" Jack asked.

"Kitchen cabinet."

Jack had missed the glass on his first search, and the omission didn't sit well with him. He hoped he wasn't losing his touch.

"Thanks," he said to the technician.

The man nodded, bored, and exited the apartment.

"The captain put the kibosh on pulling in pretty boy unless his prints show up," Gallina said as if the news pained him. "He said we didn't have enough to suffer the political blowback. I couldn't fight him on it."

"No surprise there," Jack said.

"So you're on your own. Let us know how that goes," Gallina said, giving Jack tacit approval to lean on Raul Vargas.

"Did you check the headshot?" Jack asked, referring to the eight-by-ten photograph of Angelica.

"Yeah, she's a looker," Gallina said.

"For prints, Sherlock."

"Fuck you, Bertolino. One set of prints, and they're probably yours."

"Anything on the cigarette boat?" Jack asked, directing the question to Tompkins, ignoring the lieutenant.

Tompkins pulled a well-worn pad from his hip pocket and read. "Hundred seventy-five or so on the list you gave us. And that's in L.A. and Orange County. The number's loose because a lot of the boats are towed and then dropped in the water when the owners want to get laid. The boats are too long to dock at most marinas. Without a hard description, we're just spinning wheels. We ran a DMV list against your list and didn't get any hard hits—"

"So, it's a dead end," Jack said, finishing his train of thought. "The other boat, the boat that crashed, is called a panga. It's a type of Mexican fishing boat the Sinaloa cartel's using to smuggle drugs and illegals across the border. Any idea why she'd choose a fishing boat used by the cartels?"

"Not everyone has your good taste, Bertolino," Gallina said.

"We find the connection, we might find Angelica."

Gallina rolled his eyes. "We're aware of that, Jack. That's why they call us detectives. We detect. Some of us still do it for a living. We already spoke to the Coast Guard. And I've got a call in to the DEA. Anyway, we sent the pictures of our vics to Interpol and struck out there, too."

"Vics?" Jack asked.

"Oh, yeah," Gallina said. "One could argue that the suicide was a victim, you know, societally."

Gallina ticked down a half point on Jack's asshole meter. Investigating the murder and disappearance of young women had a way of affecting the most seasoned cops.

"The front door isn't self-locking," Jack said. "So if she closed up behind herself, her prints would've still been there."

Tompkins went down his list. "Doesn't look like she packed any clothes or toiletries, she took her cell phone but hasn't made any calls, and there's been no credit card or bank card activity. Just feels wrong."

"Thirty days in—it stinks to high hell," Jack said.

The three men stared at the glossy photo of Angelica, her face bruised by a brushstroke of black fingerprint powder.

21

"Is it any wonder that I'm the finest male specimen seated at this table?" Mateo asked as he pulled out an avocado, lettuce, tomato, sprouts, and cheese on whole wheat that he had picked up at Whole Foods on his way to the meeting.

Jack's mouth was too busy with a fully loaded Pink's chili dog to respond. He waved his hand in a give-me-a-minute kind of way. Pink's hot dog stand was happily located between both of his men's locations, which was the reason Jack had chosen it for their sit-down. That, and he loved the food.

Cruz carefully placed his bacon-cheese dog back on his paper plate and then made a pile of ketchup-drenched chili fries disappear with manic speed. He washed them down with a gulp of orange Crush soda, let out an almost acceptable burp, and gave Mateo an appraising look.

"You're holding up pretty well for an old guy."

"Old guy?" Mateo said. "*Jefe*"—Mateo directed the comment to Jack—"do you mind if I smack this kid-with-a-mouth around a little and teach him to respect his elders?" He dug into his sandwich without waiting for an answer.

"You could do some damage," Cruz conceded. "But then I'd be forced to infiltrate your cyber world. I've got the power to turn your every transaction into a living hell."

Jack brought his associates up to speed on his conversation with Gallina and Tompkins, the panga boat, the Sinaloa cartel, the smuggling routes, and the possible connection. Also, there were still no positive ID on either body.

"Somebody has to know who these women are," he said, barely able to contain his frustration.

"Maybe Raul Vargas is back in the game," Mateo speculated.

"And branching out," Jack added. "Drugs, women . . . You know, I want to put a bug on his car. I'd love to get my hands on his cell phone. Rattle his cage and see who he runs to. He sent the pictures he took of Angelica somewhere."

Mateo pulled out a yellow pad and gave his report on the Vargas Development Group.

"Their new multiuse, two-tower high-rise development was eight years in the making. They were green-lit back in 2007, with a lot of fanfare. The mayor was giving photo ops, the governor was glad-handing Vargas, cheerleading the regeneration of downtown Los Angeles and the tax revenues it would create. The whole nine yards. But in 2006 the housing bubble had peaked, and by 2008, with the global financial crisis, the housing recession, and the lending freeze, their project was dead on arrival. The mayor had political mud on his face, and Philippe Vargas all but went belly-up."

"How did he dig himself out of the hole? What changed?" Jack asked.

"He mortgaged his properties to stay afloat. Here's a list of his commercial real estate holdings in downtown Los Angeles and his personal properties," Mateo explained as he handed a printout to Jack and Cruz. "And he brought in a partner with deep pockets. Guy named Malic al-Yasiri. It was reported he had connections to Middle Eastern money. Anyway, it was enough for a turnaround."

Jack looked at Cruz, who had been doing research on Raul Vargas.

Cruz dumped his oily paper plates in the garbage, pulled his iPad out of his leather knapsack, and took center stage.

"The first thing I want to say is more of an observation. This guy has to be walking around with one major target on his back. I mean, he's the only man, one out of fifteen indicted, who received a sentence commutation, even though he was the ringleader. Some seriously pissed-off dudes behind bars must want him dead."

"I know how *that* feels," Jack said. No humor intended and none taken. The team understood the gravity of Jack's personal situation with La Eme.

"He was busted for transporting a thousand pounds of cocaine to Detroit," Cruz went on, "where it was turned into crack. Sweet guy. They say even his own lawyers were surprised he was cut loose.

"He lives in a condo in Brentwood and, as you know, works for his father's company now. I guess Dad wanted a return on his investment.

"He drives a Mercedes CLS coupe, a nice ride if you've got seventy grand. And his parking space is thirteen oh six in the parking structure of the KPMG Tower at the Wells Fargo Center in Bunker Hill. I already placed an order for two GPS bugs—they're being overnighted to my dad's shop for a Sunday delivery—and talked to a German mechanic friend of mine who gave me a heads-up where I can place them so that Raul will never be the wiser. Monday morning I can get an all-day pass in the parking structure for ten dollars. We'll have Raul on our computer screens by lunchtime."

"Great work, men," Jack said as he stood and dumped his paper plate and empty can of Diet Coke. "Get some rest tomorrow, I've got a feeling things are going to start heating up. Oh, and add Malic to the list. He's a person of interest," Jack said to Mateo. As he rubbed his gut, he elicited a laugh from his friend, who genteelly folded his vegetarian sandwich wrapper and flipped it into the trash.

"It's time to exert some pressure."

———

Jack was sitting in a Coffee Bean parking lot, drinking an iced Americano, cell phone to his ear, stuck on hold, waiting to hear how much longer he'd be driving the rental BMW. He was leafing through the list of Vargas properties, annoyed at the Muzak, when one of Philippe Vargas's two home addresses caught his attention.

The property was on Zumirez Drive and the zip code was 90265. Jack was almost sure it was a Malibu zip code, a suspicion that was confirmed when he entered the address into the GPS system. He threw the car into gear and headed toward the beach. If his hunch was correct, the Vargas estate had a clear view of Paradise Cove. The target on Raul Vargas's back had just gotten larger.

An hour later, Jack did a drive-by of the Vargas estate. Thick ten-foot hedges ran the length of the property. An ornate V, painted in faux gold leaf, served as the center medallion on a black wrought iron gate that obscured the view of the house and the ocean beyond from undeserving eyes. In fact, the entire road was hidden behind overgrown shrubbery, bamboo groves, masonry walls, and privacy fences. If there was an ocean view to be had, the owners clearly didn't want to share.

———

"Oh yes, that's Raul Vargas. I call him the silver-spoon shark," Maggie Sheffield said with disdain as she tossed her red mane of hair—giving new meaning to the term *windblown*—off her face.

Maggie had been the only witness to the boat wreck at Paradise Cove, and Jack was confident that her wary eyes could be counted upon to document the comings and goings of her tight-knit beach community.

"His father, Philippe Vargas," Maggie continued, "owns an estate right up the beach. Big place, cliffside. God forbid you call the man Phil. He'd eat you alive."

"So, you see his son around?" Jack asked, trying to keep the woman focused.

"He stops by the bar late at night, an hour before closing for a nightcap, to troll for the drunk, desperate, and needy. Takes off if there's no action."

"Does he live at his father's place?"

"I think he comes and goes. He may have another place in town. I see him a lot on the weekends. There's more fish in the pond, so to speak. Just the way a shark likes it."

"Does his house have a view of the cove?"

"Picture-perfect."

"Do you remember seeing Raul the night of the boat crash?"

"Can't say that I do, but it doesn't mean he wasn't around. Hey, can I pour you a cocktail?"

Maggie's voice took on a husky tone, and Jack wouldn't swear to it, but the zipper on her workout suit seemed to have magically drifted lower, exposing more cleavage than he needed to see.

"Thanks, but I'm on a tight schedule, gotta run."

"You haven't lived until you've seen the sunset from my porch. It's quite a show."

Jack didn't doubt her for one second.

"I'm going to leave another card. Just in case you see Raul. I'd appreciate a call."

"Your wish is my command," Maggie said with a voice that could make a hooker blush.

"Just a call would be fine," Jack said, smiling as he started back down the hill to the parking lot. He hardly noticed the view. Jack was getting a surge of electricity on the back of his neck that only occurred when a case started to gain momentum.

Raul Vargas was dirty; he could feel it.

Jack believed in redemption. That it was possible. Mateo was a perfect example. He was a bad man who had turned his life around and come out the other end an asset to society and a trusted friend. He'd wanted to change and Jack had provided him the opportunity. Jack didn't think Raul was a seeker.

The murder at Paradise Cove appeared to be a warning to Raul Vargas. For what? From whom? Was there a connection between Raul and the dead woman? Was someone in his crew setting him up? Somebody wasting away in a jail cell while Raul was out living the high life? Jack didn't have a clue, and he also didn't care what third party had Raul Vargas in their crosshairs.

Jack planned to take him down first.

22

Chris's petulance filled the Skype screen as Jack forwarded the names of two specialists in the San Francisco area.

"The neurologist, Dr. Pick, said he'd squeeze you in on Monday if that works. He sounds like a good man and came highly recommended."

"I've got a lit test. I'm playing catch-up as it is."

"Then the day after. It's important you make time," Jack said, trying to keep the impatience out of his voice. "You shouldn't be walking around in pain at this point in the healing process. It worries me."

Chris's silence hung heavily in the air. He wasn't maintaining eye contact with the computer's camera.

"Chris?"

The silence stung Jack to the core.

"Dr. Leland is waiting for your call. She understands the need for discretion and promised me that she took doctor-patient confidentiality very seriously. She sounded, uh, comfortable. Easy to talk to."

"For a shrink . . . Maybe you should see her if she's so easy."

"Is that a note of humor I detect?" Jack said, trying to lighten the mood.

"All right, Dad, I've gotta go. I'll let you know what the doc has to say. Thanks for setting it up, and thank Tommy for me. And stop worrying. It doesn't help." Chris abruptly clicked off.

His son's image disappeared from the screen as quickly as Jack's smile.

———

"Speak of the devil," Maggie Sheffield said over the glow of her Marlboro. She lipped it off to one side of her mouth, keeping the smoke out of her eyes as she peered down at the parking lot directly below her deck.

Raul Vargas had just gotten out of his Mercedes and glanced up the cliff at the blowsy woman with the crazy red hair.

"Are you talking to me?" he said, brimming with attitude.

"You're popular all of a sudden. A person of interest, as Don Johnson used to say."

Raul's eyes darkened. "What the hell are you talking about? Are you drunk again?"

"What's it to ya?" Maggie stood up on unsteady legs and tamped out her smoke in an overfilled ashtray. "Happy hunting." She walked inside, locking the door behind her. She freshened her cocktail, dialed a number on her cell, and walked back out onto her balcony.

Maggie stopped short, her breath caught in her throat. Raul Vargas was standing in the shadows. Intimidating. Stone still.

"Explain," he said quietly.

Maggie fought to keep her hand from shaking and spilling her drink. "A cop was asking questions . . . about you."

"What cop?"

"What's it to ya?" she said, her voice rising in volume.

"What cop?" Raul took one step forward.

"Jack Bertolino," she answered quickly.

"What did you say?"

"I said you were a shark. Always cruising. Was I wrong?"

Raul took another step toward her.

"You wanna talk to him?" She thrust her cell phone out to keep him at arm's length. And then said, taunting, "I've got him on the line."

"You gotta fucking be kidding me." Raul grabbed the phone from her hand. "Who the fuck is this?"

"Jack Bertolino here. Is there a problem, Raul? You strike out at the bar? She's a little out of your league, don't you think?"

"Fuck you." He tossed the phone at Maggie, who fumbled for it, dropped her drink and the phone. It clattered onto the wooden deck and landed in a growing puddle of gin and tonic. By the time she had grabbed it and wiped it off, Raul Vargas was a shadow walking briskly down the path toward his car.

Maggie was still shaking as she dialed the phone again. Praying that it still worked.

Jack was standing outside Hal's Bar and Grill. He had just finished dinner and was headed for home. He was genuinely concerned as he answered the phone again.

"He scared the bejesus out of me," were the first words that spilled out of Maggie's mouth.

"Is he still there?" Jack asked, pressing.

"No, the little prick just sped out of the lot and—" She stopped as she heard the sound of metal scraping concrete. "Yup, good, he just bottomed out his fancy car on that first speed bump. Couldn't happen to a nicer schmuck."

"Are you okay? Do you need help? Should I call the cops?"

"I wouldn't say no if you wanted to take a ride over and tuck me in."

Jack had to smile. "You sound fine."

"I've got a Colt special next to my bed, and I know how to use it."

"Good to know. Now lock your door and call me if he comes around again."

"Good night, Detective."

Maggie lit another cigarette and took one last look at the reflection of the moon on the still water of Paradise Cove through an exhale of smoke.

23

Polished brown granite sheathed the monolithic KPMG building on Bunker Hill. Jack stopped in front of the glass atrium that connected the two towers that comprised the Wells Fargo Center, sipping a Starbucks, watching the flow of well-dressed professionals enter and exit the downtown high-rise.

He knew that Raul Vargas was securely ensconced on the thirty-eighth floor because he had followed him from his father's estate in Malibu, right into the lobby, and then watched as the elevator carried Raul all the way up to his father's corporate offices.

"Hey, Bertolino."

Jack turned as Tim Dykstra appeared behind him. Jack wasn't surprised to be approached by the mayor's head of security and main fixer. He hadn't expected the hammer to drop so soon, though.

"Just the person I wanted to see," Dykstra said, wearing a tight smile as he proffered a handshake. It was as hard as the man's disposition and reminded Jack why he'd turned down the mayor's job offer.

"The mayor didn't come right out and say it, but I know he'd be pleased if you'd let up on Raul Vargas," Dykstra said, running his hand through his gray, military-cut hair. His probing eyes were unblinking, as if he could control the outcome of this conversation with sheer willpower. "The kid paid his debt to society, and the mayor holds Philippe Vargas in high esteem."

"So, tell me, Tim, what did Vargas have on the mayor that got him to intercede in the release of his son? A letter to the president, no less?"

"Don't go there, Jack. You're a political animal. Don't be naïve."

"And the cardinal? And two members of the city council? Did Phil butter all of their bread?"

"You made the right decision, Jack."

"How's that, Tim?" Jack held his gaze until the old warrior blinked.

"Not coming on board. You're not a team player. You've got to go along to get along in this world, Jack."

"I'll keep that in mind." Jack caught Cruz out of the corner of his eye exiting the parking structure in Jack's BMW and driving up Grand Avenue, away from Jack and his unscheduled street meet. The kid had great instincts, Jack thought as he turned to walk away.

"You can take the wop out of the neighborhood—"

Jack spun on his heel. "What'd you say?"

"I vetted you, Jack. There were rumors circulating that you were dirty. A hired gun for the mob; I guess they were more than rumors. Another greaseball on the pad."

Jack struck like a cobra. Grabbing Dykstra's lapels, he muscled all two hundred pounds of the man off the pavement and slammed him up against a nine-foot steel sculpture that rang like a bell when his head whiplashed back.

"Call 911!" someone in the gathering crowd yelled. Jack knew this was the wrong time and place for an extended confrontation.

What he didn't know was Peter Maniacci was standing in the crowd, all eyes and ears.

Jack let Dykstra's feet touch the ground and stepped back, assuming the stance as two armed security guards exited the building and strode in their direction. Tim Dykstra, red-faced and apoplectic, straightened his shirt and wisely fought the urge to charge.

"Stay away from Raul Vargas. And uh, when you go down, Jack, I'm gonna be there to pound the first nail in your coffin."

"Send my regards to the mayor," Jack said through a relaxed grin. He casually sauntered away, blending with the flow of pedestrian traffic to meet Cruz at the Music Center, their fallback location.

———

Raul Vargas had worked himself into a manic froth by the time he slid behind his desk and drained the last of his coffee. Who the hell did Jack Bertolino think he was, asking questions about him on his own stomping grounds? Defaming his name. Bertolino had to go. First he'd try to enlist someone in Malic's gang to do the dirty work, but if Raul had to take matters into his own hands, he would. Bertolino was tenacious, and if he continued to make waves, Raul ran the risk of losing his father's support.

Somehow, Bertolino had connected him to the dead woman at the cove, and he had clearly tied him to the kidnapping of the Cardona girl. As he'd known for several weeks now, Angelica was a liability. As long as she was alive, on American soil, his freedom was in serious jeopardy.

Raul told himself to calm down. He was due in a meeting with the entire staff, and he had to appear cool and collected. He wasn't well liked by the rest of the Vargas organization, which he could live with, until he had rebuilt his nest egg. But Malic was a different story. He had to be brought on board and dealt with in a calm, controlled manner, or the man could be his undoing.

All Malic had to do was send his sex video to the police, or to one of the local news hounds who were always snooping around, and Raul would be tied to the death of one woman he had raped and the disappearance of another. The evidence would be circumstantial on both fronts, but a jury would convict him out of pure malice. Everyone hated the rich kid. He would spend the rest of his days as some Rufus's boy toy until there was nothing left of his ass, his dignity, or his life.

But come to think of it, he wouldn't last a night in prison if Vincent Cardona heard that he had set up his only flesh and blood. With the Mafia's connections in the federal prison system, Raul would be dead by first light.

He had to be smart. He couldn't let that happen.

"Halle, could you be a sweetheart and bring me a cup of coffee?" Raul said into his phone. "And are we still meeting in the conference room?"

"The meeting started ten minutes ago. I thought you were already there."

"Shit!" Raul said as he gathered himself, grabbed a file, and ran down the plush carpeted hallway.

———

Cruz was tapping out an inscrutable beat on the dashboard as Jack pulled to a stop at 201 North Figueroa. Mateo was just exiting the City of Los Angeles Department of Building and Safety, where he was doing research on the Vargas development project.

"You're going to love this," he said as he jammed Cruz forward and squeezed his six-foot-two frame into the tight backseat. "No worries, I'm fine," he said, giving Cruz a hard time for not relinquishing the shotgun seat. "Straight ahead and make a right onto Second. I'll tell you when to pull over."

Mateo directed Jack to stop in front of the Regent Hotel. The fifteen-story building might have been tony in the twenties, but it looked tired now, and ready for the wrecking ball. The brick façade was stained almost black; the signage was missing the *E* in *Hotel*. Men and women who looked more transient than genteel walked through the pitted brass doors while small groups congregated on the sidewalk in front of the building, smoking, furtive eyes tracking for dealers, hoping to score. Jack knew the unmistakable look and body language.

"I thought you were staying at the Hyatt," Jack tossed out dryly.

Cruz barked a laugh. Mateo batted the back of his car seat.

"It's a revolving door," he said, referring to the hotel. "They get busted for possession or public intoxication, spend a few dry nights on the county, and when they get out, they check back into the no-tell hotel, where it's one-stop shopping for crack."

"And we're here why?" Jack asked, knowing there was more and wondering where he got his info.

"Well, the woman at the records counter got very chatty. Her name's Cathy; I think she's a lapsed Catholic."

"If she wasn't before she met you . . ."

"She *was* having unclean thoughts," Mateo said in agreement.

"And her religion is germane to the discussion because . . . ?" Jack asked.

"The L.A. archdiocese owns this property. And it's the cornerstone of Vargas's new development project. It went from being a tax and insurance liability to being worth ten times its appraised value. Philippe Vargas made the cardinal a true believer and coerced the august man of the cloth to write a letter to the president extolling the virtues of his drug-dealing son."

"A win-win," Cruz chimed in.

"The mayor's also a very happy camper. He can take credit for eradicating a blight on his new downtown, raising tax revenues, and cleaning up a drug-infested cesspool, which is a drain on local law enforcement."

"And that's why two members of the city council were also pulled into the letter-writing loop," Jack said.

"That's right, *jefe*. The Catholic Church is happy, Vargas gets what he wants, and the mayor and city council members get reelected for fulfilling campaign promises to rejuvenate their City of Angels."

"And Raul Vargas is a free man," Jack said tightly as he pulled away from the curb.

"Where to?" Mateo asked.

"I'm dropping you at the Hyatt. Cruz and I are going to track Raul. What time are you having dinner with 'Chatty Cathy'?"

"I'm not going to dignify that question with a—"

"What time?"

"Six o'clock, straight up."

The three men shared a laugh.

———

Raul looked ragged from the day at the office and had no idea that the BMW that shadowed him to his condo in Brentwood contained Jack Bertolino and Cruz. A BMW in Los Angeles was so common, it didn't raise any alarm bells.

Cruz had his nose buried in his laptop, admiring his handiwork. The GPS system he had planted on Raul's car was working like a charm.

Jack drove past the condo building as Raul pushed his electronic key out the window, swiped the pad, and drove down into the secure underground parking garage. Jack took note of the alleyways and surrounding buildings in case he had to do some up-close-and-personal surveillance.

Jack was double-parked on San Vicente while Cruz made a Starbucks coffee run when the laptop emitted a pinging sound, alerting Jack that his quarry was on the move again. He paged Cruz, who hustled out of the store with two iced coffees and a bagful of doughnuts.

Five minutes later, they were traveling south on the San Diego Freeway, wiping powdered sugar off their lips. Jack finally eyeballed Raul's Mercedes traveling ahead of them. Jack corrected his speed to follow at a safe distance. Cruz shared a small fist pump before returning to the moving car icon on his computer.

Raul's Mercedes would have looked out of place in the tired strip mall he pulled into in the city of Costa Mesa if not for the other incongruous cars that populated the lot. Over a million dollars' worth of exotic cars. The sun was oblong and looked like a Dalí painting dripping below the horizon. The orange glow did little to dress up the string of faded yellow stucco retail shops that called the strip mall home. A hair salon, liquor store, video rental, and head shop completed the loop. It was a classic sixties spread, without any pretension of architectural detail.

Jack continued past the lot as Raul exited his vehicle. Jack executed a U-turn on Pomona Avenue before pulling to the curb a half a block down on Nineteenth with a clear view of the mall.

Raul had already disappeared inside one of the shops, and unless he was getting his hair permed at Raphael's hair salon, he was probably headed to the very end of the L-shaped complex.

The red-lacquered door had no name over the entrance and no windows. With his cell phone Jack took a photo of an address painted over the door in black. It was a private club, bar, or restaurant of some kind. Jack wouldn't know until he got a look inside. He snapped off a few quick shots of the nearby license plates and made a mental note to run them by Nick Aprea.

He ducked down in his seat as another car pulled into the lot and parked. Two men exited a silver Porsche 911. They checked out the neighborhood before walking the length of the concrete lot and disappearing behind the red door.

"Guy on the left was packing heat," Jack said, "wearing a shoulder rig. You get a fix on their ethnicity?" he asked Cruz, who had mirrored Jack's movements and was sitting low in the car's leather seat.

"Middle Eastern."

"You sure?"

"No."

"But you think?"

"Yeah."

"Me too. What the hell is Raul doing out here?"

"There's only one way to find out," Cruz said knowingly.

"Too risky at this point. We sit and wait."

"I'm starved."

"You just ate three doughnuts."

"Yeah, but that was an hour ago."

Jack laughed and his own stomach growled loud enough to set Cruz to laughing. It got instantly quiet when a Lincoln Town Car pulled into the lot and an impeccably dressed, dark-haired man slid out of the backseat, walked directly up to the red door, and stepped inside without ever looking back.

"Hmmm," Jack said. "*El jefe* has arrived."

———————

The odd grouping of hard, armed young men who were seated at multiple tables scattered around the room stood as Malic made his entrance. It looked like a meeting of Saddam Hussein's Republican Guard. Yet Raul remained seated, a slight not missed by the eighteen Iraqi gangsters. Malic ignored him and shook a few hands, clasped a few shoulders, and shared a few whispered comments with his men, who seemed lifted by his attention.

A fully stocked bar lined one end of the room, and Middle Eastern music played softly in the background. Raul finished his Grey Goose on the rocks and went to pour himself another while he waited for an audience with Malic. In the office they were business partners; in the Iraqi social club Malic was the *man*.

Raul stood at the bar and drank until he felt Malic's presence next to him.

"I've got a problem," Raul said as he locked eyes with Malic.

"Make it quick, I've got a pickup tonight," Malic snapped.

Not the way Raul had played the conversation in his head. He took another sip of his vodka to save face but knew he wasn't fooling anyone.

"Jack Bertolino," Raul stated. "He's asking a lot of questions. Too many questions. About the girl, about Paradise Cove, about me."

"And this is my concern why?"

"Because if my problems bleed over to the Vargas Development Group, it will affect your bottom line. The deal is tenuous at best. Bad publicity will bury us. He needs to go."

Malic seemed to give that some thought. Raul couldn't read the man. His eyes were like black pits. Raul wanted to scream. If Malic hadn't killed the girl at Paradise Cove, there wouldn't have been a trail leading to his doorstep. If he hadn't kidnapped the Cardona bitch, none of this would have been happening.

"It was on the news. A gangbanger tried to take Bertolino out. A drive-by on a cycle, for crissake. We could do it the same way, and they'd take the heat."

Malic finally spoke. "It should all be handled by the end of next week," he said, no inflection in his voice. "The girl will be out of the country and no longer our concern. If Bertolino remains an irritant, we'll handle him then."

The imposing man turned on his heel and walked away, leaving a red-faced Raul standing impotently at the bar. Also not missed by the young Iraqi gangsters.

———

Jack snapped a tight photo of Malic's face as the red door swung open. He took another picture of Hassan, the red-bearded driver, who emerged from the limo and opened the rear door for his boss.

"Definitely Middle Eastern," Jack said to Cruz. "Iran, Iraq. Some-damn-where in that part of the world. We'll find out."

"The guy with the red beard had crazy eyes."

Jack nodded and photographed Raul, who stormed out of the club, jumped into his car, and did a tire-burning exit.

"Doesn't look like our boy's riding high," he said as he threw the BMW into gear. When it became clear that Raul was driving toward Malibu, Jack peeled off 10 West and headed for home.

24

Malic piloted the cigarette boat with one eye on the Garmin GPS color display screen and the other peeled for fast-moving cargo container ships that had crossed the Pacific from Asia, headed for San Pedro, Long Beach, and L.A. harbors to off-load. He had inputted the coordinates of the meet but was running behind schedule. Malic was totally in his element piloting his fifty-foot go-fast boat. The Marauder SS, with its dual-charged Mercury Racing engines and acceleration that was mind-numbing, sliced through a three-foot wave like a steak knife through butter.

Unimpressed, Hassan was seated next to him. He wanted to take care of business and slip back into the warmth of his own bed. He ran the back of his fist across his copper-red beard and prayed that all would go well tonight. He didn't like being out on the open sea when it was choppy, although it did offer a small measure of safety from the Coast Guard's radar if they were out cruising the coastline.

"There," Malic shouted over the thrum of the engines.

In the distance both men could see the faint blinking green light. In seconds they pulled alongside a white wooden panga, sunk dangerously low in the water with four hooded occupants aboard. Hassan tied off onto the panga and the men made short work of off-loading seventy-five bales of marijuana with a street value of three quarters of a million dollars. When the precious cargo was secured in the holds of Malic's craft and business had been concluded, Malic reached out a hand as one, and then a second person, stepped carefully from the panga onto his luxury craft.

"Welcome to America, girls," Malic said graciously with his slight English accent. Two hoods were pulled back, revealing a startling, fresh-faced blond and a raven-haired beauty.

"It is very pleased to be meeting with you," the raven-haired woman said.

She couldn't be more than seventeen, Malic thought. It only increased her value. He would sample his latest acquisition and then place her in one of his clubs, where she would work off her sale price, the cost of transporting her illegally from Eastern Europe into Mexico and then across the border into the United States. The manager of his club, who worked the girls, would subtract the cost of her illegal papers, clothes, room, and board—an added tariff—the cost of doing business.

The girls took their seats, both excited and apprehensive that their journey was coming to an end. They had traveled halfway around the world looking for a better life. Hassan untied the ropes and took his seat as the two vessels drifted apart.

Malic pushed the throttle forward and the million-dollar customized boat rocketed back toward the safety of his compound walls.

———

Jack was kneeling, shirtless, on his bed as he undid the first button on Leslie's silk blouse and started working his way down. He was making sure she'd never forget how good it could be. When he fumbled with the fourth button, she unbuckled his belt, undid his fly, and dropped his pants below his waist on a three count. As he unfastened her bra and tossed it across the room, she grabbed his aroused self, which was peeking out the top of his Jockeys, and squeezed to just this side of pain, making him growl.

Jack rolled onto his side and kicked off his pants. Leslie helped dispatch his briefs, using her feet when they got stuck around his ankles. He slipped his hand against the arch of her lower back and pulled her close, feeling the warmth of her breasts burn against his chest and her sex rubbing against his. She pushed in tighter, and their lips and tongues and moans and beating hearts started syncing up.

The four phones that were scattered around his loft rang as one. Louder than hell.

Undeterred, Jack moved from one luscious breast to the other, blinded by the moment. Lost in the scent and the sensuality. The phone finally went to voice mail.

Then Jack's cell phone rang and vibrated on the granite kitchen center island like a windup toy. They rolled onto their backs to catch their breath until it also went to voice mail.

Then Jack's fucking landlines rang again.

"Get it, Jack. Get it over with and come back to bed," Leslie said, totally annoyed.

"I hope I'm not calling at a bad time," Carol Williams said, not waiting for an answer, "but you're not going to believe what I found on YouTube. Well, I didn't find it, but I have it now."

"Who is this? And do you know what time it is?"

"It's Carol Williams, and you told me explicitly to call twenty-four/seven if I had anything to report. I know that because I take direction very well. Believe me, you're going to want to have this conversation."

"It better be good, Carol."

"Angelica Curtis is alive."

Jack's mood changed instantaneously. "That's better than good."

Leslie, not being a part of the conversation, was less than thrilled and didn't hide her frustration as Jack walked naked into his office.

"Hey, so I just got off the phone with Barry Freid, and *the great teacher* is not one to make home phone calls," Carol Williams said. "Barry's assistant found it surfing the Web, and, well, I'm the only one who saved your card."

"Are you sure it's Angelica?" Jack asked.

"I sure as hell am. It's Angelica, all right, and she's doing a monologue, and she's good. Really good," she said with a trace of envy. "You can't take your eyes off the screen. She was never that plugged in in class. It's short, but it's Angelica, all right."

"This is great, Carol. You did good."

"Well, thank you, Mr. Detective. Maybe you should offer me a job. This waitressing thing is killing my feet."

Jack let that one pass.

"Can you send it over to me?" he asked.

"I'm sending you the URL as we speak. Don't know where it was generated from, but it shouldn't be too hard to track down."

Jack's computer dinged, letting him know an e-mail had arrived.

"Got it, Carol. Thanks. I'll get back to you if I have any questions."

"Hey, call me anyway when this is over. It appears, according to my ex-boyfriend's critique, that I might be sexually repressed after all. Why don't you come over and try and heal me? You know, a mercy mission. For the greater good."

Jack could hear the smile in her voice and was glad he didn't have the Skype screen turned on, as he was sitting in front of the computer in his birthday suit. "Maybe in ten years," he answered.

"Hell, in ten years you'll be too old to help."

"Ouch."

Carol laughed as she hung up the phone.

To his amazement, Angelica Cardona's image filled the computer screen. Her eyes blazed with controlled intensity. She was smiling, but there was no joy in the eyes of "Maggie the Cat." It was a nuanced performance. A woman drowning and fighting for her life.

The recording was no more than ten seconds long, and Jack viewed it twice, concentrating on the background more than the performance. Trying to ascertain a location. Something about the camera work was off. Jack couldn't put his finger on it.

"Is that your missing person?"

"Angelica Cardona," he said as the clip went to black.

Leslie handed Jack his robe, which he gladly shrugged into and hit Play again.

"Big Daddy shares my attitude toward those two! As for me, well—I give him a laugh now and then and he tolerates me. In fact!—I sometimes suspect that Big Daddy harbors a little unconscious 'lech' fo' me . . ." And the screen turned to black.

"She's beautiful," Leslie said. "It's from *Cat on a Hot Tin Roof.*"

Jack nodded in agreement. "I saw the script in her apartment. Does she look like she's being held against her will?"

"Hard to say. I don't see any bars on the windows."

"I don't see any windows." He checked the screen for the origin. "A Jahmir 8 posted it two days ago." Jack keyed up the video again. The person posting had written, "My new girlfriend." Nothing added under personal description. Category: Entertainment. License: Standard YouTube License.

"Shouldn't be too hard to track down," Leslie said.

"Look at the background. At the wall, the tile work. It's blurred but intricate. And is that the edge of someone's head? In the far right corner of the screen?"

"You find tile work like that in mosques. It looks Middle Eastern."

"Iraq?" Jack asked.

"Didn't you see any of the pictures of Saddam Hussein's castles? Yes, Iraq works. But don't jump the gun. It could've been shot in a building from the forties with Moroccan architecture in Hollywood."

"I'm just saying. I'm pretty sure Raul Vargas sent the pictures of Angelica to a second party. Is that someone's head?" Jack asked again, pointing at the screen.

"I wouldn't swear to it in a court of law, but it's a definite maybe."

"God, I love lawyers."

"Prove it."

Instead Jack phoned Cruz, who was a night owl and picked up on the second ring, totally oblivious to Leslie's glare as she walked out of the office. This was the break in the case he'd been waiting for. The video might be proof that Angelica Cardona was still alive and Jack was riding an adrenaline-fueled high. After bringing Cruz up to speed he forwarded the URL and they watched the video together in real time, in slo-mo, and then again.

Cruz was confident it was someone's head on the edge of the screen and promised to track the origin of the video in the morning.

Before Jack could sign off, he heard the front door open and close, the lock being thrown, and the sound of Leslie's carry-on luggage wheels vibrating down the exterior hallway toward the elevator.

Jack made no move to stop her.

25

Malic dried off from his shower, taking note of his impeccable body, and slipped into an embroidered silk smoking jacket and ornate slippers.

His wife was already in bed, watching *Late Night with Seth Meyers*. Kayla looked up as he exited the bathroom and knew from her husband's demeanor that he wasn't headed to bed. He had many late nights, she thought. Too many. Their sex life had been nonexistent since the birth of their daughter. Not that Kayla particularly cared. Her husband was a selfish lover, interested only in getting off. The attacks were more about power than pleasure.

Malic had approached her about a second wife when they were still in Iraq. She had responded with such ferocity that the discussion was never brought up again. And now, living in the States, it was no longer legal. Not like that had ever stopped her husband before.

Malic bent down, brushed her blond hair off her forehead, and kissed her there. "Don't wait up, my love," he said briskly. "I have to come up with the final figures before tomorrow's meeting. If we don't have sufficient funds in place to pay for this quarter's interest on the construction loan, the bank could step in and shut us down."

"You work too hard," Kayla said with genuine concern.

"The deal will be consummated by week's end," Malic said. "I have it under control."

She trusted that he did, as with every other aspect of their life together. Kayla was comforted by the knowledge that Malic was a good provider, and shifted focus. Seth Meyers was interviewing Amy Poehler, and Kayla wasn't even aware that her husband had left the room.

———

Malic had felt strong, gazing at his image in the bathroom mirror and understanding where he had come from and what he had become. As he walked out his French doors, past his infinity pool, he felt the power growing, an electric charge in his loins. When he witnessed Allah's miracle of a moon reflected on the serene Pacific, he was humbled at all he had achieved. As he entered his office, he felt like a lion, the master of his domain.

The computerized lights snapped on with the turn of his key. Malic stopped for a moment to appreciate Matisse's artistic genius. *La Pastorale.* His joy. Then he walked to the back of the room, hit a hidden switch, pulled open the hinged mahogany bookshelf—home to his first editions—and stepped through, gaining entry to his most private life.

A white-tiled tunnel was exposed and then disappeared as he closed the secret door behind him.

Artisans Malic had flown in from Iraq had constructed the underground masterpiece. They were ignorant as to the location of their employment and happy to be earning a huge salary plying their trade. Saddam Hussein had been fond of tunnels, and there was an abundance of engineering work while he was alive. It dried up faster than the Tigris River in drought season after Saddam was caught hiding in a rat hole by the Americans and brought to an ignoble justice. The men were flown back home upon completion of their task, richer for their effort, without ever visiting Disneyland or even knowing they had been living for six months of their lives in Orange County, California.

———

Malic's wife slipped out of bed—after Seth Meyers finished the segment—and into a silk robe that accentuated her statuesque body. She walked past her daughter's room on the way to the kitchen. Saarah's door was open a crack to let the ambient hallway light in, just the way her daughter liked it. Saarah slept like an angel. Pure of heart, Kayla thought as she poured hot water out of the massive Sub-Zero refrigerator's door for a cup of her favorite tea, Sleepytime. She decided in that very moment that she could kill in order to protect her sweet girl. She didn't know where thoughts like that came from and attributed them to her time spent in Iraq during the invasion.

Kayla happened to look out the window, past the wide lawn and the glow of the aquamarine pool, and realized that Malic wasn't seated behind his desk. She stepped through the French doors into the backyard, pulling her thin silk robe tight against the damp air, in order to make sure that the office was empty. Maybe he was talking to one of the security men who patrolled the perimeter of the property at night, she thought as she retreated into the house, shivering as she locked the door behind her. She grabbed a tea bag and submerged it in the steaming

155

water. She glanced through the window again, struck by his odd disappearance, and walked back to her bedroom.

———

Malic strolled with his hands clasped behind his back as he walked deeper into the rocky cliffside. He was in no hurry. With every step he felt he was delving deeper into his own psyche. He stopped from time to time to appreciate the antiquities he had pillaged before his flight from Baghdad and carefully transported with the help of the State Department. Malic had many secrets to share about the inner workings of the new Iraqi government, and the Americans succumbed to his charm and knowledge. As a consequence they turned a blind eye when it came to transporting his wealth. His treasures were displayed on pedestals cut into the ornate tiled wall and lit with micro spots that made the gold figurines gleam and the precise Mesopotamian sculptures come to life. The fact that his eyes alone could enjoy these priceless national treasures gave him a sexual charge.

At the far end of the tunnel were two steel-plated doors. Malic thrust the second key on his ring into the door on the right and stepped through, throwing the bolt securely behind him. He continued on for a short distance and keyed yet another door open.

He stepped inside an Arabian fantasy. Pure eye candy. A dazzling room, out of *Lawrence of Arabia*. Multicolored, gold-threaded brocade cloth covered the walls and draped gracefully down, creating the illusion of a Bedouin sheik's tent. A damask-covered bed dominated the room, which was the size of a small apartment.

The raven-haired beauty sat naked in the center of the woven opulence. Her blond companion exited the shower room wearing only her youth. She climbed up onto the bed and waited expectantly next to her friend.

Malic stood still for an extended moment, taking in the scene, and then let his robe fall open, exposing his erection. The young blond woman leaned over her counterpart and kissed her full on the mouth, never breaking eye contact with Malic, who dropped his robe to the Persian-rugged floor and joined his newest acquisitions in his grand bed.

———

Angelica startled awake as she heard a door open and then clang shut. Was she dreaming? She sat up in bed and concentrated on the sound emanating from outside her prison walls.

And then . . . there. She was sure that she could hear something. It was the sound of young feminine laughter and Angelica thought she might go insane. She shot out of the bed. The blood rushed to her head. She was afraid the heat would overwhelm her and hoped in that instant that it would.

Angelica saw her reflection in the Plexiglas wall. She was afraid that she was having a nervous breakdown and started keening, and then she started to scream, the veins in her neck and temples swollen and throbbing.

"They're no-neck monsters, all no-neck people are monsters . . . !" Angelica dropped to the floor wracked with emotional pain, tears flowing, nose running, chest heaving.

26

"Was she good?" Jack asked over his shoulder as Mateo entered the loft. Cruz was set up at the center kitchen island with his laptop, iPhone, and a large iced Americano. He'd been stymied trying to find the origin of the video and picked idly at the remnants of a toasted bagel that littered a small plate next to his computer. Jack was in the office sipping a cup of coffee, staring at his computer screen as Mateo set his things down on the dining room table just to the left of the front door.

Jack had put calls in to Gallina, Tompkins, and Nick Aprea, and brought them up to speed on the YouTube video. Then he pulled Mateo into the hunt. Not a bad way to start the day, Jack thought. Wasn't sure how he was going to deal with Vincent Cardona. He didn't want any interference but knew the man had to be reckoned with. Might give him some relief, he thought. Jack knew how he would feel if it were his son.

"No, *jefe*, she was spectacular," Mateo answered. "It's been common knowledge, ever since I was in the Franciscan Preparatory School, that these repressed Catholic girls have pent-up sexuality. It's the nuns' influence. Now, add a civil service job to the mix and let's just say the good woman gave up all of her secrets."

Jack was waiting on a Skype call from Miami. He had sent the YouTube video to Kenny Ortega, a DEA agent and an old friend. Kenny was responsible for bringing the government into play on the 18th Street Angels case Jack had broken a month ago and was always ready to lend a hand. That was a two-way street, as far as Jack was concerned. They had taken down more than their share of cartel scumbags through the years and put some major drugs on the table. He'd always have Kenny's back.

Jack's landline rang, and Jack announced, "It's Gallina," putting the call on speakerphone.

"Are you fucking with me, Bertolino?" was his opening salvo.

"That wouldn't even be sport, Lieutenant. Why do you ask?"

"The video you sent me. The proof our missing person is still alive . . . that YouTube account was set up in the name of an eight-year-old boy."

Gallina gave that a moment to sink in before he continued.

"The word I get from our IT team is that even if the kid posted it three days ago, it was a video of a video. It could have been sent to him via e-mail, or Facebook, and he only posted on the date provided. The original could have been generated six months ago. It blows our time line. But did you hear me, Bertolino? The kid is eight years old. Jahmir 8. That's why the camera angle's so low. Either that or the guy's a fuckin' midget. And here's the kicker—"

"I need a location," Jack interjected.

"I'm getting to that. The kicker is, you know where Anbar Province is?"

"Iraq."

"Good for you. You get a gold star. But you don't get the girl. Not yet. And as for your theory that it should be easy to track, not so much. We only got the Anbar location off of signage on one of the kid's earlier postings. At a horse race, of all things. Who takes their kid to the track for his birthday?" Gallina wasn't looking for an answer. "My guys are striking out with Google. They own You-Tube and are being less than forthcoming. Hell, they're in a war with China over privacy rights. It's like poison coming out of my mouth, but if we don't get the feds involved with a court order, we are shit out of luck. And I'll need more linkage between the three women to have a chance in hell."

"Stay on the address," Jack said, "and I'll work it from my end. I've still got some juice with the feds. But the kid could have shot the video in real time, and the time line could hold."

"It's possible, Bertolino. But eight years old? I can't wrap my head around that. If I stumble on anything of interest, I'll call. I expect the same. Later." Gallina hung up.

"Eight years old, what the fuck?" Jack mused as the Skype screen trilled, and Kenny Ortega's face lit up the computer screen.

"Mi hermano!" Kenny said joyfully. "And who's that I see in the background?"

"It's me, you old hound dog, Mateo."

"How's Miami?" Jack asked. Kenny Ortega could put a smile on a storm cloud.

"I bought a new boat. Twenty-seven feet of heaven. I never see the water, though, because you got me a bump in grade and a pay raise, and I actually have to work for a living."

Jack introduced him to Cruz and then methodically filled him in on the case: the two dead women and their physical similarities, the disappearance or abduction of Angelica Cardona, his connection with Vincent Cardona, his suspicion of Raul Vargas, the delivery of the video, and the phone call with Lieutenant Gallina.

"I'll put the squeeze on Google for an address. I don't think they'll want to get on the wrong side of a sex slavery ring, if that's how this plays out, or worse yet, culpability in the death of a third woman. And if there's any traction, the DEA has feet on the ground in Iraq."

"Hey, Kenny, could we find out who set up the YouTube account? My guess is an eight-year-old couldn't register himself."

"Till later, *mi hermano*." And Kenny Ortega clicked off.

"Iraq, huh?" Jack said, turning to the room. "Not so strange. You've heard of harems."

Cruz looked up from his computer and added, "Iraqi men can have four wives. I just Googled it. Sharia law was written into the new Iraqi constitution. This is post-Saddam we're talking about. It's not so common anymore, but it's totally legit."

"Sounds like a living hell," Mateo said.

He wasn't going to get any argument from Jack, who added, "Didn't the sultan of Brunei get some nasty publicity a few years back for paying to have women delivered to his palace and then holding them against their will?"

"He did," Mateo said. "And he can't be the only one who's twisted enough to play that game."

"So, if it's a sex ring, why are they killing their bottom line?" Jack threw out to the team.

Cruz looked up from the screen again. "They kill greyhounds when they start losing races."

"That's cold," Jack said. "But I can appreciate the train of thought."

Mateo jumped in. "The first girl did OD. Maybe Angelica was picked up to fill an order."

"A definite maybe," Jack said.

The men took a moment to process that piece of ugliness.

"When did that guy, Malic . . . ?" Jack asked, looking for a last name.

"Al-Yasiri," Mateo gave him.

"Right, when did Malic al-Yasiri come to work for the Vargas Development Group?" Jack asked, shifting gears.

"Two months before Raul Vargas was released from federal prison. And he's Iraqi," Mateo added, knowing where Jack was going. "I got the whole story from Chatty Cathy. She said it dominated the gossip around the watercooler for weeks. This was right around the time that Philippe Vargas was fighting to keep his head above water. He'd mortgaged all of his properties and they were about to topple like dominoes. An office pool at the Department of Building and Safety was wagering on when the Vargas Development Group would go belly-up. And then at the eleventh hour, he found the golden goose."

"Malic al-Yasiri," Jack said.

"The same. Word around the office was that Malic immigrated to the States after the fall of Baghdad with a bag full of cash. Rumor was, he had some juice with the State Department. Clean bill of health as far as anyone knows, but I'll do some digging."

"Do we have a picture of him?" Jack asked.

"Nothing yet."

"Now, all the while Vargas Senior was struggling to maintain," Mateo went on, "he was fighting and calling in every favor owed to get his kid out of jail. No easy feat."

"Let's see if there's any traction between the hiring of Malic and the release of Raul," Jack said. "Philippe's political connections might have been enough to work the magic, but a well-placed call from the State Department could've sealed the deal."

Jack started to pack up his MacBook Pro.

"Where you headed, *jefe*?"

"Beverly Hills. The Chop House."

"Early lunch?"

"Vincent Cardona. It's time to reacquaint father and daughter."

27

The heavy metal door that led to the basement, meat locker, pantry, and storage area of the Beverly Hills Chop House swung open, and a man with a burlap sack over his head, cinched tightly around his neck, was shoved down the short flight of metal steps and tumbled hard onto the cement floor below. Vincent Cardona's cousin Frankie followed, closing the doors to the alleyway behind him, shutting out the light. Fluorescent bulbs lent an otherworldly edge to the room. His jowly face tightened as he punt-kicked his captive and then lifted the man off the floor with remarkable ease.

Vincent Cardona was standing next to the large thick-glassed meat locker, where sides of beef were butchered and steaks were air-dried and aged to perfection. He held the double-sealed door open and gestured with a nod of his head.

"In here, Frankie."

His cousin roughly pushed the whimpering man into the cold room, muscled him down into a chair behind a butcher's table, and ripped off the burlap sack.

The young man had black hair, piercing eyes blinking wide

with fear, thin fine features on a handsome face. Both of the man's arms were tattooed with bright greens, yellows, and reds—an ink rendering of a rain forest. The bright blue tail of a parrot wound gracefully around one forearm. Yet amid the sweeping vines were the track marks of a heroin needle.

"I'm sorry, Mr. Cardona, it'll never happen again," he said with an upper-class French accent as he rubbed his neck where the tape had ripped off skin. "I promise you on the life of my son. Never again."

Cardona signaled to Frankie the Man, who backhanded their prisoner, knocking snot, tears, and spit out of every bruised orifice.

Vincent Cardona closed the door to the meat locker, keeping the chill in and the sound out. He unzipped a fine leather carrying case and spread the flaps open onto the wooden cutting table. Five finely honed Japanese carving knives of different lengths and thicknesses were held in place by orange silk sheaths.

"Which one's your favorite?" Cardona asked as if he really cared.

The young chef tried to answer, but his mouth was too dry to speak. He pointed at a small paring knife. He knew where this drama was headed, and his choice of the shortest blade almost made Cardona laugh. But not quite.

"I'm going to be reasonable here. Not sure why. Maybe because you're a great chef."

The young man's face turned beet red. Tears started to pour down his cheeks.

"Pick a finger," Cardona ordered. "You know where I'm going with this."

"Please." His voice was a rasping tremolo. "It's my trade; I'll work off the loss. I've got family."

Cardona grabbed the man's wrists and pounded them down onto the wooden tabletop. "Which hand did you use to steal from me again? Not just me, all the other men and women who put in an honest night's work here. Which fucking hand did you use to manipulate my fuckin' receipts?" he said, snarling.

The young Frenchman's eyes started to roll back into their sockets. Cardona gave way as Frankie slapped him back to consciousness. Frankie had the skill set to beat a man just short of unconscious, keep him lucid enough to feel more pain, or hit him hard enough to end his life.

"Think hard and clear now," Cardona hissed. "You've got one last chance. You control your destiny. If it's dealer's choice, my choice, you'll never hold a knife again."

The Frenchman screamed.

"My left hand, my pinky finger!"

Japanese hardened steel flashed in a lightning strike, impaling the man's pinky finger to the wooden cutting block. He looked down at his hand, and before he could scream, Vincent Cardona pounded on the dull side of the knife with his meaty fist and the razor-sharp blade severed the joint of the finger just above the fleshy part of the hand, like a chicken bone.

The popping sound the blade made, cutting through bone and sinew, turned the Frenchman's red face to white. He let loose with an animal wail. Frankie slapped a piece of duct tape over his mouth.

Cardona tossed the knife onto the butcher-block table and stepped back as blood spurted from the man's mutilated hand. He gestured to his cousin, who threw the thief a towel.

Cardona looked down at his shirt and spotted a bloodstain.

"Shit!" he said as he slapped the Frenchman on the side of

the head. "I'm buying a new shirt and it's coming out of your next paycheck."

The young man wrapped the finger with the towel and tried to stanch the flow of blood.

"You caught your hand in the dumbwaiter. No one will believe you, but no one will steal from me again. If I didn't like your kid, you'd be a dead frog."

Cardona looked to Frankie. "Get him cleaned up, take him to Cedars, and put the bill on my MasterCard." Then he looked down at his handiwork. "Put the finger down the disposal. I don't want them to find it and sew it back on."

The Frenchman was going into shock as a pissed Cardona dabbed at the stain on his silk shirt, closed the glass door behind him, and started for the stairs.

Peter came rushing down, glanced at the scene in the meat locker and then back at Cardona. "Bertolino's here. I said we were closed. He said he's got news. Gotta show you something important."

Vincent Cardona tucked his shirt back into his pants, buttoned his sports jacket over the bloodstain, and walked up the stairs to his restaurant.

Jack, standing at the bar, watched the six-panel wooden door swing open and Vincent Cardona fill the door frame before heading in his direction. His eyes were heavy-lidded and cold. Jack saw a red crease across the meaty part of Cardona's hand as he thrust it forward to shake.

Peter entered the room behind his boss but never gave Jack eye contact, which wasn't the norm. He moved beyond the two men and slid into a red leather booth, picked up a *Los Angeles Times*, and buried his head.

"I've got something you'll want to see," Jack said. He couldn't swear to it, but he thought the big man smelled of testosterone and violence.

"It better be good."

So much for small talk, Jack thought as he opened his sleeping laptop, pulled up the URL of the YouTube video, and hit Play.

Angelica Cardona's beautiful face filled the computer screen with dialogue from *Cat on a Hot Tin Roof*. Cardona's mouth fell open, he stood rock still, and tears started to roll down his face. No other emotion showed. The only chink in his armor was the tears. When the video came to the end, he said, "Play it again."

Jack complied. When it ended and froze on Angelica's face, Jack asked, "Have you ever seen the room that she's in, or the room behind the television screen?"

"Never."

"Does she look distressed? Does she look like she's being held against her will?"

"She looks different. What's she talking about?"

"It's a scene from a play she was working on."

"When did you get this?"

"Yesterday."

Cardona's head jerked in Jack's direction. "And I'm just seeing it now?"

"I didn't want to get your hopes up until I had more information for you. The video was posted three days ago, but it might have been generated six months ago. I'm still trying to ascertain a location."

Vincent Cardona grabbed a bar napkin and swiped the tears off his fat cheeks. The button on his sports jacket popped open when the big man raised his arm, and Jack spied a smear of blood on his silk shirt.

"You have an accident?" Jack asked, gesturing toward the stain.

Cardona spoke without looking down. "I was cutting steaks. You want me to wrap up a few to take home?"

"I'm good. Do you know anybody in Iraq?"

"One of my guys. His kid's in the army. Why?"

"We think that's where the video originated. An eight-year-old boy posted it. We know the general area, but we're waiting on an address."

"It was his father's."

Cardona's remark came out of the blue, and Jack said, "What?"

"The video on the TV screen was his father's. The kid shot it. I stole a nude picture out of my father's drawer when I was about that age. Took it to school and got dragged to the principal's office when I passed it around class and Mrs. Stern grabbed it. What do you think?" he asked, referring to the tape.

"Makes sense, Vincent. That's why we need an address. I'm working on it. Just know, if she's alive, I'm gonna find her."

"I'd like to be there," Cardona said murderously.

"Don't count on it." Jack knew how that would turn out. The guilty party would never see the inside of a courtroom. "But this *is* good news, Vincent."

Cardona stared at his daughter's face on the computer screen. "She looks like her mother." And then, "You're doing good, Bertolino. I knew I didn't make a mistake reaching out. Get her back."

Jack nodded as he shut down the computer and headed for the entrance. His gaze drifted to the six-panel door leading to the restaurant's basement. His cop radar, which kicked in as he walked past, left him with an overwhelming sense of dread.

28

Thirty minutes later Jack was motoring down the San Diego Freeway, going over all the things on his to-do list for the rest of the day: calls to make, traces, follow-ups, surveillance to set up.

The Marina Freeway turnoff loomed a quarter mile ahead and, at seventy miles an hour, was closing fast. As he started to merge onto the off ramp, he had a sudden thought about his son, Chris. He vividly recalled Cardona's reaction to the video of his daughter. Following his instincts, Jack veered sharply to the left and continued down the 405 toward LAX. Everything else would have to wait.

———

The early spring light illuminated the most mundane objects from the window of the Boeing 737. Emerald-green hills were alive with development and industrial commerce surrounding the iconic skyline of San Francisco. Sailboats with multicolored spinnakers heeled to one side in the choppy waters and shared sea lanes with cargo-laden freighters. The Golden Gate Bridge glowed brightly in the afternoon sun, an architectural wonder that could put a smile on the most cynical face.

Jack barely noticed. He was worried. He had put in two un-answered calls to Chris as he waited to board the plane and was now going to show up unannounced and knock on his son's dorm room at Stanford.

Chris had warned him in no uncertain terms to stay away, to let him go through his emotional trauma alone. But Jack had to make sure Chris understood that he *wasn't* alone. Not in his fear, not in his recovery, not in this lifetime. He had family who loved him. Maybe his drug use was just a momentary lapse, self-medicating to make the pain in his healing arm go away. If not, Jack was going to make sure that he reached out.

After landing, Jack checked back into the Garden Court, the only hotel he knew in town, and then walked up Campus Drive toward Klein Field at Sunken Diamond and watched the baseball team practice, hoping for a glimpse of his son some-where in the stadium. Chris wasn't there, which Jack found dis-turbing, and he still wasn't answering his phone. Jack headed over to Florence Moore Hall, better known as FloMo. Within the asymmetrical grouping of seven separate student houses, Chris lived in Alondra. His building was all freshmen, coed, and the tab was entirely picked up by his athletic scholarship. It was a high honor.

Jack walked through the front door and took the stairs to the second floor. It was late-afternoon quiet and Jack stood for a mo-ment outside of room 2B, raised his big fist, and then knocked. He listened. Not hearing any movement, he knocked again, a lit-tle harder. Jack's heartbeat started to elevate; he was getting upset, a little light-headed, not knowing where Chris was, imagining the worst. He knocked one last time, hard. A young man three doors down opened his door, looked out, saw Jack's state of mind, and just as quickly closed the door. As Jack turned to walk away, 2B was yanked open and he heard, "What!"

Chris appeared in the doorway with disheveled hair, torn T-shirt, red-rimmed eyes. He had obviously been asleep. At four in the afternoon. He'd dropped more weight in the past week, his pupils were dilated, and he was clearly high. Chris shook his head, exasperated, and walked back into the room. Jack followed him in and gently closed the door behind them.

Chris turned on his father. "What the hell are you doing here?" he said with total disgust that cut Jack to the quick.

"You're stoned," Jack said in a controlled tone.

"I am not. Answer my question. What the hell are you doing here? Why didn't you at least call?"

"I called. I left two messages. But you were too high to answer your phone." Jack wished he hadn't said that, but there it was.

"Dad, I'm not stoned!"

"Your team is out on the field. You were asleep. You tell me."

"I don't sleep at night. I told you to stay away."

"Yeah?"

"Yeah," he delivered like a punch to the heart.

"Do you know who you're talking to?" Jack said, bringing a little attitude into play.

"What?"

"Do you think you're the only Bertolino who's got a thick skull?"

Chris let out a labored sigh, and Jack wanted to slap the shit out of his progeny. But he fought to control himself and the energy in the room. "Has your mother ever, ever once in your entire young life done what you told her to do?"

"Yes."

"Bullshit."

"My laundry."

"You *ask* her. You'd be wearing crusty Jockeys if you ever *told* your mother what to do. And she'd be right. You hear me? She'd be damned right."

Chris sat down on the edge of his bed, his head low. The cast on his arm jutted out at an uncomfortable angle.

Jack leaned back against the small desk that dominated the dorm room and felt claustrophobic, too large for the space.

"You think I'm gonna be *told* to do anything?" he went on. "Do you think that was my reputation at work? A detective who did what he was told?"

"No."

"I think it's time to rethink your strategy here. This is not a winning strategy."

Chris leaned off the bed and pulled two bottled waters out of a mini-fridge that was an arm's length away. Just about everything in the dorm room was an arm's length away. He handed one to Jack, who accepted the offer, screwed off the top, and took a long pull, diminishing some of the heat in the room.

"Where did you get your drugs?"

"I'm not doing drugs."

"Where did you get your pills?"

"From you."

That actually made Jack feel better. He knew better than to trust a user, even his own son, but if Chris was still taking the pills he stole from Jack, he might not be too far gone.

"Tommy went through a lot of effort to set you up with good doctors, where you'd feel safe, away from campus. Now, do you have him on retainer off of money I wasn't aware you possessed?"

"Dad . . ." Chris sounded like a boy again.

"Then why did Tommy do it, Son? Call in favors for you."

"He loves me."

"Why am I here?"

"You love me."

"You wanna get rid of me?"

"Yeah."

Jack smiled and his eyes got moist.

"Let's call Dr. Leland and see if she can fit you in this afternoon." Jack knew that she'd make the time. He had called her office as soon as he landed. "I'll drive you over. If you two don't get along, and I think you might, we'll find someone else. But just know, we won't stop until you find someone that works for you."

Chris took a swig of water and looked out his window. He didn't say yes, but more important, he didn't say no. Jack took that as a win and soldiered on.

"How's the pain?" he asked, referring to his son's arm.

"Comes and goes. Two in the morning, three."

"Dr. Pick has an opening tomorrow at eleven. He thinks if it's physical, it might be as simple as changing the angle of your brace."

Chris jumped up off the bed, red-faced. "Physical! What the hell does that mean? You think I'm making this up? It's psychological? I'm a nutter?"

"I misspoke! Muscular, not physical. Muscular, and not nerve damage. Chris, I'm trying, I make mistakes."

"No kidding."

"No kidding."

Chris turned back to the window and Jack did the same. Dr. Pick, a neurologist, could give Chris something for the pain that wasn't addictive, if Jack could get him to his appointment.

"What's her number?" Chris finally mumbled.

Jack pulled out his phone, accessed the number, and hit Dial. He handed the phone to his son, who grabbed it and waited for Dr. Leland to pick up on her end.

Father and son stared out the window and watched normal college life pass them by in the quad below.

29

"The neurologist took X-rays, MRIs, the whole enchilada and said he couldn't detect any nerve damage. He applied a new cast that was fastened in place closer to Chris's body. He thought there was a good possibility that the pain was migrating from the strain on the kid's shoulders and back, down his arm."

"How about the shrink?" Nick Aprea tossed back a shot of Herradura Silver and chased it with a bite of lime that puckered his mouth slightly and put a grin on his face.

"Noncommittal, but he made an appointment to see her again next week. About as good as could be expected," Jack said with a tone of optimism. He took a sip of Caymus cab, but he could have been drinking Cribari. He was spent.

They were sitting at the Beachside Restaurant and Bar, attached to the Jamaica Bay Inn in Marina del Rey. The water was still and the small lights on the boats' decks played off the protected water of the marina.

"I don't know," Nick said. "Being in narcotics and all, if my daughter, God forbid, started using, I don't know, maybe a nunnery."

"That's what Vincent Cardona said about his daughter."

"Cut out my tongue." And then, "Do you trust her?"

"Who?"

"The shrink?"

"Yeah, I do, but that's not the issue, is it? The kid has a bad case of PTSD. If she can help him get a handle on that, and if Pick can get to the bottom of the pain, and if Chris can get some sleep . . ."

"Lotta ifs, Jack. But hell, he's a Bertolino. You call your ex?"

"Rather poke my eyes out."

But Jack knew he would have to make the call. Just a matter of time.

"Wouldn't do any good, you'd still find trouble with both hands. Speakin' of which, do you get a lot of pleasure poking hornet's nests?"

Jack was stirred out of his exhaustion. "My mind's a little too fried for abstractions."

"The pictures you took of the license plates in front of that strip mall in Costa Mesa. One of the plates, on the black GMC Yukon, was a Detroit plate."

"Good detecting, Aprea."

"I am impressive, and possess twenty-twenty, but there's more. Every immigrant group brings along some good and some bad when they step off the boat. You know, the bad comes in the form of homespun gangsters, like the Mariel boatlift from Cuba or the Russian mob. Instead of getting a job when they come to America, they get into the protection rackets in their neighborhoods and . . . you get the drift. A lot of these mobsters make the Mafia look downright genteel.

"Well, there's an Iraqi gang that set up shop in Detroit. Big

Iraqi population there. We heard rumors of an L.A. connection but haven't been able to nail it down. You might have stumbled onto the hornet's nest."

Now Jack was all ears. "Interesting. Detroit was one of Raul Vargas's cocaine destinations."

"I think it might get better. The Sinaloa cartel's providing the Iraqis with coke, pot, and weapons. They're into all the good stuff. Oh, and uh, did I mention prostitution?" Nick asked rhetorically. "And guess how the drugs and guns and illegals and whores are coming into the States and traveling east?"

"Panga boats," Jack answered.

"Wasn't that how the second blond chick got snuffed? You know, her vehicle of choice. Her death chariot."

"You are a poet and a detective, sir."

"I'm gonna give myself a raise." Nick signaled the bartender for another round. Jack passed.

"The YouTube video was generated in Iraq," Jack mused, and let that notion drift in the air to see where it landed. "And now with the connection between Raul and the Iraqis, maybe an Iraqi gang. Could be."

"Who knows? The punk is a drug dealer of record. You're the detective, find the linkage."

"Any hits on the men I photographed?"

"Nothing local and no hits on ViCAP. The limo is registered to a personal corporation."

"I'll have my guys run it down."

"Speaking of which, you still have that CI working for you?"

"Mateo, yeah, he's good people."

"Fuckin' rogues' gallery on your team."

"Meaning?"

179

"Eh . . . I don't trust him."

"He's quick on his feet, smart, loyal to a fault."

"If you say so."

Jack finished his glass and decided to order another round. Nick licked some salt, swallowed the tequila, and sucked on the lime. He wasn't grinning this time. Jack knew he was bothered.

"He's losing money staying in town. Just doing it to help me out."

"I don't like it."

"So you said."

The bartender placed another glass of cabernet in front of Jack, who nodded thanks and took a sip. He placed two shot glasses in front of Nick and told him one was on the house. Nick didn't object.

"There's always an angle with those guys," Nick said.

"Well, if you figure it out, I'm all ears, but at this point in time . . ."

"Dude sold a lot of poison. Mateo and Raul, cut from the same cloth," Nick said, surly now. "Silver spoons, educated, they both chose the low road."

Nick licked a pinch of salt, tossed back the Herradura, and bit into a lime like a man biting off the head of a snake.

"I opened the door for Mateo," Jack said. "He stepped through. Raul, he's toxic."

"Gut check, Jack. Raul's complicit in the disappearance of the Cardona girl?"

"He's good for it."

"Bring me something, and I'll be there with you to take him down."

Jack raised his glass, and Nick picked up his last shot. They clinked as friends do, disagreements left on the playing field, and they polished off their drinks.

————

Tufts of gray-white clouds peppered the night sky and star field. The moon was vivid without the light pollution. Its reflection seemed to dance on the chop of the black Pacific. The Ferris wheel—with its computerized psychedelic colored-light patterns—was his heading.

The feel of Leslie's arms around Jack's waist as he piloted the boat beyond the breakwaters toward the Santa Monica Pier was just what the doctor ordered. She was excited and recounting her day in court, her mouth dangerously close to his ear. He was glad he had fielded her phone call.

"I eviscerated him, Jack. Do you have any idea how that makes me feel?"

"Horny?"

"As hell, Jack. Horny as hell. You really didn't have to take me out on the water to seduce me. I would've done it in the backseat of a taxi."

"You're such a romantic," Jack said, smiling. Glad to have Leslie's energy to bounce off of. Happy to get out of his own head for a few hours.

DDA Leslie Sager had been prosecuting a rape and attempted murder case, where the suspect was acting as his own defense attorney. The defendant had stalked an Asian woman who worked a self-selected neighborhood in Venice collecting aluminum cans from Dumpsters and filling a cart she pulled behind her bicycle.

The suspect had run up behind her, grabbed a handful of her hair, and yanked her to the ground, where he started beating her mercilessly, punching the woman's face until she was unrecognizable.

While she lay in a coma, he ripped off the woman's clothing from the waist down, put on a rubber, and forced himself into her frail body.

The woman was sixty-nine years old.

The truck driver, with two out-of-state priors for sexual assault, was fifty-eight.

The attack took place in a dark grassy area bordered by a four-story apartment complex. A woman on the third floor testified that she heard something strange that made her feel uncomfortable, like a hand punching flesh. She looked out and saw what appeared to be a man from the back. The woman couldn't tell if he was puking, heaving, or having sex, and then she heard him punch the woman again. The horrified witness dialed 911.

The man was still raping his victim when the first cop arrived.

As more patrol cars swarmed the scene, the police subdued and arrested the defendant, still wearing the prophylactic filled with his DNA. It should have been an open-and-shut case, Leslie had explained.

But when a defendant represents himself, the court and prosecutors have to take extra care to ensure that there's no room for appeal. Leslie had been very impressed with the way the judge handled the defendant and was confident the case was tied down.

Leslie had delivered her closing argument, and after two hours of deliberation, the jury returned a guilty verdict.

Leslie was riding a high that Jack well understood. All the hard work, grueling hours, and court gamesmanship had paid off. The innocent victim, who was still in recovery, would know that justice could be done and her attacker would never see the light of day.

"I put another scumbag away, Jack."

"You're starting to sound like me."

"Like a drunken sailor?"

"Like an ex-cop."

"I am damn good, Jack."

"No argument from me."

"My contract review comes up end of the month. I'm up for a promotion, a raise, the entire enchilada."

"You'll make a fine DA."

"You're preaching to my choir. Oh, I ran into the mayor at the courthouse today. He wanted to know if you'd stop by his house in the morning. Ten-ish, he said. I told him you'd be there."

Jack's head snapped around. "You what?"

"I hope I wasn't talking out of school, but you're a smart man and the mayor of Los Angeles is not a bridge you want to burn, Jack."

Jack wasn't sure that Leslie hadn't set up the meeting herself, but the damage was done.

"I know what you're thinking, Jack. You're good, but not that good. I didn't orchestrate the meet. Don't shoot the messenger." Leslie bit his ear, her hands drifted below his belt, and he started to get aroused despite his anger at being manipulated.

Jack throttled down a mile offshore from the pier and dropped anchor. Then he wrapped his arms around Leslie and drew her into a hard kiss. The sea had flattened to an easy roll. A flock of gulls squawked and glided overhead, their white bodies fading into the black sky as she spun around, leaned her back against Jack's chest, and pulled his arms even tighter.

Jack nuzzled the back of her neck and then bit the lobe of her ear. She growled, "Owww," but pushed back against his groin, demanding more. The scent of her perfume, the salt air, the distant lights, the sound of the ocean lapping against the boat's hull, and the feel of her body moving against his were driving him crazy. He slid his hand under her sweater and then her bra. Her nipples were rock-hard from the cool night air.

The Ferris wheel mesmerized as it changed colors and patterns and then surprisingly blinked out.

"Now, Jack."

Jack took Leslie by the hand and led her into the teak-paneled, amber-lit cabin, where they dissolved into the soft flannel sheets on the bunk. Their clothes came off in a fury. Their bodies were hard and cold but their lovemaking was hot, and as Jack slid into Leslie's wet sex and as she wrapped her legs around his waist, pulling him deeper, and as they moved and rolled and came together in perfect rhythm, Jack and Leslie were overcome by a wave of pure, sexual, orgasmic release. Angry sex for Jack. Victory sex for Leslie. Plenty of fury, sparks, and chemistry.

Jack fell onto his back. The amber glow of the wall sconce played on their gleaming bodies like candlelight.

"Nothing wrong with that," Jack said, breaking the silence, breathing hard.

"That was damn near perfect, Mr. Bertolino." Leslie's delivery was the only thing dry in the bed.

"Hmmm," he said through a smile. Jack rolled onto his side and put his lips close to her ear. His ragged breathing telegraphed his intentions. "Then how about we double down and let it ride," he suggested, already rising to the challenge.

Jack got no argument from the deputy district attorney.

30

The exterior of the Spanish colonial house was as deceptive as the mayor's political sensibilities. Modest and self-effacing at first glance, its grandiosity was revealed as Jack stepped through the thick distressed-oak front door.

Jack was dressed to impress in a gray Donna Karan suit, with a striped blue shirt he left open at the collar.

An overweight Hispanic woman with intelligent brown eyes, wearing a starched black uniform, answered the doorbell. She gave Jack the once-over, taking her responsibilities very seriously, before allowing him entry. Jack liked her immediately. The woman looked as if she could handle the mayor's household, he thought as he was ushered through the grand two-story foyer into a living room the size of Jack's loft.

The room was furnished with ultramodern Italian furniture, and the mayor, whose smile sparkled brighter than the white wall paint, beckoned Jack over with an outstretched hand. He was sitting military straight in a black Eames lounge chair. A young man, who was taking measurements of the mayor's face, stepped back deferentially as Jack shook the proffered hand.

"Mr. Mayor."

"Jack. They're taking my measurements for Madame Tussauds wax museum," the mayor said, as if having his face replicated in wax was an everyday occurrence. The room smelled of pastries and fresh coffee, and breakfast foods had been set up on a Noguchi coffee table. He hadn't had time for breakfast, but he knew why the meeting had been arranged and didn't think he was going to be staying long enough to eat.

"Thanks for coming in," the mayor said as the wax sculptor adjusted his head back into proper alignment. Then he circled him snapping digital photographs of the mayor's head and zoomed in on specific features.

"You look busy," Jack said, hoping to bring a quick end to the meeting. It was not to be.

"Oh, come on, Jack," the mayor said, gesturing to the blank wax head propped on a pedestal, next to a laptop, that the young artist spun, measured, and made notations on. Next to the head sat an open briefcase filled with hair samples that went from blond to black, multicolored glass eyeballs, and an array of false teeth in varying shades. "Lyndon B. Johnson used to hold meetings in the crapper. Don't let this little circus throw you off your game. No offense meant." He directed his last comment to the artisan, who smiled, adjusted a steel caliper on the mayor's right ear, and then inputted his findings into the laptop.

It didn't escape Jack that the mayor had just compared himself to an ex-president. Lofty aspirations, big ego—no surprise to Jack, who waited for the reason he'd been summoned to be revealed. The mayor sneezed, pulled out a monogrammed cloth handkerchief, and blew his nose.

"You've been treated well since your move to L.A., haven't you, Jack?"

"You mean, other than being arrested for murder?"

"Water under the bridge. My job offer still stands. You should take it."

"A very generous offer, Mayor, but I'm afraid I'd be a political liability."

"Let me worry about the politics, Jack." And then as an aside, "I've got someone I'd like you to meet. Maria."

The wax sculptor was adjusting the caliper over the mayor's left ear as Maria appeared from the foyer. Jack followed her out of the living room and down the hallway past the oversized professional kitchen, to a room in the rear of the house. The wooden door was closed, and when Jack turned around, Maria had already moved silently back toward the kitchen.

Jack turned the brass knob, opened the heavy door, and stepped in.

The wood-paneled room smelled of Cuban cigars, aged scotch, and saddle-soaped overstuffed leather armchairs. Big-screen television, two landlines: this was the room where deals were consummated for one of the most influential cities in the world.

A man of the cloth was standing stone still by a window that looked out on a sprawling manicured garden and lawn. The cardinal stood six feet tall, thin but not frail, and his red robes appeared to glow in the soft spring morning light that filtered through the white gauze curtains. The tableau looked too studied to be accidental, Jack thought wryly.

At first glance, Cardinal Ferrer appeared lost in prayer, unaware of Jack's presence. Until he turned around. His fine brown skin shone like translucent parchment paper, his clear gray eyes

blazed, and Jack understood that the man of God was just search-
ing for an opening gambit.

"Welcome, Jack—it is all right if I call you Jack?" he asked,
making the question an inevitable statement of fact. His voice, a
rich baritone, had an educated Spanish lilt.

"Jack works for me, Father."

"Call me Cardinal, Jack."

Jack shook the man's hand. It was smooth and dry, with un-
usually long, slender fingers. When they're steepled in prayer,
they must wield some power, Jack thought. He was already uncomfortable with the tone of the conversation but chose to remain respectful.

"You look like a good Italian-American Catholic. Are you
still practicing, Jack?" the cardinal asked.

"I got a lot of practice when I was a kid. I think the designa-
tion at this point in my life is *fallen*."

That elicited a thin smile from the cardinal. "That can be rectified," he said with firm conviction.

"Good to know."

"Father Geary?"

"Excuse me?" Jack said as old memories came flooding back.

"He was your priest at Queen of the Most Holy Rosary?"

The cardinal had done his due diligence. Jack wasn't happy
about the snooping, but he wasn't surprised.

"He left the priesthood and ran off with a wayward nun," the
cardinal said, his tone condescending and dismissive.

"We were all rooting for him. Geary was a good guy, deserved
to be happy."

Jack could sense a slight change in the cardinal's controlled
demeanor and enjoyed his discomfort.

"He didn't have the right stuff. Religious fortitude. He was a quitter." The cardinal put the emphasis on *quitter*, as if the perceived slight against God was a personal affront.

"If you say so, Cardinal."

"You played baseball in high school and then for a year in college. Your transcripts said you had promise. Why did *you* quit?"

Jack was getting pissed now. "A tailing fastball I couldn't control. What can I do for you, Cardinal?" Jack asked, wanting to get the hell out of Dodge.

"We don't quit on anyone, Jack, we Catholics. If you ask for forgiveness, we forgive. It's a benevolent system. Redemption is the glue that has bound our religion together for over two thousand years."

The man was charismatic, Jack conceded begrudgingly. The rich tone of his voice demanded attention. It must have been effective from the pulpit, but it wasn't working on Jack.

"So, again, what can I do for you?"

Jack had stared down gun barrels, psychopaths, politicians, and fools, but the cardinal was good. Jack knew that he hadn't worked his way out of the ghettos of Mexico City and ascended to the nosebleed heights of the Catholic Church's hierarchy without possessing a steely core. Jack had also done his research.

"The homeless population in Los Angeles County is pushing ninety thousand at last count. It's a blight, personally, spiritually, and economically. Drugs, prostitution, rape, murder, all by-products of living on the streets. I witnessed it every day of my childhood growing up. The Catholic Church changed my life; the Vargas Development Group is going to change the fabric of life in downtown Los Angeles, and they have our full support. Their architectural plans call for two hundred low-income units to exist alongside upscale condos in one tower and then commercial spaces in the second."

"Very white of them," Jack uttered as if it left a bad taste in his mouth.

"Excuse me?"

"So the Catholic Church is in the turnaround business?" Jack asked, fighting to rein in his attitude.

"Save a soul, save a child, save a city."

"Make a good bumper sticker."

"Do you want some coffee, Jack?" the cardinal asked, trying to diffuse the energy in the room. He gestured toward the mayor's desk with his long, elegant hands, where a silver tray had been set up with an ornate silver coffee urn and white bone china. Jack shook his head and the man of God poured himself a cup.

"If the mayor's offer isn't rich enough, come to work for the church. We have a well-equipped security department with international reach. We could use someone with your exemplary background."

"As long as it's hands off Vargas."

"Eight years of work, Jack, cleanse a neighborhood, lives saved. Do you know how many children live on skid row?"

"I think I'm about to be educated."

"Sometimes in life, one makes decisions based upon what would serve the greater good. No?"

Jack knew he was being quoted. Serving the greater good had been his rationale for going into business with drug-dealing confidential informants. It was all in his files.

But instead of taking the bait, he looked past the cardinal and focused on a black-framed picture that was displayed on the mayor's power desk. It was a publicity photo taken at a ribbon-cutting ceremony on an empty lot that was located directly beside the transient hotel, the Regent, that Jack knew was owned by the Los Angeles archdiocese. A man Jack intuited was Philippe Vargas stood holding a Gulliver-large pair of scissors. The smiling mayor mugged directly into the camera to his right. Then Jack spotted a man he was sure he had seen before.

An electric charge sparked on the back of Jack's neck and shot down his spine. He could now put a face with the name. The last time he had seen the polished, swarthy man standing to the right of Raul Vargas was outside of the Iraqi club in the city of Costa Mesa. It was Malic al-Yasiri, Vargas's golden goose.

The cardinal followed Jack's gaze toward the photograph and air-tapped his long finger to make his point.

"Philippe Vargas is building a school and day-care center where the hotel now stands so that their mothers can be retrained and join the workforce. Two acres of the development will be green-zoned parkland for the residents with children and dogs."

Jack stopped him before he could go on. He'd heard just about enough.

"I think Philippe Vargas might be guilty of pushing Pope John Paul the Second out of line."

"I'm not following you." The cardinal's laser eyes were searing; no benevolence now.

"For sainthood, Father. For sainthood. Sorry, but I'm not buying. His son is a drug-dealing scumbag who may also be a kidnapper, a rapist, and a killer. I'll back off when I run him to ground."

The cardinal's face turned as red as his vestments.

Jack nodded and started to leave.

"Oh, Jack . . ."

"Yeah, the conversation never happened," he said over his shoulder as he pushed through the heavy doorway and left the man of God to dwell on what was to come. It might not be as divine as he'd hoped.

Jack winked at Maria, who blushed as he passed the kitchen, and stopped at the entrance to the living room. The mayor was standing now, and the blank wax head had been propped on top of a mannequin, a clone of the mayor, wearing one of his signature suits. On the laptop computer was a 3-D picture of the mayor's face covered in green grid lines and numeric measurements.

The mayor raised his eyebrows in a question. "How did it go?"

"He didn't threaten me with eternal damnation," Jack responded.

"Give him time," the mayor added with no humor as the young artist tightened a tape measure around his neck.

Jack strode crisply out of the mayor's house and picked up speed as he jumped into his car and powered away. He was heading straight for the marina to scrub some of the stench from the meeting off his pagan soul.

31

"The prodigal son . . ." Philippe Vargas said with all the recrimination a powerful man could muster with three words.

Philippe, patriarch and founder of the Vargas Development
Group, had the look of a patrician nobleman. Shoulder-length
silver hair that shined like the metal. Piercing brown eyes that
looked down on the world through wire-rimmed blended bifo-
cals and unblemished skin that spoke of male vanity and tonics.

Raul took after his mother.

"What?" was all Raul could come up with to combat his father's attitude. He glanced over at Malic, who sat at the opposite
end of the fourteen-foot teak conference table, his expression
masked.

"Water under the bridge," Philippe said disingenuously while
he glanced down at his platinum Rolex Day-Date. "Sit, sit."

Raul obeyed his father and grabbed a seat in the middle of
the table. He drummed the thick, black-glass tabletop idly, staring out the thirty-eighth-floor window, wishing he were dead.

"Malic al-Yasiri," Philippe went on, "our beloved partner in
this endeavor, just dropped a million five into our bank account,

guaranteeing the construction loan and ensuring that eight years of development will not go up in flames. Guaranteeing our place in the pantheon of Los Angeles developers. The Vargas Development Group is going to change the downtown skyline of the city with the fourth-largest economy in the nation. We," he shared grandly, "are going to be the architects of great change."

His father loved to hear himself talk, Raul thought through a haze of disinterest. He always felt diminished by his father's charisma. He fantasized about throwing the old prick out the window. Then the empire would all be his. He could handle his mother. A shame, he mused, the windows didn't open in this fucking airtight building.

"You seem underwhelmed," Philippe said.

Raul snapped back to now, wishing he'd done a second line of coke.

"No, Dad, it's terrific. Malic, you're the man. You did it again. We're forever in your debt."

Of that truth Malic was sure. And he didn't expect to wait too long for payback.

"You don't look well," his father said to Raul, feigning interest, shifting the focus away from Malic.

"I'm fine, Dad. Insomnia."

"I've set a preliminary meeting with you and McCarthy and Associates for next week. Halle has the particulars. I'm putting you in charge of the leasing campaign."

No visible response from Raul.

"Raul?"

"I thought we were working with Stein."

"Cardinal Ferrer called last week. He highly recommended McCarthy and I know it's in our best interest to take the meeting.

Their group has a stellar reputation. Stein was understandably annoyed, but that's business. It's a small price to pay for the support the cardinal provided when you were incarcerated."

Raul glanced at Malic, who was giving him the eye. Malic's connections at the State Department had closed the deal and brought him home.

To his father, ignoring the personal jab, he said blandly, "It's a big opportunity."

"It's an important position, maybe *the* most important. It's not enough to say that 'if we build it they will come.' We all know the current realities. Commercial vacancies are running at twenty-eight percent and residential sales are just starting to recover. We've got to do better. *You* must do better. We're counting on you."

"I look forward to the challenge."

"You have our utmost faith." But the words rang hollow.

Raul broke eye contact with his father, glanced at Malic again. Malic's wishes were painfully obvious. There would never be a good time to initiate Malic's desired conversation, and so Raul bit the bullet, cleared his throat, and dove in.

"Have you brought Malic up to speed on the Spring Street project?" Raul asked, trying to sound collegial but failing miserably.

Philippe's silence hung like a burial shroud. He gave away nothing, not a blink or an exhale of breath. What he couldn't control was the crimson blush that spread from his neck to his ears. His stony gaze never left his son as he spoke.

"One contract at a time, Raul. Malic's plate is presently full. When this project comes to fruition, the sky is the limit moving forward. Not for you to worry about." It came out as an unveiled warning for his son to keep his fucking mouth shut, only harsher. "Spring Street isn't open for discussion at this time."

"It just seems—"

"Thank you, Raul. Talk to Halle and she'll give you McCarthy's contact information. Malic and I will want a full report after your meeting."

Malic abruptly stood, pushed away from the table, and started for the door.

"I'll leave you to your family business." His tone was crisp and icy.

Philippe stopped him. "Malic, you and your beautiful wife will be sitting on the podium with the rest of the Vargas Development Group at the Wilshire Gala on the fourth."

"She will be pleased." And he was gone.

Philippe Vargas turned on his son with such ferocity that Raul flinched.

"If you ever sandbag me again, I'll throw your worthless ass off the top of this building."

Raul choked back a nervous laugh. He wondered if his father could read his mind and decided that it was a like-father-like-son exchange. What really pissed him off was that his father wasn't afraid to verbalize his threats. And the *worthless* barb stung.

"You think this is funny?" Philippe pressed.

"I brought in Malic," Raul countered, his skin-deep emotions erupting. "And if I hadn't been incarcerated, as you constantly throw up in my face, I never would have shared a cell with his cousin, and you would now be living in a rental apartment in Reseda! You don't owe the Catholic Church, you owe Malic. He saved your ass and you saved face. How about a little respect?" His father's expression showed total contempt, but Raul pressed onward.

"Smart money is on you doing the right thing and making him a partner before he puts a stop-payment on his check and the mayor's goons throw both of us off the roof for making him look like a fool for a second time."

His father was loath to admit it, but he knew that his son was correct. It was only a matter of time before he'd have to dip into Malic's well again. Vargas Development Group's credit rating had suffered during the recession, and without Malic's infusion of cash, the Spring Street project might well be a nonstarter.

He responded by picking up his phone. "Halle, Raul is headed your way. Can you give him the particulars on his McCarthy meeting? And make sure he gets there on time." Philippe let out an exasperated sigh. "I leave that to you. Do you enjoy your position here, Halle?" His tone was growing in intensity. "Then give him a wake-up call if necessary."

Raul exited the room before his father could slam down the receiver. The meeting was over, and not one second too soon. He didn't want to add patricide to his burgeoning résumé.

Raul startled when he saw Malic waiting just outside the doorway. He had gotten an earful and looked at Raul with a modicum of respect before walking silently down the hall and closing his office door behind him.

Raul walked to his own office, locked the door, pulled out a small brown vial, and tapped out a thimbleful of cocaine onto his glass-and-chrome desk. With a shaky hand he fashioned a line with a razor-sharp letter opener shaped like a dagger. With a rolled twenty he snorted half of the drug in one nostril and the rest in the other. When he realized his hands were still shaking, he did a second line—and then cut his tongue as he hungrily licked the rest of the powder off the dagger's edge.

Malic thought about evading the phone call from Sheik Ibrahim but decided he should face the lion if further negotiations were in order. The sheik had always been a skittish negotiator. If Malic hadn't brokered his deal with Halliburton, the little man wouldn't have had the discretionary wealth to buy the Arabian three-year-old that crossed the finish line by a nose to win the eight-million-dollar purse. Malic thought he deserved 10 percent of the winnings for setting up the deal.

But if the sheik wanted to crow, Malic would be gracious. After all, his million eight had already been spent. Angelica's blood test had turned up negative for cancer and negative for STDs, her cholesterol was perfect, and she was the very vision of health. There was no way the little man could weasel out of the deal.

Malic glanced up at the solid-gold figurine he had stolen from the basement of the National Museum in Baghdad, purported to bestow good fortune, and clicked on the line.

"What are you doing up so late, my friend?" Malic's voice, pure honey.

Sheik Ibrahim strolled down the center aisle of his air-conditioned stables. The wooden walls and flooring were tongue-and-groove ebony, milled and imported from Africa. The stable floor reflected the amber light that spilled from eighteen-karat-gold sconces handcrafted in Turkey that were evenly spaced on either side of the individual equine enclosures, creating golden pools of light that ran the length of the twenty stalls. At the far end of the multimillion-dollar structure was the sheik's garage, filled with a collection of exotic cars that could have put a smile on Jay Leno's face. Fuel-injected, lacquered metal sculptures that made the sheik feel taller.

The sheik's favorite stud was eyeing him in anticipation of a treat and whinnied lightly, shaking his lustrous blue-black mane from side to side.

"Hold for one second," the sheik said into the phone as he pulled a carrot from the pocket of his silk robe like a magician. The large beast bent down to reach for his favorite snack. From a distance the sheik would have looked like a child attending the magnificent horse.

"I received a call the other day that ruined what was otherwise a remarkable victory," he said with an easy tone.

"Your thoroughbred won," Malic stated.

"You saw the race?" The sheik sounded pleased.

"I live vicariously through your many exploits, my friend."

The sheik accepted the praise without a blink of his moist eyes and licked his pink lips before continuing.

"My phone rang during my champion's victory lap," he said. "Someone named Bogdanovich from the DEA. He's attached to the Legal Attaché's Office and used the name of the regional security officer at the American embassy to try and muscle me."

"What did he want?"

"He asked about a video that had gone viral on YouTube."

"And?" Malic prodded, failing to keep the irritation out of his voice.

"I told him I had no idea what he was talking about and the phone call was ill timed. He told me to download the video and get back to him."

"Please get to the point."

"The point is"—the sheik enunciated every word like a petulant child—"it was our girl, Malic. The woman I purchased. The video you played for me," he said, matching tone for tone.

"That's impossible," Malic said dismissively.

"Ah, but you're wrong. It is the woman I have paid a large sum of money for, and when you get off the phone, you can go online and verify my veracity. Then you can call me back and kiss my Arabian ass for wasting my time by questioning me."

"How could this have happened?" Malic said, ignoring the verbal slight. "The video I transmitted was in real time and never left my room," he said, struggling to still his beating heart.

"Let's both calm down, my old friend. As you know, my son is only eight, but he is cunning. He recorded a few seconds of my new girl on his iPhone. Over my shoulder when we were negotiating. I don't think any harm was done because the video could have been shot anywhere in the world. They wanted to interview my son and myself, and of course I denied their request."

"How does an eight-year-old post on YouTube?"

"His tutor set up the account. He thought it would expand my son's experiences. I couldn't argue the point. My son is testing at a ninth-grade level."

"Has the tutor seen the video?"

"Two thousand people have seen it, Malic. Not to worry. A sudden large windfall will keep his lips sealed. Between you and me I'm sorry to lose him. My son will be sad."

"He'll recover. And this Bogdanovich?"

"He seemed appeased when I refused. He's got two thousand other leads to follow."

"And now?"

Sheik Ibrahim's silence stung like a lash. "I was going to cancel the order, but this woman is very desirable. She came to me in a dream."

"And did she bring you the fax I sent? Her most perfect medical report?" Malic asked, sarcastically hammering the point. He wanted this deal to be over.

"After my champion arrives from Dubai, I will send my jet. Early next week. It will give us time to see if there are any more complications."

Malic was afraid that if he opened his mouth he would say something that would permanently damage their business and personal relationship.

"Are you there, Malic?" the sheik asked calmly.

"We will proceed as planned, my friend. Dream well." And he clicked off.

Sheik Ibrahim walked back down the aisle, turning his gaze from side to side, looking in on his exquisite beasts. His smile was impish. The sheik loved toying with his old friend's emotions. But he would happily drop the hammer if necessary. The Matisse that hung in Malic's study, he judged, would look superlative on his own bedroom wall.

32

Jack gritted his teeth and his stomach roiled as the chopper lurched upward, defying gravity, until it reached cruising altitude, tilted forward, and headed away from the Santa Monica Airport toward the Pacific Ocean.

Mateo was strapped comfortably into the club seat next to him, and Cruz was secured in the front next to the pilot, who was talking into a mouthpiece attached to the headphones connecting the four men. The pilot pointed out the Santa Monica Pier on the right and Venice Beach directly below, before executing a stomach-wrenching left and traveling south at a leisurely 120 miles an hour.

"This baby'll do a hundred and forty knots if I push her, but it's a beautiful day, so sit back and relax, gentlemen," the pilot said.

Easier said than done, Jack thought.

They were flying in a candy-apple-red Bell helicopter that seated five. It was commonly used by upscale real estate companies who sold estates and mansions from Malibu to San Diego. Mateo had built enough of a reputation in the Miami real estate market to pull a few strings on the West Coast. Jack could have done without the running commentary, but Cruz was like a kid in a candy shop on his first flight. He didn't want to miss a thing. Jack just wanted to get back in one piece.

Still, now that he was going to place Malic al-Yasiri under a microscope, he wanted to get a feel for how the man lived. Google maps were good, but a flyover was better.

Jack didn't fear flying as such, but he was unsettled by the fact that if anything did go wrong with the chopper's engines, there was no glide time. Just a gut-wrenching spiral of death and an unplanned burial at sea.

As if the pilot were prescient and reading Jack's mind, he said in a voice tinged with pride, "Rolls-Royce engines. Good as gold."

Jack started to appreciate the day once he settled in. The sky and sea were azure, and it was hard to tell where one plane started and the other finished. The pilot pointed out a pod of dolphins skimming the water and breaking the surface with graceful, playful dives.

"I'm doing something wrong with my life," Cruz said, looking at the enormous mansions that populated the coastline. "Where the hell do that many people get that much money?"

"We attract wealth from all over the world," the pilot said cheerfully. "The Chinese threaten Taiwan, the Taiwanese consolidate their holdings and pump their money into Southern California real estate. Trouble in the Mideast, they trade their oil wells for American terra firma. All of those jokers keep me and my company flush."

He steered the chopper closer to the growing cliffs for a bird's-eye view of the multimillion-dollar estates. "That's Senator Jefferies's spread. Retired from the Senate last year, flush with cash. And the architectural monstrosity up ahead, that's Carmen

Bellow's pied-à-terre," he said, enjoying his own humor. "Led the Averia Group into Chapter Eleven, negotiated concessions with the unions, turned around and fired five thousand workers, and landed comfortably here on her golden parachute. House is as cold as her body temperature."

"Dog eat dog," Mateo said without judgment.

Jack was a union man and wasn't at all pleased with the alarming antiunion sentiment that was sweeping the country. It had recently hit Detroit especially hard. Turning Michigan into a right-to-work state amounted to union busting, he thought, but he had more pressing issues on his mind. Specifically, Malic's connection to Detroit.

"What's up ahead?" Jack asked the pilot.

"Palos Verdes Peninsula, and that's the Terranea resort."

Jack could see the shadow of their chopper moving along the sandy beach and playing over the sunbathers, and the multicolored umbrellas and beach chairs that were set in neat rows by the resort staff.

"That's where the first body floated ashore," Jack said, trying to imagine how the newlyweds must have felt having a dead body crash their honeymoon. "How far to our destination?" he asked the pilot.

"Five minutes, give or take a few. When do you want me to start shooting the video?"

"As soon as the property is in range." And then to his men, "Doesn't make sense he'd dump a body so close to home."

"Unless there were riptides. Currents could have worked against them," Mateo said.

As the chopper powered over cargo ships filled with red, green, yellow, and blue containers, sailboats with swollen spinnakers, and surfers bobbing like shark bait waiting for the perfect wave, the pilot pointed up ahead in the distance to Malic al-Yasiri's compound.

"It's the third mansion in that grouping, cliffside."

Malic's massive house was a modern take on a Greek revival. Stark white, with four massive columns that flanked the front entrance and supported a porch that ran the width of the house. It should have been overlooking the Potomac River, Jack thought.

All three estates shared a promontory that jutted into the Pacific. They were fenced and walled, built on huge expanses of property. Stairs were constructed into the sides of the cliff giving the owners access from their compounds to the water below. The steps at the first house led to a small private beach. The last two properties, including Malic's, had wooden docks precariously built out into the ocean.

"You can start rolling now," Jack instructed the pilot.

"I'll take some wide shots and then push in tight when we get overhead," he answered.

All three men took in the house as they approached. Up from the fragile wooden dock, at the top of the stairs, was what looked like a scene from *The Sound of Music* playing out on the expansive green lawn behind the compound walls and the sheer cliff.

A woman was running after a child, her silk hijab head scarf billowing like a nun's habit. She was chasing a little girl, Jack realized as they came closer. The woman scooped up the girl, laughing, and held her tight. The woman's face darkened, and her eyes narrowed and locked on the candy-apple-red helicopter executing a slow flyover. It hovered in place for a moment as the pilot pushed in with his gyro camera, which was filming on the undercarriage of the bird.

"Pull up," Jack said, not happy they'd been made. "Let's push on down the coast and we'll do another pass on our way back. Was she a blond?"

"Oh, yeah," Mateo answered. "Very unusual for an Iraqi."

"If she's homegrown," Jack said.

"Could be a bottle blonde," Cruz tossed in. "Other than the color she looked like Sally Field in *The Flying Nun*."

"You're too young to be able to reference that show," Mateo said, amazed at the kid's brainpower.

"Hulu," was Cruz's response.

Jack was struck by the similarities between what appeared to be Malic's wife, Angelica, and the dead women. He didn't buy into coincidence.

"They're used to seeing real estate birds flying in the neighborhood," the pilot said as he powered the flying machine past the main house, the garden, the pool and pool house, and a large guesthouse tucked into the rear corner of the property.

"What is it about rich folks and walls?" Cruz asked.

Jack looked back at the compound and could now see the woman urgently pulling her child by the hand. She glanced nervously over her shoulder at the receding aircraft and disappeared into the main house, shutting the door behind them.

The chopper flew down the coast a quarter mile, and the pilot executed a wide, banking, vertigo-inducing turn and powered back. Jack tried to unclench the tension in his jaw. From his new vantage point he could see the wooden stairway that had been built into the cliff face. There were no visible openings where the stairs met the eight-foot wall, Jack noticed, as if the rickety stairs were a vestige of a past owner's design.

"Malic bought the property for eighteen mil," Mateo said, answering Jack's unspoken question. "Couple of months before he started infusing cash into Vargas and company."

"Looks like they've got armed security on patrol."

The men spotted what Jack had seen. A black car was moving slowly up the street and slowed in front of the compound's entrance before continuing to the next property. It had the feel of a cop car without the numbers. There was only one street leading to the compound. It fed into another road that circled around the other two estates on the protected promontory before dead-ending. Surveillance would have to be done at the mouth of the road.

"And a guard shack," Cruz added, the consummate professional now. "I see multiple camera setups around the perimeter. It has to be a state-of-the-art system. Throw in the eight-foot wall, the steel front gate, and the guard shack." They could now see directly beneath them as they hovered above a circular driveway that could accommodate twelve cars. "If you don't have an invite to the party, if you're not on Malic's guest list, you are shit out of luck."

"That must be the guesthouse," Mateo said, pointing to a large dwelling that was built against the wall on the side of the property hidden from the main house and the pool house.

The pilot powered up and then away, and the craft's massive blades created a pounding downwash of air that left a billowing cloud of garden detritus and grass clippings in its wake.

"Some people build walls like that to protect themselves, their families, and their wealth," Jack said, answering Cruz's earlier question. "And some people build walls because they have something to hide."

Jack had a strong suspicion the latter was the case, and he

wasn't going to stop until he found out what secrets were hidden behind the eight-foot wall.

————

Angelica couldn't hear anything other than the muted silence in her glass cage. But the steaming water in the bath she had just filled suddenly rippled, like a pebble being thrown into a pond. She walked out of the bathroom into the bedroom, cinching her bathrobe tight around her waist.

It was the wrong time of day for a visit from her jailer, she thought. She listened, confused, for the metallic sound of a key being inserted in the exterior lock. Silence. She looked back into the bathroom and her tub water was still again.

Steeling herself, she shrugged off her robe and stepped into the hot water. She knew she was being watched and didn't know what was expected of her.

Angelica slipped down into the water until only her head was above the surface and started soaping her body, her gaze drawn to the message again. Desperate childlike letters that had been carved into the bathtub caulking with someone's fingernails.

HELP.

There was no mistaking the urgent missive. She could read the fear in the rough markings.

Angelica prayed that the message had been answered. She caught herself doing that a lot lately. She didn't know if her prayers would be answered. But she knew one thing with absolute certainty. She swore on the grave of her mother that she'd do whatever was necessary to stay alive and then find a way to punish her captors.

Retribution was something the Mafia had always excelled at. In this, Angelica was her father's daughter.

————

Kayla locked the heavy door to her husband's office behind her and turned in a circle, taking it all in. Dark paneled walls. Mahogany shelves filled with leather-bound books. An ornately carved desk in front of the window overlooked the garden, pool, and house. She hadn't been inside Malic's inner sanctum since the day the workers finished converting the pool house into his home office. He was very particular about his belongings and demanded one private space in the glorious house he had provided, and Kayla couldn't have cared less. She called it his man cave, something she had heard about on *Dr. Oz.*

Her husband's disappearance the other night, and the helicopter earlier in the day, had left her feeling uneasy. Kayla had brushed aside her fear, grabbed the spare keys that he kept hidden in the laundry room, and decided to have a look around. One key opened the door and the second key, larger, more ornate, remained a mystery.

Malic's desk was as imposing as her man. No loose paper, nothing at all on the burnished top except his iMac computer. Not even a photo of his daughter. The drawers were locked, as was the mahogany file cabinet. Kayla wasn't sure what she was looking for. A sliding panel directly under the desktop pulled out, and she uncovered the computer's keyboard and a few assorted buttons. She pushed one at random and a mahogany panel to her right slid open, revealing a pin-spot-lit painting. It looked like a Matisse.

The oil painting on the wall was stunning, and Kayla wondered at its authenticity. Still, she wasn't here to critique art. She pushed the button again and the panel slid back into place. She wasn't about to telegraph to her husband that she'd been snooping behind his back.

She looked at the mahogany bookshelves that filled the back wall, but they didn't contain anything out of the ordinary. Just his collection of first editions, many of which were works of historic importance. She suspected they came from the archives of the National Museum of Iraq.

Kayla looked at the fax machine in passing and then stopped and pulled a few sheets of paper out of the tray.

She noticed they had the letterhead of Dr. Khalil, their general practitioner. It looked like the results of a blood test. Everything listed on the two sheets of paper had been checked normal.

Kayla wasn't aware her husband had been to see the family doctor, but he'd been less communicative of late. As she looked closer at the document, she realized that the blood test wasn't for Malic but for an unnamed female.

Tests had been run for STDs and then one for HPV, the human papillomavirus. Kayla knew that the test was for the virus that causes cervical cancer; she'd been discussing the vaccine with her gynecologist.

Kayla's stomach did a slight flip as she replaced the blood test in the fax tray and sat back down behind the desk. She was overwhelmed by a surge of panic.

She had suffered a similar feeling when her family had been surreptitiously evacuated from Iraq in the middle of the night with no prior warning. Saarah was only three at the time, and Kayla remembered the silence in the limousine as it delivered her family to an awaiting American jet moments before Ba'ath Party operatives broke down the door of their home and destroyed it. Their neighbors had reported that the automatic-weapons fire that tore apart the tiled walls and fixtures was meant for her family. If the American State Department hadn't interceded and secreted them out of the country in the dead of night, it would have been their last.

She remembered the city lights of Baghdad spread out beneath her as they circled the airport in the military jet and then roared over the desert. Kayla knew she would never return to her homeland and vowed never to succumb to fear again.

Still lost in her thoughts, she pulled out the sliding panel under Malic's desktop again and hit a second button.

A television was revealed behind another wall panel and the flat screen blinked to life.

Kayla made a noise that she didn't recognize. It radiated from her throat but sounded disembodied.

She was staring at a naked woman bathing in a tub. That wasn't the most unsettling part, though. The woman was blond and looked like she could have been Kayla's younger sister. Or even more dreadful, Saarah's older sister. Kayla couldn't be sure, but it felt like the bather was in close proximity, in the next room. But that was impossible, she thought. The only other door in the office led to Malic's bathroom.

Angelica Cardona appeared to be staring straight into Kayla's eyes, and her intensity caused Kayla to blink and look away.

She glanced out the window and startled as she saw her daughter running from the nanny across the lawn and around the pool toward the office.

Kayla hit the button again and the television snapped off and disappeared behind the mahogany panel. She jumped to her feet, checked to make sure nothing was out of place, and stepped out into the bright sunlight and locked the door just as Saarah leapt into the safety of her mother's arms.

"Owwhh, Mommy, you're squeezing too tight."

Kayla marched past the pool, sliding her daughter onto one hip. She glared at the Guatemalan nanny and disappeared inside the house, slamming the French doors behind her.

Kayla stood at the kitchen window, her gaze drifting to Malic's office and her troubling find. She had read in *Cosmopolitan* magazine about female college students who augmented their tuition by setting up cameras in their dorm rooms and charging men a fee to watch them in their daily routines. It was voyeuristic only. Maybe that is all this was, she thought hopefully. That, she could live with.

But the naked woman Kayla had seen did not look happy. In fact she looked troubled, frightened even. Who would pay to watch such a woman? And why Dr. Khalil's blood test? She could call him and ask, but then Malic would know she was spying on him and she refused to deal with his anger. Kayla decided to say nothing. Not yet. Maybe never.

33

Kenny Ortega was overworked as usual but carved out a fifteen-minute block for his old friend and comrade. His face lit up the Skype screen. His tie was at half-mast, but that was the only thing loose about his countenance.

The front of Jack's loft had been turned into command central. A large corkboard had been set up on an easel near the dining room table, where Mateo was spread out, and Cruz had his laptop, iPhone, and iPad on the kitchen island. Crime-scene photographs of the first two victims had been pinned to the top of the board next to a recent eight-by-ten headshot of Angelica Cardona. A reminder of why they were assembled and what their mission was.

Also mounted were photos Jack had taken doing surveillance outside the Iraqi club, and an arrogant Malic stood front and center. To his right was a picture of a pissed-off Raul Vargas exiting the same club. Hassan's photo was pinned under his boss's along with an array of cars and license plates that had populated the club's parking lot. A time line ran down the left side of the board, indicating the dates the women were found, Raul's release from prison, and when Malic entered the country and started working for the Vargas Development Group. The board would get more complicated as the days went on.

Jack was seated at his office desk finishing off a Jersey Mike's Italian sub. His stomach had finally settled down from the reconnaissance flight, and Kenny Ortega always put Jack at ease.

"I see you're still into that health food kick," Kenny said through a smile.

"Old habits," Jack said.

"So, the pug's name is Sheik Ibrahim. He's a Sunni tribal leader, and he stonewalled Bogdanovich. Refused to let him talk to his son, the eight-year-old boy who posted the video. Said he didn't recognize Angelica and wouldn't travel back to Anbar Province to be interviewed in person. He threatened to file charges with the U.S. consulate in Baghdad if Bogdanovich continued to harass his family. It seems the man's well connected."

"Since when is asking a few questions that might save a life harassment?" Jack posited.

"When the aforementioned harassed has something to hide. Not a steadfast rule but enough to keep me in the game."

"Is the sheik well-heeled?" Jack asked.

"He's part of the oil ministry and has done extensive work with Halliburton," Ortega said, as if the name *Halliburton* left a bad taste in his mouth. "Bogdanovich got him on the phone in Dubai, where one of his three-year-old thoroughbreds took the World Cup. It had a purse of eight million."

"Nice work if you can get it," Jack deadpanned. "I wonder if he's a ladies' man?"

"One wife of record. And probably not willing to sacrifice his life to enjoy seventy-two virgins."

"Not when you can buy them with Halliburton Monopoly money," Mateo added from across the room.

Ortega laughed and then said, "Sad but true, my friend. Now, Jahmir is the sheik's kid and the one who posted Angelica's video under the moniker Jahmir 8. The YouTube account was set up by the tutor."

"Was the tutor willing to talk?"

"He was in the wind, but Bogdanovich grabbed him as he was boarding a United Emirates flight to Paris. Tutor was a font of information. He'd been teaching the kid, Jahmir, for a couple of years, and get this: the sheik has two homes. Not unusual for a rich prick. But he lives in one with his wife and keeps his women—that's *women* in the plural—at the second abode."

"That's good, Kenny. Anything new on Malic?" Jack asked.

"Not a well-liked man. Left the country under a cloud of suspicion. One step ahead of the rabble. State Department paved the way for his exit."

"Why the animus?"

"A lot of looting went on while Baghdad was being shelled to hell and back. And then again when Saddam was on the lam. The Iraqi people took umbrage that the National Museum was picked clean of priceless antiquities. Malic is rumored to have enriched himself at the country's expense. He left a long line of angry academics, curators, and legitimate politicians in his wake."

"As if," Cruz tossed out with the emphasis on *if*.

All three men looked at Cruz waiting for an explanation.

"Legitimate politicians?" he said quickly.

"Oh, good one," Mateo gave him.

"What was in it for the State Department?"

Jack stayed the course, knowing Ortega's time was too valuable to waste.

"Malic was a fixer. A procurer. The U.S. needed an in, and Malic provided our government access to the right people. People who could say yes. Halliburton was awarded the no-bid contracts to rebuild the Iraqi infrastructure and oil refineries the U.S. had destroyed during the war. Malic wasn't a Halliburton alum of record but greased the wheels, fed the contract to his buddy the sheik, and got very rich in the process. As for the State Department's involvement, it was a favor owed. Although they'll never admit to it."

"He stepped off the plane with enough cash to drop eighteen million on his compound in Orange County," Jack said.

"Zillow says the property's only worth twelve now," Mateo threw out.

"That's a major hit," Ortega said.

"Maybe enough of a hit to go back into procurement," Jack added.

"Gotta run." Ortega pushed back from his desk, hand-ironed the wrinkles out of his pin-striped shirt, and cinched his tie. "I asked Bogdanovich to stay on it, exert some pressure. He's friends with another tribal sheik over there and will try to do an end run and get some face time with Ibrahim when he's visiting his girls."

"Not too much pressure, Kenny. If a deal's been struck, then it means Angelica is still alive. If we hold the sheik's feet to the fire and he gets scared off, he could pull out and Angelica becomes a liability to Malic."

"Good thought. We'll play it as it lays, and I'll ring you back if anything comes of it."

"Thanks, Kenny," Jack said.

"*Hasta la* bye-bye, *mis amigos.*"

Kenny clicked off. The computer screen snapped back to the screen saver.

Cruz glanced up from his laptop.

"I just pulled Sheik Ibrahim's profile on LinkedIn. Says he graduated from the University of Oxford with a law degree. I went to the school's site and got a full list of the sheik's graduating class. Malic's name was prominent. An MBA. Graduated with honors."

"So we have a link. And if Malic is feeling pinched," Jack said, referring to Mateo's Zillow quote, "then he has six million reasons to come up with a big-ticket item to sell to his old school chum who likes to collect girls."

"Especially if his function at the Vargas Development Group is to guarantee the cash flow," Mateo chimed in.

Jack walked over to the corkboard, thinking out loud, eyes narrowed as they settled on the photos of the three women.

"Our first vic died of an overdose. If she was being readied for a flight to Iraq and the sheik's harem, and spoiled Malic's plans by dying, then I like Mateo's train of thought. Angelica might have been picked up as the fallback girl. Another woman, same age, same type to fill the order.

"We have the video of Raul taking Angelica's picture in the club the night she was abducted. Remember, he sent it to someone, and that might have been to get the approval for the matchup. If Malic and his State Department connections were used to provide Raul a get-out-of-jail-free card, then maybe this was payback. The fixer was in trouble, and Raul found a way to help."

"Sounds like a win-win for Raul," Mateo said. "If the Vargas

Development Group goes bust, he's out on the streets. His only real skill set is dealing drugs. Not an impressive résumé. If Malic can keep the business solvent, then Raul stays in the chips."

"What about the second woman?" Cruz asked.

"She didn't have much time left on this mortal coil. If Malic discovered she was terminal, stage-four breast cancer, she wasn't much good as a commodity, but she could have been used to send a message. I don't think it was an accident that she turned up on Raul's doorstep."

Cruz closed his laptop. "What's our next move?"

"I want you to take a good look at the video we shot today. I keep flashing on the dock. What the hell is it there for? If Malic is dealing in drugs and women, would he risk having them dropped off at his home? With a wife and a kid?"

"The stairs go up to that monster wall. The bridge to nowhere," Cruz said.

"We need to find a way around the alarm system. See if you can identify where the external motion detectors are located. We need another way onto the property we haven't discovered yet." He turned to his two associates, feeling greater certainty as they talked out what they'd found.

"It's all about Malic. We shadow Malic. We can't lose sight of Raul, but I want to know what's inside that club, what his gang's up to, whether they're tied to Detroit, and what's behind those compound walls." A new idea came to him, and he threw it out. "If the opportunity presents itself, let's put a kill switch on the Yukon with the Detroit plates. If that's the car used to transport the drugs, and we time it right, we might be able to cause Malic some serious distress."

"I can get us inside the club," Cruz volunteered. "Their alarm system's a dinosaur. Give me five minutes on the telephone pole closest to the strip mall and thirty seconds on the alleyway door, and we can get in and wire the place for sound. In and out in fifteen minutes."

"The young man's impressive," Mateo said with a knowing grin.

No argument from Jack, who nodded in agreement. "Let's move. If Malic fielded a call from the sheik, the clock is already ticking."

34

The hazy moon was crowned with jagged wisps of clouds the color of lead. It barely afforded Cruz enough light to see from his perch atop the telephone pole two doors down from the strip mall that housed the Iraqi social club. He was dressed entirely in black, as were Jack and Mateo. They had big plans for the night and wanted to blend with the shadows.

Jack was standing outside the alleyway door to the club, waiting for Cruz's signal. Mateo kept watch on the front of the building in case any of Malic's men decided to return for a nightcap, but at two a.m. it wasn't likely. They had gone back and forth as to who should break into the club, and Jack made an executive decision. He wasn't as good as Cruz, but he was good enough. He wasn't going to put his young charge into extreme jeopardy until Cruz was fully vetted and licensed. Jack wasn't crazy about breaking the law, but to save a life he would operate in the gray zone between what was needed and what was legal.

All three men were in communication on Bluetooth devices, and true to the young man's word, five minutes after climbing the pole, Cruz gave Jack the all-clear signal.

The last time Jack had done a break-and-enter, his foot had done the talking, and he'd kicked in the door. This time, with neighbors on the back side of the cinder-block safety wall, the B & E required more finesse. After five minutes of manipulating the lock picks Cruz had provided, working to keep the tensioner tight, Jack heard a familiar click, and he was in.

He pulled out his Glock nine-millimeter and listened to the silence. There was the odd creak and maybe a clock ticking, but no live bodies in this side of the club. Given the lack of windows, Jack chose to use a small Maglite instead of turning on the over-heads. He found himself standing in a catchall room filled with store supplies, cardboard boxes, garbage bags, brooms, mops, buckets, and miscellaneous cleaning supplies.

He cautiously opened the door and advanced into the main room. It, too, was empty. He traced the light beam across a fully stocked bar, wooden tables and chairs, a flat-screen television, and a sound system. A large espresso machine perched on one corner of the bar. It reminded Jack of a Mafia social club he had stumbled into when he was a rookie cop doing undercover work in Manhattan.

Jack made short work of secreting a listening device under one of the central tables and then a second one on the underside of the bar's thick wooden overhang.

"All clear in front," Mateo reported as planned.

"All clear in back," Cruz echoed.

"Copy that," Jack fired back.

He had to keep moving. He walked quickly toward the front of the main room down a narrow hallway lined with three red lacquer doors, one on the left and two on the right. Jack carefully opened the first door on the right, his Glock leading the way into the room. He couldn't risk that someone might be sleeping off a drunk. The room was thankfully empty. It was clean but not luxurious. It had a bed and a small bathroom with a modern sink, toilet, and shower. Used towels were tossed in a pile just outside the glass shower surround. The smell of sex, perfume, and men's cologne hung heavily in the air. It was clear the room was used for one purpose only.

It explained the function of the two women Mateo had taken photos of entering the club an hour before Malic and Raul arrived. Both men had seemed in a jovial mood as they exited their cars. Maybe they were looking forward to more than a cocktail before heading home for the night.

One of the women had jet-black hair, Mateo had explained, giving Jack and Cruz a blow-by-blow of who was entering and exiting the club. The second woman was blond and a ringer for Angelica. Could have been her sister.

Jack continued down the hallway. The second room on the right was the spitting image of the first. Only it had a small closet where a few pieces of men's clothing hung haphazardly. Men's toiletries were strewn about the sink in the bathroom.

"It looks like someone might be crashing here. Keep your eyes peeled."

———

Jack hadn't expected a twofer as he and the team sat surveillance on Malic outside the KPMG Tower earlier. He'd placed a call to the front desk to confirm that Malic was indeed in the building and clicked off when the receptionist put through the call.

Mateo had been sitting across the street in a black Ford Explorer with black-tinted windows that totally obscured the identity of the driver. Jack and Cruz were posted farther down South Grand Avenue in his rental BMW.

At six o'clock sharp a Lincoln Town Car had pulled to the curb, and Malic exited the building with Raul hot on his heels. A terse exchange occurred between the two men as red-bearded Hassan jumped out of the car and opened the rear door for his boss. Malic slid in and Raul double-timed it down into the parking structure.

Jack tailed the limo, and Mateo, with his computer opened on the seat beside him—showing the GPS icon of Raul's car bleeping—followed at a safe distance.

They realized in a very short amount of time that both men were headed south, in the direction of Orange County. The fact that both men were traveling to the Iraqi social club in Costa Mesa, Jack's ultimate destination, was pure unexpected gravy.

———

Jack opened the single red door on the left and stepped in. He found himself in a stuffy, overcrowded office. He could see from the doorway that the room was clear, and he holstered his weapon and went to work. He turned on a PC with a twenty-seven-inch screen that dominated the wooden desk and slipped in a flash drive, tapped a few keys, and downloaded the hard drive.

The file cabinet next to the desk was filled with papers written in a language that meant nothing to Jack. He flipped through the top and bottom drawers—all the same round scribbles.

He had better luck with the small drawer under the top of the desk. He pulled out what appeared to be a handwritten ledger. He spread it open and took photos with his iPhone. He'd discover if any of the entries were of interest when he found someone to translate the info on the hard drive.

As he was closing the drawer, he noticed a refrigerator magnet stuck to a small compartment that held pens, paper clips, and rubber bands. He shone his Maglite on the plastic gimmick. It was embossed with the logo of a sailing yacht plus the name of a marina with an address and a phone number. It advertised dock rentals. Ballpoint-penned on the magnet was the number 207.

Jack knew from experience that many people hid their passwords somewhere near their computer in case they forgot. If an accountant or a gang member was paying the bills for a rental at the marina, they would have to include the slip's number on the check. That's where 207 came in. Just in case they forgot. Jack texted the information to Mateo and Cruz. Carefully, he placed the magnet back into the drawer in the exact place he had found it.

"Get out, Jack, now," Mateo suddenly announced, trying to sound calm.

Jack instantly sprang into motion. He pushed the drawer back in, pulled out the flash drive, turned off the computer, pulled out his gun, closed the door silently behind him, and headed for the rear entrance.

"It's the Yukon and a silver Porsche. They're parking, and one man is already out of the Yukon, headed for the door. Get the fuck out, Jack. Let me know when you're clear."

Cruz, still on the pole, listening to the exchange, was a whir of motion. He had to reattach the wiring, or whoever was entering the club would know the alarm had been breached.

The driver of the black GMC Yukon, a dark-haired Iraqi, put

the key into the front door lock and turned. It stuck. He muttered something under his breath, pulled it out, shoved it back in, jiggled it—and the key turned.

Cruz respliced the cut wire and wrapped it in electrical tape with the precision of a surgeon.

The front door yanked open as Jack ducked out the back, locking the door behind him.

The red light on the alarm box began flashing and beeping. The man punched in a code and the blinking red light turned to a solid green. The heavy lacquered door slammed shut.

"Talk to me, Jack," Mateo implored while he checked the load in his automatic.

"Clear," was all Jack needed to say. Mateo let out his breath and holstered his nine-millimeter.

Jack waited in the shadows while Cruz wrapped up his tools and shimmied down the telephone pole.

"They're on the move again, Jack."

Mateo watched as the dark-haired man locked the front door, jumped back into the Yukon, did a three-point turn, and with the Porsche dangerously close on his bumper, headed out.

"Follow them," Jack said. "Stay in touch. We'll catch up with you later."

Mateo waited until the two luxury vehicles hung squealing lefts onto Pomona Avenue before putting the Ford into gear and following a safe distance behind.

"Scared the shit outta me," Cruz said, smiling nervously as he hugged the pole, tossed Jack his bag of tools, and jumped down the last five feet. With the state of Jack's back, that jump would have sent him to the chiropractor, he thought. He'd already downed four Excedrin with cold coffee while sitting surveillance. He shied away from Vicodin when he was doing this kind of work, but he'd pay in the morning for not staying ahead of the pain.

The two men walked to the BMW, parked on the suburban street that ran perpendicular to the alley and had afforded them an unobstructed view.

"You did real good, Cruz. Real good. You saved my ass."

The neighborhood was closed up and fast asleep. No movements or sounds except for the distant thrumming of a helicopter's rotors, a wailing siren in the distance, and the odd bark of a family dog.

"What now, Jack?"

"Gotta talk to a man about a boat."

Both men piled into the Beemer, and Jack swung a U-turn and powered off into the night. Jack had a strong feeling that if they could find berth 207 at the marina, it would give up its secrets.

———

Mateo followed the Yukon and Porsche to an upscale parking company that shuttled business travelers to John Wayne Airport, filled their gas tanks, and detailed their cars, all for a hefty fee. It was situated in the Irvine Towers, next door to the Irvine Marriott.

Both cars entered the garage, and after fifteen minutes the Porsche exited the building with the dark-haired man in the passenger seat.

Mateo texted the info to Jack and then followed the men back to the club, where the passenger got out of the car, patted the roof of the Porsche, and disappeared inside the club.

The Porsche peeled out of the strip mall lot, laying down twelve feet of black rubber and smoke before rocketing away.

Good riddance, Mateo thought as he headed back to the parking structure to keep an eye on things and wait for his crew.

————

The number 207 wasn't marked on the six-foot fence meant to keep out anyone who wasn't a member of the yachting community, but rusted plaques for 205 and, farther down, 206 were still attached to the chain links. The next number in line was conspicuously missing in front of the last slip. Coming closer, Jack noticed a clean rectangular space on the weathered fence where a plaque had once been attached. Definitely 207. Brilliant deduction, Sherlock. You're one hell of a detective, Jack thought, almost laughing through his fatigue.

He powered down the windows, clicked off the car's lights, and took in the scene. The heady smell of salt water was mixed with the chemical odor of gasoline that bled off the motors, leaving an iridescent sheen on the brackish water.

Slip 207 had easy access from the parking lot, yet it was far enough away from the retail stores and restaurants to be safely hidden from prying eyes. The clacking of halyards against aluminum masts and water lapping on the sides of the yachts, cabin cruisers, and high-end powerboats that filled the marina was all they could hear. At three o'clock, the lot was empty, but live-aboards might well be sleeping on their crafts.

A canvas enclosure hid whatever was docked in slip 207, but Jack could see what looked like a hydraulic lift sticking out of the far edge. The last time Jack had seen a rig like that, he was chasing down go-fast boats bringing cocaine into Miami in the dead of night.

A corrugated metal shed the size of a cargo container stood just beyond the canvas tent. It was secured with a heavy-duty Master Lock padlock.

As Jack stepped out of the car, the safety light on the bottom of the door panel illuminated a small pile of cigarette butts. He picked one up and examined it. The ash was still intact and the paper was clean. Jack knew it had been smoked in the past few hours. Cruz vaulted over the low fence on a one-count. Jack followed suit and stopped in place to make sure they were still alone. He gave Cruz the all-clear sign and walked over to the canvas enclosure as Cruz headed for the shed.

Jack pulled back the canvas flap. He wasn't surprised, but he still got a thrill when he was in the hunt and downwind of his prey.

A tricked-out cigarette boat with three thick stripes, all shades of blue that ran the length of the boat, was perched on the hydraulic lift. It bristled with power and looked like it was doing forty knots standing still. Jack gave the boat a once-over, being careful not to leave any prints. If he could tie the boat to Malic, he'd let forensics check it out. See if any traces of the dead women had been left behind.

Jack snapped some photos of the boat using his iPhone. He felt certain this was the boat Maggie Sheffield had seen powering out of Paradise Cove after someone had orchestrated a young woman's sadistic murder. She had been chemically paralyzed, wide-awake as the boat she sat in crashed onto the rocks. She was an unwilling witness to her own brutal death.

That's some sick shit, Jack thought.

He stepped out of the canvas enclosure and found Cruz standing just inside the opened door of the compact metal shed.

Cruz had a silly grin on his face when Jack passed him on the way in.

"Ganja," Cruz said.

"I defer to your wisdom," Jack answered, but after twenty-five years chasing down drug dealers, he had no doubt that the shed had been used to store marijuana. And very recently, from the thick pungent smell. Other than a few life jackets, fuel tanks, hoses, and fire extinguishers, they discovered nothing more of interest.

"They were here tonight. My guess is, the Yukon is gassed up, loaded, and ready for a trip to Detroit. It's time to bring in the law."

35

"You know if I bear witness to what you're doing, I'm gonna have to run you all in," Nick Aprea said with an early-morning rasp.

"Where are we, on the Ponderosa? You're gonna have to run us all in?" Jack said, straining to extricate himself from the back end of the Iraqi's GMC Yukon without touching anything. The car was heavy with marijuana ready for transit.

Cruz laughed and then stifled it when Nick leveled his dark gaze in his direction.

"I'm really tired," Cruz said by way of explanation, and immediately focused back on his laptop, his fingers flying over the keyboard.

The men were standing inside the parking structure, watching Cruz work his technical wizardry. He had already broken into the vehicle electronically and disarmed the alarm. While Jack searched the car, Mateo drank 7-Eleven coffee the guys had brought along while they waited for Nick to arrive.

"From what I could see, there's gotta be at least twenty bales," Jack reported while he stretched to one side, then the other, trying to loosen his back. "What are we talking? Five fifty, six hundred pounds. Depending on the grade, it could be a quarter million? Three fifty?"

"Sounds about right," Nick said, anticipating the righteous bust to come. He was giving off the sweet smell of tequila, and that was the only thing sweet about him. He'd been roused from a liquor-induced sleep and the warmth of his young wife, and he wasn't an early-morning person.

"I was a little surprised Dick Trammel answered the phone," he said. "His wife—how should I say it?—was less than pleasant when I knocked on their door. Although at four a.m., who could blame her?"

Dick Trammel was the LAPD's resident electronic genius and gadget-meister, to whom Nick could reach out in times of need.

"We got lucky," Jack said.

"Tell that to Trammel," Nick shot back. "He's married to the woman."

Chuckles from the guys.

"I owe him one, and now you owe me a major one, and it's you who's gonna pay first. Trammel said if the bust goes bad, I should tell that Bertolino fuck that he doesn't want any blow-back."

Laughing, Jack grabbed a container of coffee and burned his lip on the fucking plastic top.

"You know what I say. If the door's open, step on through. The drugs will be halfway across the country if we wait on a search warrant."

No argument from Nick, who turned his cranky gaze in Cruz's direction.

"So, where did you acquire this particular skill set?"

Cruz thought before he spoke, afraid if he said the wrong thing he might incriminate himself.

"Self-taught," he ended up with. He quickly changed the subject to what they were trying to accomplish here. "Okay, I finished hacking the OnStar system. So now I'm gonna hijack the ECU—"

"English," Nick said tightly.

"The electronic control unit."

Cruz felt Nick's eye roll from behind the mirrored sunglasses and pushed on.

"So with the scrambler Dick Trammel provided and my laptop, we now control any function OnStar provides."

"You're shitting me," Nick said.

"We can start the car, turn off the power, lock the doors, unlock the doors, pop the trunk, and deploy the air bags. This bad boy is basically our bitch."

"Stopping the car is the point," Nick said. "Popping the trunk could bring it home. And you're comfortable with the setup?" he asked Jack, knowing this wasn't his maiden sting.

Mateo jumped in. "We took a million five off a Colombian laundering cell up in Great Neck, same basics. Used a cutoff switch that was attached under the hood. With the new technology, we don't even have to get our hands dirty."

"Too late for that," Nick said without humor. "Guys like you are the reason the cops are always one step behind the scumbags."

Mateo stiffened. "I thought we were fighting the same war."

"Right."

"Maybe we'll stay lucky," Jack interjected, trying to diffuse the direction the conversation had taken. His back was knotted up and firing currents of pain up and down his spine. "But in case it doesn't work"—Jack pierced a rear taillight with a Phillips-head screwdriver—"you can pull him over the old-fashioned way."

Nick held out his hands, gesturing *What the fuck, Bertolino?* and shook his head in exasperation. As tired as Jack was, he took the time to enjoy the moment.

"All right," Cruz said. "I just got the ID on the transponder. Now we'll be able to pick up the car's GPS signal."

"Range?" Nick asked.

"You could be sitting in your living room. As long as you've got my laptop, you're good to go."

"Let's wrap it up," Jack said. And then to Nick, "We'll track the Yukon, and when we're a safe distance from the club, so they don't trip to there being a connection, you give us the go-ahead and we'll disable the car. Then it's your scene. We're only there in case of a fuckup."

Cruz reengaged the alarm system and locked the doors from his computer while Mateo closed up the back and wiped the car clean of prints.

"This has gotta play out like a bad-luck bust, just the shitty luck of the draw," Jack said. "We want the gang to go back to doing business as usual. I wanna twist the knife, keep Malic off balance, but I don't want him running for the exits just yet."

———

Jack had taken the first watch while he let Cruz sleep in the back of the Beemer, and in the end he was in too much pain to fall out himself, so he let him sleep.

Jack never minded surveillance work when he wore a badge. He could sit for days outside a cartel safe house until he had logged the license plates of all the clients and had proven without a shadow of a doubt that the house was loaded. Then he'd call up his team, and they'd execute a warrant and shut down the entire drug or money-laundering cell.

Jack was into career building during his son's first year of Little League and missed far too many games. He lived with the guilt and was still trying to make up for being an absentee father.

Jack would call him after the game, keeping one eye trained on the drug house, while Chris gave him the cold shoulder over the phone. But Jack could always break through. The love of baseball, and a father's love for his son, won out.

Chris would loosen up and narrate a play-by-play of every hit, every run, every pitch he threw, every strike, walk, and tag-out he made, like a young Howard Cosell.

Now Jack had second thoughts every time he picked up the phone to call.

Chris had met with Dr. Leland, the shrink, but Jack had no idea how the session had gone or whether he'd even shown up for his second appointment. The cast on Chris's arm had been re-aligned in an attempt to stop the night pain, but Jack didn't know if the procedure had been successful. The neurologist had also prescribed some heavy-duty, non-narcotic pain medication. Jack prayed it worked.

Chris had promised he was clean, and if he wasn't too far gone, Jack thought, it might be the truth.

———

The men were all in foul, pissed-off moods three hours later when they shook themselves awake, revved their engines, and prepared to hit the road. The adrenaline that usually came before a takedown did little to buoy the energy in the three cars.

Mateo was parked around the block, reclined behind the wheel of his Explorer, and Nick was in his mammoth black Expedition on Airport Way, surly, hungover, and waiting for a go signal. Each car was equipped with a walkie-talkie provided by Dick Trammel. Jack made a mental note to take the man out for a steak dinner when the dust settled.

Normally, Jack would have run a classic progressive surveillance on the Yukon, stagger their three cars and when one driver radioed the Yukon's position, that car would leapfrog ahead of the target and be replaced by the next member of the team. That way if the target became suspicious of being followed, he'd never make the tail, because it was constantly changing.

Now that the GPS signal had been hacked by Cruz, the group could hang back at a safe distance and wait until it was time for the takedown.

The first complication appeared after the silver Porsche roared by and entered the parking structure. A Jaguar XK that Jack had taken a photo of outside the Iraqi social club was trolling down Von Karman Avenue, checking the parked cars, looking for anything suspicious.

Jack caught the maneuver in his rearview, turned off his engine, and slid down in his seat. While hunched down, he warned Mateo. Cruz didn't have to be told and Nick wasn't directly in the line of fire.

After the man in the Jag had made a full sweep of both sides of the block and was satisfied all was clear, he pulled to a stop outside the enclosed parking structure at Irvine Towers with his engine idling. Jack saw him raise a cell phone to his ear and a few seconds later lower it.

The silver Porsche barreled out of the enclosure with the

black Yukon so tight on its bumper it looked like a killer whale closing in on a seal. The Jaguar squealed away from the curb and assumed the rear position. The three-car motorcade traveled northeast on Airport Way and hung a tight left onto MacArthur Boulevard.

Nick reported that he had a visual and followed five cars back as Jack and Mateo played catch-up.

In the wee hours while the others were asleep, Jack had pulled up on his laptop three main routes to Detroit, highlighted on MapQuest. His guy would likely take one of the two overlapping routes because they both passed through Vegas and Denver before splitting off toward the Motor City. And Jack had never met a gangster who could pass up a night on the town in Vegas.

After talking with Nick, they decided that they would pull the trigger where the I-15 crossed I-10 in Ontario. Nick knew the local cops and could call for backup if needed.

They hoped that the trailing cars would carry the Yukon until Jamboree turned into the CA-261 N, a toll road and then drop off when it crossed under the I-5. That didn't happen, and Jack and the men started to worry. Engaging the armed entourage would be a total cluster fuck. They might have to rethink their strategy and let the drugs slip through their fingers.

The only thing that made sense, unless all three cars were going to Las Vegas, was that the Iraqis would now peel off when CA 91 E crossed the I-15, which was a straight shot to Vegas. And that's exactly how it played out.

Jack's heart rate quickened, and Cruz's foot tapped nervously on the floorboard as they watched the two exotic cars disappear down the exit ramp—heading for home, Jack expected.

With approximately five miles to go, Nick backed off the gas and Mateo sped past the Yukon. He would stay a few hundred feet ahead and then pull over when he got word that the target was disabled and he was out of the Yukon's line of vision.

Jack would pull to the side of the highway a few hundred feet behind and raise his hood, feigning motor trouble.

Nick would arrive a few minutes later and engage the driver. Ask if he could be of service. Bad luck breaking down on the highway, that sort of thing. Keep it light. Then he'd flash his badge and ask to see license and registration. As soon as the bearded Iraqi opened the door, the smell of marijuana would give Nick probable cause, and he'd slap on the cuffs. No muss, no fuss. A clean bust.

That was the plan.

Jack's BMW pulled about ten car lengths behind the Yukon, and when the I-15 approached I-10, he gave the go signal.

Cruz tapped a few strokes into the computer.

He banged Enter.

The Yukon shuddered, swerved, and then started to decelerate. The driver frantically tried to merge to the right. With his power steering gone, the wheel leaden in his hands, he fought to navigate a safe exit from the freeway.

Jack pulled onto the shoulder with the Yukon still in his line of vision but far enough back to assuage suspicion.

Mateo disappeared around a bend in the highway, waiting for an all-clear over the walkie-talkie.

The Iraqi pumped his brakes and executed a gravel-spitting stop on the side of the I-15, unaware that his rear brake light was smashed. He immediately jumped out of the vehicle with a phone plastered to his ear and slammed the car door. His anger could be read at a hundred paces.

Nick passed the BMW, pulled comfortably to the side of the highway, and parked behind the Yukon.

Nick was a good actor when called for, and Jack could tell by his body language that he was offering friendly help, just a Good Samaritan, but the Iraqi was shaking his head, friendly enough, but not taking the bait.

"He won't open the door," Cruz said.

Jack knew they were shit out of luck without entrée to the car. The bust wouldn't stick.

"You said you could lower the windows and pop open the back. Do it now."

Cruz tapped a few keys and hit Send.

Nick and the startled Iraqi turned toward the Yukon as all of the tinted windows powered down and the rear panel yawned open.

Nick pulled out his badge as the dark-haired Iraqi pulled a nine-millimeter from a shoulder holster.

The passenger door to the Yukon flew open, and the raven-haired woman leaped out, ran, stumbled, and scrabbled down the side of the grassy embankment toward I-10.

Jack sprinted toward Nick, a bullet in the Glock's chamber. He fired one into the air to get the Iraqi's attention, and when the desperate man flinched, Nick punched him in the side of the head and drew his own police-issue.

The Iraqi went down, rolled, and came up on one knee firing, putting the Yukon between his body and Nick's gun.

Nick ducked behind his Expedition as his side windows exploded, raining shards of safety glass over his head and hair, really pissing him off.

The silver Porsche and the Jaguar screamed up the road

doing 120. They both went into power skids and chattered to spinning stops in the middle of the four-lane highway. The Iraqi gangsters jumped out of their vehicles and laid down suppressing fire.

Jack, being fully exposed, hit the deck.

Bullets punctured Nick's Expedition.

Traffic screeched to a dead halt in both directions and then the sound of metal smashing metal, a panicked chain reaction of fender benders, punctuated the firefight.

Jack, wary of collateral damage, scrabbled closer, looking for a clean shot, but was forced to hold his fire.

Mateo rounded the bend but couldn't pull the trigger without the risk of hitting his own men or the civilians caught in the logjam.

The dark-haired Iraqi jumped to his feet and fired his weapon, forcing Nick farther back, then bolted away, running a zigzag pattern toward his comrades, who continued to provide protective cover. He leaped into the Jag, slapped in a fresh clip, and started shooting out the window, covering his men as they jumped back into their vehicles and executed tire-spinning exits.

Jack ran up to check on Nick, who was already in the middle of the highway in a two-handed stance. He fired once and was forced to hold up because Mateo stepped into his line of fire.

"Get the fuck down!" Nick shouted.

But Mateo was in the zone.

The Porsche and Jag were pushing sixty as they hit the bend in the road, slid, and rocketed past. Mateo raised his weapon and fired, fired, fired, missing the Jag but scoring direct hits into the rear engine block of the Porsche.

The silver sports car went into a death spin. The forward

momentum caused the car to go airborne, flip, and careen end over end until it came to a metal-wrenching, spark-gushing stop. Smoke billowed out of the engine compartment, and Jack and Nick immediately raced to the scene. The door was locked, the driver unconscious.

Jack used the butt of his pistol to break the window and open the door. Nick pulled the unconscious driver out and dragged him a safe distance before the car became fully engulfed in flames.

Jack, Nick, and Mateo looked on as one hundred and twenty thousand dollars' worth of luxury vehicle exploded in a massive ball of fire.

Commuters jumped out of their cars, dialing 911, talking excitedly, and taking videos and photos with their smartphones.

"That went well," Nick said, bone-dry.

Two police helicopters appeared overhead and circled like vultures.

"Good shooting," Jack said to Mateo, who accepted the compliment silently.

"He missed the Jag," Nick said, not expecting a response and not getting one. They all knew he was talking schoolyard bullshit.

While they surveyed the carnage, Cruz stumbled up over the ridge, dusty, bruised, and dragging the obstinate raven-haired beauty by the arm.

"Least the kid got lucky," Jack deadpanned.

"We've got a lot of explaining to do," Mateo said.

"They shot my fucking car," Nick added through clenched teeth.

No sympathy from the crew.

The Ontario police arrived en masse, lights flashing, sirens wailing, and too many guns drawn to count. Nick badged the onslaught, but all five of them were ordered to throw down their weapons and assume the position until the Ontario police sorted things out.

So much for friends in the department, Jack thought, as he lay spread-eagled on the hot pavement of the I-15.

36

Rarefied air, Malic thought as he looked over the Lucite screen where the Azure Architectural Firm was finishing off a Power-Point presentation in Vargas's conference room. The screen had been set up in front of an expansive window on the thirty-eighth floor of the KPMG building and showed how the present skyline would be altered with the addition of the Spring Street complex.

Philippe Vargas looked imperious in his gray pinstripe Armani suit, commenting on the fine work as if he had come up with the cutting-edge design himself.

Raul sat mute, pleased he had forced his father's hand. Malic was now a full equity partner in Vargas Development Group. His job was to protect the flow of money and guarantee the financial feasibility of all future projects.

After Philippe's frosty introduction of Malic as the newest member of the Spring Street team, Malic induced a slight thaw in the proceedings by suggesting the project be renamed Vargas Towers.

Malic's cell phone vibrated, and when he looked at the incoming message his smile was wiped clean. It was a 911 text from

Hassan, who knew better than to interrupt his boss unless it was a dire emergency.

Malic didn't hear the end of the presentation. It became white noise as he rolled around the possibilities of what had gone wrong. But he stood at the appropriate time, shook hands with the architectural team, and then politely excused himself.

————

Malic had his cell phone pressed to his ear before his office door closed behind him. He glanced at the gold idol, which was not bringing the luck the Sumerians believed it possessed. If he hadn't stolen the damned thing, he'd have demanded his money back.

Hassan hated to be the bearer of bad news, but he gave his boss the play-by-play of the bust, the shoot-out, the confiscated drugs, and the arrest of their man and newest girl.

Malic sat behind his desk, expressionless. The only part of his body that moved was the pulsating vein on his temple. He played all of the possible permutations that had led to the bust like a chess grandmaster.

Finally, he spoke.

"The money can be replaced. Move the boat, clean out the club, destroy the Jag, call Robert Jacobs at the law firm and have him set a bail hearing for Mustafa and make sure he gets out of the hospital in one piece. I want Jacobs by his side when the police interrogate him. Have him take control of the girl, Hassan, deal with immigration and then move her to a safe house before she can say too much. No loose ends. And when you talk to Robert, tell him I want the names of the men responsible for the arrest.

"I'm stuck in meetings until three, and then we'll talk again. You are my right hand, Hassan. Make me proud."

———

The company line was that Jack had been working a missing-persons case and tripped to the drugs. He had called in Nick Aprea at the eleventh hour. They followed the GMC Yukon, and when it pulled to the side of the road with engine trouble, Nick exited the highway, offered help, and then badged the driver questioning him about the broken taillight. All on the up-and-up.

It went bad when the raven-haired woman popped open the back of the Yukon and made a run for it. The Iraqi panicked because of the drugs in the vehicle, pulled out his nine-millimeter, and fired the first shot. Nick, Jack, and his team returned fire in self-defense.

The fact that six hundred pounds of marijuana with a street value of over three hundred fifty thousand dollars was recovered—plus, there were no dead bodies—went a long way to soothing the Ontario police department, who were happy to take full credit for the bust. No arguments from Jack's team.

They decided that Nick, Jack, and Mateo had shown great restraint while returning fire in order to save innocent lives and went the extra mile, putting their own lives in jeopardy to save the life of an Iraqi gangster who tried to kill them. That and the fact that Jack's and Mateo's gun permits were in order sealed the deal.

Still, Jack was totally pissed. The time line was all fucked up now, and Angelica Cardona, if she was still alive, was in greater jeopardy. He hadn't wanted Malic tripping to the surveillance or the bust. He wasn't sure if the other gunman had made him, but the driver of the Porsche would lawyer up when he came out of sedation, and Jack's name would become a matter of record.

If Angelica was still alive, she was a definite liability, and Malic would have to dispose of her one way or the other.

The raven-haired beauty told her story through a Ukrainian interpreter. She was an illegal alien who stubbornly insisted that she spoke no English. The young woman stated emphatically that she had no idea who had sponsored her trip to the States. It had been arranged over the Internet. She was unaware of the drugs in the vehicle and had, in fact, just met her driver that morning. She had no idea about her destination, only that she'd been promised a good job as a cocktail waitress in a big American city. The innocent young woman had come to the USA looking for a better life, and there were any number of Ontario's men in blue who were more than willing to lend a helping hand.

Of course, she was lying through her bleached teeth and her true journey had only just begun. The photo of her entering and exiting the Iraqi club while Malic was present would open the door to questioning him.

The driver of the Porsche was in surgery for multiple broken bones and a fractured skull. Nick would interrogate the girl, and then the driver, the moment the gunman's eyes blinked open.

Then he'd drop in on Malic al-Yasiri to pay a friendly visit.

Nick's car was DOA, having taken multiple rounds in the engine compartment. The windshield and side windows were history, and one of the front tires was shredded.

Leslie corroborated the men's bona fides but didn't hide her irritation. Jack couldn't blame her, because these phone calls were becoming all too frequent. She did agree to help procure a search warrant for the Iraqis' club, the cigarette boat, and the metal shed where the drugs had been stored.

The LAPD was highly suspicious of Nick's story, but they

couldn't argue with the drugs he put on the table. An arrest warrant was initiated for the driver of the Yukon and the owner of the Jaguar for attempted murder of a Los Angeles police officer. They wanted a full report at headquarters ASAP.

Jack rang up Lieutenant Gallina, brought him up to speed on his suspicions, and talked him into starting a paper trail on the cigarette boat docked at Newport Harbor. Gallina promised to get a tech crew down there as soon as the warrants were signed, and Jack suggested that they post an officer at the dock ASAP so that nothing mysteriously disappeared.

Gallina agreed to start his search at the Iraqi club after Jack reported seeing the blonde and the raven-haired girl enter the premises the night before. The blonde fit the description of the two dead women and Angelica Cardona.

He'd let Gallina run with the ball because Jack already had the hard drive and ledger from the club, and it would take some time to discover any latents or DNA traces of the dead women on board the cigarette boat docked at Newport.

After five hours of interrogation and filling out reports at Ontario PD, the men were released. Nick hitched a ride with Jack, and Mateo drove Cruz.

Jack had been awake for thirty-six hours and was in dire need of food, sleep, and a shower. Not necessarily in that order. He dry-chewed two Excedrin, holding off on the Vicodin until he was safely home.

Twenty miles outside of Ontario, Jack fielded a call from Lieutenant Gallina, who was standing in front of the Iraqi club, search warrant in hand. In a very un-Gallina-like move, Jack and Nick were invited to the party of Jack's creation. They accepted.

Jack now had a link between Malic, the drugs, and a woman

he was sure had been smuggled into the USA aboard a drug-laden panga boat.

Given Malic's powerful connections, they didn't have enough evidence for an arrest warrant, but Jack was tightening the screws. He was certain that Malic al-Yasiri was in the flesh trade and good for the kidnapping of Angelica Cardona. Raul had done the scouting, and Malic had dropped the net. Jack just had to prove it.

———

"Looking for something in particular?" Gallina asked as he entered the main room of the Iraqi club from the back alley.

Jack struggled up from a crouched position in front of the bar. The listening device he'd planted was gone, along with the device he'd secreted under one of the wooden tables that populated the room.

"Just a hunch," Jack answered, almost relieved. It would have been a hell of a thing to get busted for an illegal listening device that hadn't paid off, he thought.

"Uh-huh," Gallina said, smelling a rat but not pushing the point. "Oh, I got a call from the lab on my way over. The wine bottle we grabbed at the Cardona girl's apartment tested clean. But there were trace elements of Rohypnol in one of her wine-glasses."

"So, that's how they grabbed her," Jack said, not happy about the news. Rohypnol, referred to as the "date rape drug," induced amnesia in the unsuspecting victim. Angelica might not remember a thing from the night of her abduction. If she was still alive, he thought, knowing the odds were stacked against her.

Jack walked down the hallway and opened the first red lacquered door on the right. It had smelled of sex and perfume the night before, and now it smelled heavily of Lysol disinfectant. The bed had been stripped, the mattress cleaned.

"They bleached the drains, sink, and shower. No residual hair or soap or any-fucking-thing," Gallina said through a growl.

Nick was combing the second bedroom, where the clothes and toiletries had been, and Jack didn't expect him to find anything of value.

Jack stepped past the disgruntled lieutenant and made the left into the office.

"We already tore it apart and came up empty," Gallina said.

"Second set of eyes," Jack replied mildly.

"Whatever." Gallina marched up the hallway into the main room.

The computer on the wooden desk was gone. The ledger in the small drawer under the desktop, gone. The refrigerator magnet from the marina, gone. The file cabinet, empty, as was the garbage can under the desk.

Jack had forwarded his iPhone copy of the handwritten ledger to Kenny Ortega and downloaded the contents of the flash drive to his own computer.

He made short work of placing the microdevice between the back leg of the desk and the wall. Might as well bring the LAPD's IT crew into the mix, he thought. Time was not Jack's friend.

Nick entered the room and found Jack bent over. "Whattaya got?" Nick asked, keeping the suspicion out of his voice.

"Caught something," Jack said over his shoulder as he picked the flash drive back up off the floor. He examined it as if for the first time and handed it to Nick.

"What?" Gallina barked, suddenly appearing in the doorway with Tompkins crowding the hallway behind him.

"Jack found this, must have fallen behind the desk," Nick said, covering for his friend.

"We looked everywhere, goddamn it!" He threw a pained glare toward his partner, who raised his empty palms in frustration.

"Looks like a flash drive. They must've had a computer in the room," Jack said.

"All right, my fucking eyes aren't worth shit." He snatched the memory device and walked out muttering, "Good catch." He turned to leave the club, almost bumped into Tompkins, and stopped.

"You interviewing the girl?" he asked Nick.

"First thing tomorrow. She's already lawyered up. Her and the driver, if he's out of surgery."

"Mind if we sit in? We got a hit on the first victim. The OD. Her parents are flying in from the Ukraine to identify the body and ship it home, and they sent a few pictures along. Might shake something up."

"Bring the coffee," Nick replied. They'd interrogated another suspect together in the 18th Street Angels case, and things had gone well enough, as long as Nick ran the show.

"We need to tie her to Malic," Jack reminded the crew. "We need to tear his compound apart until we find something. He's a dirtbag hiding behind a thousand-dollar suit."

"I ran it by your girlfriend," Gallina said. "And she said it wouldn't fly with the DA."

Jack bridled at the personal reference but let it go.

"Not until we get a direct link between Malic and the dope," he went on. "Or Malic and one of the women. We got nothing substantive at this point except the stench."

Gallina nodded curtly at Nick, and he and Tompkins split.

"It's not nice making the police look bad," Nick said.

"Eh, just a lucky find."

"Right." But Nick's wolf grin said that he knew otherwise.

———

Jack stood at the kitchen island in his loft, reviewing the helicopter footage of Malic's compound. He was too tired to sleep, and his back was roaring with pain. His hair was damp from the shower, and a half-eaten turkey sandwich remained on a plate next to an empty glass with red wine residue.

Something was off. He couldn't tell if he felt that way because he was so tired or if he'd really seen anything. No, it was the cliff, he decided. He rewound the digital recording back to the beginning and then fast-forwarded and hit Stop just before the chopper crossed the water and passed over the dock, the wooden stairs, and then the compound wall.

Cruz had been struck by Malic's staircase, Jack remembered. He had said the stairs went up to that monster wall and called it the bridge to nowhere. Jack thought it might have been some kind of relic from the past because he had seen no visible opening or gate built into the perimeter of the wall to access the compound from the stairs.

Jack rewound again and then he saw it. That was it . . . right in there, he thought. Something looked wrong about three-quarters of the way up the cliff's face. Jack wasn't sure if it was an anomaly in the rock, a reflection, or a glitch on the tape, but he could see a small grassy outcropping that hugged the sheer wall. That's where the texture of the cliff changed. It was subtle but different.

Sleep was out of the question, so a boat ride down south seemed reasonable. Jack was going to get up close and personal and find the damn answer.

37

Angelica Cardona sat barefoot at the small round dinette table, nursing a cup of coffee. She was wearing an immodestly short skirt and a revealing blouse, one of many that had been provided for her. Her trim nails clicked against the edge of her cup. Her feet tapped nervously in the plush gray rug. She looked tired and confused, and her voice was a tightly wound band.

She blew over her coffee cup to cool it and took a tentative sip as if the dark liquid would infuse her with enough strength to go on.

"I'm losing my edge," she said, and nodded her head, acknowledging the fact that she was finally talking to herself.

"I'm thirty-six days and nights into, I don't know the fuck what!" And then, "Into my own nightmare."

Her voice trailed off, and she sucked in a ragged breath and sipped some more coffee, the caffeine finally kicking in. If anyone was watching and listening, she'd give them an earful.

"I didn't want to disappoint. I never set out intentionally to disappoint. But I have guilt. I withheld smiles and love; it's the only way I can say it. I can't say that I understand it, but I withheld what my father wanted. What he needed. I did that. I take full responsibility for that.

"But he'll forgive me. But you." Angelica flashed a deranged smile. "You, he'll hunt down. You can go to the bank with that piece of information. He'll never forget me. And he'll hunt you down. And you're gonna wish you had never been born."

Angelica's green eyes pooled. Defiant, she tried to will them dry but failed.

"Ah shit," she said angrily. "I need a nap. And maybe when I wake up I'll be gone."

Angelica took the coffee cup over to the sink, where she methodically washed it, dried it, and set it on a bamboo rack. Then she walked to the bed, sat on the edge, and rolled onto her side, pulling the pillow against her chest. Angelica Cardona closed her eyes, tried to sleep, but they snapped open. She rolled off the bed and started humping out push-ups.

———

Jack pulled back on the throttle, did a wide languid turn, and motored north. His back was a sheet of pain and the Vicodin wasn't providing relief.

His engine whined at a higher pitch as the boat cut against the current until he feathered the throttle back and glided assuredly toward the dock in the distance.

The phone call he'd received from Lieutenant Gallina had knocked him off his game. By the time uniformed cops arrived at slip 207 at Newport Harbor, the cigarette boat that had transported the drugs and the women was history. Along with any direct connection to Malic other than a picture of him entering and exiting the club.

Consorting with criminals still wasn't an illegal activity in this country unless there was a RICO order in place. And Jack knew the case against the Iraqi gang wasn't far enough along to get a judge to sign off on that.

Angry about Malic's instant moves to thwart further damage, Jack slammed the throttle back, shutting off his engine, and let forward momentum carry his boat toward the fragile wooden dock.

His philosophy when investigating a crime was to do enough of the right things, always thinking three steps ahead, and a case would eventually come to fruition and he'd take the guilty party down. He wasn't sure if it was his back or the fatigue, but he was worried Angelica Cardona was getting away from him. The gauntlet of obstacles was taking its toll.

He shook off the momentary depression, flipped out the rubber bumpers, and jumped a second before his craft hit the dock. Jack made short work of tying off his boat forward and aft.

He inspected the metal dock cleats. They were aged and pitted on top but smooth dull silver where his ropes were securely tied. This dock had seen recent activity.

His eyes drifted up the cliff face, which shone burnt orange in the late afternoon sun, to make sure he was alone. Nothing in his sight line and no sounds but the mocking screeches of gulls circling overhead and the rhythmic pulse of the sea slapping lazily against the rocky shoreline. From here he couldn't see anything abnormal on the rock face above.

Then he spied, caught in a splintered crevasse in one of the dock's weathered boards, a small clump of dried mud with a blade of grass attached. Still green. Jack remembered the small grassy outcropping from the surveillance video. Time to take a look, he thought, and started up the wooden stairs.

He jacked a round into the chamber of his Glock just to be safe and reholstered the weapon in his shoulder rig.

What he couldn't have known about was the wireless alarm system that pulsed a silent warning on Malic's iPhone in his office on Bunker Hill. At the same time his security team was alerted that an intruder had breached the perimeter of Malic al-Yasiri's property.

Once Jack reached the grassy level above, he realized his eye had indeed spotted an anomaly. A metal camouflaged door. He snapped a series of pictures with his cell phone and pushed hard on the heavy locking mechanism. It looked impenetrable. He had to admire the craftsmanship. With the flaking camouflage paint, the door blended perfectly with the rock facing.

Jack didn't know what was behind the door or where it led, but he would be coming back. First he needed to confer with Cruz and outfit himself with the right tools.

Before he made his escape, he checked beneath his feet. The grassy landing was larger than it appeared on the video or from the water. A man's boot had left an uneven impression and chewed up the wild grass some. The impression was recent and caused by a big man, Jack thought. At least a size eleven. Jack snapped a picture.

As he pocketed his iPhone, he caught a reflection from underneath the stairs' handrail ten feet above his head leading up to the compound's perimeter wall. It was a round-mirrored globe.

A security camera.

Jack instinctively lowered his head to his chest and started back down the stairs two at a time, keeping his face out of direct camera range.

Knowing that a security team could show up at any moment,

he quickly untied the boat and fired up the engine. The wind had started to pick up. He let the tide and the ocean breeze carry him away from the dock, did a loose turn, and throttled forward, setting a course north.

Two men appeared at the compound wall brandishing rifles. One jumped the wall and pounded down the stairs. The second man, binoculars to his face, tracked Jack and his cabin cruiser as it disappeared up the coast.

———

There was something peaceful and reassuring about passing the breakwater entering the jetty at the mouth of Marina del Rey and powering down to five miles per hour as he turned into the central channel.

The San Bernardino Mountains looked like a painting on the cloud-strewn horizon. A hell of a long way from Staten Island, Jack thought without a trace of nostalgia for the East Coast.

He had decided to make a stop at the Coast Guard station and talk to Captain Deak Montrose, the officer who had been so helpful and informative about drug smuggling and illegals aboard the panga boats. As he eased to a stop and tied off on the dock in front of their headquarters, he was treated to a new piece of technology enlisted for the war on drugs.

Deak walked down the dock, wearing a starched uniform. His face lit in a huge grin as he recognized Jack.

"Is she cool or what?" He stuck out a firm hand to shake.

Ah, youth, Jack thought. But like a teenager admiring an eight-cylinder road rocket for the first time, Jack was immediately taken.

The armor-plated gunboat looked like a retrofitted fishing

craft, but it teemed with power, guns, and armor. All in a tight twenty-eight-foot package. It probably made up for its size with stealth, speed, and weaponry, Jack thought.

"Feels like Christmas," Deak said. "Just arrived from Florida. They use them on the Rio Grande patrolling the U.S.-Mexican border for drugs, and we got our hands on one."

"A thing of beauty," Jack said.

"So what can I do you for?"

Jack followed Deak into the office and downloaded the pictures he'd taken of Malic's boat from his iPhone. He filled him in on the drug bust, the women, and the general area where the exchange might have transpired. Captain Montrose promised to keep an eye out for the cigarette boat, check with the local marinas to see if any new dock space had been rented to a boat fitting the description, and share the intel with his men who patrolled the local waters. He also promised to take Jack out for a spin in his new toy when the dust settled.

By land or by sea. Jack remembered thinking that a few days ago. As he boarded his boat, he realized the expression had taken on a new meaning. He was going to catch Malic by whatever means it took—and with only one road leading to Malic's compound, the sea was starting to look like a valuable option.

38

Jack was suffering early-evening traffic driving south on Glencoe in his rental. The car was growing on him, but he wanted his Mustang back. The BMW was understated and the American muscle car was anything but. Raw power was more to Jack's liking.

Jack saw the sign for Bruffy's Tow when he was half a block away from his loft building, and then he let out an involuntary sigh.

Fighting to look inconspicuous was Peter Maniacci. Black hair slicked back with razor-pointed sideburns, black pegged pants, black pointed boots, and a worried expression.

He picked up Jack at a hundred yards, and as the Beemer made a right into the driveway, he ran around the car and up to the driver's-side window.

Jack reluctantly powered the tinted window down.

"Yo, Jack."

Peter's left eye was still swollen, purplish red tinged with green, from where Jack had planted his fist during the Cardona dustup.

"Peter."

"You don't wanna go up there."

"Peter, my ass is dragging here. I don't have time for this."

"That Dykstra dude. The one you tussled with downtown. He's standing in front of your door with a restraining order. Thought you'd want to know."

Jack decided not to ask how he knew Dykstra, but clearly, Vincent Cardona had more information about the case than Jack had been willing to share.

"Restraining order from who?"

"That Raul scumbag and the raghead that works with him."

"Malic al-Yasiri?"

"Very much the same, Jack. Oh, and Mr. Cardona would appreciate a phone call at your earliest convenience. That pretty much means now."

"Thanks, Peter."

Jack rolled up the window, did a three-point turn, and headed back to the marina and the safety of his boat. He wanted to avoid Dykstra, but he'd call Cardona only when he had something to say.

———

"She's here, Dad," Chris said.

"She's where?"

"Well, right now she's on a power walk with Jeremy, said it helped with jet lag, but she's here on campus. Said it was a surprise."

"That's an understatement," Jack said, trying to keep the sarcasm out of his voice.

Jack was sitting on one of the canvas deck chairs in the open cockpit of his boat with his laptop resting on the small dining table. Cruz had set up the boat with wireless Wi-Fi, and Jack was Skyping with his son while he tended to a small New York steak on the gas hibachi grill attached to the boat's stern.

"Women, huh?" Chris said.

"Yeah," Jack said, glad Chris could make a joke. "You all right with it?"

"She told me you warned her off, but she said her maternal instincts took over, and so it really wasn't her fault that she showed up on my doorstep."

"That's a good one," Jack said through a smile as he took a sip of cabernet.

"Thanks for running interference."

"For all the good it did. How's it going?" Jack asked, trying not to pry but needing reassurance.

"Well, I slept . . . the whole night. Till eleven o'clock. Missed two classes, but I didn't hurt."

"Great news, great."

"Did you ever kill anyone, Dad?"

"What the—?"

Damn, if Chris wasn't the master of the non sequitur, Jack thought. He took a sip of wine before answering what must have been a question weighing heavily on his son's mind.

"Only men that needed killing," Jack finally said. Even that answer sounded glib and he tried again. "To save a life, or to save my life."

"The man who hit me?"

"Arturo Delgado, you mean," Jack said quietly.

"Did you regret it?"

"My only regret is that he could only die once."

Chris thought about that and then said, "Okay."

His son seemed satisfied with the answer, but Jack wasn't comfortable. He stared into his son's eyes, wanting to divine his feelings, wanting to make sure he wasn't adding to the scar tissue.

"I'm not crazy, Dad."

Jack fought to keep from welling up with emotion. "I know, Chris. But you had a traumatic event. Situations like that, well, they damage more than the body."

"That's what the shrink, Dr. Leland, said."

"Any soldier will tell you, it takes time to heal. You've got support, a family that loves you."

"Yeah, I know about that. Talk to you later, Dad."

And Chris clicked off. His image was replaced by a graphic photo of the planet Earth, taken from space. Blue and green with white swirling clouds against a black background, evoking infinite possibilities. Jack hoped it was true.

He pulled the medium-rare steak off of the hibachi, tented it in foil to let it rest for ten.

His cell phone rang when his wineglass was inches from his mouth. He took a quick sip, checked the incoming number, and let it go to voice mail.

Vincent Cardona was on the other end of the line, and Jack didn't need the aggravation. He'd talk to his client when he had something of value to share.

Jack barely had time to sit back, trying to clear his head of the gunfire out on the highway, when he heard, "Yo, Jack."

Jack closed his eyes and hoped the offending voice would go away along with the offensive person it emanated from.

"Yo, yo, Jack. Vincent Cardona would like a word."

No such luck. Like a bad dream, the Lincoln Town Car rolled to a stop, and Vincent Cardona stepped heavily out of the rear of the car. His cousin, Frankie the Man, was late getting around the car to service the boss.

Peter cleared a path for the big men and gave Jack the *It was outta my fuckin' hands* look.

Seven hundred pounds of horseflesh, Jack thought as he saw the two wiseguys standing at the chain-link fence. And that's all they could be from the look of them. No confusing the two bruisers for schoolteachers.

Not wanting to delay the inevitable, he crossed up the dock and turned the lock on the gate.

"Jack, you don't answer your phone. Too busy?" Cardona said with all the humor of a black mamba.

Thankfully, his cousin Frankie stayed up top with Peter.

Cardona started in even before he lowered his three-hundred-fifty-pound frame into a canvas chair. "Start talkin', Jack. I don't like being kept in the dark."

"A childhood thing?" Jack said, going for comedy.

"We got the mayor's office protecting the drug-dealing wannabe hoodlum. Explain that to me for a starter, Jack. Whatta they got on 'em?"

"I don't think it's that."

"Enlighten me."

"It's more a relationship of mutual needs. That and turning a blind eye. Real estate, tax revenues, reelections, and bragging rights."

"So, his father buys a pardon and now the kid's the anointed one. And what's the tie-in with that al-Yasiri guy?"

Jack took a sip of wine and decided to play it straight. He prayed he wouldn't live to regret his decision.

"From what I've put together, Raul was the spotter the night Angelica disappeared. I have him on tape taking a picture of your daughter and then forwarding her image to a second party. We think it was sent to Malic al-Yasiri."

"Whattaya got on al-Yasiri?"

"I've got him tied to a sheik in Iraq who collects horses and maybe women. His eight-year-old son's the one who posted Angelica's video."

"You told me that at the club, and I pegged the father for it. What's the connection?"

"Malic and he were school chums. It's too much of a coincidence without some involvement there. I just haven't nailed down the exact connection. Malic is protected by the State Department, Raul is protected by everyone else."

"They filed paper on you. How're you gonna get close?"

"It's what I do, Vincent. I'll get close and they won't know I'm there. Everything is coming to a head and I don't want to force them into doing anything rash."

"You mean other than kidnapping my fucking girl?" Vincent said.

"I need forty-eight hours, Vincent. A few more days. I need you to trust your instincts. That's the reason you reached out to me in the first place and not Vinnie Badda-Bing up there."

"He's my cousin, Jack. A little respect."

"I lost my head," Jack deadpanned.

"Could happen. It's all I'm sayin'."

Jack leaned forward, wanting to bring an end to the discussion.

"I'll bring Angelica home. I'm getting close. But I want you to hear me on this: if I push too hard, it's your daughter who's going to feel the pain."

Vincent wanted to say something, but his emotion got his tongue.

"Go home, Vincent. I'll call as soon as I have something to report."

"Don't blow smoke up my ass, Jack."

"I want to shut these guys down for good. I'm all in."

Vincent Cardona lifted the edge of the tinfoil, took in Jack's steak, and rolled his eyes.

Everyone's a critic, Jack thought.

"Forty-eight hours, Jack, if you can stay alive that long."

"Hell of a vote of confidence."

"Prove me wrong, Jack."

Vincent Cardona pushed his massive frame up and out of the canvas chair. The boat dipped as he stepped off.

"And if that Vargas prick laid hands on my girl, I'm gonna take his hands. Eye for an eye. It's a Sicilian thing. Same goes for the raghead."

Jack knew it wasn't an idle threat.

———

Vicodin, Excedrin, and a hearty red wine had dulled the pain in Jack's back. The throbbing was always present, just below the surface, waiting to make an appearance.

The waves of gold, gray, and flamingo pink that streaked the early evening sky helped Jack momentarily forget about the ugliness at the root of this case. Jack had experienced slavery before, but in that case the master was a drug. A drug-dealing scumbag who ran a crack empire in Long Island City got his entire family hooked on his drugs, and then he allowed them to run his business to stay nose-deep in crystal-white powder.

Slavery fueled by drugs and greed. Not far off the mark from his present case. Throw sex into the mix and he had the trifecta from hell.

———

Leslie rolled on top of Jack, holding tight, not wanting to lose contact. She bit his lip, and tugged at his long hair, and tightened and pulsed and moved in a maddening rhythm. Their breathing and heartbeats, one.

Then a shrill car alarm echoed from the parking lot adjacent to the boat's slip. The mood was altered, but the lovers persevered, not wanting to break the rhythm toward the release that was so close. Yet the insistent clanging went on. And on. When it shifted tones, and started to beep and wail, both of them grew still.

"What the . . . ? Really? Whose car is that?" Leslie asked breathlessly.

"Damned if I know." And then, "Shit, it could be my rental."

A warning note—not just from tonight but for all the other nights that had come before—entered her voice. "Well, shut it off, Jack. Goddamn it. And come back to bed."

Jack jumped off the bunk and eased into a pair of jeans, commando. He grabbed his nine-millimeter and walked shirtless and barefoot out of the cabin onto the dock. He walked gingerly to avoid splinters and made his stealthy way to the parking lot. Sure enough, his black 335i's headlights were blinking, horn wailing.

Pulling the keys from his pocket, Jack pointed and clicked the fob until the fucking alarm went silent.

Thank God, he thought.

Jack saw the muzzle flash from the side of the marine sales building before he heard the sickening sound of automatic weapons fire puncturing the metal body of his BMW.

Jack fired once where the light erupted—and then clicked on an empty chamber. He hadn't reloaded since the firefight in Ontario.

Instantly in motion, Jack ducked and ran. The bullets arced across his car, ripping metal, exploding glass, setting off other car alarms in the lot, and then tearing into the Lexus parked next to his as he ran by.

That was Leslie's car, Jack thought as he spun, doubled back, jumped the fence, and sprinted down the dock. The aged wooden slats splintered as the automatic rounds traced Jack's movements. They were closing in.

Leslie was standing in the open cockpit wearing one of Jack's T- shirts, a phone to her ear.

"Run! Now!" Jack said as he dodged to the left, grabbed her hand, and pulled her down toward the end of the dock an instant before cop-killer bullets peppered his boat in the spot where she had been standing. High-caliber intensity smashed the cockpit windows, chewed up teak and equipment, and then nipped at their heels.

Jack and Leslie leaped off the pier.

They splashed down and disappeared below the water's surface. The sea was dark, murky, and Jack pulled her away from the deadly bullets that thwacked and corkscrewed into the water and then went silent.

They surfaced three docks down, spitting oily water and taking in huge gulps of air. They hugged the damp pilings and each other while they waited for the second assault that never materialized. All they could hear were car doors slamming, tires squealing, and then, thankfully, a siren in the distance growing louder as it moved closer.

39

Malic was seated behind the ornately carved desk in his home office. The side of his face reflected the blue light emanating from his television monitor. He watched two of his men, who were now being housed in his guest quarters, walk leisurely past the aqua-marine water of the Olympic-sized swimming pool, checking the loads on their MAC-10 submachine pistols. His face changed color as he fought to control his seething rage. He turned back to his computer screen and the obsequious image of Sheik Ibrahim pacing in front of his own flat-screen television—in Iraq—with his blue, white, and gold–tiled living room as a backdrop.

"I blame you, not my *son, you*, for being so dramatic you felt the need to send the tape of the girl's theatrics to sell me in the first place." The sheik's voice was pouty, defensive, and ugly. "I was sold," he continued, hammering *sold*, "when you told me she resembled Kayla. I should never have let that one get away."

It was the sheik's condescending reminder that he had bed-ded Malic's wife first when they were college students. Malic would've been happy to kill the man for making him suffer the boring repetition.

"That being said," he droned on like a bad dream, "now that the legal attaché is involved, it wouldn't be prudent to consummate the deal."

Malic's ears started to buzz and his heart beat with an unhealthy rhythm as he saw his deal disintegrate. He turned in his chair and stared at the perfection of Matisse's *La Pastorale*.

"They have the local police in their hip pockets and could make my life very difficult indeed."

The sheik paused for dramatic effect.

"Once they pull that first thread in the rug"—he mimed with his pudgy forefinger and thumb—"all that is left in the end is a dusty floor. And I cannot risk that, Malic. More to the point, I will not risk that. Not for this woman, not for any woman. And not even for you, my old friend. Are we clear?"

The sheik had worked up his own head of steam, and the little man's coy demeanor had been replaced by deadly venom.

"I wired you the agreed-upon sum in good faith. Now I expect the money to be deposited back in my account by day's end or you better start packing the Matisse. I shall enjoy its company until such time as you can repay your debt. That is more than fair, already agreed upon, and nonnegotiable."

Malic was swept up by a sudden, overwhelming urge to feed the sheik his own beating heart on the end of a dagger. But Malic was a pragmatist. And his course of action would be guided by current events.

The death of Jack Bertolino would buy him some time on his end. His quick mind would discover a way to assuage the sheik.

His revenge would be total, but in its proper time.

Malic acceded to the sheik's wishes and promised to call back before the end of banking hours. He signed off abruptly as he caught sight of Hassan running across the lawn with a tragic look on his face.

"He's still alive," Hassan said, the ugly truth barely able to pass his lips.

It was last call at the Paradise Cove Beach Café's bar. Raul Vargas had lost count of his drinks consumed and the time. He'd emptied the joint and couldn't get over the feeling that the bartender was happy to see him go. Fuck him, Raul thought as he walked on unsteady legs to the far side of the parking lot, where his car stood alone. Parking there was the only way to keep his baby from getting scratched. The midnight-blue paint job looked almost purple in the reflection of the security light, and he dug it.

Raul didn't see the faint red glow of Maggie Sheffield's Marlboro up on her cliffside porch, or Maggie herself, sitting in the dark, looking down as he unzipped his fly and took a leak on the cinder-block wall in front of the Mercedes. He didn't hear the slight clacking of her ice in the red metal goblet she used for her late-night gin and tonics, or the pleased murmur as her favorite liquid slid down her throat.

He did hear an engine spark to life. Before he could shake off his dick, a squeal of brakes erupted behind him. As he fumbled to zip himself up, a burlap sack was thrown over his head. Two beefy men grabbed him and dragged him, kicking furiously, into the back of a white step van, already on the move before the door slid shut. The van powered into a sliding U-turn and roared past the empty security shack, bouncing violently over the speed bumps up the winding service road to the Pacific Coast Highway.

The red tip of Maggie's cigarette glowed brightly as she took a languid drag and chased it with a pull of her favorite elixir. Something about the smell of the juniper berry mixing with the salt air spelled heaven on earth to Maggie. Maybe one more, she thought. After all, the night had turned out far better than she expected.

———

Jack was standing on the twenty-third-floor balcony of Leslie's condo in the Wilshire Corridor. On the horizon a salmon-pink glow was bleeding into the night sky. Wilshire Boulevard was eerily silent, a dark ribbon all the way to the Pacific. His hair was still damp from his recent shower, and Leslie was finishing up in the bathroom. She had been silent the entire drive from the marina, sitting in the back of an LAPD black-and-white. She'd uttered not a word of recrimination as they watched both of their destroyed cars being towed away. They were alive and for the moment it put everything else in perspective. Leslie desired the safety and comfort of her own bed after the events of the night, and she got no argument from Jack. The more time he spent away from his loft, the more time he had to pursue the case unencumbered by the pending restraining order.

Jack was dead on his feet but not dead. The adrenaline had worn off and his back was spiking with white pain that trumped his drug cocktail.

Leslie walked out of the bathroom wearing a thick white cotton bathrobe she had purchased at the Ventana resort in Big Sur.

It made her feel pampered and centered, she had told him. Jack hoped it would work its magic in the wee hours. It was not to be.

She didn't reach out, and Jack stood pat.

"Three cars in the past week? New record, Jack?" Her eyes crinkled into a smile, but there was no humor.

"Not my proudest moment."

"Get the feeling you're in the wrong line of work?"

"Crossed my mind."

"Hmmm."

Leslie gave Jack an appraising once-over. Trying to formulate a decision.

"You saved my life, Jack . . . that goes in the plus column."

"But if you hadn't been with me . . . ," Jack said, finishing her thought.

"Exactly."

"Cops got it wrong," he said. "It wasn't the Mexican Mafia."

"You know best? You might be too close to the case. Skewing the evidence to fit the crime."

Jack didn't like the implication. "It has Malic's stink all over it," he said defensively, wishing he had held back.

The police who arrived at the scene weren't convinced. They pulled up a copy of the complaint Jack had filed after the first attempt on his life and decided it was case closed.

Jack looked into Leslie's hazel eyes, trying to get a handle on where the conversation was headed. He couldn't read her and fought the urge to reach out.

"You know I love you, Jack?"

His heart sank. The first time this beautiful, intelligent, strong woman proclaimed her love for him, and he knew it would probably be the last.

"But I don't see there being a *you*," she went on. "If you don't change. And I think change might kill you . . . tell me I'm wrong, Jack."

For the first time since the attack, Leslie's eyes welled up, and she pulled her robe tighter around her neck trying to keep herself from unraveling.

Jack's silence told Leslie everything she needed to know.

40

South Coast Plaza was the jewel in the crown of luxury mall shopping in Southern California. It dressed and pampered and catered to the 1 percent of the world's population that could afford the high-end retail and boutique merchandise. Though its reputation was international, for day-to-day business it strained the credit cards and egos of the men and women who aspired to a Newport Beach lifestyle.

Jack's loafers clicked sharply on the polished white marble floors of Nordstrom. He had been lagging twenty feet behind Malic al-Yasiri's wife and daughter, waiting for an opportunity to engage, when the pair stepped into the Marketplace Café.

Saarah was fully engrossed with her iPad, working studiously on a coloring app, while Kayla rearranged her recent acquisitions and then picked up the lunch menu.

Jack advanced to the table, and Kayla ordered the wedge salad without looking up. When it became clear Jack wasn't the waiter, Kayla was both amused and startled.

"Can I help you?" she said, trying to recover.

"Mrs. al-Yasiri?"

"Do I know you?"

"My name is Jack Bertolino," he said, flashing his most benign smile, trying not to intimidate.

Kayla was getting uncomfortable, and he quickly followed up. "I don't mean to be a bother, but I was wondering if you could give me a moment of your time."

Jack pulled out a picture of Angelica Cardona before she said no and placed it on the table next to her menu. "Do you recognize this woman, Mrs. al-Yasiri?"

Kayla's eye twitched, and she grew very still. Jack knew in his gut that she recognized Angelica. She glanced down to the left before looking up. A "tell." Jack knew when someone was preparing to lie.

Her daughter looked at the headshot and said, "She's pretty, Mommy. She looks just like you."

It was true. An uncomfortable, disturbing likeness, Jack thought.

"She does," he said. "She's a beautiful woman."

"Did you follow us here?" was Kayla's answer to the question, not acknowledging the flattery.

Jack knew he had to make his pitch.

"Mrs. al-Yasiri, I work for the distraught father of this young woman. She's been missing for five weeks now, and he's very worried she's come to harm. You would be doing my client and myself a great favor if you would take another look at her picture."

"I've never seen her before," Kayla said without shifting her gaze, "and I'd appreciate it if you would leave us now. We're about to order lunch."

"What about this woman?" Jack placed a picture of the OD victim, who was in her early teens when the picture was taken, on the table. The photo had been faxed to the States by her grieving parents, who were en route to escort their daughter's body home for burial.

Jack stepped to Kayla's side and lowered his voice to protect her daughter.

"She washed up onshore around the time that Angelica Cardona went missing," he said. "I really need your help. I'm afraid for Angelica's life. Your daughter's correct, she does look remarkably similar to you. Her father loves his daughter and is desperate for any help you could provide."

"Mr. Bertolino, are you the police?"

"No, ma'am. Retired NYPD inspector. I do private investigations now. We have every reason to believe this young girl is in grave danger."

"Her eyes, Mommy. Like yours."

From the mouth of babes, Jack thought. Yet the momentary thaw in Kayla's demeanor had hardened. She turned in her seat and motioned angrily for the maître d'.

Jack slid his card toward Kayla and picked up the photographs.

"If you can think of anything at all that might help, please call. Anytime. Day or night. It could save this young woman's life."

Jack showed Angelica's photograph again to both Kayla and her daughter before turning to the officious maître d' who had arrived to run interference.

"Beautiful place," Jack said. He flashed a menacing smile and took a step toward the maître d', who backpedaled. Jack wasn't going lightly. After dodging her husband's bullets, meant for him and the woman he loved, Jack wasn't going down politely.

"So, how about that Sheik Ibrahim?" he asked over his shoulder.

"What?" It came out like a choke.

"Mommy?" Saarah asked, concerned.

"Keep painting, sweetie."

The young maître d' took a half step closer to Jack and had to look up to feign menace as Kayla smiled tightly and waved him off. He looked relieved but walked to his station at the front of the café and picked up a house phone.

"He's the reason I'm here," Jack said. "His eight-year-old son posted a video of Angelica Cardona on YouTube."

She was rattled by this new revelation. "What are you saying?"

"Your husband and the sheik went to college together. They're in business together. Thick as thieves. You're a smart woman. We believe the sheik and your husband are responsible for the disappearance of Angelica Cardona."

"But I don't know—"

"The sheik's a collector. Horses, cars, and women. Think about your daughter, Kayla. You can help me save this young woman's life."

"I've never seen her before."

He added some police grit to his voice. "Help me or else you will go down with the evil." He pointed meaningfully with a finger. "Hold on to my card and call me. You can still get out of this."

Jack passed two intent mall cops on his way out the door. He blended with the well-dressed, upscale patrons. His message had been delivered.

———

Malic sat in his thirty-eighth-floor office with the killer view, waiting on the meeting with Philippe Vargas and Raul to go over the agenda for tomorrow night's gala, being held at the Bonaventure Hotel. Philippe wanted everyone representing the Vargas Development Group to be on the same page. A uniform front, he had said. A dog-and-pony show, Malic had thought. But he'd be politic and his wife would be dazzling, and he would cement his place in the Los Angles political hierarchy.

His stomach was a little off, though, and Malic couldn't really remember the last time he'd felt at ease.

It wasn't the act of killing another woman that weighed on him. It was the number three that had become worrisome. Not because of any guilt. No, the proliferation of young women was proof of mistakes made, and it correlated to a diminishing bottom line. If the money continued to dry up, so would the salaries of his men and so in turn would his power.

Malic had learned through the years that a man would only sacrifice his own life and kill when ordered out of fear, greed, or religious fervor, which was the world's greatest decimator. He knew he could only control *his* men with the almighty dollar.

Malic was pulled out of his contemplation by angry voices in the hallway. They were moving closer, and getting louder, until they stopped directly outside his door. He pulled open the upper drawer of his desk and slid his hand around the mother-of-pearl grip of his Beretta. The door was knocked open and in walked Nick Aprea with Halle, the receptionist, hot on his heels.

"I'm so sorry, Mr. al-Yasiri, I tried to stop him."

"Nick Aprea, sir. LAPD. I just need a few moments of your time."

Nick was talking fast, but his right hand had already flipped the leather strap off his revolver and his eyes never left the drawer with Malic's pistol in it.

"Pull out the weapon, Malic, and put it handle-first on top of the desk."

Malic complied.

"You have a permit?"

"And license to carry concealed."

Nick let loose an engaging smile. "Then this is the first day of the rest of your life."

"I don't understand."

"If that gun had made it out of the drawer, your brainpan would have been splattered all over the white wall behind you." Nick came over, looking down pointedly at the gun. "Now let's start again. I need to ask you a few questions. Are you all right with that? The caveat being if you're not, we'll continue this at headquarters. Your call, Malic."

"Here's fine. Thank you, Halle. I'll call if I need anything."

"Are you sure, Mr. al-Yasiri?"

Nick did a slow turn and the look in his eyes was all the response needed as Halle retreated rapidly back down the hallway.

"That's better," Nick said, closing the door. He pulled out his ID and badge just to keep things by the book. "Lemme see the paperwork," he said, referring to the gun.

Malic went through his wallet, found the correct card, and handed it to Nick, who gave it the once-over.

"Fine, now stow it."

Malic carefully picked up the gun and placed it back into his drawer and closed it.

"Lotta men get killed with the same weapon they buy for protection."

"I wasn't aware of that," Malic said, not enjoying the scrutiny or having to follow this cop's orders.

"Speaking of accidents, your friend had a doozy. Surprised I didn't see you at the hospital. He's pretty knocked up."

"I'm not sure who you're referring to."

"I had an in-depth discussion with your bud Mustafa this morning."

"My bud?"

"Mustafa belongs to your club."

"I'm at a loss."

"That's one hell of an understatement."

"Can we get down to what you want, Detective Aprea? I've got work to do, and you didn't make an appointment."

Nick was pleased by this piece of officiousness. "That's one of the great things about being a detective in the U.S. of A. When I'm working a murder investigation, I don't need no stinking appointment," he said like a bad Al Pacino. And then continued in his own voice.

"I've got pictures of you entering the club around six p.m. two nights ago. Mustafa entered the club twenty minutes later. And then two women. A blonde and a dark-haired beauty. And then, same night, we have you exiting the club around nine with a shit-eating grin on your face. You and your butt-boy, Raul Vargas. We got the dark-haired broad in custody, but you already know that, right? You set Mustafa and her up with a lawyer your group keeps on retainer."

Malic contained his rage. "It's a social club with an extensive membership. It's a place for Iraqi nationals to get together and enjoy the camaraderie of the old country. I'm not on a first-name basis with all of the members, nor am I responsible for their actions."

"An important man like yourself? Here's his mug, might shake your memory."

Nick handed off his cell phone, featuring the photo of a bruised but very much awake Mustafa sitting up in his hospital bed.

"The pain meds, they loosen the tongue like crazy," he observed mildly.

"I've seen him, never to talk. And as you inferred, I was otherwise engaged that evening. Is it now a crime to have an extramarital affair in America?"

Nick gave the contrite man his wolf grin. "You just buried yourself, Malic. We'll get an age on our black beauty, and if she turns up underage, you just confessed to an officer of the law that you had relations with a minor. If she's underage and illegal, then yeah, it's a fucking crime."

"I prefer blondes." Malic delivered it as if he'd said *checkmate.*

He handed the cell phone over to Nick, who stepped back and snapped a few shots of Malic and the gold idol that appeared to be sitting on Malic's left shoulder, staring down on the proceedings.

"You don't know him? I'll take your word for it. That's good news for you. He wasn't very talkative at first. He hit his pumpkin head and couldn't remember too good, until I reminded him about his attempted murder of a police officer, aiding and abetting a drug distributor, and transporting an illegal minor across state lines for the purposes of sex. His memory came back like . . ." Nick snapped his fingers for punctuation.

Keeping Malic off balance, he took a verbal left turn.

"Beautiful statue, that." Nick snapped another picture of the idol. "Looks like the real thing."

"Don't I wish."

"I guess. Something that valuable could bring a person a lot of grief. But hey, I've got a bud over at UCLA got his doctorate in the lost treasures of Iraq post-Saddam. He's gonna be all over that thing. Sumerian, isn't it?" Nick walked behind Malic and picked up the statuette. "They do some great knockoffs these days; this has got some heft," Nick said, almost dropping the sculpture for effect. He handed the idol back to Malic, who remained icy calm.

"You're having quite a string of bad luck, Malic."

"How so?" Malic answered smugly as he gestured to the view beyond the window.

"World's your oyster, huh?"

Malic didn't dignify the question with a response.

"Well, you're operating in the right town."

"Explain."

Malic expected Nick to shake him down, ask for money. It was how business was conducted at home, and he would pay to grease the wheels if needed.

"You're a good actor," Nick said, "I'll give you that. You lose three fifty in dope, value of your house tanks, you tried to take out a friend of mine and failed, and here you sit, like, 'Made it, Ma, top of the world.'"

Nick started for the door.

"That's all I got right now. Enjoy the rest of the day." And Nick was gone.

Malic sat perfectly still, staring at the pure-gold idol. He rose from his seat, and the only clue to his mental state was the slight tremor in his hands as he placed the priceless artifact back up on its pedestal. He'd melt it down for scrap if it came to that.

———

Jack stepped off the elevator at the lobby of police headquarters in downtown Los Angeles. Leslie was nursing a Starbucks, having finished her own interview and deposition about the attack the previous night. She shot him a look usually reserved for defense witnesses. Cool. "They're sure the Mexican Mafia is good for the gunplay," Leslie chided.

"Not brain scientists, the lot of 'em. So al-Yasiri's Teflon? It was him. He knows I'm getting close."

"That may be," Leslie said, not convinced, "but he'll be sharing the podium with the mayor, the cardinal, the city council, the downtown redevelopment committee, and the rest of Vargas Development Group tomorrow night. He's one of the guests of honor. He's a success story, Jack. Iraqi immigrant moves to the States, makes good, and gives back to the community. Speaks well for Los Angeles."

"He's dirty and I'm gonna take him down."

"Any confusion as to why I didn't invite you?"

"The DA's office has a table?"

Jack had to admit being left out stung. She hadn't even thought to mention it, he was that much of a political liability.

"Along with the police chief and half of the force. I'll be there eating rubber chicken and hobnobbing with the elite, the up-and-comers, and the wannabes."

"I'm hurt," he said, making light of it. "I can hobnob. What the hell does that mean, *hobnob*?" he said, vamping, trying to get a handle on what he was really feeling. "Tommy already talked to my insurance company. You'll love the new Lexus. It's got more horse—"

"Bertolino!" Jack heard after the ding of the elevator door whooshing open.

"Christ."

It was Tim Dykstra, the mayor's security chief.

"You're one slippery dude," Dykstra said as he pushed through the crowded lobby and walked up to the couple. And then mock deferentially, "DDA Sager."

Dykstra stepped too close to Leslie, who wasn't a fan; extended his hand, which she shook; and side-passed the restraining order to Jack, who wanted to punch the guy out but accepted the document.

"So, you're served. You know the drill: fifty yards away from Malic al-Yasiri and Raul Vargas, their persons and dwellings, and you are not to harass the aggrieved parties or anyone else in their families or on their staff."

"Later," Jack said to Leslie, and started out.

"Not done. Speaking of number one son, have you seen him around?"

"Haven't had the displeasure."

"I learn otherwise, you're going down, wiseguy."

Jack wasn't going to take crap. He took a step toward Dykstra, who puffed out his chest and stood tall in the safety of police headquarters.

"Jack . . ." Leslie warned.

"Raul's gone missing," Dykstra said to Leslie. "Didn't show up for work this morning, isn't answering his phone. Missed a meeting for the gala. You get your invite, Jack?" An ugly smile oozed from his smug face. "Oh, that's right, you're persona non grata. You've managed to piss off every political ally you ever had."

Then to Leslie, "You must be proud. Your boyfriend's a real career-ender."

Jack lunged and Dykstra jumped back a step, grinning as he walked around him toward the thick glass front doors.

"I'll see you tomorrow night." He directed it over his shoulder at Leslie as he exited the building.

Leslie turned on Jack, red-faced.

"Really, Jack? You were going to punch Dykstra out in the lobby of police headquarters? He might be a major asshole, but really? Are you the only person in the room that you care about?" she asked incredulously.

Jack took a deep breath, wishing he could disappear. Embarrassed by his lack of restraint.

"You've got anger issues, Jack. And the control of a sixteen-year-old."

Leslie knew this wasn't the time or the place to continue the conversation and followed in Dykstra's wake.

Jack watched Leslie's receding figure, knowing she was right, and pushed his emotions to the side. If Raul Vargas was truly missing and not sleeping off a drunk, Jack was traversing some rocky shoals.

He might have to take down his client along with the perp.

41

Jack was driving his second rental car of the week. He went to Hertz because Enterprise wouldn't accept the liability on another premium car. Jack had a bad risk profile, they said. Couldn't blame them, he thought. His Mustang wouldn't be out of the shop for another day, and so Jack chose a fully loaded Blue Mica Lexus IS F. Might as well keep things interesting. With a V-8 and 416 horses, Jack hoped he could stay ahead of the trouble. His phone was paired to the car's Bluetooth and the GPS would get him where he needed to go.

Jack pulled out of the underground parking and was immediately caught in heel-to-toe downtown traffic. So much for 416 horses, he thought. The phone rang.

"So I rattled his cage. I didn't mention Angelica, but he's feeling the heat. I gave him a lot to think about," was Nick's opening gambit. No hello, none needed.

"Did you get anything out of Mustafa?"

"*Negativo.* Deaf and dumb. His 'suit' was sitting next to him in the hospital room and kept shaking his head. Our man Mustafa zipped it up tighter than a boll weevil's ass."

"Very graphic. And the girl?"

"Nothing."

"Shit."

"Yeah, so, after the interview with Mustafa, the lawyer escorted the sweet young thing out and away with a promise to deliver her if we had any more questions. Gallina was apoplectic, but immigration had signed off on it. Are your guys sitting on the compound?"

"We've got it covered. I've got them taking down license numbers and comparing them to the list we made at the club. He's moved in at least eight of his men. They come and go. One at the guard shack and roving security at night. He's got a guesthouse the size of a hotel."

"Doesn't seem right."

"I'm crying for him. So, I hear Raul is MIA," Jack said.

"Don't I know it. They found his car at Paradise Cove, unlocked. He never made it home."

"Maybe he got lucky and was too wasted to drive."

"The bartender reported he was feeling no pain, but he left the bar alone. Doesn't mean he didn't meet someone in the parking lot. Security camera doesn't shoot a frame that wide. Some uniforms interviewed a few of the neighbors who live in the doublewides up on the cliff, but no one saw dick. Whatta you think?"

"I think the prick's getting more attention in twelve hours than the dead girls got in a month. I don't like where this is heading."

"I know where you're going with this. But don't jump to conclusions. A long list of people have him in their sights."

"What was your take on al-Yasiri?"

"Piece of work. He's like the head of the snake. Kinda guy

that walks around with a smile on his face while he's gutting you. Always looking for an exit play."

"I feel like I'm running on empty. I've got to get inside the compound."

Nick's tone shifted. "You're looking at jail time."

"And Angelica Cardona's looking at a grave. You mind reaching out to Dick Trammel?"

"What do you need?"

"Cruz said it's something called a negative pulse disrupter. He also called it an EMP. Says I slap it on the main computer, it scrambles everything in the house and the security cameras on the system go belly-up. I can cut the juice leading into the compound. Cruz has that in pocket. It's shutting off the computer systems that might be tied into an auxiliary power source I need help with. I'll need some time to get in and out of there in one piece."

"Time frame?"

"An hour max. Eight to nine. When Malic is tuxed up and basking in the limelight."

"I don't like the odds."

"A pair of night-vision goggles wouldn't hurt."

"Trammel drinks Macallan."

"Tell him I've got a bottle of Eighteen with his name on it."

"I can't promise."

"Later, pard." And Jack clicked off, knowing Nick would deliver if possible.

Jack didn't have a plan B. It wasn't his preferred way to operate, but it had never stopped him before.

It was time to face the lion.

———

Kayla stood in the kitchen, a keen eye trained on the pool house. She had witnessed Hassan cutting across the lawn from the guesthouse with a suitcase and entering Malic's private office.

She wanted to investigate, but she was wary. She strolled by the pool, pulling her hijab tight around her face. She clipped a few yellow long-stemmed roses, trying to look normal, and made a mental note to remind the gardener to dust for mildew. When she glanced into the pool house window, the office appeared to be empty. Her heart started racing. She was so overwhelmed, she didn't remember walking back into the house.

By the kitchen sink she clipped every thorn off the roses so that her sweet daughter would not prick her perfect fingers. As she snipped, her mind drifted to the missing girl's father and what he must have been feeling.

While she was arranging the elegant flowers in a jade-green cloisonné vase, Hassan exited the office, locked up, and walked rapidly across the lawn, lost in thought.

And empty-handed.

Kayla heard the limo's engine turn over in the front of the house, ran into the living room, and peered through the gossamer curtains. Hassan waved to an unseen man as he drove past the guard shack onto Seaside Lane and back toward the main road.

Kayla dialed Malic's number at the office and was told by Halle he was up to his neck in meetings until five and, oh, that she really looked forward to seeing her at the gala.

It was now or never.

She checked on Saarah, who was taking an afternoon nap while her nanny read a magazine. Kayla grabbed the spare keys that were hidden in the laundry room, stepped through the French doors, and walked rapidly across the lawn past the garden and pool. Inserting the key, she quickly closed the heavy door behind her. She looked out the window and checked that all was clear.

It was quiet in the office, but she didn't feel safe. She knew she should have her head examined, snooping around like this. But the man she had met that morning, Jack Bertolino, had seemed sincere. He'd made her think on the drive home. Thoughts she had never entertained before came to life. Nor could she deny what she had seen. On Malic's own television. In this very room. And the woman's blood test was for what, her well-being?

Kayla had to have answers one way or the other. She started her search in the bathroom and came up empty. The walls were solid and she found she had a hard time staring at her own image in the mirror. Was she ashamed, or afraid of what she might find? Afraid of the truth?

She wasn't raised to be afraid. It wasn't the example she wanted to set for her daughter. Her mother and grandmother were strong, independent women. Under the thumb of no man.

But she'd fallen into a very comfortable life with her daughter. Safe from the bombs and political and religious strife at home, living in luxury under the protection of the U.S. government. Did she really want to keep digging? Was she crazy? All she had to do was put the keys back where she'd found them and everything would return to normal.

No, that was no longer assured. What did that man say today? Help him or she would go down with the evil. Kayla knew what she had seen. She couldn't erase the young girl's image. But could she live with the truth?

Kayla walked back into the office. Her hands rifled through the leather-bound books. They flew over every surface of the mahogany bookshelves in the rear corner of the room.

She found it on the second pass, on the second row from the top. Kayla had to stand on tiptoes to reach it. A smooth button on the side of the wooden panel.

She depressed the button and that section of bookshelf hinged open a crack. A faint light emanated from the other side.

Kayla sucked in a breath, pulled the secret door open wider, and stepped through.

———

Angelica Cardona stood stone still as she heard a key turn. The sound came from the steel door on the right side of the exterior hallway. It had never been opened once in the thirty-seven days of her imprisonment, and now, it had clicked twice in a half hour. She felt nothing but dread.

Kayla took one step past the door into the hallway, turned to face the Plexiglas wall, and stared straight into the eyes of Angelica Cardona.

Neither woman spoke.

Kayla's striped hijab hung loose, and Angelica could see she also had blond hair, and a remarkably similar face.

Angelica wore a short skirt, sleeveless blouse, bare legs and feet, looking younger than her years. A half-filled suitcase lay open on the bed behind her.

They stood frozen. Time seemed frozen.

"My name is Angelica Cardona, and I need help," she finally said, breaking the silence. "Please help me," she added slowly, not knowing if the woman who stood on the other side of her clear prison wall spoke the language.

Kayla wanted to run, wanted to scream, but she stood silent. It was all true. Worst-case scenario. The father of her child was a flesh peddler. She had to force herself to breathe. Her ears were ringing and her breath erupted in short silent gasps. She reached out to steady herself, to keep from passing out, and pressed her hand against the Plexiglas wall. She knew the room for what it was. A prison cell.

Angelica instinctively put her hand on the other side of the Plexiglas and mirrored Kayla's hand.

"My name is Angelica," she repeated, her voice steady and measured.

Kayla pulled her hand away as if she'd been burned.

"I've been kidnapped, and I don't know where I am or where I'm going. I don't want to die. I'm being held against my will. Do you understand? Please, for the love of God, please open the door and let me out."

Kayla's cell phone rang. The electronic tone echoed in the hallway and startled them both. She grabbed the phone out of her pocket, looked at the incoming call, and her frantic eyes lasered back at the girl.

Angelica could read her indecision. "Please."

Kayla sucked in a ragged breath, her eyes taking in the hallway, the locked door to the cell, and the steel door at the far end of the hallway. Then she backpedaled out of view.

"Don't go!" Angelica shouted, her voice thick with desperation. "Please help me! I don't want to die, please . . ."

Help me was the last thing Kayla heard as she slammed the steel-plated door shut and locked it with the ornate key.

The phone call was from Malic, and she ran. Her eyes filled with tears, and she stumbled and fell down hard, cutting her knee and the palm of her hand as her phone skittered forward on the tiled floor of the tunnel.

"Shit! Shit!" she cried as she rose to her feet and picked up her cell phone. Her eyes were awash with tears that turned the gold statues displayed along the wall of the tunnel into surreal ugly forms. She ran to the mouth of the tunnel, stepped into Malic's office, and pushed the secret door closed behind her.

42

"Don't be such a stranger, Mr. Bertolino," Arsinio, the consummate waiter at Hal's Bar and Grill, said as he placed the bill on the table.

"Sometimes life gets in the way of good living," Jack said as he pulled out some cash and added a healthy tip.

"With my two boys, don't I know that to be the truth? Always something."

Jack, Mateo, and Cruz were sitting at Jack's favorite booth in the rear of the restaurant. It had a straight-on view of the entire room. They'd just finished dinner and were strategizing. In the NYPD it had been called a TAC meeting. The night before deployment, Jack liked to go over *tactics and tactical*, make sure all the questions had been answered, all the duties assigned, and the safety of his team enhanced.

Jack was sipping a Benziger cab, Mateo was nursing a Stoli on the rocks, and Cruz banged back the dregs of a Dos Equis and politely waved off Arsinio, who offered a refill before moving on.

The place was raucous, patrons stood three deep at the bar, and every table was filled.

Jack had his cell phone on the table with a close-up photo of the camouflaged metal door at Malic's compound.

"I ran it by my father," Cruz said deferentially. His father was a walking encyclopedia when it came to locks and keys and safes, and he had tutored his son well. "Semtex would work, C-4, or a half hour with a heavy-duty diamond-tipped drill."

"So if I blow the lock, I could kill anyone standing behind the door," Jack pointed out sourly.

"Could happen. And that would obviously defeat the purpose."

"Next."

"The lock was Turkish-made, used in detention centers and jails. Durable, not impenetrable. But with the drill and your skill set, security would know you were there before you gained entry. Why don't you let me do it?"

"Not a chance," Jack said. "Case closed. After you knock out the lights, I'll go up and over the wall. I want you back at the main road keeping an eye out. We don't need any surprises. We'll all be communicating on Bluetooth. Check your batteries. Mateo, you only enter the fray if things get hinky."

"You're the boss. Whatever you need, *jefe*, I have your back."

Jack knew that to be true and was grateful. The three men gathered themselves up and walked out of Hal's.

"Mateo, you up for another drink?"

"Yeah, what do you feel like?"

"I want you to go to the Chop House on Canon Drive near Wilshire. Let me know if the usual suspects are there. As you walk into the place, a six-panel wooden door leads down to their coolers, where Cardona ages his beef and his guys butcher the steaks."

"What am I looking for?"

"Just keep an eye out. See who comes and goes. I'll be on my cell."

"Where are you headed?"

"The beach."

"Don't forget your sunscreen." And he hung a right on Abbot Kinney.

"I'll call you when I'm set up in the a.m." And Cruz hung a left. Jack wanted him to catch some shut-eye and get down to Orange County first thing in the morning.

As Jack headed across the street to the liquor store he fielded a call from his son, Chris, and answered on the fly.

"Chris."

"I'm packing it in, Dad. Quitting school and hitting the road."

That made Jack pull up short outside the store. He flashed on the cardinal who had painted Jack with a quitter's brush.

"Relax, Dad, jeez, just a little hyperbole. I picked that up in English lit. *Hyperbole.* Didn't think I'd get to use it in a sentence so quick."

"You got me," Jack said, smiling. "You are gonna pay for that, young man." Jack was relieved, but more importantly, his son sounded normal.

"It's your ex-wife, Dad. She's killing me."

"That's your mother you're talking about." Mock scolding.

"I've already got two doctors who actually went to medical school."

"Point well taken. Look, why don't you tell her I'm driving up with a date. That'll scare her off."

"You bringing up Leslie?"

"I don't think that's in the cards, Chris."

"Oh. Sorry," he said, not wanting to pry. "But are you really gonna come?" he asked gently.

It sounded like an open door to Jack. "I have some business to clean up down here, and then, try and stop me."

"Okay, Dad. I'll tell her you're coming up with a hot blond bimbo. That should do the trick. Except then Jeremy will want to stay and check her out."

That elicited an honest laugh from Jack, who was protective of his ex-wife in front of his son, but her boyfriend, Jeremy, was fair game.

"Let me know how that works out, Son. And I'll see you in a couple of days."

———

Maggie Sheffield was reclining in a wicker chaise lounge. Her ever-present Marlboro dangled from her red-painted lips, accenting her wild mane of red hair, which was haloed by her porch light. Her manicured fingernails were long in the extreme and . . . red. She didn't seem surprised to see Jack, and she said hello on a smoky exhalation.

Jack stepped up on the porch wearing a tight black leather jacket, black jeans, and black boots, doing his best Don Johnson impersonation. With his long dark hair hanging over his collar, he looked more like Sylvester Stallone in *The Lords of Flatbush*, but he'd driven this far. It was worth a shot.

"Maggie," he said by way of hello, handing her a fifth of Bombay Sapphire gin.

"How did you know?"

Jack pointed at Maggie's kitchen window, where the distinctive blue metal cap that topped a bottle of Bombay could be seen.

"You're good," she said. "Can I pour you one?"

"I'm good."

"So I said. Let me pour you a drink?" But she didn't get up. She was just flirting. "What brings you to my little piece of paradise?" she asked, knowing the answer.

Jack wanted to get home. "Just looking for anything you can tell me about the disappearance of your favorite shark."

"Nothing to tell. I already came up with nada for the police."

She pulled another cigarette out of the hard pack and lit the new one off the stub of the old.

"But those guys, they're not like the two of us," Jack said, watching a wave roll in, the moon reflecting silver on the curl.

"How so?" Maggie asked.

"We're stargazers. Night owls. They weren't aware you were the only witness to the death of that poor girl. About the same time of night. No, even a little bit later, I think. The bar was shut down for the night."

Maggie nodded in agreement, not wanting to relive the tragedy of that night.

"And then there's the two of us being creatures of habit."

"Whatever do you mean?" she said, enjoying the sound of Jack's voice and his scrutiny.

"My guess is, no one saw you sitting up here on your chaise, having a ciggy and a nightcap the night Raul disappeared."

Maggie took a deep drink of gin, the ice sliding up the metal goblet.

"You sure you're not Sicilian?" Jack asked.

That one threw her for a loop, and she demurely wiped her lips and hid her smile. "Why do you ask?"

"The way you hold a grudge. The way you sleep with a Colt special next to your pillow."

"You're good. You should become a PI."

Maggie took a long drag of her cigarette and exhaled, tracking the smoke as it curled up into the clear night sky. The echo of the waves crashing onto the black rocks provided the sound track of her life.

"Anything you want to share?" Jack asked. "Anything?"

"Nothing really." But Maggie knew the game was over. Jack was going to leave sooner than later, and she'd be alone again.

"I *didn't* see two sumo wrestler types, had to weigh in at three fifty, brown-bag him and toss the piece of shit into a beat-up white van with no windows in the back and no writing on the side."

Sounded like Cardona and Frankie the Man to Jack.

"Just dirty white. And a skinny dude with pointy sideburns drove them out of here like they had someplace important to be."

And Peter Maniacci makes three, he thought.

"Sorry I wasted your time," Jack said. "It's too bad you didn't see anything. Might have saved our friend some pain."

Jack was letting her know he would keep her confidence. He stood up and stretched, taking in the scenery for the last time before hitting the road.

"Sure you're not Sicilian?" he deadpanned, nailing her with his smoky eyes.

Maggie laughed despite herself as Jack stepped off the porch. He could feel her eyes stripping him naked as he walked down the path toward the Lexus.

A small price to pay, he thought. He got what he came for. The last thing Jack needed was to barge in on Vincent Cardona if Raul Vargas had really been set up by one of his pissed-off, incarcerated gang members.

You have to be in the know, Jack told himself, if you plan on breaking down the door of your client. Especially if your client is a mobbed-up gangster with a button man for a cousin who weighs in at three hundred and fifty pounds.

43

Mateo was sitting at the first-floor bar, nursing a Stoli on the rocks with seven other patrons who were feeling no pain. A sixty-year-old dowager was giving him a heavy-lidded come-on. He had just gotten off the phone with Jack and filled him in on the lay of the land.

He had seen no activity at the six-paneled door until ten minutes ago, when Frankie stepped out, wiping sweat off his brow, and walked heavily up the stairs to the main floor of the restaurant above. Vincent Cardona was still up on the second floor glad-handing his VIP clients. The piano player continued to take requests and tips, and the din of happy patrons rose and fell with his Broadway musical selections. Last call was moments away.

Mateo advised Jack to make his move now.

The alleyway behind the Chop House accommodated parking for fifteen, and in the far corner, sharing space with Mercedes and Porsches, was parked a nondescript white van with no back windows. It fit the description of the vehicle Maggie had seen, and if Jack had cared, he probably could have found traces of Raul's blood on the sheet-metal floor inside.

The delivery door to the basement was locked, and Jack pulled out the tools Cruz had provided. After fiddling with his wire probes, he was relieved to hear the click of the lock disengaging. He eased the door open, stopped to listen, and then stepped down onto the metal stairs. Reaching up overhead, he closed the door behind him, making sure the lock stayed disengaged in case a quick exit was in play.

The basement felt tomblike, Jack thought as he edged down the stairs and onto the cement floor. He passed stores of olive oil, flour, salt, paper products, pasta, and cases of liquor used daily in the food and beverage preparation of a major Beverly Hills restaurant.

The main room was lit with fluorescent lights. He couldn't hear any sounds from above as he checked the stairwell that led up to the restaurant. He noticed that the lock was off on the walk-in, thick-glass meat locker. As he approached, the hair on the back of his neck stood at attention.

He opened the six-inch-thick insulated door and took in the grisly scene.

Raul Vargas's limp body was hanging from two meat hooks, pinioned by leather straps wrapped around his wrists. His ankles were bound, his body positioned directly above an industrial drain that channeled the dripping blood and juices from the four sides of beef he presently shared cold storage with. His eyes were closed and his hands were blue and swollen.

A single overhead light dripped with condensation and cold smoky vapor.

A thick, square butcher-block cutting table sat next to Raul with a pair of bloody pliers laid next to five broken, jagged fingernails with bits of cuticle and flesh still attached. A hacksaw, drill, cleaver, and blowtorch shared the tabletop, waiting their turn.

Cardona's cousin had done one hand and was probably giving Raul time to contemplate his existence before starting in on the other.

Jack walked up and slapped Raul across the face. One eye was swollen shut, but the other blinked open and registered surprise and then recognition.

"Did you talk?" Jack asked in a forced whisper.

Raul shook his head no.

"Did you tell Cardona that his daughter's at Malic's compound?"

Raul shook his head and then his one good eye went wide with terror. If Jack talked, he had just signed his own death warrant.

Jack was feeling the pressure of the clock as he muscled Raul up and slid his damaged hand off the meat hook, eliciting a haunting groan. Then he released the good hand, which was frozen and useless.

Jack was struggling to get Raul ambulatory when he was stopped short by the thick New York accent of Frankie the Man.

"Drop that piece of garbage where he's at. Right over the fuckin' drain works for me."

Jack did as ordered.

Raul's knees buckled and he went down like a sack of flour. The primal moan that he emitted was more chilling than the temperature.

Jack turned slowly and found himself staring down the barrel of a cannon. With the single bulb lighting the scene, Frankie's fat cheeks and heavily lined forehead, which had its own rolls of fat, gave him the look of a deranged Neanderthal. His feral eyes were as hard and lifeless as ball bearings.

"Now get the fuck out while you still can. You're fired. Vincent will have words with you later."

Suddenly, Frankie the Man went silent. The barrel of his Colt lowered from Jack's kill zone. He straightened uncomfortably tall as he felt the cold metal of Mateo's gun pressed against the base of his thick skull.

"It has a hair trigger and my hand's a bit shaky. I'd drop your weapon before they're hosing *your* blood down that drain."

The big man was not totally stupid and wisely complied. The Colt crashed to the cement floor. Jack cringed, hoping it wouldn't discharge, as he deftly attached two pairs of plastic flex-cuffs to Frankie's fat wrists, knowing one wouldn't do the trick.

Mateo cut the tape that bound Raul's ankles, cuffed him, pulled Raul to his feet, and started toward the door. Jack stopped him with a nod to the burlap sack.

"Don't," Raul whined. "I can't breathe in that shit." But he was in no position to negotiate.

Mateo grabbed it and slid it over Raul's sweat-plastered hair, a move not lost on Frankie the Man.

Jack took Frankie's cell phone and his weapon and muscled him to the concrete floor.

"Call Vincent in fifteen minutes," Frankie wheezed. "After you've cleared the joint, let him know I'm in here. Least you could do."

Jack nodded and stepped out of the freezer, locking the door behind him.

———

A hooded Raul Vargas was complying with Jack's order to stay down on the backseat of the Lexus. If he didn't, Jack had warned, he could travel in the comfort of the trunk. Raul let out involuntary moans as the car hit speed bumps and made hard turns. No sympathy from Jack.

"They fucked up my hand," Raul said, his voice muffled by the burlap sack.

"I'm crying for you. You'll never play Beethoven again."

"Take off this fucking bag, man. I'm sweating, I have allergies."

"Don't bleed on the leather."

"Fuck you, man."

"Did you say 'Thank you, man, for saving my sorry ass'?".

"Where are you taking me?"

"Depends on your next answer."

Jack let that roll around his desperate brain before going on. He made a hard left turn and Raul let out a plaintive yelp.

"Is Angelica Cardona alive?"

"I told you, I don't know the girl."

Jack made a tire-squealing right turn and Raul rolled onto his bad hand, which had been wrapped in Mateo's T-shirt. The scream was primeval.

"I'm gonna puke. A little compassion here."

"Is she alive?" Jack said simply.

"I never heard anything to the contrary."

"What am I gonna do with you, Raul? Will you testify against Malic?"

Raul's laugh was tight and crazed. "Not if I want to see Tuesday."

"I tied you to the girl."

"I'm the only one in the world taking pictures of pretty women with their cell phones?"

"I drop you off at the hospital, what are you going to say?"

"That I was set up by my friends I left in the dust at the big house. They think I'm sitting on a pile of money instead of house-sitting for my father. They sent guys who jumped me and took me around the corner to my father's beach house. There was no pile of money and they took me somewhere else and tortured me as payback. When they went out for a smoke, I ran, got lucky, and ended up in the ER," he said, hoping his story would come true and he wouldn't end up dead in a ditch off of Mulholland.

"Works for me," Jack said, and Raul emitted a muffled sigh of relief. "But if Angelica turns up dead," Jack continued, "or she doesn't turn up, or if you warn Malic, or his men, or your lawyer, or talk to the cops, or any-fucking-body, you're going down for kidnapping and murder with aggravating circumstances, a capital offense. With your record, it behooves you to remain silent. It's time to put your game face on, Raul."

Jack reached back and yanked the burlap sack off Raul's head. He hung a hard left into the lot at Saint John's emergency entrance and pulled to the curb. Jumping out, he cut the flexi-cuffs off Raul with a Leatherman and hauled Raul up and out of the backseat.

Raul stood on wobbly legs, wiping burlap threads out of his eyes and mouth with his one good hand.

Yet once Jack jumped into the car, Raul slipped down on one knee, started to wail, and went Shakespearean on him. "Help! Heeelp me! Police! Jack Bertolino fucked me up! Help! I have a restraining order and he tortured—"

A man rushed toward him, intent on business. He slid an arm

around Raul's neck and squeezed tight enough to shut off his air-flow.

"Keep your yap shut, boyo," Nick Aprea said, leaning down, his menacing face inches from wide-eyed Raul. "You called for the police?"

"You're squeezing too tight," came out like a rasp.

Nick let him go, and Raul slid to the pavement.

Jack rolled down the passenger-side window, and Nick winked.

"Thanks for the heads-up." And he tossed in a brown paper bag.

Jack had Nick phone Mateo and send him home for the night.

"The eighteen-year-old Macallan did the trick," Nick continued. "You better disappear yourself until this is over. You won't be much help sitting in a jail cell."

Jack nodded his thanks and peeled out. In his rearview mirror Jack saw Raul reach out for help standing and then howl at the moon as Nick grabbed his bad hand, squeezed it tight, and pulled the ex-con to his feet.

"I know what would suit you, Sheik. I know you better than you know yourself."

Malic was sitting in his home office, wearing his tie at half-mast with uncharacteristic dark circles under his coal-black eyes.

"But why would I need an electric car?" the sheik asked. "It's not as if gas is an issue for me."

The sheik's image was choppy and pixelating this evening. Maybe a solar disturbance, Malic thought.

"You need it because the Tesla Roadster is a work of art, a

perfect one hundred percent rating in *Consumer Reports*, and it takes you from zero to sixty in three point seven seconds. Silently. Like a stealth bomber."

Malic worried he was pushing too hard, but it was crunch time. His world was coming apart, and he was feeling pressure from all sides. His wife had been acting very strange, he didn't think Detective Aprea was going away without a fight, and Jack Bertolino was a thorn in his side that kept piercing.

He was getting pressure from the Sinaloa cartel, which had fronted the drugs. They wanted their cash and wouldn't be denied. They were nobody to fuck around with, Malic knew. The Cardona girl was an albatross and would be dealt with in the next twenty-four hours, or she could literally bring an end to life as Malic knew it. And he wasn't totally convinced that Mustafa hadn't talked to the police. Would he cut a deal to stay out of prison? Malic knew he himself would if it were politically expedient. And now his old friend, for whom he had generated so much wealth, was turning a deaf ear.

Malic watched the sheik walk back and forth before the Skype camera like a preening peacock. Malic had always prided himself on controlling his own fate, and now it was in the soft, pudgy hands of Sheik Ibrahim.

The sheik knew full well why Malic was offering the exotic car. He lived for moments such as these and couldn't wait to bury the knife.

"Two of my men scouted it in Anaheim and will take possession in the next few hours." *Take* being the operative word. "I'll have it detailed and it will be ready for transport when your men arrive," Malic said. "Sadly, I will not be home to greet them."

"And then let's say we float the loan for a thirty-day period.

I'll be forced to do some creative bookkeeping but will deliver as I have always done."

The sheik looked like he was actually thinking about accepting the proposal and then . . . was that a smile Malic detected?

"I will hold the Matisse for the thirty days until payment is rendered, my friend. I have the perfect wall already picked out. My men will be landing at John Wayne Airport at seven p.m. Have the painting wrapped and ready."

That was not the demand he wanted to hear. "Tomorrow is not good. I have an event that must be attended."

"Cancel it."

"Impossible."

"Then make other plans. You are a powerful man with many friends. Have your driver, Hassan, take care of your business, but I will have what has been promised and what is now mine. Are we clear, my old friend?"

Sheik Ibrahim stepped so close to the computer that his face became distorted, but his eyes showed clear resolve. Malic knew there was no way out. He had given his word.

"Hassan will be here waiting. I'm not a happy man. We have a long history. I have made you a fortune and never let you down."

"Our relationship will remain strong as long as we fulfill promises made. Our friendship is too valuable for me to compromise.

"And hold the car, Malic. It is a grand gesture, but I am a man who loves a combustion engine. I've learned that silent power isn't as fulfilling as the roar of a lion."

———

Jack docked his boat at slip 207 in the Newport Marina, the one that had housed Malic al-Yasiri's cigarette boat. He needed a safe place to spend the night and gather his thoughts. There wasn't much chance that Malic or his men would be returning any time soon, and so he tied up close to the canvas-covered hydraulic boat lift and spent the better part of an hour cleaning up the mess the MAC-10 bullets had made of his side window and teakwood instrument panel.

The pain in his back was acute, and his self-medication was a full step behind the hurt. He needed sleep. Leslie had rung him up twice, but Jack chose not to answer. He didn't want to lie if asked what he was up to.

Nick was going to keep Raul on ice for as long as possible. But if Raul decided to spill his guts to Malic about what had really transpired, the element of surprise would be gone. Jack risked prison time or death if things blew up.

If all went according to plan, Jack would invade the compound and leave with Angelica safely in tow. His debt to Vincent Cardona paid in full. Malic would be arrested for kidnapping, murder, and human and drug trafficking. As for Raul, hopefully Jack would have enough to put him back in the slammer.

Just in case the operation went bad, Jack checked the load in his Glock semiautomatic and packed two full clips. Then he pulled out his old throw-down .22 and made sure it was locked, loaded, and stowed in his ankle rig, ready for the worst-case scenario.

Jack didn't remember falling asleep and wasn't aware of the rain until his cell phone beeped and dragged him from a deep REM sleep. He fumbled for the phone and read the text.

I have information. Will contact tomorrow. K.

44

"Get out of bed and get dressed," Malic ordered Kayla, who looked as if the king-sized bed had swallowed her whole. She was lying with the gold-threaded brocade duvet cover pulled tightly up to her chin. Her knuckles white, her eyes red-rimmed from crying.

"I'm ill," she spit out. "I vomited an hour ago and I still have to vomit. You are not helping me."

"This is an important night," he said, trying to control his anger. "How will it look if I show up alone?"

"I don't care how it looks, Malic—"

Kayla leaped from the bed and ran into the bathroom. She knelt at the bowl with her back to her husband and stealthily slid her finger down her throat until she puked. Long and hard.

Malic looked away in disgust.

Kayla stood slowly, holding herself up at the lavish sink. Weakly, she splashed water on her face and rinsed out her mouth. She walked silently back to bed and slipped under the covers, ignoring her husband's scrutiny.

"Is Mommy sick?" little Saarah asked, sticking her head in the doorway.

"She'll be fine, my love," Malic said as he struggled to button his heavily starched tuxedo shirt. "Go back in with Adelina."

"I love you, Mommy," she said.

"I love you too, sweetheart."

That was good enough for Saarah, who galloped back into the living room with the nanny.

Malic gazed at his wife, who was crying again and looked pitiful. He started to upbraid her but grabbed his Armani tux jacket and stormed out of the room before he said something he would live to regret.

Kayla dried her eyes and checked the time on the bedside clock.

Malic walked briskly across the lawn, looking like an ad from *GQ*. The man was so self-absorbed, he didn't have a clue as to why his wife was crying. He was seething and Hassan took a reflexive step back from the desk, where he had been working when Malic pushed through the doorway.

The mahogany wall panel that hid the Matisse was open and lit. Malic knotted his tie as he looked at the empty space and felt a surge of rage. He would get his life back in order and fly to Iraq personally to pick up his work of art when the sheik's one million eight was safely returned to his account.

He couldn't bear to watch as Hassan picked up the bubble-wrapped parcel that contained his treasure and placed it in a Zero Halliburton aluminum suitcase that had been lined in memory foam to protect the masterpiece.

Malic sat down behind his desk and hit one of the buttons on the pull-out panel. The television set was revealed and as it blinked on, Angelica Cardona could be seen lying on the bed, in much the same position as his wife, seemingly lost in thought.

Malic had an impulse to smash the set. What he really wanted to do was sample the wares, but it was not to be.

"One bullet to the back of the head," he said without any feeling. "If she doesn't become shark bait, it will look like a mob hit to the police, and her father will have to look at his own organization for revenge. Did you fuel up the boat?"

"Both tanks," Hassan answered. "More than enough to get to the back side of Catalina and home. And Raul? What did he have to report?"

"Retribution for his early release. He was beaten and will still be sitting at the dais tonight. He should have been an example for Kayla."

Hassan dared not go there. He knew a wise man never interfered in another man's marital strife.

Malic keyed a sequence into his desktop computer, and sixteen different cameras fed sixteen different squares on his computer screen, providing different views of the compound. His wife in her bed, his daughter in the living room, his cigarette boat safely tied off at the dock, the front gate, and every other square inch of his protected domain. All was good.

Malic stood tall, straightened his jacket, and snugged his bow tie. "If I don't leave now, I'll be late." He stopped at the door. "Hassan, you are a good man. My right hand. Your loyalty will be rewarded. I will have a handsome bonus for you and your family at the end of the month."

Malic walked out without looking back.

————

The yellow sun dropped below the horizon, leaving a darkening blue sky as Jack paddled his inflatable Avalon away from his boat.

He had moored it around the bend of the promontory, away from prying eyes. The ocean was glassy, the air clean after last night's rain. He tied off on the neighbor's dock and felt his blood pressure rise at the sight across the way. Malic's cigarette boat was docked, and bright security lights surrounded the compound.

Jack was dressed entirely in black with black running shoes and a black watch cap. He checked the time and started up the stairs to the top of the neighboring property.

The seven-foot tall, locked metal gate and security fence, both topped with razor-sharp spears, had been built five feet below the cliff's edge so as not to tarnish the view from the estate above. The left side of the rusted gate had been anchored securely into the shear cliff face. The fence to the right, welded at a forty-five-degree angle, jutted out eight feet over empty space and the rocky shoreline below. A convincing deterrent to unwanted visitors.

Jack threw a canvas bag with his equipment over the gate and made his move. He clambered hand-over-hand across the fence's uppermost crossbeam. His legs dangled precariously over thin air and the rocks fifty feet below. Jack gripped the base of the metal spear at the end of the fence, reached around the outer edge slick with condensation, grabbed hold, and carefully made his way back. When the fence met the gate he pulled himself up and stepped safely onto the stairs.

Jack grabbed his bag, bound up the last few steps and squat-ran along the cliff's edge to Malic's compound wall, where he caught his breath and waited in shadow for full darkness to descend. A crescent moon was on the rise, merely a slash in the night sky.

Kayla's text had been cryptic. *I have key,* was all she shared— besides where they'd meet.

He texted Deak Montrose, the Coast Guard captain, alerting him to the coordinates of Malic's cigarette boat, and put his phone on vibrate.

Jack cupped his hand over the Bluetooth device in his ear, his eyes narrowing as Cruz reported a stretch limo traveling toward the compound gate at a slow rate of speed.

Malic had been spotted driving alone in his Town Car toward the city an hour earlier, and Jack wasn't happy to hear about surprise visitors.

But he was going in regardless. Tonight was the night. If Malic was being forced to clean house, sitting in front of a thousand witnesses was the perfect time to do it, Jack thought. No, Jack knew. He felt it in his bones.

———

The black stretch limousine pulled to a smooth stop in front of the massive steel gates protecting Malic's compound.

The sheik had sent three of his men to do the job of one. A not-too-subtle show of force if his old friend decided to renege on their deal. And a reminder that his reach was vast.

The uniformed guard in the gatehouse was gazing at the monitor that had multiple views of the property, minus the main house. Kayla had demanded her family's privacy from the security team, and Malic had reluctantly acquiesced. The Iraqi gang member tapped one particular square, and the image of the limo idling at the front entrance enlarged to fill the entire screen.

The guard signaled to another member of his security team, who slid out a side door to check out the occupants of the stretch. Then he banged on the gate, which swung open, and trotted in behind the car as the gates closed securely behind.

Hassan, having been notified of the men's arrival by security, stepped out of the pool house with the metal suitcase in hand, locking the door behind him. He knew how upset Malic was, losing a prized possession, but Hassan had more on his mind than a rich man's emotional attachment. He had to kill his prisoner.

Hassan hoped Malic was serious about the bonus. After losing the shipment of drugs and now the painting, he wasn't sure where any surplus would come from. His wife had been badgering him about a new car. It would be good to shut her up, he thought as he walked past the pool toward the front gate. He never sensed Kayla standing at the kitchen sink, tracking his movements.

———

Malic al-Yasiri stood in a tight knot gathered next to Philippe Vargas, his attention on the mayor, who was holding court in the front of the Catalina Ballroom on the third floor of the Bonaventure Hotel. The cardinal, in his red finery, nodded in appreciation at something of import the mayor shared, and then the men broke their huddle and made their way to the head table.

Raul was already seated. But not at the head table with the mayor. He had been placed with McCarthy and Associates, the group recently hired to run Vargas's leasing campaign. One of his eyes was swollen and ringed in a purple-green. His damaged hand was completely wrapped in gauze. The other held a drink.

Philippe Vargas walked past his son's table as if he were invisible and took his seat next to the man of the cloth, forcing Malic to accept the chair on the end.

Malic glanced down at his cell phone, which he had put on vibrate, but he spied no text messages. Therefore no bad news. It did little to assuage his mood. His future was supported by a house of cards, and he was overleveraged. He thought about the sheik's analogy of pulling a single thread out of a rug and being left standing on a dusty floor. In an uncharacteristic moment of weakness, he prayed that losing the ten-million-dollar Matisse wasn't the beginning of his end.

Malic chastised himself for harboring negative thoughts and then waved off a waiter's offer of wine. He took in the room, filled with the wealthy, powerful, and politically connected, and reminded himself that he belonged. Glancing at the members of the media in the back of the room, Malic steeled himself for the accolades to come and his time at the microphone.

The lights dimmed. The mayor stepped up to the spot-lit dais, and the room went silent.

45

The bright lights on the peninsula blinked once and then snapped off, blanketing the three massive estates and four square miles of Orange County in total darkness.

Jack leaped over the compound wall, night-vision goggles in place, and ran to the edge of the main house, slipping inside the French doors, which had been left purposely unlocked.

Kayla startled at the sight of Jack in the night-vision goggles but handed off the two keys and pointed across the way.

"These open the doors to the pool house."

"Is she there?" Jack asked.

Kayla looked fragile, ready to crumble.

"Kayla?" Jack said, wanting to keep her on point.

She heard her daughter cry out in the other room. Jack watched Kayla steel herself and then nod a tight yes.

"There is a button on the bookshelves on the back wall, second row from the top on the side of the wooden panel," she said. "Oh, and I saw Hassan, Malik's driver, walk toward the guard house."

"Do you have a safe room?"

"Yes."

"Run. Take your daughter and the nanny and lock yourselves in until this is over."

Thoroughly frightened, Kayla hurried through the darkness toward Saarah's frightened cries.

Jack slipped out of the house, checked that all was clear, and ran across the lawn past the garden and pool toward the pool house.

He inserted the larger, more ornate of the two keys. Wrong one. Jack could hear men shouting now. On the far side of the house a headlight blinked on. He tried the second key, and the door unlocked. He fastened it behind him just as the screen of the desktop computer blinked on. Powered by a backup generator, sixteen security cameras came to life. He could see the face of the Iraqi in the guardhouse looking frantic and shouting silent orders to someone off camera. Jack slapped the magnetic negative pulse disrupter onto the back of the computer, and the screen blinked and then thankfully went dark.

The pitch-black room was an eerie green through his night-vision goggles as Jack walked over to the bookcases and ran his hands along the mahogany shelves, disrupting leather-bound books until he found and depressed the hidden button. The secret door hinged open a crack, and as Jack pulled it wider to step through, he sensed movement behind him.

The door to the pool house exploded off its hinges.

Jack dove into the tunnel as Hassan filled the doorway, holding an AK-47 at his waist. He sprayed the dark room with high-powered rounds, splintering mahogany wood and first editions. He missed Jack Bertolino by a razor's edge.

The sheik's limousine sat idling, headlights on.

It took a gun to the head to force Malic's guard to manually open the gate and let the sheik's men escape with the painting.

The stretch limo made a wide turn in the circular driveway, smashing into the rear of a Maserati, sending it spinning off to the side, clearing the way. The sheik's gunman jumped into the back of the limo on the run.

The long car powered out onto the street—and was instantly T-boned by a Lincoln Town Car. Glass exploded, rubber squealed, and the limo stalled, blocking the entrance to the property and prohibiting the gates from swinging shut.

Two of the shaken Iraqis jumped out, firing wildly at the offending vehicle. The limo driver leaped out and disappeared into darkness.

Vincent Cardona emerged from the back of the Town Car and fired his pistol, taking down one of the sheik's gunmen.

Frankie the Man lurched out of the passenger seat, using the door to block incoming fire. The window shattered, and as he spit out glass he traded shots and took a bullet in the meat of his arm. Undeterred, he grabbed the gun with his good hand and kept on firing.

The third man slipped out of the backseat of the stretch with the suitcase. He crouched low and fired a round. With the sudden support from Malic's men, who were firing at Cardona from behind the gate, he made a mad dash around the Italians and up the road, away from the compound, carrying the sheik's treasure.

Peter jumped out of the driver's seat, fired twice, and took off running after the sheik's man.

———

The deadly barrage of Hassan's bullets went silent in the pool house. He ejected his spent clip and slapped in another.

"Call in the troops," Jack shouted to Cruz, using his Bluetooth as he poked his weapon through the opening and blind-fired, emptying his clip. He pulled the secret door shut behind him and took off running deeper into the tunnel. He took the opportunity to slam a fresh clip home into his Glock.

Jack couldn't help but register the Iraqi antiquities that lined the tunnel wall. He knew where they came from, and his rage grew the deeper he went. But he had to stay on point. In mere seconds Hassan would be on his tail.

He was confronted by two metal doors at the end of the passageway. Jack keyed the door on the right with the larger key. It opened on another short hallway. He crossed those few steps and opened the door at the far end, entering a room that looked like a set from *I Dream of Jeannie*.

It was fucking empty.

He dashed back outside, opened the steel-plated door on the left, and stepped through. As he turned the key, locking it behind him, it was pounded with deafening, clanging cop-killer rounds from Hassan's AK.

Jack stopped short, looked through a Plexiglas wall at what must have been a jail cell. It looked like someone lived there. It was windowless, freakish and unnatural, he thought.

And then he remembered: it was the room where he saw Angelica acting in the YouTube video.

But it was empty.

Was Angelica in the limo? Jack worried. Maybe the sheik was still on board and they were flying her to Iraq.

Then Jack saw movement through the opened bathroom door, and he felt a wash of relief.

Angelica Cardona peered around the doorjamb and then pulled back, hidden from the hallway.

Jack unlocked the door to the glass cage.

"You're going to have to kill me here," Angelica said. "I'm not leaving—"

"Angelica," he cut her off. "I'm Jack Bertolino. Your father hired me to find you. I want you to come right now."

Jack heard a key turning in the metal door, and as it pushed open a crack, a single beam of light refracted through. Jack aimed and fired. The first bullet sparked off the metal; the second made it through the opening, and Jack could hear a curse as the flashlight clattered to the tiled floor.

"Now," he said with quiet strength to Angelica as he reached out. She gripped his hand with desperate power as he helped her out of the pitch-black room.

Jack fired another round that echoed in the hallway.

"To the left," she said, guiding Jack toward the camouflaged exterior door.

Jack said a silent prayer that the larger of the two keys would work. Angelica cried out as the heavy cylinder clicked and the door swung open, revealing a clear star-filled sky.

He slammed the door shut, locked it, and broke off the

thick key with the butt of his gun. They could hear muted pounding on the door behind them and gunfire from the property above.

Jack ripped off the night-vision goggles, led Angelica toward the slick wooden stairs twenty-five feet above the rocks and pounding surf below, and made a mad dash to freedom.

46

Nick Aprea came screaming up the road in a massive SUV with a lone cherry-top spinning. Three police cars with sirens wailing, red, white, and blue lights flashing, followed in his wake.

Nick was the first man out of his vehicle, weapon drawn.

"Police!" he shouted, aiming down on Cardona and Frankie. "Stop firing. Drop your fucking weapons!"

Vincent Cardona and his cousin were smart enough to hold fire when the bulls arrived. They tossed down their guns and were arrested on the spot.

Malic's men answered by firing at Nick. The uniformed cops raised their police-issue nine-millimeters and returned fire as Nick led the charge past the crippled limousine and deployed inside the compound walls.

Peter Maniacci was arrested by the next wave of cops arriving on the scene. He was beating the shit out of the sheik's man, whom he'd tackled running down the road with the aluminum suitcase and the ten-million-dollar Matisse.

The exit through the gate and the only way out was partially blocked by the crashed limo. One of Malic's men panicked when the cops arrived, jumped in his Porsche, and tore across the lawn past the pool, ripping up the rose garden. The desperate man spun a one-eighty at the compound wall, spraying a rooster tail of dirt and grass, and then jammed the transmission into first and roared back toward the front gate.

Nick stepped into the center of the destroyed garden and fired. His automatic jammed. He fired again. An empty click.

The driver shifted into second. He cracked a tight smile as he rocketed toward Nick.

That's when Mateo stepped out of the shadows and fired three rounds.

The driver took a bullet to the forehead and slumped sideways. The weight of his dead body pulled the steering wheel crazily to the right. The Porsche veered away from Nick, ramped up the coved edge of the pool, and splashed ass-down in the deep end, the car's headlights burning skyward like klieg lights.

Nick ejected his jammed clip and slapped in another. He nodded his thanks to Mateo, who headed back to the front of the property.

Nick pulled a flashlight off his belt, saw that the door to the pool house had been kicked off its hinges, and ran in that direction.

Hassan exploded out of the pool house door with a loaded AK. He saw Nick pounding the turf in his direction and let loose with a short burst of automatic firepower.

Fully exposed, Nick fired on the run and then dove into the pool. The AK bullets followed, puncturing the skin of the Porsche as a wild-eyed Hassan ran past to the far end of the property and leaped up and over the compound wall.

———

Angelica, in a short skirt, diaphanous blouse, and bare feet, moved gingerly over the rocky shore toward the inflatable boat tied off on the next dock. She didn't want to let go of Jack's hand, but he had another thought and headed toward the cigarette boat to disable it.

As he stepped onto the dock, an arcing trail of bullets splintered the wooden slats in his direction and forced him to move back, hug the cliff, and join Angelica at the inflatable. All he could see in the dark was the muzzle flash. With manic strokes he oared the boat out into the waves.

Hassan had started his descent from the top of the cliff, just below the compound wall, firing as he struggled to maneuver down the slick wooden stairs in his leather boots.

He jumped off the stairs onto the grassy outcropping and sighted in on the Avalon inflatable, disappearing in the distance. He let off a tight burst that fell short as Jack paddled safely around the bend of the peninsula to his moored boat.

Hassan felt a bullet invade his space before he heard the discharge. A divot exploded out of the cliff face. Hassan arched his back, swung his automatic sky-high, and fired over his shoulder at Nick Aprea, who was raining bullets on him.

Hassan knew that if Angelica got away, he would spend the rest of his life in prison, and that was not an option. He spun around; sprayed the top of the cliff, forcing Nick back; threw the AK over his shoulder; and took the stairs down three at a time.

———

Jack stepped on board his craft first. He reached out a hand to pull Angelica up, but she slipped into the water and swam to the transom, where he all but lifted her onto the deck. Angelica's blouse stuck to her body like a contestant in a wet T-shirt contest. She stepped into Jack's embrace, wrapped her arms around him, and squeezed.

"Thank you," she said, nailing him with her blazing green eyes.

When Angelica stepped back, she glanced down at herself, as did Jack. She was very beautiful and very exposed.

"If I'd known you were going to save me, I'd have worn a pair of shoes."

Jack's grin was tight as he pulled up the anchor, started the engine, and headed north toward Marina del Rey.

"There's a towel in the head," he said over the roar of the engine. Angelica walked into the dimly lit cabin, throwing an appreciative look back at Jack as she closed the bathroom door behind her.

He was running on pure adrenaline from the rush of the assault. Because of the natural curve of the landmass, he chose to power into deeper water for a more direct route home. The lights of the Terranea resort shone like a beacon in the distance. Jack could see a cargo container ship moving from San Diego north in his direction, but it was still in his rearview.

Then the deep thrumming of a high-powered boat turned his stomach to water. He glanced over his shoulder but couldn't make out the cigarette boat on the dark horizon. Hassan was running without lights. Jack instinctively reached for the radio and then remembered that his equipment had been smashed to hell after the attack in the marina.

He pushed the throttle to max, checked the load on his Glock, and pulled the .22 from his ankle rig. As Angelica walked out on deck with a towel wrapped around her hair, he handed the gun to her.

"You know how to fire one of these?"

"It's not over?" she asked fearfully. Yet in the next moment the slight crack in her resolve turned to ice. She unwound the towel and threw it over one of the deck chairs. "It's just point and shoot," she said with the ease of a mob wife. "Uncle Frankie," she said by way of explanation.

"Right."

Jack pulled out his cell and handed it off. "Dial 911 and have them patch us through to the Coast Guard."

She dialed the phone and then looked up. "No bars, Jack. We're in a dead zone."

"Not on my watch."

Jack vowed not to let that reality come to pass.

47

Hassan had untied the cigarette boat while he fired one-handed at Nick. Turning the engine over, he threw the throttle into reverse and roared away from the dock and the killing range of Nick Aprea's bullets. He knew he would have seen Jack's boat pass if it were going south, and so he headed north, knowing it was just a matter of time before he outran them. He popped a fresh clip into his AK-47 and made sure his pistol was fully loaded.

Hassan planned on killing them both, torching Jack's boat, and then disappearing until things settled down. Maybe a trip to Detroit, visit his brother. If he shaved his beard and dyed his hair black, he'd look like just another Middle Eastern cabdriver, he thought.

He was doing fifty knots and skimming over the water when he decided to delay his report to Malic. The boss was probably just sitting down to dinner, so why spoil his big night? He could see the lights of Terranea ahead as he rocketed across the calm ocean, the wind whipping his copper-red hair.

Up ahead in the darkness, he spotted the faint glow of green and red running lights. He smiled at how close he was. It was finally time for the kill.

————

Jack was out of options. Hassan would be on their tail inside of three minutes. To the right were stark cliffs and the black rocky shore. No way, no time, to beach the boat and make a run for it. They'd get cut down like animals. If they were forced to jump ship, Hassan could pick them off like fish in a barrel. To the left was the open sea. The cargo container ship was gaining ground and would arrive about the same time as Hassan, blocking them in. Jack knew he'd be outgunned in a straight-up shooting contest.

The cargo container ship was twelve hundred feet long and a hundred feet tall, and plowed through the waves at a frightening twenty-five knots. Jack suddenly had an idea. Forget about being boxed in. He killed the lights on his Cutwater 28 and abruptly changed course. He headed straight for the massive ship.

————

Hassan saw the green and red lights blink out, then the change in Jack's direction, and corrected his own course accordingly. He stood strong at the wheel, weapon ready.

"What are you doing, Jack?" Angelica asked, seeing the monstrous superstructure looming ahead, dwarfing their craft.

"An end run."

Jack headed straight for the bow of the cargo ship. His cabin cruiser maxed out at twenty-eight knots. There was no room for error.

Angelica snapped a look behind them.

"Here he comes, Jack."

"Hold the wheel and keep the heading."

Angelica stepped up without argument. Jack braced himself, assumed a balanced stance, and fired.

————

Hassan came flying up on the port side, hitting Jack's wake, and let out a wild spray of bullets that landed high. In contrast, Jack's rounds found the windshield of the cigarette boat. Stung by the explosion of shattering glass, Hassan pulled up sharply. He'd have to come around again for a second assault.

"Jack!"

They were on a collision course with the container ship.

Switching his focus, Jack grabbed the wheel from Angelica as the looming hull and Jack's boat moved dangerously close. Jack's angle of attack had to be perfect. The spray being kicked up by the container ship showered their boat's windshield and side windows, rendering them all but blind.

Jack pulled hard on the wheel.

He cut in front of the behemoth.

The sheer mass of the ship blacked out what little light there was.

Angelica let out a cry.

Jack held his breath.

His engine strained against the current.

And then they were on the other side.

Jack's cabin cruiser cleared the lane seconds before the big ship crushed them. The wave thrown up by the massive hull propelled Jack's boat forward and out of harm's way.

Jack cut to the left toward the stern of the ship, and five hundred feet down he turned his bow toward shore, threw his boat into neutral, and waited.

Hassan was seconds behind Jack but too late to follow. From his vantage point it looked like the steel monster had swallowed Jack's boat. But he wasn't sure. He changed course and powered slowly toward the rear of the ship, hoping to surprise Jack when the cargo ship cleared the lane.

———

It all happened in a second. The hundred-foot wall of steel was there and then gone.

Jack throttled forward, hitting the double wake at the stern of the ship. His boat went airborne and splashed down hard, sending Angelica sprawling. Jack flew toward Hassan's craft to ram it.

"Hold on, Angelica. Grab on to something," Jack shouted.

———

Hassan hit the power and lurched forward as Jack's boat cut across his wake, missing him by inches.

Hassan cut a hard power-right, sending a shower of water onto the deck of Jack's boat. Jack white-knuckled the wheel and fired his nine-millimeter, tagging Hassan in the thigh.

The strong man howled but did not go down.

Jack set a direct course for the Palos Verdes Peninsula.

"Stay down," he shouted to Angelica over the sound of the engines and the increased roar of the cigarette boat.

Angelica got up on one knee, hugging the side rail.

Hassan's boat nosed closer, ready for the kill.

He raised his AK-47. He had a clean shot at Jack.

He didn't see Angelica, though. She emptied her pistol at her jailer, praying for a solid hit. One of her bullets found its mark, slamming into his shoulder.

Hassan growled but held on to his automatic tightly. He fought through the pain, lifted his AK again, and let loose. Angelica dove to the deck as Jack's boat was assaulted.

Jack pulled hard on the wheel as Hassan's bullets splintered wood in a straight line across the stern of his boat and then lurched upward, puncturing the propane tank on the hibachi grill, which saved Jack's life but burst into flames.

The sky lit up, and then pools of light played over the water as a thousand-candle spotlight on the undercarriage of a Coast Guard helicopter moved in, sweeping patterns over the deadly scene playing out below.

The flames on the Cutwater 28 were gaining in intensity.

Hassan was coming in for the kill.

Jack's boat was now a floating torch heading straight for the cliffs.

"On a three count we jump," he shouted.

Angelica grabbed Jack's hand as flames licked their heels.

"Hell with the count," she shouted, and pulled him up and over the side.

The two splashed into the dark icy water and slipped below the surface.

Hassan flew past, chasing the boat. He emptied his clip into the cabin cruiser before realizing there was no longer any pilot. He throttled back, did a tight turn, and scanned the water.

He ignored the disembodied orders from the PA system on

the helicopter to turn off his engine. Instead, he drew his pistol and fired at the chopper, causing it to pull up and away. He cruised forward, hunting for his targets.

The chopper's searchlight crossed Jack and Angelica's position in the water as it banked around and Hassan now had them in his sights.

He raced forward and was hit in the face by a high-powered spotlight flying toward him at incredible speed.

Captain Deak Montrose and the Coast Guard's armor-plated gunboat sliced through the choppy water on a direct course.

Momentarily blinded, Hassan yelled, "What the fuck!" He smashed the throttle forward, grabbed the wheel with both hands, and rocketed away. If he couldn't shoot Bertolino and Cardona, he sure as hell could cut them to ribbons. He saw them bobbing in the distance, and he straightened his heading.

Deak assessed the situation and ordered his men to fire. Heavy-duty rounds from mounted machine guns strafed the side and then the back of Hassan's cigarette boat as it flew past.

One hundred yards from Angelica and Jack and closing. Hassan was losing blood and wanted theirs.

Angelica squeezed her arms around Jack's neck as they bobbed in the water. Jack computed the depth they'd have to dive to in order to clear the propeller blades of the cigarette boat.

Another prolonged burst of machine-gun fire from the Coast Guard's gunboat punctured one of Hassan's full tanks of gas.

It ignited.

The fire spread to the second tank of gas.

———

The force of the first explosion lifted Hassan and the million-dollar craft out of the water. The second percussive explosion lit up the sea and the night sky in a mushroom cloud of death. It tore apart man and boat. Shrapnel, flames, and chunks of debris rained down on Jack and Angelica, who were forced underwater to escape the onslaught.

The chopper's spotlight moved in a slow circle where the pair had gone under.

More fiery debris splashed down like napalm, but no bodies appeared.

The spotlight probed the area.

The ocean rippled with the downwash of the chopper's blades.

Jack and Angelica broke through the water's surface into the spotlight, spitting water, coughing, and fighting for breath.

The sound of the chopper was thunderous, but Jack couldn't mistake the sound his boat made running aground against the rocky shore. He spun in time to see the sky lit up by the third explosion of the night.

Jack pulled Angelica in tight, amazed at her strength, relieved he had saved her life, and happy to be alive.

———

Deak piloted his armored vessel into the pool of light. His men carefully pulled Angelica and then Jack out of the water and onto their able craft. The young sailors handed Angelica a blanket and politely averted their eyes until she was wrapped, warm, and safely strapped into one of the rear seats with a bottle of water.

Deak immediately headed back to the marina. An EMT unit was standing by to transport Angelica to Saint John's Health Center.

"The bird will stay put until emergency vehicles arrive and contain the scene. Sorry about your boat."

"Worth the sacrifice," Jack said, glancing back at Angelica, who was staring mindlessly out over the water. He had seen that look before. Shock had finally set in.

"Got a call from your friend Detective Nick Aprea. Sorry I missed your text. It's hard to hear sometimes out on the water."

Jack clapped him on the shoulder. "You are the man."

"Nick's going to meet us at the marina, said something about unfinished business. Said you'd understand."

Jack did. It was time for payback.

48

"How's this for timing?" Nick said to Jack. "The fat lady's singing."

Jack and Nick were standing in the foyer on the third floor of the Westin Bonaventure Hotel. Music could be heard bleeding through the doors of the Catalina Ballroom.

Jack's hair was slicked back from his time in the water. He was still dressed in damp black clothes, and his five o'clock shadow was pushing thirty-six hours. Nick looked the worse for wear, having splashed down himself. Neither one of them gave a rat's ass. They were hopped up on adrenaline, ready to grab the prize. These were the moments they lived for.

They had conferenced with the event's security team, who were off-duty police officers, already on high alert because of the dignitaries in attendance. Everyone understood the play; all the exits were covered. The only thing they asked for was discretion.

Jack and Nick agreed. A simple arrest. By the book.

The placard on the easel next to the door announced the "Downtown Redevelopment Gala."

The guests of honor: the Vargas Development Group.

A rotund soprano from the L.A. Opera was regaling the crowd with an over-the-top rendition of Adele's "Someone Like You."

Classically trained singers trying their hand at pop music felt like fingernails on a chalkboard for Jack. But he wasn't there to critique the music. Then again, he couldn't help himself.

"A thousand damn dollars a plate. I'll bet the chicken was as bad as the music."

"Let's go see," Nick said with boyish fire in his eyes.

They stepped through the double doors and waited in the back of the ballroom to let their eyes adjust to the dimmed lights and get the lay of the land. A sea of black ties, white tablecloths, and pastel gowns filled the room.

Uniformed waiters were placing crème brûlée in front of the diners. Wine and coffee were being poured, and all eyes were on the soprano, who held an impossibly long note.

And there—Jack lasered in on the raised podium—was the man of the hour.

Malic al-Yasiri.

The devil in a three-thousand-dollar tux, his face still infused with the blush of success.

Being recognized for excellence by the mayor of Los Angeles was a personal best, Malic thought. He glanced down at the honor the mayor had presented him with: a simple sculpted piece of glass with his name embossed in gold. It filled him with pride. It helped him brush aside his annoyance at Hassan for not keeping him in the loop. He trusted that one of his pressing problems had disappeared by now. He would be more discerning when picking his women in the future. But everyone needed a bit of recreation, he told himself. The rules were different for powerful men.

He thought of his wife, Kayla, and again was forced to temper his anger. Her lack of respect would not be tolerated in the future.

Losing the Matisse was a minor setback, one that would be rectified. If he was capable of achieving citywide recognition in a two-year period, his future was limitless. His face was sure to grace the real estate trade publications, and that alone would thrust him onto the national stage. The media coverage and connections made at tonight's gala guaranteed his future.

———

Jack wondered if he was enjoying himself too much as he watched the dog-and-pony show playing out on the stage. Nah. Malic al-Yasiri was basking in the limelight, unaware that his wife had turned on him, that he'd never walk his daughter down the aisle, that his loyal soldier was dead, his million-dollar boat destroyed, and the glass award sitting in front of him would ultimately raise more money than its worth on eBay, because he was about to be exposed as a notorious killer.

Raul sat at the B-table, swollen and glassy-eyed, nursing his bandaged hand, which Jack knew was throbbing despite the drugs he was taking.

As the guest of honor, a smug Philippe Vargas shared the power table with the mayor and the cardinal, whose spot-lit red vestments oozed salvation. The mayor leaned over and whispered something amusing into his fine girlfriend's ear. He winked and then stepped in front of the podium. He was all smiles and goodwill as he adjusted the mic and gave thanks to the opera singer, eliciting a subdued round of applause.

Two cloth scrims hung on the wall behind the mayor. One depicted a black-and-white panoramic photograph of downtown Los Angeles from the 1920s.

The second scrim, hanging directly behind His Eminence, depicted a modern downtown skyline, in vibrant color, with the Vargas Development Group's new project digitally overlaid and magnificently highlighted front and center.

Jack's money was on Malic jackrabbiting. The man wasn't going down without a fight. Too much ego, he thought.

After twenty-five years of law enforcement Jack still didn't understand the fight-or-flight response. The criminals never got away, he mused. They rarely won. In the high-speed car chases that played in a loop on the local news, the bad guys never escaped, and they watched a lot of television.

Lieutenant Gallina and Tompkins stepped quietly through the ballroom doors with arrest and search warrants in hand. Gallina gave Nick the go-ahead nod. This was one time Gallina, a political animal, had no desire to take the lead.

"I would like to thank everyone here tonight," the mayor said, oblivious to the drama about to play out on the ballroom floor. "All of my friends. You are an inexorable force for change."

Malic's smiling eyes shifted from the mayor to the subtle movement in the rear of the ballroom. He narrowed his eyes, not sure what he was observing. Then his smile vanished.

Malic al-Yasiri locked eyes with Jack Bertolino.

He took an impulsive drink of water as he watched his adversary walking in his direction.

"And in this case," the mayor continued, "the change is positive. We will save lives, create jobs, educate the poor, and improve the quality of life in the City of Angels. We will let our city truly become worthy of its namesake."

Some of the well-dressed attendees started to turn in their seats and follow Malic's darkening gaze. The Los Angeles district attorney's table turned as one, and the DA lurched forward, whispering something to Leslie Sager.

She leaped out of her seat and charged over, stopping the men in their tracks.

"Jack," she whispered heatedly. "What in the hell are you doing? Whatever it is, this is not the right time."

"We're good," he said.

"If you don't turn and walk out of here," she said, looking from Jack to Nick and back again, "you're both finished, and there's nothing I can do to help."

This was the wrong time for explanations, Jack thought.

"No, we're good," Nick said.

Leslie looked a final heartfelt question at Jack, who gave her a tight smile. Incredulous, she shook her head and walked back to her group.

When Jack glanced up at the head table, Malic's chair was empty. The cloth scrim depicting the Vargas Development Group's new Los Angeles fluttered in the breeze behind the mayor.

Jack pounded up the aisle with Nick fast behind.

Tim Dykstra, the mayor's head of security, and a few of the mayor's cohorts rose to stop them, but Nick flashed his badge, running interference.

A crash of plates from behind the scrims attracted Jack's attention, and he ran toward the sound. Behind him the voices in the ballroom rose in a wave of panic.

The mayor stopped talking, and if looks could kill, the cardinal would've ended Jack's life then and there.

Jack pushed through the two scrims and found a uniformed waiter on his hands and knees surrounded by broken glass, silverware, and crockery. He jumped over the man, banging the door to the kitchen open, his gun leading the way.

A security guard was down, bleeding, his hands wrapped around the hilt of a steak knife protruding from his stomach.

Two stunned dishwashers jabbed their fingers toward a side door.

"Where does it go?" Jack asked.

"The dumbwaiter. To the bar, to the basement."

"Call 911, get an ambulance now," Jack said as he pushed through the door. A stairwell was located next to the small service elevator. Jack pulled the dumbwaiter's safety door open and looked up the shaft. The dumbwaiter was headed up to the revolving bar on the thirty-fourth floor of the hotel. It was tight quarters, and already too far up, he thought, not sure Malic could have even fit.

Nick ran in as Jack was opening the stairwell door. Jack pointed upward with his Glock. Nick nodded, pointing down. They split up and Jack started up the stairs.

One flight up, the fire door was ajar. Jack slipped through. It opened to the fourth-floor pool deck, where a wedding was in progress. Five hundred people were gathered around a brightly lit blue pool. The bride and groom stood in front of a female minister, reciting modern vows.

Jack held his gun down at his side as he skirted the perimeter of the pool. The groom caught his eye and gestured with his head to the side of his flower-strewn platform. The bride gave him a snarky look as two cops entered from the main doorway.

Malic burst back through the crowd, sending a knot of unsuspecting wedding guests splashing and screaming into the pool.

"Freeze," Jack ordered, his gun trained on Malic's kill zone. But Malic, gambling that Jack wouldn't risk the shot, juked to the right, blasting through the central doors leading to the atrium.

Jack raced after him. In a matter of a few steps he was right on his heels. Jack leaped and bulldogged his prey to the marble floor.

Jack's gun skittered over the edge of the walkway and splashed down into the koi pond four stories below.

Malic twisted his body around, and Jack hammered his face with a bone-splitter, bouncing his head off the marble floor, a punch that would have taken most men out. Yet Malic answered with a four-inch paring knife he'd grabbed from the kitchen on the run. His muscled arm pistoned upward.

Jack caught his wrist with his left hand, stopping the honed steel blade inches from his face. He landed a powerful right to the side of Malic's head, stunning him. Jack grabbed the knife hand with both of his and, summoning all of his two hundred and thirty pounds, muscled Malic's hand sideways, bending his arm at an unnatural angle. He pressed farther until a sickening snap occurred. The knife clattered to the marble floor. Jack snatched the weapon as Malic silently keened.

Jack grabbed the killer by the scruff of his neck, forcing his anguished face to look directly into his eyes. Then he pressed the blade to Malic's cheek just below his eye socket.

"I could kill you right now," Jack said with dangerous calm, breaking the skin and drawing a drop of blood, "but then you'd win. You'd be dead, but you'd take me with you."

"Do it," Malic said, his voice gravel, his eyes taunting.

"Not on your life."

Jack pulled the knife away and pushed himself up on stiff legs. The two uniformed police officers came running in from the pool deck as Nick Aprea stepped off the elevator.

Nick holstered his weapon as he looked at the unnatural angle of Malic's broken arm, his lifeless hand, and his face, which was devoid of color.

"How in the hell am I gonna cuff him, Bertolino?"

"By the neck works for me."

Nick let out a grim laugh and let the two uniforms deal with Malic until an EMT arrived. He'd have a police escort to the hospital and then on to Central Jail. They heard one of the cops reading him his Miranda rights as they started to walk away. Nick pulled up short.

"So, your friend," he kind of blurted.

"Who?" Jack said.

"You know . . ."

"Who?"

"Your bud," Nick said.

"Mateo?"

Jack knew where this was headed and let Nick swing in the breeze.

"What?" he repeated, suppressing a grin.

"He did good," Nick said low.

"I must be going deaf. What?"

"Fuck you, Bertolino. Your guy did okay."

"Rogues' gallery my ass, Aprea."

Jack laughed and Nick turned beet red.

"I think this is yours, wiseguy," Nick said as he grabbed Jack's gun from the small of his back.

Nick handed the Glock, handle first, to his friend, and both men watched as pond water drained out of the barrel of Jack's favorite weapon.

49

The press conference the next day turned a PR nightmare for the mayor into a law-and-order triumph. The headlines read A MONSTER IN OUR MIDST and HIDING IN PLAIN SIGHT.

A sex slavery ring had been broken up, a killer brought to justice, and a treasure trove of priceless Iraqi artifacts would be returned to the National Museum of Iraq. The president of France called the mayor personally to thank him as soon as word leaked that the masterpiece *La Pastorale* by Matisse, a national treasure that had been stolen in the Musée d'Art Moderne heist, had been recovered.

On a political roll, the mayor was thrown softball questions about the honor he had bestowed on Malic al-Yasiri the night of his arrest. Brighter men than himself had vetted him, the smiling mayor said self-deprecatingly. Mistakes were made, but the greater good was served.

Nick Aprea was front and center sharing the camera with Gallina, the mayor, the district attorney, and a beaming chief of police. They even paraded Captain Deak Montrose of the Coast Guard up on the stage, extolling the virtues of interagency cooperation. Nick reminded everybody in the room that Jack Bertolino had brought all the forces together.

The district attorney tried to downplay Jack's involvement, but Nick was having none of that. Gallina uncharacteristically joined the choir and announced that it was Jack Bertolino who broke the case of the Jane Does and saved the life of Angelica Cardona, who had been kidnapped by the animal Malic al-Yasiri and imprisoned against her will for thirty-eight days.

The YouTube video had already surfaced, and the image of Angelica being held in a glass cage was enough to set off an international press frenzy. A Hollywood bidding war was in play for Angelica's life story before the first telecast stopped rolling.

DEA agent Kenny Ortega led a multiagency, early-morning raid, dismantling the Detroit faction of Malic's Iraqi gang. It was initiated by information provided by Jack Bertolino, who had come into possession of a handwritten ledger that tied the Los Angeles group to their Detroit relatives. It contained an orderly accounting of drugs and women shipped across state lines, from Los Angeles to Detroit, on a monthly basis.

Vincent Cardona and Frankie the Man had been arrested, bonded, and released. Their lawyers had been assured that all charges would eventually be dropped after the specifics of the case came to light.

―――

Mateo got word from Chatty Cathy that the Vargas Development Group's project was moving forward without a hitch. Two A-list investors had stepped forward, offering to replace the tainted money that Malic had pulled from his private reserves.

Cruz stayed one step beyond police scrutiny, which was

just the way he and Jack wanted it. The electrical anomaly that blacked out a four-square-mile section of Orange County had been chalked up to faulty wiring and an act of God.

Kayla al-Yasiri was in hiding. Her lawyer read a prepared statement on her behalf. "Kayla asks for privacy for herself and her daughter at this time of great emotional distress. She offers sincere condolences and prayers to the victims' families and begs forgiveness for the sins of her husband."

She did make a deal with the district attorney's office. In exchange for testifying against her husband, the state wouldn't put a lien on her property.

———

The wealthy always landed on their feet, Jack thought with some bitterness as he scored the bottom of his last homegrown tomato and dropped it into boiling water for sixty seconds before the requisite ice bath.

The garlic, onions, and fresh basil were already working their magic, and fifteen minutes later the skinned and seeded pulp was being hand-crushed and added to the pot.

Jack was starting to relax. The Vicodin and Excedrin had finally caught up with the harsh pain in his back, and Jack decided not to turn a victory into defeat.

Camera crews were camped out in front of Bruffy's Tow and the front of his loft building waiting for a glimpse of the "hero." Jack's mug had made the national news and CNN and would be fodder for the tabloids for the immediate future. So much for anonymity. All things being equal, he thought he looked pretty good on camera.

Jack hadn't tried to contact Leslie. From his point of view, she had chosen sides. She'd become the district attorney's heavy. Tried to use her personal relationship with Jack to interfere with a righteous bust. And for the worst of reasons, he thought. Politics. Jack understood, he just didn't like it.

Almost twenty-four hours had passed and Leslie hadn't reached out.

Jack thought about calling her, had picked up the phone more than once, but couldn't bring himself to dial the number. Best to give it some time, he thought. Let it rest, and then see how it played out.

Tommy had once called him damaged goods from the aftermath of the divorce, and maybe the label was still apropos.

Whatever.

Jack crushed the last ripe tomato and put it on a low simmer. The tomatoes were so sweet they could have been served salted and lightly sautéed, but Jack liked a more complex depth of flavor, and since he was cooking for one, he could do whatever the hell he felt like.

The only fly in the ointment was Raul Vargas.

That asshole was sticking in his craw, invading his calm.

Because of the Rohypnol, Angelica couldn't remember a thing about the night she was kidnapped after leaving the club. And therefore she couldn't incriminate Raul.

There was still no direct linkage tying Raul to the kidnapping or any other illegal enterprise Malic al-Yasiri had been involved in. And Malic wasn't talking.

Raul's cell phone had disappeared the night of his abduction. Plus, he said self-righteously, it wasn't a crime to take a photo with a cell phone. No one could argue the point.

No link had been found on Malic's computer or landline or

cell phone. The theory being floated was that he used a dedicated safe phone and destroyed it when things started heating up. The tech squad would tear everything apart in the coming weeks, but as of now, Raul was tanning himself at the Malibu house.

Jack cracked open a bottle of Benziger. The taste of the rich cabernet and the smell of the sauce infiltrated his mind and teased him away from thoughts of . . . fucking Raul! Jack needed a break, that was all. Nothing a short cruise on his boat couldn't cure . . . but his fucking boat had been scuttled.

There was a firm knock on the door, and Jack pulled it open, too quickly, thinking it might be Leslie.

"Yo, Mr. B."

Jack had to laugh. Peter's black eye had faded to a yellow-green. "Good work with the Matisse," he said.

"Yeah, not bad, Mr. B. They say it's worth ten mil. There might be a reward of some kind. Maybe a trip to Paris."

"One can hope."

The sheik's man had started talking before the cuffs came out. When he was finished, a call went out to Kenny Ortega in Florida, and then to his man on the ground in Iraq, Bogdanovich. The fed knocked on Sheik Ibrahim's door in the early-morning hours and arrested him on the spot. The State Department confiscated his plane at John Wayne Airport and was presently working on extradition papers.

"Vincent Cardona understands the delicacy of your privacy issues at this moment," Peter said, "but he was wondering if he could have a few words."

"I'm cooking here."

"Yeah, smells like Grandma's gravy. Down at your dock, say a half hour?" Peter turned and headed to the elevator.

Presumptuous little shit, Jack thought as he took a spoonful of sauce. It burned his lip, but he sucked it down anyway. Then he clicked off the heat and banged a cover onto the pot.

Jack had made arrangements with Platinum Auto Body earlier in the day. They had finished replacing the door on his Mustang and agreed to let him store it on their property until the feeding frenzy died down.

Jack jumped the wall at the back of his building, bypassing the paparazzi; picked up his car; and arrived at the marina in the allotted time.

It felt reassuring to be behind the wheel of his own car, Jack thought as he pulled to a stop behind what looked like a brand-new Lincoln Town Car. The windows had been blacked out but couldn't hide the outline of Frankie the Man in the driver's seat. Frankie powered down his window and gave Jack a thumbs-up.

Jack walked past Peter, who was standing sentry; keyed the lock on the chain-link fence; and looked down on the lone figure of Vincent Cardona, sitting in a director's chair he had probably "borrowed" from a neighbor's yacht. He was smoking a cigar, staring at Jack's empty slip. A second chair had been placed next to the big man.

Jack grabbed the seat.

The two men sat in silence.

A nice breeze was blowing, a few sailboats drifted by, a flock of seagulls mocked no one in particular. It was springtime-perfect in Marina del Rey.

"I was gonna buy you a real boat," Cardona said, breaking the silence, "but I thought better. I'm honoring our deal."

Jack took that in, not knowing how to respond.

"There was some reward money I promised after talking

to that prick Gallina. I figure, your men, no reason to punish them."

"I could live with that," Jack said.

"Big of you."

Jack flashed anger.

"I'm just sayin', good for you." Vincent Cardona sounded tired, like a weight had been lifted and not a minute too soon.

"You've got quite a daughter," Jack said finally.

"You're tellin' me. Been through the wringer. She'll do all right."

Jack didn't look at Cardona, but in his peripheral vision it looked like he was swiping at his eyes.

"Very thankful, she is. And me."

Jack accepted the thanks with a nod.

Cardona pulled a butcher-paper-wrapped package from below his chair. "Have some steaks."

Jack thought about Raul hanging from the meat hooks next to four sides of beef and gave his stomach an involuntary pat.

As if Cardona could read his thoughts, he smiled and lifted his heft out of the chair. "That's aged meat, don't throw it out." The two men appraised each other for the first time since Jack had arrived at the dock. "There's something special wrapped inside."

Vincent Cardona took a long pull of the cigar, nodded his head, and walked up the dock, a little lighter on his feet. He stopped and turned at the gate.

"Oh, Jack, that little contractual issue you had with the Mex-icans. It's over. *Finito.* Enjoy your life."

Cardona pushed through the chain-link gate, nodded at Peter, and stepped onto dry land. Frankie the Man, with one arm in a sling, moved to open the car door for his boss, but Vincent Cardona waved him off. He opened the rear door himself.

Out stepped Angelica Marie Cardona, the most sought-after international news story of the past forty-eight hours, carrying a single long-stemmed red rose.

Peter held the gate open for her as she stepped through and walked the length of the dock to greet Jack. She was wearing jeans, a blue work shirt, running shoes, and no makeup. She looked younger and more fragile, Jack thought.

"I'm sorry about your boat."

"No worries."

She handed Jack the rose. "It was all I could think of to say thank you."

"It's perfect. Very thoughtful."

Jack looked from the red of the rose to her clear green eyes and was suddenly at a loss for words.

Angelica filled the silence. "I'm moving home for a while, until things settle down."

"It's a circus out there," Jack agreed.

"They'll get bored and move on. They always do."

Jack was amazed at Angelica's composure. He knew she was in for a rocky ride, but he was pleased she seemed grounded under the circumstances.

"How are you feeling?" he asked gently.

"I'm not sure. I'm better than I would have been if you hadn't stepped into my life."

"I'm really glad it worked out, Angelica."

"Me too. Really glad. I'm going to lay low. Maybe talk to someone."

Jack knew she was referring to a therapist. "That would make sense."

"I'll let Dad run interference. He's good at that." She shared a secret smile with Jack. "I'll let you know where I land, if that's all right."

"That would be fine."

They both stared at the empty slip for a moment.

"You're a good man, Jack Bertolino." She stood on tiptoes, took Jack's face in her young hands, and gave him a soft kiss on the lips. She nailed him with her killer eyes, turned, and walked back up the dock.

Something stirred in Jack's chest as he watched the black Lincoln pull silently away from the curb.

———

After one of the best spaghetti dinners Jack had ever eaten, he went to the fridge and pulled out the butcher-paper-wrapped steaks. He cut the string with a knife, slipped his finger under the tape, and the thick paper flapped open. On top of eight perfectly trimmed and aged New York steaks was a Ziploc plastic sandwich bag.

Inside the bag was an unmarked DVD.

Curious, Jack grabbed his wine, walked into his office, and loaded the disc into his computer.

The first shot was of a naked blond woman in her early twenties. She was clearly unconscious. Could've been Angelica, could've been Kayla. Jack was positive it was the girl who had been killed in the boat crash at Paradise Cove.

Then a naked, swaggering, fully erect Raul Vargas entered

the frame and went to work on the drugged woman. He raped and defiled and brutalized her. Jack shook with rage but forced himself to watch the entire sadistic film. And at the end, he was clear on one thing.

Raul Vargas was going down hard.

Acknowledgments

The author gratefully acknowledges the many people who lent their time and expertise in making this the best book possible. Karen Hunter, for staying the course and keeping the faith. Brigitte Smith, Melissa Gramstad, and the entire Simon & Schuster team for their continued support. John Paine, for another brilliant edit, and Aja Pollock for an impeccable copy edit. My attorney, Les Abell, whose support is invaluable and always appreciated.

Thanks to Bob Marinaccio, Annie George, Gordon Dawson, Deb Schwab, Kathryn Solórzano, Molly Miles, and Diane and Deborah Lansing for great notes on early drafts. And retired Air Force colonel Jeff Barnett, for sharing his knowledge of the FBI's presence in Iraq.

Special thanks goes out to Vida Spears. She kept me on the straight and narrow with her support, love, and patience as she listened to every word written with grace under fire.